Fractured Hope

Kristine Endsley

KE Fantasy

ALSO BY

The Exile's Paradox

Fractured Hope
Jaded Loyalties
A Twisted Fate
Series Novella
Shattered Fate

Fractured Hope

The Exile's Paradox/Book Three

Cover Art and Design by Cristiana Léone

Editing by

http://www.arrowheadediting.com

http://markedandread.com

Published by KE Fantasy

ISBN E-book: 979-8-9930512-0-8; Paperback: 979-8-9-897685-8-5; Hardcover: 979-8-9897685-9-2

First edition September 2025

To my husband, Adam
Thank you for always being beside me

CONTENTS

Dubois Famille

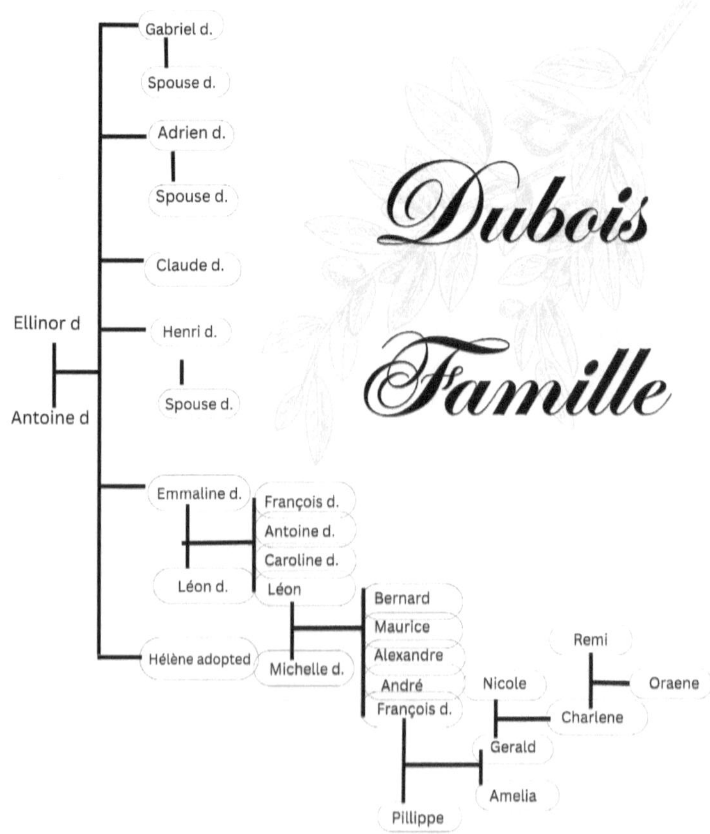

Index of Common Words

Aeminan— Citizens of *Aemina*

Aemirin— Language of the *Aeminan* people

Ai— Expression or exasperation, like "oh"

Amura Ore— Governing council in *Aemina*

Aore— Senior *Amura Ore* assembly member

Avrel — Lieutenant

Basean — General

C'yo— Cuss word (hash 4/5) (Yo- short version 2/5)

Catia— *Aemina* ambassador

Cesaya— Ninth day of the week (weekend no school!)

Dirgiserin—the disease that the *serilesoda* virus is responsible for

Enda— Elf

Endae— The elven realm

Endaen— Elven

Esamia— Greetings and partings (like aloha)

Ginem — *Private*

Hallë— This is Nolan's name for Hally, only he uses it

Hinam — *Captain*

Hoaya— First day of the week

Imolegin— An *enda*'s magical signature

Itaya— *Second day of the week*

Laro— Father

Lataya— Fourth day of the week
Lidean — Major
Loret— Junior *Amura Ore* assembly member
Majut— Cuss word (harsh: 4/5)
Meril— An *endaen* magical amulet
Mesaya— Third day of the week
Muranilde — Rare soulmate-like bond Hally and Nolan share
Murë— Mother
Neseaya— Seventh day of the week (weekend, no school!)
Nol— This is Hally's name for Nolan, only she uses it
Pae-lesoda—The name Aswryn gave her cursed-plague
Pesset — *Sergeant*
Quaya— Fifth day of the week
Recesdan — Colonel
Rosava— Earth
Sajé— A comforting word like "shh"
Savile— Title of an exile (again, not capitalized when using gender version)
Sercae cumo— Cuss word (harsh: 5/5)
Serilesoda—The ancient, original virus responsible for thousands of deaths. Zayuri are believed to be immune to it
Somaya— Sixth day of the week
Sudome — *Commander*
Tesaya— Eighth day of the week (weekend no school!)
Tullaca— (*Tulla* for short) Cuss word (harsh: 5/5)
Tuma juvaë— Cuss word. It can be split up (harsh 5/5)
Urro— Cuss word (harsh 1/5)
Wyuendell — Mid-season celebration
Yalurë (Yalu)— Paternal grandmother (Grannie/Grandma)
Yaluro— Paternal grandfather
Z. serilesoda.— The altered serilesoda virus that a Zayuri's immune makes. It attacks the original serilesoda virus within his/her system — killing the virus at an exponentially faster rate.
Zaris — Spring
Zayuri— Organization of samurai-like warriors

Word Endings:

-ë— female

-o— male

-e— neutral or title

-i— plural

Remember! These are English translations for the convenience of English speakers. Please don't assume the characters are speaking English just because you're reading English.

For a full ever expanding and evolving translation list visit my website: https://kristineendsley.com/extras/

Endaen Characters

An'di — Nolan's big sister
Aswryn — Antagonist
Bren — *Zayuri*
Carena — elven friend killed by prank
Edvic — Nolan's dad
Estwyn — Junior Member of *Amura Ore*
Evazella/Zella Inara — Hally's grandmother
Gileal/Gil — Hally & Nolan's best friend
Hally Dubois/Hallanevaë Inara— Protagonist
Jenne — *Zayuri*
Junae — Senior member of *Amura Ora*, district of *Rudairn*
Lahiem — elven friend killed by prank
Leda — Antagonist
Nyda — Antagonist
Onaeris — Hally's grandfather
Orin — Hally's father
Rajamë/Raj — Hally's childhood friend
Sanae — Nolan's dragon (not an elf but still in *Endae*)
Savis — Antagonist
Tamden — Commander of *Zayuri* (Nolan's commanding officer)
Tiaë — Hally's mom
Tolwe — Nolan's uncle

Nolan/Twynolan Madorean — Second protagonist/Hally's *muranildo*

Wennië — Nolan's mom

1

Nol raised his hand once again and my eyes closed—I swear, involuntarily! The sun was already in my eyes and he was using it to his advantage. I prepared myself for the harmless-but-annoying little zap of a spell we were using for practice. Instead, Nol used something that shoved me off my feet. On instinct, I flung my hand out to catch my fall and my ass hit the hard ground.

"Nol!" I shouted—okay whined—as I shook the dirt off my palm. "That was not a zap!"

"Don't close your eyes then." His scolding laced with amusement. "Besides, if you'd thrown up a ward, you wouldn't have fallen."

I stood, brushing pine needles and dirt off my jeans. "Let's face it, I'm never going to do it on command." We'd been trying for a month and a half and I could count on one hand how many semi-successful wards I'd thrown up when we practiced.

From above us on my back deck, sitting on his lounge chair, safe and away from retaliation Mateo hollered down, "Where's your winning attitude?" Mateo gave me a broad smile, white teeth bright against his brown skin.

I pointed at him. "Watch it mister, I'm planning your bachelor party."

He held up his hands in mock surrender, but his eyes widened just a hair. A warning.

I turned too late. Nol zapped me with the spell we'd been using for practice. The spell Nol and Gil used to toss around when we were kids.

Gil.

Our best friend. The only one who understood the bond Nol and I shared. After I was banished Nol and Gil relied on each other even more. The friend Aswryn killed two months ago as he protected my *muranildo*—

"Hallë!" Nol called, the same pain in the ass *muranildo* who'd needed that protection two months ago. He waved his hand in front of me. "Are you going to work or are you going to daydream?"

He had no clue where my thoughts had gone. I scrunched my nose and with a thought, no spell calling or warning, I did my own made-up version of the zapping spell. Nol shook his hand from the shock and he pressed his lips together, determined to get me back now. With a sparkle of mischief in his eyes, he flexed his hand, trying to hide his fingers as he drew the symbol for the spell, which he could've done mentally, and flicked the spell at me. My hand went up to about waist high and I jumped to the side, as if that'd help. But it might have...because I didn't feel any zap.

Nol's cinnamon red eyebrows shot up, his mouth an *O* of surprise. "That wasn't a ward."

"Well, yeah, I didn't have time to think of a ward." But I hadn't gotten zapped. "Or...you have bad aim?"

His shoulders dropped with exasperation. "You never have time to think, it needs to be instantaneous."

I pointed at him. "*You* don't always throw one up in time. Stop judging me."

"Judging?" Nol muttered something under his breath.

I inhaled to say something, but stopped when my phone vibrated in my pocket. I held my hand out for a time out as I pulled it out and checked the caller ID. Friday evenings weren't his typical time to call—which was three in the morning in Paris. I pressed and lifted the phone to my ear.

"Gerald?"

"*Tante* Hélène?" Gerald's rapid breathing blew into the phone.

"*Ce qui est faux*?" *What is wrong*? Charlie's father did not panic, he had a calm, stoic personality. But when things did break through his shell they were big.

"It's Léon. He's had a heart attack."

Gerald's grandfather, the boy I'd helped raise since birth, my ninety-eight-year-old nephew, had had a heart attack. I stopped breathing, and everything narrowed down to just me, the phone, and Gerald.

"Did you hear me?"

At Gerald's words, everything came back into focus. I lifted my eyes and found Nol standing in front of me. He didn't speak French, but he heard the shock in Gerald's voice. There was no time to panic. None. "Yes. Tell me, where are you? Is Nicole with you? And are you with Léon now?"

"Nicole and I are walking into the hospital now." He seemed to calm as he answered my questions. "The ambulance took him. I'm not sure how severe it was."

"I'm coming."

"Thank you, *Tante*. I can't believe this happened. I should, but you never think it will happen. There's someone coming our way. I need to go. I'll keep you updated."

Gerald hung up without saying goodbye, like his grandfather. The phone slipped from my ear and my arm dropped as I stared into Nol's pale-blue eyes. "I need to get to Paris."

Nol's eyes widened in surprise. He looked behind me and up to Mateo and where Charlie and Ray were in the house. "How soon? What has happened?"

Pressing my lips together, I tilted my head toward the house. He followed me to the steps.

Mateo had already climbed out of his lounge chair and met us at the top. "What's going on?"

"That was Gerald. Come, I'll tell you both along with Charlie."

Mateo and Nol followed me past the creaking back door and into the mudroom/laundry room. To the left a door lead to our pantry and out into the kitchen.

"Charlie?" One boot thunked on the floor, then the next.

"In here!" Charlie called, her voice drifting through the pantry from the kitchen.

I followed her voice, leaving the guys to trail behind me. As I came around the corner I found the refrigerator door wide open. My nieces were standing at the counter, their backs to me as Charlie stood over her four-year-old daughter. I closed the door, re-trapping the cold air.

"Everything all right?" Charlie asked without turning around. She said a word to Ray, maybe "yes" or "one sec". She pressed her hip against the step ladder to keep Ray from falling then turned to face me, flour on her nose and cheekbone. Her large, brown eyes curious, face open and happy.

"No."

Charlie's face hardened into a frown, ready for anything. And this year...she was about prepared for anything. Mateo and Nol shuffled in behind me and I moved into the dining room, giving the kids space for their work, or maybe avoiding the flour and sugar mess on every surface. I placed my hand on the stool under the counter of the peninsula, and pushed it close to the cabinet. I wasn't in the mood to sit.

Mateo came to stand next to me and Nol leaned against the fridge, pressing against the pictures posted on the doors. Smiling faces, happy moments. We'd even had the chance to add the recent new additions: one with Nol and Quinn, another with Ray and Seamus playing. All of the humans in my life would get old, just like Léon.

My eyes fixed on Charlie with her flour-coated nose. "Gerald called. Léon had a heart attack a short while ago. Your father—"

"Go. You need to be there with him," Charlie blurted as I said, "Your father needs me there."

Charlie's dark eyebrows scrunched together. "Papa needs you there? Amelia and mom are there with him, Tatie. *You* want to be there for Léon. And that's okay."

"I need to...help. They..."

"Tatie—" Charlie glanced up and behind me. "Yes. I'm sure they'd love your help and support."

The weight lifted off my shoulders and I could breathe again. Charlie got it. She knew they needed me.

Charlie brushed her hands together, flour sifting to the counter. "What do you need right now?"

My brain flipped through all the requirements of traveling. Passport, ticket—shit. I'd need to tell Queen Orlaith and...my shoulders slumped. I'd have to get permission from Queen Brigid and King Domhnall, my boyfriend's parents. Damn, how'd my life get so political? "I'll take a cookie if you have any made."

Ray huffed, drawing my attention to her for the first time. "I guess you can have a cookie early, Tatie. If it makes you feel better."

Nol cleared his throat as he tried not to laugh, but Mateo couldn't hold it in. He leaned over the counter, getting his shirt floured, and gave my little, adorably smart-mouthed niece a kiss on the head. "Can I have one, too?"

"HALLY JUST SETTLE DOWN and eat," Mateo snapped. Not in a harsh mean way, in a harsh encouraging way. One that was a bit tired of my attitude.

I glanced at Mateo and then at my casserole. My chair squeaked as I tried to get comfortable. Silverware scraped against the plates and still no one spoke.

My phone dinged, normally we didn't use our phones at the table, but the circumstances trumped my rules. I stood and snatched it from the counter behind me. Charlie's and Ray's smiling faces appeared on the screen, but the message box covered the lower half of the picture. My interest diminished when I read the sender. The penis cups for Mateo's bachelor party would arrive tomorrow. Good, but not helpful.

My family dropped their eyes back to their plates when I shook my head. I set the phone back down, dropped down in my seat and stared at my meal. Even the asparagus had no flavor.

How could I settle down when the boy I'd raised since he was a baby was in a hospital halfway across the world? Sleeping in a hospital bed and hooked up to machines? No answers, lots of tests.

Quinn, or rather Foreign Relations Officer Delany, assured me he'd go through all the right channels and get me an answer, yes or no, that I had permission to see Léon. Until then, the others wanted to continue as planned: Dinner with Nol and Mateo, Sam would pick Mateo up in an hour, after he'd gotten done with his late-night meeting with some hotshot client in some other country. It wasn't our business, just that Mateo wasn't a fan of being alone much.

Mateo's silverware clanked as he almost slammed them on his plate. "Why don't we go pack?"

"There's not much to pack."

"Toothbrush? Deodorant? Undies? Yes, there sure as hell is enough. I can't stand your moping."

"Mateo, I don't even know—"

"You know your Prince Charming will come through."

"Don't call him that."

Mateo stood and set his napkin on the table. "He's charming as all hell and he's a prince. That's how it is, get over it. Now, up." He pointed and flicked his finger at me until I stood.

Before he could come all the way around I pushed my chair in and met him at the head of the large eight seater table. Mateo's eyebrows shot up, daring me to talk back, but I wasn't a child, so instead I followed him through the living room and into the hallway.

The wood planks creaked as Mateo stepped on them. Other than that, our socked feet barely made noise going up the steps. Again, Mateo stepped on the other creak in the wood floor that I avoided. He turned to check on me with a mischievous look. He knew the noise made my eye twitch every time. I frowned, but didn't say anything.

"Listen." Mateo kept his voice low as he pushed the door to my bedroom open. "They can do a lotta things about heart attacks now." He shut it while I dropped onto the bed. "My dad's brother, Stan? He's had four heart attacks *with* surgeries. He's still kickin'. I'm not saying all heart attacks are non-life threatening, but you don't *know* how bad it is."

"That's the thing, Mateo. We don't know." As I tried to convey how my heart felt at that moment, I reached for my bracelet, the small engraved luggage tag with the old Dubois family's address in Paris, sold... a century ago. The only thing I had left of them. The only thing left of my sister, except Léon. "I've lost two of Emma's kids. Léon's sister and Léon's daughter. I promised her..." I looked down at my hands. "I swore to my sister, as she lay dying in my arms, that I would protect her children. Even if Léon pulls through this, I feel like that's breaking my vow to her." I looked up and met Mateo's dark brown eyes. "Does that make sense?"

Mateo dropped onto the bed beside me. "It does." He wrapped his arms around me and rested his head on my shoulder—no easy feat with our eight inch height difference. But that didn't matter, he was my best friend.

After a moment of sitting in my dark room, I let Mateo help me pick out some clothes. I had an apartment in Paris, but it didn't seem to matter to Mateo. "You've got clothes from the *nineties* there." His eyes bulged. "You need to bring emergency outfits just in case there's nothing fashionable for this decade."

I laughed at his dramatized reaction. "It will be fine."

As he opened his mouth to protest I interrupted. "Two outfits, okay? Two."

He crossed his arms and pouted. "Fine."

I hopped into my walk-in closet, an upgrade from the nineteen twenty style it used to be. I'd had the upgrade years ago. "Everything is black. That's not *normal* over there. Or business clothes, I am not wearing pleated trousers and a blah blouse. I'll just—"

Mateo hurried in, grabbed one hanger from the right side and then another hanger from my side and held them in front of me. He knew my closet like it was his own. To be fair, I knew his pretty well, too. "Take this."

"Oh..." I took the two hangers from him. I'd forgotten I even had these. It wasn't professional attire, it wasn't black, and there were no rips or holes. Dark green, wide-leg trousers. I ordered them years ago, and worn them maybe twice.

I lifted the top higher. "This is...I can wear this on the plane."

Mateo held up a finger, his lips pursed, but a knock on the door interrupted whatever he was going to say. Instead, he threw his hands up and walked out to open the door. "Dear lord, woman. Yes—Hello, handsome, come to take me away?"

Had it been an hour already? Time did fly with Mateo around. "Hi, Sam," I hollered from inside my closet as I shook the top, determining if would I need something under it. No, I decided. The brown, cream and olive crop sweater would hang below my ribcage. I didn't give a shit if it showed my belly and lower back. Regardless, it'd be acceptable in Paris.

"Actually, this contemplative numminess is here for you."

Not Sam? Quinn? No, Mateo would never call Quinn that. I popped my head out of my closet, clothes still in hand. Nol, of course. While Mateo had quit his matchmaking bullshit between Nol and I, he played favorites. And I had to agree, his favorite did look contemplative.

Nol's head quirked to the side. An eyebrow arched high. "Contemplative?" Nol's *Aemirin* accented voice questioned the unfamiliar word.

"Broody?" I suggested as I threw my clothes on the bed.

Nol still looked clueless. "What is broody?" He pulled out his phone. A few clicks later... "I'm not a chick— Oh, the other definition. That would make sense. *C'yo*," Nol whispered under his breath in *Aemirin*. "*Contemplative* is a better description. I have been thinking, but I wouldn't say lost. I was hoping we could talk."

"Oh, honey, you could talk to me about anything."

Nol's dimple showed as he smiled for Mateo. Wait, was he blushing? Not Nol. "Um, sorry Mateo, Sam said no."

My bark of laughter startled them, but when the two guys looked over at me with serious looks, I had to wonder if they were serious about Sam. Not my business. I would not go there.

"Sorry. What's on your mind, Nol?"

His shoulders tightened and he glanced at Mateo. Nol shuffled his feet. "I've been thinking about your trip to Paris."

When Nol didn't elaborate, I glanced at Mateo. He shrugged and tilted his head at the door to let me know he was going to give us some time to talk serious stuff. If he could avoid serious talks he would. Except with me. It took me a year of coaxing to get him to talk to Sam about his depression. Soon after that was when Sam asked him for his hand, again. Long story.

"I'll leave you two alone. No funny business, though."

"Mateo that wasn't why—" Nol tried to explain but Mateo was already standing in front of him.

"Nah, Sam will be here soon anyway." He kissed Nol on the cheeks. "See you at work tomorrow."

As Mateo kissed my cheeks Nol dropped his gaze to the floor and didn't lift them even after we were alone.

"Usually when one asks to talk, they start the conversation," I said.

"I know, but, I'm being selfish and I don't want you to be mad."

"Did you talk to Quinn or something? Does he think I shouldn't go? Do you think I shouldn't go. I'm going to be with Léon. Whatever you two come up with."

"No, Hallë. Stop. That's not it. I don't know what Quinn thinks."

That wasn't a denial of his opinion, though. "What about you?"

Nol winced. "If you go—"

I crossed my arms and cocked my hip. He was not going to change my mind. "When I go."

"Your family hates me." He swallowed.

"Some of them blame you, I wouldn't go as far as hate, though. What's this about? I'm not expecting you to come with me."

He glanced up at me then back down. Apprehension didn't suit him. "That's the thing. The distance might be too great for the slave band. I think, I need to come, too."

"We don't know if that's too far." We didn't know much about it at all, except Aswryn had tricked me into putting it on to save Ray. For three weeks, we searched and my grandmother in *Endae* searched for any scrap of knowledge on a damn slave band. Slaves, yes. Slave band?

Nothing. Then we met Lord Gavin, an ancient fairy who recognized what was permanently attached to my arm. "Besides, it wouldn't kill me, as long as we're in the same realm."

"*Ai*, Hallë, surviving being sucked through space doesn't mean you wouldn't be hurt. The point is a slave isn't supposed to leave its master! Don't you think that slave—*you*—would be punished for leaving her master—*me*? You'd survive, but how much damage would it—" Nol scowled when he couldn't find the English word. "*C'yo!*"

"Inflict." I gave him the correct word as he paced my room, his hands clenching and unclenching. He hated that he was the reason I couldn't take it off. He killed Aswryn and the ownership of the band transferred to him. And until we found the word or phrase that released me, Nol was stuck "owning me".

He paced my room for a few more seconds as I stared not knowing where this conversation went wrong. Or had it gone wrong? "So what are you saying? Are you asking to go with me or are you asking me not to go?"

"I don't *know*. I just know it's a bad idea to separate." He stopped in the middle of my room, between the bed and the wall. "To go with you." He nodded as if that finalized his answer.

"Ahem. Hello?" Charlie poked her head around my door. "Um, I hate to interrupt, but Sam just picked up Mateo. And um, Ray has requested Uncle Nolan read her a bedtime story. When did that happen?"

Nol moved until his back was to the wall opposite the bed so he could see Charlie at the door and me, standing near the foot of my bed. At the uncle comment, Nol's face brightened. Everything was right in the world. "She asked me if she could call me uncle when I first arrived today."

Charlie paused for dramatic effect, her chin lifted as if she were considering the allowance of such a thing. "You better get in there and read your niece a book, then."

Nol shifted, one moment he stood near the wall, the next moment he was standing by Charlie at the bedroom entrance. "I like the sound of that. Niece."

Charlie jumped, but he was gone before she finished the reaction. "Good god that man can move."

"*Endao*, never man."

"You know what I mean, Tatie." Charlie plopped on my bed and saw my clothes I'd thrown there. "Are these the clothes Mateo pick this out? He said you liked them."

I took another look at them. "They're my clothes, of course I like them."

"Right. Hally Dubois likes it. Would Hélène Roux wear this, though?"

I scowled. Changing identities ruined everything. "I'll ask her later."

Charlie snorted. "It's just a thought, Tatie. I don't think the TSA will be considering your choice of outfits.

"Shut up." I sat down beside her. "How are you doing, love? We haven't had a moment to catch up in weeks." It wasn't like I hadn't seen her, but other than Sunday dinners, where she passed out before we could catch up, we only saw each other in passing.

Charlie huffed. "Yeah, working at the fae lab really screws with your time. I'm glad I took that sabbatical leave. And do not give me the sad eyes, Tatie, this was my choice." Charlie looked up at the ceiling. "Let's see. The Dublin crew has a fae virus with a similar protein sequence to the virus Aswryn cursed."

I knew about the collaboration. She was always talking about Collin, the fae boy who came from Dublin. I wasn't too certain about why he called himself fae instead of fairy, but I wasn't going to ask either. Charlie pulled her legs onto the bed and hugged her knees. "We sent them *my* virus samples of Aswryn's curse, *Paedigin*–no, that's not...I get all the fucking names confused." Her eyebrows shot up as she scoffed. "God, they fucking give me crap about it all the time. They're lucky they have your translated notes at all."

"What happened after you sent them the samples?" I encouraged after she had stewed long enough over their mistreatment of her work.

"They haven't said anything. Collin said they'll get back to us. That was two weeks ago. Ish." She muttered the last word. "I'm about ready to go over there myself and check. Not a fucking word. Can you believe it?" But she was in her own world, staring a hole into my wall.

I shook my head and waited for her to continue.

She sighed after a minute. "I just wish I could have gotten the data Gil was going to bring me. I hate that we lost him."

"Me, too, love."

My phone chirped before I could think of something to break up the melancholy moment. Being closer to the bed side table and charger, Charlie reached over and grabbed it.

As she slid it over we both saw the caller ID. Quinn. My thumb shook as I pressed the little green button.

"Hey, Quinn?"

"Speaker, speaker—" Charlie hissed as she fanned at my phone.

I groaned. "Hang on." I pulled the phone away from my ear. The sound of rushing cars came through the tiny speaker so both of us could hear. "Are you driving?"

"Uh, yeah. So are you ready for the news?"

My fingers brushed my dragon ear cuff as I settled my hair back in place. A hundred and nineteen year habit to hide my ears. "Yes. Yes, of course."

I heard the amusement in Quinn's voice. "I'm giving you the green light."

My insides flipped with excitement, and I turned to Charlie, as she bounced up and down with me, our movements shaking the bed. It was so much easier than I'd dreaded. "They said yes? Without stipulations? No hoops?—Wait, you said *you're* giving me the green light?"

"Yeah, I did. I am. They called me home. I'm leaving before you and I'll talk to them."

"Are you in trouble for asking? Are they going to make you *stay*?" I asked.

Stay meant no Seamus for Ray. No boyfriend for me or friend for Nol. Stay meant no international relations officer for Orlaith. Fuck, was Orlaith going to be pissed at me?

"They might ask when I plan to come home, but they won't make me stay. Here's how it'll probably go, in my experience. They'll talk to me and set up a meeting for you to meet them formally. You might meet another person or two, but I'll push for minimal disturbance."

"I hear a *but* coming," I said.

Movement at the bedroom door caught my attention. Nol was leaning against the door frame, arms crossed and listening.

Our eyes met just as Quinn added the condition. "You need to take Nolan."

"Is that coming from you or your parents?" Nol asked, startling Charlie, who hadn't seen him hovering.

"Me," Quinn answered, nonpulsed. "When you come for the visit, a stronger, united force will look better. Trust me."

We did, because he was our only source of fae information. I already went to him for job advice.

"Did you know you are the best boyfriend ever? Unless your parents hate me and say no because you gave me permission before they could."

Quinn's smooth, low chuckle reminded me of why I was in trouble and over my head with him. "You're all good. Remember, I'm used to this."

"I'm gonna owe you, aren't I?"

"Oh, tenfold. You get to pay for dates for a year."

I caught myself laughing at Quinn's joke. Wait. "A year?"

"I'm not a cheap date, either. We're going full Monty. Weekends in Iceland and—"

"Iceland?" I almost couldn't get the word out, was he serious? He came from a different life from me. A prince could use his wealth ostentatiously, while I stowed mine away for the future. There was no telling what circumstances I'd find myself in. But things were different now that we'd met the fae. I wasn't alone, even when Nol had to leave.

"You'll see." Quinn's assurance brought me back to the here and now.

I nodded, forgetting he couldn't see me. "Okay. Thank you, Quinn."

"What are boyfriends for if not for this?"

"I can think of a few other things," I teased. Charlie giggled and Nol shook his head with a smile.

Quinn chuckled again. "Me, too. I'll talk to you soon."

Again, I nodded. "Bye."

I sighed as I pulled up my travel app. "Looks like it's been decided for you, Nol. Let's get our tickets."

2

A RUSTLING IN THE dark hall downstairs gave Charlie and me pause, until Nol knocked on the wall moments later. With a lot of nagging after the first few times he'd crept in through the shadows, we'd convinced Nol to announce himself. It set off Charlie's panic attacks when she heard a strange noise that didn't belong or saw a movement in a semidark corner. The *Zayuri* skill of traveling through the shadows, or *Zamecaten*, was a bit unsettling when he appeared out of nowhere. However, it allowed Nol to go back to his apartment without us driving him there.

Nol's bag slid off his shoulder as he stepped into the room. "What?" He looked straight ahead at Charlie, sitting on a chair to slide her boots on.

When I followed Nol's gaze, Charlie was just closing her mouth, her brown doe eyes blinking. "You clean up nice."

Unfamiliar with the phrase, he frowned. His gaze flicked from his hands to her. His shower damp hair looked almost brown instead of its normal cinnamon-red, and he seemed to think that was what she was referring to.

Charlie watched, enjoying his adorably confused face.

"It's a compliment, Nol. She's saying you're dressed nice." That was an understatement. I'd told Nol not to wear his uniform on the plane. It would look out of place. Now he would stand out for a different reason.

He'd chosen a slim teal button-up that I hadn't seen before. The color deepened his pale blue eyes and accented his tan skin tone. And the brown slacks almost matched the color of his *Zayuri* jacket. I wouldn't fight him over it if he wanted to wear the jacket on the plane. It held his sword in a sheath, attached and hidden by magic on the back. Mateo loved finding clothes for him, and Nol let him do it as long as they went somewhere new once in a while. Their last excursion had been to Portland.

"Then thank you, I think. You..." Nol began scrambling for a word and dropped his bag at his feet. "Your sweater looks nice."

"This?" She tugged on the bottom of her favorite gray sweater, that was too worn for her to wear in public. "I didn't dress up to take you to the airport. Tatie wore something different, though."

Nol glanced up and down my outfit. "The clothes from the bed? How is that different?" Then without a second thought, opened his jacket.

"See?" I lowered my voice as I looked at the sleeping child on the couch. "It looks too gothic."

"No, it doesn't." Charlie argued again.

"So find something else." Nol shrugged, dismissing my concern.

"Hélène Roux doesn't show her midsection. You were right before, Charlie, it doesn't suit her!"

He reached into his sleeve, messing with the straps of the scabbard. "Who is Hélène Roux?"

How many times did I have to tell him I had to change identities? "Me."

He reached into the other sleeve. "Do not go as someone else. We won't be there that long, will we? If so, I must update my employer. I told him I'd be gone a week for a family emergency."

"I can't..." Or could I?

"No, you are used to changing it. But did you not go to France to bring Charlie and Ray home as Hally Dubois four years ago? As you keep pointing to it, technology is getting more...sophisticated. What is it called, the face identity? Will—" He paused, checking another area inside his jacket. "Ah, there it is. Will that technology not...identify you as who you are here?"

I stared, dumbfounded. He was too damn smart. "How the hell did you figure all this shit out in six months?"

He slid his jacket on and rolled his shoulders, checking his adjustments. "Seven months. Observation. It's all observation and asking questions. *Tullaca. Sye, seta pivenaca etanalu,*" *Fuck, this isn't adjusting correctly,* Nol growled under his breath, except with a few more colorful words I couldn't translate.

"I don't think that's possible," I teased. "Just take the sword out."

Nol glared at me, frustrated and stressed. He glanced at Ray, still asleep on the couch. "Fine."

The leather-wrapped hilt of his sword wavered into existence as he touched the back collar of his jacket. I'd seen it twice, four if I counted the times he'd used it in the dark. Not only was there a spell on the scabbard to keep it hidden, but the matte black metal held the *Zayuri's* unique magic. Like a magic trick, his sword grew as he drew it out at a left angle, until he had to drop his jacket. It curved like a katana but wider—a beautiful, deadly sword.

Nol looked around before he lifted it and settled the blunt side in his palm. He walked to the fireplace mantle on the wall between Charlie's lab and the hallway entrance, he gently set his sword down, which took up the entire length, and at its widest point, the entire width, of the mantle.

Standing in front of the fireplace, Nol picked up his jacket. He worked on the straps, turned it around, pulled on the seams, and slid it on again. He rolled his shoulders and frowned. "No matter what I do the straps are tight."

Charlie came forward and reached out. She waited until he nodded before touching his jacket. "You've bulked up going to the gym with Mateo. I'm assuming your training at home doesn't involve weights?"

"It does not," Nol said.

"You might have to get a new jacket."

"Are there any protective spells in it?" I asked. "Maybe I could fiddle with it."

He inspected the sleeves. "Nothing that would affect altering—I don't think."

Oh, so reassuring. "If I fly across the room, I get to beat you."

He cocked his head to the side, exasperated. "That wouldn't happen."

"Whatever you do, we need to be quick," Charlie said, always the prompt one. "I want to be on the road in ten minutes." Okay, maybe she got that from me. Still, SeaTac wasn't far and we had an hour before we had to be there.

"Then I'll give it a shot, but I'll need to see the stress points first before you can take it off."

He lifted his arms and waited, granting me permission.

I didn't understand it, but I felt nervous as I reached into his jacket. He found it funny to make me fidget. Once, he even admitted that he liked it when "he made me breathless." Nol had asked to talk about our odd feelings back in March, but we'd worked through the classic awkwardness that came with reconnecting after so long when he moved out. Crisis adverted, to talk needed. Not to sound corny, but we knew an intimate relationship would end in sorrow. He was leaving, for Pete's sake. I breathed through the feeling and focused on the task.

With our height difference it was easy to see the underside of his arm and the back of his jacket as he stood. Closing my eyes to feel the leather on my fingertips, I found several thick braided straps of *endaen* silk and leather, attached to the seam across the top of his shoulder blades and the seam down his back. Each one branched out to under the arms, over the shoulders, around the housing of the sword or down to the small of his back. The adjustable portions were under his arms and shoulders. Charlie was right. His bulkier muscles were straining the leather. He needed more strap length, more leather, and wider sleeves.

"Cool," I whispered, breaking the nervousness. "I didn't realize this was how it all works. Now I get why you keep rolling your shoulders. Doesn't the weight of the sword pull backward?"

"It's balanced magically so I don't always have to keep the jacket closed, but it isn't perfect."

I touched the adjustable part under his arm. "I think I can fix it, but it's stressed at multiple points. Even if you keep it on, which would be easiest, it's highly likely—"

He tilted his head, and I saw his face in the corner of my vision. "Hallë? Trust yourself. I do."

I chewed on my lip. Did he really, though? I saw the doubt on his face sometimes, but he always changed it when he realized I'd noticed.

"Okay, but don't get pissed at me if I screw up and you have to get a new one."

"You won't screw up."

Worn leather had less give than new leather, but I'd try. Starting with the back, my magic seeped into the pores of the old skin and caressed the smallest parts, maybe at a cellular level. Charlie would know how to explain it. If every part gave a little, the leather would stretch enough. After each pull, I wrapped a protective spell around that part to keep it from tearing.

I took a deep breath as I pulled my magic back, without even a whisper of lightheadedness. The practice I'd been doing to strengthen my magical endurance was working.

Stepping back, I opened my eyes. "How's it feel so far?"

Nol licked his lips. "That was amazing, Hallë. The back feels looser. And the magic was...delicate."

"I have to keep it light in order to"—I cleared my throat and searched for a less awkward word—"fix it. How much time do I have, Charlie?"

"That only took two minutes. You've got time."

I gawked, then picked up my jaw. "Two minutes? It felt like ages." I shook my hands out and got ready to do the rest, then got an idea about his straps. If I did it right, he'd never have to adjust them again. They'd move and breathe with him. "Let's do this, then." One part down... many more to go.

Minutes later, grimacing, Charlie and I stood shoulder to shoulder, watching Nol inspect my work.

He moved one shoulder, then the other. "The straps...I don't feel them."

Without meaning to, I let out a nervous chuckle.

He raised an eyebrow in suspicion. "What did you do?"

"Well." I pressed my lips together. Full disclosure. "The straps are kinda part of the leather now. It won't get loose and..." Squinting, I hoped he wouldn't get upset with what I'd done. Beg forgiveness, and all that. "You can take the scabbard off."

"Pardon?"

Oh, shit.

I stilled my fidgeting fingers. "I thought it would be nice if you could wear it without the sword every once in a while. I know it's always there, even if we can't see it, and it's heavy, so..."

"It could fall off."

"No." I pointed at him. "It won't stretch, or rip, or fall off, or get too small again. Ever. I promise."

His face didn't change from that disbelieving shock.

"You said you trusted me."

"I-I do."

"Then why are you questioning me with that look?"

"That's not it. I'm in awe." He traced the leather with his fingertips. "The straps are a common problem for everyone.

In awe? "Maybe I could help others, too."

His head snapped up, eyes wide. "No."

"Come on. If you say it's a common problem, what's the matter?"

He scraped his bottom teeth against his upper lip and looked away. "Do not take this wrong."

"Uh-oh," Charlie muttered, and I got nervous again. This did not bode well.

"But I think it would be a bit awkward."

I crossed my arms at his stalling. He saw my patience wearing thin and waved his hands in front of him, placating me.

"I said the magic you used was delicate, and it is. And I know you didn't mean it this way, but that could come across as—"

I gasped. "No."

Charlie laughed but shut herself up before she woke Ray.

"—intimate."

"By no means—" I had to walk away. "Nuh-uh. We're past that."

He nodded. "We...are."

"Then it shouldn't have felt that way."

He held up his fingers, pinching the air. "It did. I'm sorry."

"You should have stopped me."

"I didn't want to make it awkward while you fixed it. Not to pry too much, but have you and Quinn—"

"That is none of your business."

"I'll take that as a no. Talk to Quinn about it. Not this. Do not mention what happened here if you want to keep that relationship."

I hid my face in my hands. I was so confused, but like hell I was going to ask what the difference between *it* and *this* was. All I knew was that what I'd done made Nol anxious.

"At least this was with me and not a stranger. And in front of Charlie. I really am sorry."

Was he serious? I lifted my face, blinking at him while I tried to decide if he was messing with me. Everything he said just made the situation worse, and he wouldn't shut up. He took a few steps toward me, and I held up my hand.

"Too soon, too soon." Comfort was not what I needed. Distance. I needed distance.

"Would you rather I'd remained silent and let you discover this with someone else? You would be much angrier with me and embarrassed. Neither of us would want that." His face fell as he looked at the floor. "I'm your *muranildo*. I can tell you anything. This shouldn't be awkward to tell you how it felt, especially after the fact. We've gone through this shit before, Hallë. Every part. Except the *Zayuri* part."

"But it is awkward." Talking about sex in any form with Nol was uncomfortable. Nol was...not mine in that way, and I'd rather have not thought about it. "Because we agreed not to be that this lifetime."

He straightened, challenging me. "Did we?"

Pausing, I thought back. "Yeah...didn't we?"

He crossed his arms. "When?"

"Before Gileal moved to Rudairn"

"Ooh, things just got real." Both of us looked at Charlie, curled up in a chair, enjoying the show. Damn the little brat. "I'm gonna go put the luggage in the car while you"—she waved at Nol—"get to have a heart-to-heart with your soulmate."

"We aren't soulmates," we said together.

"Well, you're something more than friends, and you need to figure it out before you"—she pointed at me—"get any more involved with Quinn." She pointed to Nol. "And you, either plan to stay longer than two decades or before they're up, because you're not leaving and breaking her fucking heart."

We'd worked on this. We'd talked about this lifetime. When that was, I couldn't remember, but I swore we'd made that decision.

"I'm not. I won't break her heart."

"Yes, you will. It may not be this way. But you will break her heart when you leave. Get it together. You're two hundred and fifty...something years old. Even Hally acts older than you." She paused. "I mean, not here..."

"Hey." I took offense to that.

Charlie got up, grabbed my bag, and glared back at Nol. "The point is, act your age."

He pressed his fingers to his chest to defend himself. Then stopped and looked at the ceiling. "I'm sorry, Hallë. I should have found a different way to warn you and considered when and where we were."

I cleared my throat and acted my age, too. "I accept your apology. You're right, it was good that you warned me before I tried it on anyone else. And..." I looked away, my face burning. "I'll talk to Quinn about *it*." When I figured out what exactly *it* was, but Nol was not the one to ask. This kind of shit was what I'd robbed myself of when I killed my friends and got exiled. If I'd stayed in *Endae* I could ask my mother—no, I probably would have talked to An'di and Raj, but, I'd missed out on all the "girl" talk that I needed to know to become a full fledged *endaë*, a woman in human terms. "Truce?"

He nodded. "Truce."

"And?" Charlie urged.

Nol looked as confused as I was. "And what?"

"Hally, do you want this relationship to become more than platonic in this life?"

Even the thought made my face burn. "No. Just-just *muranildi*."

"Nolan?"

He looked at Charlie, then at me, silent. Holy shit. Shit, shit, no!

"No." His brow furrowed and he looked away. "But, if I'm being honest, I can't see"—Nol swallowed hard—"myself anywhere right now. Hallë is just here, and comfortable, and—" He shoved his hair back and squeezed his eyes shut. "*Tuma juvaë,* Nol swore, "*Osye in-egam enetal fontuaconi juvede setade lasi,*" *My heart can't handle this right now*, Nol mumbled under his breath, but I heard it. Now I knew the problem. Someone had broken my *muranildo's* heart. And if I ever saw them, I would punch them in the fucking face.

I threw my hands out. "This is done. It's a truce. Charlie, leave it alone. I'm sorry. I know you're not ready." I hurried over and hugged him. "You don't have to say another word."

It took him a moment, I think, to realize I'd given in and taken the loss. He'd won, and I didn't care. I turned my face to Charlie and mouthed, "Go." She took my bag and left out the front door, where she'd pulled the car around.

Nol's breath shuddered, and his arms went around me. "*Ma-hayem,*" *I'm sorry*. "I don't know what's wrong with me. Please, forgive me," he whispered in *Aemirin*, too emotional for English.

"There's nothing to forgive," I whispered back. I didn't understand why he'd begged my forgiveness, and I wouldn't until he talked to me, but I had to be patient.

TEN MINUTES LATER, FIVE more after Charlie wanted to leave, I locked the front door. Everyone was in the car with everything packed by the time I made it over, the low heels of my booties clacking on the damp cement.

"Okay, got it." I shook my cell phone, which I'd run back in for.

Nol still had his door open, a foot out as he fiddled on his phone. Instead of getting in, I came to stand in front of him. His eyebrow rose as he lifted his head to look at me.

I grabbed his arm and squeezed. "Things will work out."

"That is what you say." His look darkened into that broody thing Mateo had pointed out. I opened our bond to comfort him, sending a little energy his way in the hope of putting him at ease. Nol gave me a small smile when he felt it slip into him. He patted my hand and tried to put on a brave face. Sighing, he put his phone away and pulled on his seat belt. "You have more important things to worry about than my selfishness. I'm sorry for screwing everything up."

"Stop apologizing. Shit happens." I leaned in and kissed his temple. "You can talk to me whenever you need to. About anything," I whispered, emphasizing the last part.

"*Sitam,*" *I know*, he whispered back.

I hurried into the back seat to shut out the cold pre-dawn air. Sadly, the car wasn't as warm as I'd hoped. Charlie put our eighties Volvo in reverse and turned to back out of the driveway. She winked at me. "And we're off."

3

My phone chirped just after the gate attendant announced it was our time to board.

"*Merde*," I growled and tried to whip my carry-on around to get to my phone, then remembered it was in my purse. I pressed the button and put it to my ear. "Nicole?" I caught my breath.

"*Hélène? Tu as l'air occupé.*" *You sound busy.*

"*Non*, it's fine. We're about to board. Are you all right?"

"We're fine. Um...Bernard is on the phone fussing with Gerald." Shit, the non-Hally family drama.

"I can call him on our layover." Gerald loved his wife, but I'd reminded him a thousand times, Nicole was his wife, not the family mediator and not Léon's caretaker. My one-hour layover was quickly filling up, but I needed to deal with this.

"That's all right," Nicole backtracked. "I'm sorry. You worry about your flight."

I stopped moving. The guy behind me grunted and muffled a rude comment, and I almost missed the glare Nol gave him. "Nicole? Tell me what's wrong?"

Nicole sniffled on the other end. "I found him on the floor. He-he wasn't responding, and he was all sweaty. Hélène, I thought he was gone."

I glanced at Nol and tipped my chin. "I'll be there in a minute," I whispered. He understood, hearing Nicole with his better than human hearing. Then, setting his own apprehensions and doubts aside, he pulled my bag off my shoulder, hiked it up on his, slipped the ticket out from between my fingers and took my free hand. I wouldn't have to think while we walked. The best *muranildo* ever.

"Nicole, I'm so sorry that you found him like that. Are you still at the hospital?"

"*Oui.*"

I grimaced. They'd been there too damn long. "There's no reason to be there when he's sleeping. Why don't you go home."

"Millennials," the jerk behind us snapped, distracting me from my conversation. "Always on your phones."

Nol gave him a death glare before returning to his mask of calm, dealing with tickets and airline staff even though he barely knew what he was doing.

I bit my lip, and Nol hooked my arm as we walked down the ramp. "The doctors will call if there is any problem. Besides, you're fifteen minutes away."

"I know, but—"

"What would Léon tell you?"

"*Stop fussing over me,*" she mimicked perfectly, but with a soft chuckle.

"Exactly. Please go home and rest. I'll be there in sixteen hours. I'm sorry I can't get there sooner. Do you want me to call you during the layover?"

"No. Worry about your connecting flight."

"And you'll go home and get some rest?"

"*Oui.*"

"We're getting on the plane now. I have to go. Love you."

"*Je t'aime aussi,*" *I love you, too.* "Goodbye."

Way in the back of the plane, I let Nol take the aisle seat. I'd been told it was more comfortable for tall people, and at six-four, Nol fit that. Nonetheless, his seat was too narrow for his shoulders, and his knees pressed into the seat in front of him. I winced. If only Quinn could have taken us on his private plane. But no. Maybe we could get a ride back.

The person beside us was already settled, earphones in and oblivious to the world. He looked around Mateo's size. At least his shoulders didn't stick out on both sides.

"How is Nicole? Did I hear hospital??" Nol asked once he had stuffed his bag in the overhead.

"Ah, your French is improving."

"I'd be fluent if you'd—" He wiggled his fingers and widened his eyes. "Actually, with me traveling with you, I was hoping to talk to you about that."

I squinted at him and his stupid attempt at talking about magic without saying magic. Mother help me. "I doubt I could do it."

His eyes crinkled. "You did it once, you can do it again."

"Sure, I helped a *Terrin* speak *Aemirin* to save your ass. That doesn't mean I can do it now." The *Terrin* were a dryad-type people, which Nol and I now suspected were the native people of *Endae* before the *endai* came from Earth.

My father was the *Terrin* representative on the council, and while he didn't go to every meeting, he did join the *Amura Ore* when the *Terrin* had a problem. And now where was he? Wasting away, sick with the curse Aswryn made, while I boarded a plane to fly across the world.

"*Oyi,*" Nol whispered and bumped my arm with his. "You got...um..." He looked up, searching for the right word in English, then gave up. "*Ohaesar dirodae. Vaica Léon d'wanyle?*" *You grew melancholy. Is it Léon or something else?*

"Nothing...lost in thought. When we get to Paris"— I held up a finger—"If you stop bugging me about it, I'll...help you learn French."

His face lit up. "Thank you." Nol looked around like he'd announce the momentous occasion. A moment later, his left hand curved around my right one. He lifted it and squeezed with both of his hands. "And your dad will be fine. We will find the cure in time." He knew where my mind had gone. Typical.

I shut my eyes. This whole thing was crap. Would the Mother be so cruel as to take both my father and my nephew in quick succession? Please, Mother, no. I rested my head on Nol's arm and closed my eyes. Plane rides made me sleepy, and I hadn't been able to sleep last night.

"Hallë, something is going on. They are standing in front and holding—what is that?"

I reached over and patted his chest with my free hand. "Just listen. I've heard it before."

"It's in French."

"They have an English one, too. Shh." Nol didn't like cars. What if he didn't like planes?

"They expect us to crash?" he hissed.

Fuck.

Nol chuckled and let go of my hand. "I'm just joking."

As Nol was reaching for our bags my phone dinged with a text message. I checked it right away, even though we were late and getting off the plane first. The caller ID said Amelia. I flicked the message open: *Ignore Bernard's message. He's being himself. Listen to Léon's voicemail.*

My hands shook as I swiped Amelia's message away. I'd check the voicemail after we got going.

"What is wrong?" Nol hadn't slept, and while he was used to very little sleep, his accent and contractions took a big hit. I'd get him sleeping pills for the next leg. "Take this." Nol grabbed my bag from above. "And this." He piled his jacket on top of it. The leather thing was heavier than it appeared with the sword attached. Nol tugged hard on his bag until it came loose, and another passenger's bag went flying, sort of. Nol grabbed it before it hit anyone.

Three other passengers with international connections waited behind me while we got into the covered tunnel. The plane had landed twenty minutes late, but I had to talk to Léon before we left. I had to. Those sleeping pills were looking less likely. We moved over to the side of the ramp, where Nol dropped his bag and slid his coat on.

"It's gonna be hot in here."

"I will be fine." He slid his bag back on, grabbed mine, and began walking.

"Nol!"

He raised his arms up, a bag on each shoulder. "Are we going to argue, or are we going to make our flight?"

Lips twisted, fists on my hips, I glared at him. "I can carry my own bag."

"If I do this," he teased. "You can call Léon."

Wait. "How—"

Nol looked over his shoulder and smirked. "I know you. Now, we must be faster than your normal pace. I think you can manage to talk, though. You are in good shape." We came off the ramp and found ourselves right in the middle of the largest terminal. Fan-freaking-tastic.

"We'll get a few minutes at the gate." I hoped. Security screening would be a bitch, but inevitable since we weren't in the international terminal.

"You will have more if you call now." Nol grabbed my hand and hurried away from the gate—almost a jog for me. He pulled out a ticket, looked around, and cussed under his breath.

I tugged him over to the huge map of the airport. "We're here, and we need to take the AirTrain."

"Got it." He whispered something under his breath in *Aemirin* before tugging on my hand again. "*Neda,*" There. And we were off.

I scrolled around on my phone calls and pressed the voicemail for Léon, but it didn't play. Fine, I'd try calling. Pressing the call back button was a challenge while jogging through an airport. My thumb finally touched the little button on my smartphone. Again, nothing. Nol pulled on me, and we dodged more people.

"It's not working." I scrolled through my favorites and tried that way with the same result. We'd have time at the gate. I sighed, snatched my bouncing purse, and shoved the phone in as we jogged. Except five steps later, we were at the AirTrain and had four minutes to wait.

"Would it be quicker to walk?" Nol looked up and down through the hordes of bustling travelers.

I shook my head. "No, this is the quickest way."

An AirTrain rolled up, and Nol jumped into action.

I pulled hard on his arm. "Wrong one. It goes the opposite way."

"You have gone through here a lot?" He raised his voice to be heard over the foot and AirTrain traffic.

"Enough."

The AirTrain came, and as we were getting on, a text notification from Amelia appeared, but my phone didn't allow me to open the damn message. You'd think airport wifi would be more reliable. The doors closed, and Nol began rubbing the knuckles of my hand he still held. "It is all right, Hallë."

I took a breath and accepted the comfort he offered. "I hope the phone will work enough to call when we get to the gate. I'm sure they're nervous."

"They will be fine. Did they not just help Charlie when Remi died?"

My head snapped to him. "Charlie told you?"

Nol shrugged it off like it was no big deal. The one who wouldn't talk about his monsters thought it was no big deal that someone else talked about their issues. Unbelievable. "Well?"

"Well, what?" Oh, Remi. "They did, but with Charlie's panic attack, I came in to help."

Nol didn't say anything. Maybe he didn't know as much as he thought. "Remi's parents tried to take Ray when Charlie was in the hospital with Remi." I remembered the day I'd flown in. I'd opened Gerald's and Nicole's front door, as they'd known I was coming, and came face to face with Remi's mother holding little Ray.

"Remi's parens are some fucked-up people. It wasn't pretty. They tried to steal Ray, can you believe it?" I rubbed my eyes, then stopped abruptly, remembering my makeup. "Eventually, I paid them off."

"How much?"

I hated talking about money, about how much our family actually had and how much I'd inherited from the Dubois estate. "Two million."

"Dollars?" His eyes widened. He knew the value of money."

"Francs. Sad really. That was how much their son and granddaughter were worth to them."

The AirTrain stopped, and the group closest to the doors got off. Two more stops.

Nol leaned down, his lips against my ear so he could whisper. "You have that much money and you are charging me rent?"

I shrugged. "I'm giving you the full human experience," I whispered back. "You get a fifty percent discount from the rest of the tenants." I turned to smirk at him.

He tried to hide his shock, but I caught it.

"Don't look at me like that. It's Amelia's livelihood."

His brow furrowed as he tried to piece that out.

"Amelia is the manager, but it is a Dubois company. My company. What can I say? Maman and Papa taught me well." I chuckled at his continued frowning. "And I passed that knowledge down to Léon's descendants. Don't be sore, Nol. I am doing this for your own good."

"I think I hate you right now."

I laughed, and my forehead bumped his collarbone as I leaned on him. The AirTrain stopped again, and I wasn't ready for it. Nol stayed in his spot, and I almost fell on my ass, but he grabbed my arm at the last moment.

My jaw dropped. "Rude."

"I could have let you fall." He smirked, enjoying my irritation and almost embarrassing moment. I glared at him a while longer. The AirTrain stopped again, and we followed everyone off. Thirty minutes later, screened by security, and fully annoyed, we arrived at our gate. Nol dropped our bags on a chair at the end and plopped down on another one.

"We should get you some sleeping meds for the plane." Dealing with him tired and grumpy the entire flight would drive me and the flight attendants insane.

"I will be fine."

"You're not using contractions. You're fucking tired, Nol. Stop arguing."

"Call Léon."

I pulled my phone out of my purse and pointed at him with it. "If you agree to find some sleep aids."

Nol shoved his hair back with both hands and puffed his cheeks out. "What does that even mean?"

I pointed to the closest store. "Go ask them. Flutter your eyelashes at the pretty girl and she'll help you find them."

"I do not flutter my eyelashes." He scoffed as if I'd insulted him and his flirting abilities.

"You're right. You give them all flirty smiles, and your eyes crinkle and look all cute. Go do that."

One of his eyebrows lifted, and he pressed his fingers to his chest. "You think my eyes are *cute*? How can eyes be cute? Should I be offended?"

"No! Go ask."

"I think you should pay."

"Twynolan, go get some drugs for the plane. Now. And get a book. Two. Big ones."

That got him moving faster. The fact that he didn't want to go shopping proved my point about how tired he was. The *endao* loved shopping. It didn't matter if he bought anything. He loved going to as many places as he could and seeing as much as possible. Essentially, he was a tourist, except this wasn't a vacation. He was stuck here.

After he was well on his way and getting in line, I checked Amelia's text first.

Saw you called. He was asleep.

I dropped my arms and looked up at the high airport ceiling before remembering the voicemail. I pushed play and raised the phone to my ear.

"Hello, old lady." Léon's familiar, youthful voice came through the scratchiness that came with age. "Don't worry about me. I'll be out of here in no time."

I snorted as it clicked off. He never said goodbye, or any other farewell, for that matter. I tapped the call back button. The phone thought about it for a second, and then it started ringing. Thank the Mother. I slid and sat on the floor against the window, where I could still see our luggage so people didn't freak out about unattended bags. Against my ear, the phone rang four times and went to voicemail. I tried again. We didn't have long now—ten, fifteen minutes before they started calling passengers on. I wanted as much time as possible to talk to him.

"*Tante* Hélène?" Amelia cleared her throat like she'd been sleeping or crying.

"Hello, *mon chou*. What is happening? Have you gotten any rest? How is everyone holding up?"

"We're all fine. I promise." Amelia cleared her throat a few times. "It's the guys' arguing that's stressful. On top of convincing Léon to agree to a bypass, Gerald and Bernard are arguing about company schematics again."

"They need to figure it out soon or I will close the it."

"I know. Léon warned them yesterday."

"Papa would've rather seen his company collapse than have the family fight over it," I reiterated to her for the thousandth time. *Dubois et Bercot – Maison d'Art et de Métier—* The bespoke furniture house my foster grandfather founded in eighteen sixty-eight had survived three wars, including both World Wars. Now, it was up to Léon's descendants to manage the business, but it was more bickering than management this past year. And I didn't want to step in, but I would if it came down to it. Being the silent partner had its perks.

"How is Léon? Can I talk—" I choked on my words and held my breath so I wouldn't hyperventilate.

"I'm sorry. Look at me carrying on."

"Don't be. All of you are important to me."

"He asked for you again a few hours ago. He'll be delighted." Amelia's breathing increased like she was running or walking fast. "I went to get him some pudding."

I squeezed my eyes shut, trying to block out all the noises of the airport and pretend I was walking with her. "*Merci, mon chou.*" *Thank you, my cabbage.*

"You need to stop calling me that." But she chuckled while she chided me.

I scoffed. "Never."

"Here he is. Love you."

"Love you, too."

"*Tante* Hélène?" Léon's voice brought tears of relief to my eyes, and the knot in my chest loosened.

"It's me. Can you hear me all right?"

"*Oui.*" His words were slow, reminding me of what had happened hours ago. I felt a tear start to roll, but I swiped it away with a shaky hand. "I hear you well. These new hearing aids work better than the last ones. Where are you?"

"New York. My flight will be boarding shortly. I just needed to hear your voice."

"Don't fret. It was only a heart attack." But there was a pause. We knew the reality; Léon had turned ninety-eight this month. "They're talking about bypasses. Evidently, these doctors think they can fix anything still breathing. I have to keep reminding them that I'm older than dirt and to stop worrying so much. I don't need you to come in here worrying like these young things. I think my heart doctor just got out of secondary school."

I had to laugh. Even down for the count, he tried to joke around. "Oh, Léon, let them work on you. It's good practice for these young-sters. And don't be grumpy with them. They mean well."

"Sometimes I wonder about that. Seems nowadays they're in it for the paycheck, hurrying patients in and out as fast as they can. I can't wait to get back home."

I could imagine the scowl on his face. We both hated them. Barely anything good came out of them. "Yes, well, you wouldn't be in there if you hadn't gone and had a heart attack. What were you thinking? You can't be doing things like that."

Léon chuckled. "I know. I just couldn't help myself." He paused. "I heard Nicole found me."

I cleared my throat and got serious. "Yes. It scared her, but you are lucky she got to you so soon. How much do you know about your condition?"

"Enough to know it could have been much worse. That bypass thing they want to do seems important, but I don't see the point of having surgery at my age."

"Don't say that. Think about it. You are a functioning nine-ty-eight-year-old man. You walk and make your own meals. You go to the bathroom independently."

"That's all true, but I'm so tired of it all. Gerald shouldn't have to take care of me constantly. I don't want to depend on Gerald, Nicole, and Amelia. It's stressful and they can't enjoy any vacations. It isn't supposed to be this way."

"It's called payback for all those years—"

"Not my grandchildren. I want them to be free to enjoy retirement."

Gerald thought the responsibility of taking care of Léon fell on him, after all the years Léon, his wife, Michelle, and I had taken care of Gerald and Amelia. "Then I'll come home. We'll go south where people won't recognize me."

"Hélène, I can't ask you to do that."

"You're not asking. I want to. You're my baby. Besides, I promised your mother." I swallowed before my words failed me. Mother help me, I missed my sister. I took the phone away from my mouth and counted to ten, pushing all those emotions down deep. "I miss you. You're too stubborn to talk on the phone for more than five minutes. You hate video chats! The only logical thing to do is come be with you."

"You'd be sick of me in a month."

"I'm never sick of you. Now, tell me what's going on. Paint me a picture so I can pretend I'm sitting next to you."

"Oh..." He drew out that word. "You know what these hospital rooms look like. Annoying monitors beeping at you constantly. Blankets that don't do a bit of good." He laughed. "I don't even have a window. Imagine that, if you will. The nurses are quite the lookers, except the male ones. I still don't understand that. They got my arm hooked up to little tubes, and sticky things on my chest."

"Sounds fun. Tell me more."

Nol came back, smiled, and shook the book at me while Léon gave me more details. He sat in his chair and started reading. When a voice over the intercom spoke, Nol lifted his head to listen. Fifteen more minutes until boarding.

"Where are the tickets?" Nol whispered.

I pointed at my bag and let him dig around in it. He scowled.

"One moment, Léon." I covered the speaker. "What?"

"We are in the back again." Where Nol had to almost fold in two to fit.

"Léon? I need to go. They're starting announcements."

"Sure. *Tante*? Is he with you?"

Fuck. "Yes."

Léon stayed quiet long enough that I checked to see if he'd hung up. "I want to meet him. There are things we need to discuss."

I turned to face the window. The boy had just had a heart attack. How could I deny him? "Promise me—" Wiping my tears before they fell, I lifted the phone back to my ear. "Promise me you won't yell." I wiped more tears away, knowing I probably looked like a raccoon.

"I'll stay civil. Promise."

I nodded, knowing this was as good as I'd get. An arm snaked around my shoulder from my right. I leaned into Nol with the phone to my ear, trying to hold all my emotions in, which I was epically failing at.

"Don't fret. I won't break your soulmate."

He knew it would make me smile and take the attention off himself. "I love you, Léon. Please stay well while I'm in the air? I need to see your smile."

"I'll send you a picture just in case."

A harsh bark of laughter escaped out of my chest. "Defiant little shit."

"There's my Tatie." He hung the phone up before I could say good-bye. Again, defiant.

Nol took the phone and pulled me in tighter, placing a hand on the back of my head. "*Cyesvera*," *Things will be fine.*

I shook my head. "You can't promise that, Nol."

He wrapped me in his arms and rested his cheek on my head. "*Saje, sitam, olentame,*" *Shh, I know. I will be here beside you.* "I will hold hope for both of us."

I sat with Nol for a few more minutes, before I wiped my eyes and came away with mascara and concealer. Crap.

"Here." Nol leaned in, almost nose to nose, and pressed his thumbs under my eyes. He whispered a spell and swiped out, then crinkled his eyes. "All better. No more makeup." He tapped my nose, his knuckle slid off the tip, and his eyes crinkled.

"Thanks." I leaned forward, out of the circle of his arms, stood, and grabbed my purse and tickets.

"What are you doing?"

"Stay put. I'm going to try to get you more room."

At a loss for words—because how on Earth could I make room in a plane—he stayed where he was, puzzling it out. I headed over to the counter to see about some first-class seats. Besides, I could afford it.

4

WE JUMPED INTO ONE of the airport's prayer rooms after getting off the plane. Following numerous failed attempts, I got out of my own freaking thoughts and projected my magic, with my knowledge of French, into Nol's mind. My magic was weird. A spell would have been simpler, but then I'd have to find a spell and learn it…too much time wasted. Instead, my magical energy manipulated reality to make it do what I wanted. Ugh, that sounded even worse.

Even though we had nothing to declare or any baggage to pick up, it still took a solid thirty minutes to get through customs. And we had French passports. And Nol's French was believable enough to fool them. I'm good like that.

My phone vibrated in my pocket. Amelia and I had been texting back and forth since we'd landed. I dropped my arms after looking at her message. "Amelia says she's waiting in luggage claim for us. And it's crazy fucking busy. Keep your eyes open for her."

"Did they just say a dog is on the runway?" Nol asked in his newly learned French.

"What?" My backpack slipped off my shoulder as I glanced at him to make sense of his random question.

"Over the"—he pointed to the ceiling—"speaker."

"Nol, listen!" How was that even remotely important at the moment?

He frowned. "You expect me to recognize Amelia from video calls in a crowded airport? That I'm rarely a part of?" he asked as we walked down a ramp and around a large tourist group. "I'll try, but I can't promise to succeed. See, I am listening. To you and the airport speaker." He winked at me, then made a point of scanning the crowd.

I rolled my eyes and looked around the crowded airport. There was no way to see anything other than the people directly around me. Nol could see above almost everyone, but he wasn't much help.

"Hally?" a familiar female voice shouted from my right.

Nol grabbed my hand and pulled me. After moving around three families, I saw her, close to a bookstand, waving like mad. Amelia bounced up and down like a bubbly teenager, her graying auburn hair swaying along with it. She'd cut it since the last call. Now her waves didn't touch her shoulders.

I spread my arms wide as I hurried over to my niece. I lifted my head and my chin rested on her boney shoulder as I hugged her for dear life. "*Mon chou! Tes cheveux sont ravissants.*" *Your hair is lovely.* I let her go, but snatched her hands, giving her kisses on each cheek. "Oh, how I've missed you."

"I'm so happy you're here." Amelia pulled me into another fierce hug. She leaned back, tilting me away to examine my outfit. Nothing like my other identity here.

I held my breath, waiting for her opinion.

"Your clothes suit you. Not because you are Hally Dubois and certainly not Hélène, but *you*. I love it."

"Amelia..."

She squeezed my hand and pulled me toward her again. "Now, introduce him."

Pursing my lips, I gave her a flat stare.

"You're the one who taught me my manners. Blame yourself."

Nol snorted behind me. "What a concept. My *muranildë* never behaved as a child."

I whipped my head around. "I did so!"

Nol pinched his fingers together and lifted a shoulder. "Who got banished for not listening?"

My jaw dropped. How dare he casually mention my exile. The reason our friends' deaths.

Nol leaned forward and tapped my nose. "Lahiem would have laughed."

Blinking, I considered our old friend's reaction to such things. Nol was right, she would have been beside him teasing me.

Caving, my shoulders dropped. "Fine," I grumbled. "Amelia, Nolan. Nol, Amelia."

She held her hands close together, as if holding all her emotions in. A moment later, she snatched Nol's hands. I wasn't sure if she pulled him down or Nol bent over on his own to meet her five-foot-seven-inch frame, but she planted two kisses on each cheek. Like Charlie, Amelia felt no animosity toward Nol. The girls were in the minority, however. The youngest generation was the most forgiving, as we hadn't been able to spend much time together. My family was slipping away from me.

"You're taller than I imagined," Amelia pointed out in English.

Nol's eyebrows shot up. "You speak English. I didn't expect that. You always speak French in your family meetings. Not that I listen to them all, but I've heard a few."

"I must know English if I am running two international businesses. Come, we can talk in the car." Amelia hooked Nol's arm, just like Emma used to do with mine. I smiled at the familiar reminder of my sister. "Did you both not bring any luggage?"

I shook my head. "My clothes at my apartment will do fine. Nol could have, but I guess he took my lead."

We made it through terminal 2E easily, but 2F was a mess. I grabbed Amelia's hand as she dashed between people while the crowd seemed to split for Nol. At last, getting to the elevator, Amelia mashed the button and took a long breath. "Welcome back to Paris!" She wiggled her eyebrows as I scoffed. "I won't ask how the flight was. I'm sure you're exhausted, annoyed, and hungry."

"I'm starving," Nol chimed in. "They had small portions. Hallë gave me half of her meal and I'm still hungry."

The elevator dinged, and they went in first, chitchatting away. "I imagine so! With your physique and height, I'm certain you eat much more than Hally. Would you like to stop for something to eat?"

Nol hitched his bag up higher on one shoulder then glanced at me before answering. "I would, yes."

"Tat—Hally?" Amelia corrected herself just as another traveler popped into the elevator. The traveler pressed the -1 elevator button to the car park before I could reach it. "Shall we go to your apartment to drop your things off? A shower?"

"A shower would be lovely, but I want to see Léon first."

"We'll go straight there after food then." The door opened, and Amelia's new blue BMW SUV sat three cars away, visible from the elevator.

I clapped a hand to my mouth. "How did you get such a good spot?"

"Luck, I guess."

"I'm so glad you brought your X5. As you can see, Nol needs the legroom."

"I can fit into small spaces if needed." Nol assured me as if I didn't witness it on the other flight. "Although, I did appreciate the upgrade on the second flight."

"I needed you to sleep. There was no way you could have done that folded in two." The idea of sleeping in that position made *my* neck twitch. I did have sympathy for Nol and his height, but to be just a little taller? I'd love a measly two extra inches.

"I never fly anything but first class," Amelia announced. Her chin in the air as she opened her door. The girl couldn't be snooty if her life depended on it. There was too much of her great-grandmother in her.

I opened the rear driver door, tossed my bag in the other seat, and slid in. The smell of a new car and real leather relaxed me. I liked cars—driving them. Repairing cars wasn't my thing. Okay, maybe on the side of the road, but I hired people to work on them.

Nol opened the rear passenger door, set his bag and coat down before hopping in the front seat. "Do you travel often?" he asked Amelia once they were both inside.

Amelia pushed the ignition button and pulled her seat belt on. "A few times per year. So this must mean you're rested, at least some-what."

"He passed out before the third chapter of his book."

"I didn't anticipate such a quick reaction to the pills. And they tasted disgusting." Nol looked forward, but I imagined his scowl—the same one he'd given on the plane.

"You're not supposed to chew them," I chided for the twenty-seventh time.

"As I found out afterward," he grumbled at the window, watching the empty car beside us as Amelia's car started backing out.

"I didn't think you'd need me to tell you. You read everything." Had I laughed at Nol's sour expression as he tried to drink enough water to get the taste of the pills out of his teeth? Yes. But until he passed out I'd had to hear him complain that the taste was still there. Even after food.

"I did read the directions. It said to swallow two pills with water. I didn't take that literally." He opened his mouth and licked his molars as if there were still bits in there. "I can still taste it," he grumbled when he closed his mouth.

Amelia stopped backing out and laughed. Luckily, she wasn't very far.

Huffing at her amusement and the irritation that the reminder brought, I snapped at Nol. "Buckle up and try not to freak. Amelia's driving is more...emotional than mine."

Ameilia's laugh cut off short. Both of them looked back at me.

Amelia looked offended. "Emotional?"

"What does that mean?" Nol asked at the same time with an open and curious expression.

I gave Amelia a flat look. She needed no other explanation. "Emotional. Don't worry too much, though, she's never been in an accident."

Nol's lip curled. "Encouraging."

Amelia grinned and started to drive. The chirp of her tires echoed through the parking garage.

"Now." Amelia paused and checked both ways before moving into traffic. Her eyes flicked to me in the rearview mirror between driving and talking. "Nolan, not everyone in the family speaks much English. Some not at all."

"Bernard," I offered.

"Sylvie," Amelia added. "That's Bernard's daughter."

"It is convenient that I am fluent in French, then," Nol said in French. I was wondering when he'd hit her with it. But he did love his surprises.

"What? Since when?"

"Since this afternoon. Hallë's magic worked perfectly. I have been listening to conversations and the announcements. There was a dog on the runway. They said it was delaying flights."

"Magic? Yes...magic." She paused, pressing her lips together as her eyes darted from car to car in front of her. "It's hard to wrap my head around. After all these years and then you have magic." Her hands flew off the steering wheel for a moment. "It really is real! It will take time to adjust." She then veered left to cut off the person behind us.

Nol jumped and grabbed the oh-shit handle.

Amelia righted the car and started driving normal again. She studied Nol for a moment and his white-knuckled grip on the handle. "Nolan, aren't you a warrior of some sort?"

Nol sighed, used to being teased for his fear of car rides. "I am not fond of vehicles."

"That's apparent," Amelia mumbled, then honked her horn.

Nol turned in his seat to face her then a slow smirk lifted the corners of his mouth. "I would like to see you ride a dragon."

Without a hint of surprise or even a look his way, Amelia shot back, "Hally has mentioned they exist over there. I never knew you rode them, though. How fascinating."

"Not everyone, just *Zayuri*."

"Why not more?" She made another death-defying dive into the right lane. I had to remind myself that she knew what she was doing. *She's never been in an accident. She's never been in an accident,* I chanted to myself.

"*Zayuri* and our dragons work in a harmony that is not present in other *endai* or dragons alike. Wild dragons don't have the higher consciousness to communicate. There are thousands of studies and attempts to try. Many possess formidable intelligence, certainly, but not at the level."

"What about domesticating and training them? You don't have to consciously connect with them. We ride horses and don't converse with them."

"That is not something our species would consider humane. They must choose freely. We would never force a living being into servitude."

Nol turned to look at me and reached back to touch my knee. I grabbed his hand and squeezed. That was exactly what the slave band was, and it killed Nol to be in any way associated with something so vile. Everyone was quiet for a while, not knowing what to say after that.

"Oh," Amelia said out of the blue as we made it through the tunnel on A1 into the upper outskirts of Paris. We weren't far from the hospital now. "Nolan, would you be open to fast food? It's not the most nutritious, but it'll fill your belly."

"What do you have in mind?" Nol asked.

"We just passed a McDonalds. I can veer off, and it won't cost us more than ten minutes. Hally?"

Nol looked back at me again. "Hallë? Do you mind?"

If he was asking for McDonalds, he had to be hungry. He wasn't much of a fan of greasy, over-salted food. I, on the other hand, didn't mind a chicken burger every once in a while.

"All right. Let's do it."

NOL THREW THE WRAPPER of his second McChicken without cheese or condiments into the bag and opened his door. The hospital campus, which took up a city block, was across the street from the car park.

"That is a hospital?" Nol scrunched his nose as he looked at the facility of older red-brick buildings to the right and a modern four-story gray tower.

"What else would it be?" Amelia headed for the crosswalk, leaving us to hurry after her.

"It is very red." Nol leaned over. "And narrow."

"What are you talking about?" I took a few steps back and tried to see how he saw it. "No. It's this whole thing." I swept my arm from left to right. "Look past that one." I pointed up to the huge modern building so unlike the old, long brick buildings alongside it within the walled complex. They were part of the old hospital and had various uses. "Our destination is the silver one there."

"This entire thing is one hospital? The one Hallë was in is much smaller. Why so many buildings? Is France's population much bigger than the United States?"

Amelia shook her head, standing tall. "We just have a better system."

I smirked as we headed up the ramp to the front of *Bichat-Claude Bernard* Hospital.

"What?" Amelia glared at me.

"Weren't you just complaining about the system six months ago?"

My niece scoffed. "I don't know what you're talking about."

The glass doors whooshed opened to a wide open lobby. The cloudy morning light seeped in through the floor to ceiling windows. Dozens people occupied the main lobby at this mid-morning hour—not as many as I'd expected. None of them paid attention to the comings and goings of new visitors. Maybe one or two—the security guard by the escalator, in particular. But Amelia turned left and got on the escalator to the second floor.

As we came to the top, and the people ahead of me were out of the way, my eyes squeezed shut for a moment from the sunny yellow wall. It seemed like every room on the second floor had different bright-colored walls. Some red, some lime green, and an orange waiting room wall. All with chairs that did not match. It threatened to give me a headache.

"Tatie? In here." Amelia tugged on my arm and guided me over to the—you guessed it—bright yellow elevators. No matter how many bright colors they painted things, it wouldn't brighten anybody's mood. The less time we spent here, the better. "Amelia, have they mentioned anything about discharging him? Or that bypass thing?"

Amelia pressed the number four button. "Not since I left last night. The doctors haven't been around this morning."

"Hmm." I made a mental note to ask a doctor or Nicole later. I didn't like this lack of care and communication, but I'd take it with a grain of salt. Nicole had been by his side the most. "It's nice of you to give Nicole a break. Is she doing better?"

"She's tired. She stayed with him all day yesterday. I'm sure you'll see her this afternoon."

"That would be nice."

The elevator opened up on the shining gray and blue tiles of the fourth floor. Garish orange seats were arranged in groups to make a small lobby area in front of a large reception desk with a large house plant, or more like a small potted tree. Why it wasn't on the floor was someone else's best guess. I just wanted to get to Léon. But the young woman behind the desk beckoned us over. She wore Snoopy scrubs and a fuzzy cardigan. Her short black hair pressed against her temple in little swirls, with the rest of it in an updo bun. So cute.

"*Bonjour*," Amelia and I said together. Amelia scribbled her name and I scribbled mine and Nol's names down.

When we started moving again, I realized we'd left Nol behind. I turned to find him in the reception area staring out the window toward the seventh arrondissement.

"Is that the Eiffel Tower?" Nol's finger tapped the window as he stared.

There in the distance, atop the city of white structures and red brick, stretching into the sky in the hazy light of midafternoon, stood the Iron Lady. "We call her *Le Dame de Fur*. I'm sure one of us can take you there, if you'd like."

"Perhaps. I don't want to be a hindrance more than I already am to your visit."

"Nol, the hospital has visiting hours. I can't stay here twenty-four-hours a day. If you ask really nicely and bat your eyelashes at Amelia, she might take you there herself."

Nol looked away from the window. The white of the overcast, hazy sky through the window dulled his skin and hair. "I don't bat my eyelashes. I ask nicely and am courteous."

"Is that what you think that is?" I squeezed his arm. "The French can teach you a thing or two still. Now come on."

The hallway was almost claustrophobic with its tall white and gray walls. Not that I was claustrophobic, I just hated hospitals. The gray tiles reflected the fluorescent lights above. Some of the rooms were open; most had patients and a few were empty and dark. Ahead of us, the hallways opened. A bank of windows replaced the stifling white and I could breathe.

Amelia stopped and raised her hand on the partially opened door of room 413.

"Wait." I grabbed Nol's elbow and tugged. "Do you mind waiting out here? Just at first. I think it would be good to say hello alone."

Nol's shoulders sagged in relief. "Sure, what a great idea. I'll go back to the chairs and continue my book."

"No need, there's a smaller seating area right over there next to the restrooms." Amelia pointed down the hallway. It must have been a space off to the side that we couldn't see from our angle.

I turned to Nol. "Thank you for understanding. And for all the help with…everything."

Nol touched my nose with his book. "You're welcome. Now pages must be read. Go see Léon."

"Tatie, wait. I must drop your backpacks off and get back to work. This is goodbye for right now."

"Thank you, again, *mon chou*. For everything." She'd dropped a meeting to pick us up at the airport, took us to the hospital, *and* volunteered to drop our bags off at my apartment.

"Text me tonight when you're settled in the apartment, or I'll assume you're here and come drag you out." Amelia gave me two quick cheek kisses.

"It won't come to that. I'll text you later."

Amelia hurried out, her ballerina shoes sliding against the floor with every step.

I waited until Nol found the chairs. He looked back once and waved his book at me, one of the only things he'd grabbed out of his bag still in Amelia's car. I nodded and pushed the door open. What used to be a six-foot-two, heavily muscled man was now half that size and shrinking before my eyes. The overhead florescent lights bleached Léon's already pale skin. Age spots speckled his mostly bald head. He held a large tablet in his shaking, spotted hands. The thing looked heavy. We could get him a stand for that. It was a shoebox of a room, but he didn't have a second bed. Then again, it could have looked smaller because of all the medical equipment shoved against two walls. Speaking of walls, I set a hand on my waist and cocked my hip for some attitude.

"You may not have a window, but you do have this lovely pink wall that you failed to mention."

Léon's face transformed. His brown eyes, yellow with age, crinkled, and he smiled from ear to ear. The wrinkles piled up at the top of his cheeks and across his forehead. He looked like a skeletal Buddha.

"I didn't expect you for hours yet, Tatie."

I scooted in and shut the door. "We came straight here. There's no telling when the king and queen will call for me."

"Hm, how long will that visit take?"

"It's somewhere in Andorra, so a day. Quinn bought me some time."

"Sounds like a catch."

My cheeks warmed, and Léon's smile returned. "He's great. It's nice that I don't have to hide, and I won't have to leave him in a few years. Not that I'm saying we're talking about long term. But it's nice to know I can relax and let him get to know me. Does that make sense?"

"It does." Léon patted his bed beside his leg, but I hesitated. I'd always known he'd grow fragile, but I'd kept shoving it to the back of my mind to deal with later. "My question is, what personality will he get to know?"

I looked down at my hands—mine. No matter who I was pretending to be, in whatever city I was living in, those were mine. "I like being Hally, but I'm also myself here." I walked over and sat on the bed where he wanted me to sit. "I will have to show him both and let the chips fall where they land. Do you notice a change?"

"I don't know. You just sat down. Tell me everything."

"Nonsense. I need to know the details." I ticked off every question on my fingers. "Have they said more about the surgery? When will they discharge you? What do you want to do when you're out? We can go anywhere post-surgery. Screw the doctors! If you want to travel, we will. I can see about moving back for a while. That has more factors about it, so I can't promise that with certainty, but it's a possibility."

Léon lowered his head and looked at me over his fuzzy gray eyebrows. "What about your new friends? Your tattoo shop?"

None of them had gotten to meet Léon in person, as he'd stopped traveling a decade ago. We'd talked about organizing a trip here, but it just kept getting postponed. Come hell or high water, I'd bring them this summer.

"They're very supportive." I knew Mateo would be all for it. Lewis and Yumi were a different matter. Maybe they'd come visit. "And it's Lewis's shop, too. Again, it's a factor to deal with later. What about you?"

"Surgery is not scheduled yet. I don't know much still. Gerald is advocating. Tatie, these doctors are so young! Have you seen any?"

"Not here, but I know what you mean. If you don't know much, what do you need? What can I help with?"

"Cognac and a cigar? No, I'm kidding." Léon waved a hand at me, laughing. I knew he was kidding, though. "I haven't had either in years." Léon folded his hands together and sighed. "Company would be nice. Amelia and Gerald have their businesses to run. Nicole feels guilty, but needed some time away. What about a game of Yahtzee?"

"I can do that! Do they have it here?"

"Nicole brought that along with the tablet and cards."

"Very thoughtful." I got up to search for the box. "I was thinking about getting you a stand for that block of a tablet."

"Maybe. Tatie..." Léon paused and gave me a long look. "I want to talk to him first."

I knew who "him" was. I came back to the bed and held one of his hands between mine. "Are you certain about this? You aren't well. I don't want you getting angry—"

"I've waited two months. I've calmed my anger. I told you I'd be civil and I meant it. It's time. There are some words that need to be said."

"Lee, don't hate him. Give him a chance."

My nephew's eyebrows rose so far that if he'd still had hair, they would've been hidden.

"He's my *muranildo,* and he was a child who found his friends lying on the floor dead. He very much regrets his words. Even if Nol hadn't led those professors to me, I would have been tried with the same outcome."

"He didn't need to revoke your bond. He didn't need to say what he said to you."

"You're right, he didn't need to. But he was a kid, just like me, Lee." I squeezed his hand tightly. A knot in my stomach loosened. "What are you going to talk to him about?"

"That's between him and me. Does he know about your night terrors?"

I sat up all the way, my whole body much looser than it had been moments ago. "Oh yes. I've always had them. It comes with the territory of my ability to dream walk. He can even get into them and calm them."

Léon's brow furrowed as he looked from my head to my shoulders and back again like he'd see my dream walking magic somewhere on me. He swallowed and thought about what I'd said. "Can he dream walk, too?"

I shook my head. "He can do it only with me because of our bond. We can open that bond and share thoughts, dreams, and sight even. So yes, he knows. This is a lot, I know. It's just...you know I don't keep things from you."

"But you don't share *endaen* things. It's new for you, with him here and with your magic back. What..." Léon licked his lips and reached for his cup on the side table, but I was in the way. I grabbed it and waited for him to finish drinking. "What do you wish me not to mention?"

I swallowed and looked away. "I haven't told him about Rene. I'm not trying to keep it from him, but you were too young to remember what really happened." Léon narrowed his eyes at me, remembering his own versions of those days. "Just don't tell him shit to make him feel guilty. You should already know what I mean, young man." I puffed my cheeks out, reminding myself of Nol.

"I know. Now, go get him so we can play Yahtzee."

"Okay." I stood and kissed his temple before going to get Nol. The waiting room was much closer than I thought and seemed to take only a few steps before I was there. Was that because I'd been apprehensive of seeing my nephew laid up in bed, or was it because I didn't want the two of them to meet? The world might never know; I sure didn't.

I found my *muranildo* bent over, reading the book he'd started on the plane. "Nol? Léon would like to speak with you."

Nol raised his head slowly as he closed his book. No need to use a bookmark; he remembered almost everything. He stood up and set his book on the chair. "Any tips?"

"I don't know what he's going to say." I couldn't help but lean in and hug him. "No arguing. If he pisses you off, leave. I don't know if his heart can take it."

"Promise." He laid his cheek on top of my head. "They have a right to be angry at me."

"Not at you. The system, the council's decision, but not the actions of an emotional, grieving child. That isn't fair. They know it's not your fault. You're just convenient."

Nol lifted his head and stepped away without glancing at me once.

"Fuck," I whispered to the empty space. I plopped down on the seat next to Nol's empty one.

5

After ten minutes of wringing my hands, I could've lied to myself and claimed they were cold, because they were ice cold, but the wait was making me edgy. What in all the realms could they be talking about for so long?

I'd paced, checked my phone a billion times for something to distract myself, and texted Mateo, Charlie and Lewis. But at eleven o'clock at night in Seattle, they were asleep or, in Lewis' case, busy tattooing.

My phone chirped in my hands and I almost dropped it. Finally, a distraction. Except it was my boyfriend. That meant he was done talking to his parents. I dreaded the answer even as I answered the phone. Even so, my stomach fluttered as I pictured him on the other end. Where was he? Andorra, still?

Answer the damn phone and you'll find out, Hally. I scoffed at myself, pressed the green button and set it against my ear. *"Hey, you."* I went with pleased—or rather, my brain had chosen for me.

"Hi," he answered in the soft tone that always made me smile, no matter what. "I've got news. Are you still at the hospital?"

"Uh-huh." Then I snapped out of my stupid happy zone. He was asking for a damn reason. *Get it to-fucking-gether, Hally!* Jeez, I was a mess today.

"Good. Where at? I'm walking through the doors now."

"Um...south side, fourth floor."

"Okay. I'll be up there soon."

"Wait, what? You're here, in Paris?"

"Yeah, flew in twenty minutes ago."

"I thought—"

"I'll tell you when I get up there."

"'Kay." I swallowed, my throat sticking together. This was going to be bad. He wouldn't come here if it wasn't. But then he was my boyfriend, he could be here just to support me. "See you soon." I hung up and dropped my arm and phone to my lap. Fuck.

I stood up and walked over to the window. Northern Paris spread out before me. All the famous buildings were on the opposite side of the building. A movement on the window started me until I realized it was my own reflection. I had circles under my eyes, my dark freckles stood out even more than normal with my skin paler than normal from fatigue. Paler? Freckles? Shit, Nol had taken all of my makeup off in New York and I hadn't thought to check on it. And Quinn was on his way up? He'd never seen my freckles. I always wore concealer. Well almost all the time, but I couldn't think of one time I hadn't when Quinn was around. The elevator dinged, and my heart started racing, worrying about something as stupid as makeup.

I turned toward the light footsteps coming from the elevators. Quinn made it halfway down the hall while I'd been panicking. I couldn't meet him in the middle, too nervous about the news he was bringing and maybe the freckles.

I felt my shoulders loosen at his harried expression as he slowed his pace. Maybe it wasn't that bad. Though he usually wore near impeccable clothes, his style here took him to a higher level. He rarely wore blazers or ties, but he wore both now. And he wore them well. A fitted blazer and a thin slate-gray tie with slacks—black, of course. But what freed me from my arrested, panicked state were his black leather Converse. You could put the extra fancy on Quinn, but you couldn't take Quinn out of his Converse. Quinn rolled his eyes, knowing exactly why I was smiling. He came close to me.

I tossed my hair back as I looked up at him with a few inches between us. "Hi."

"Back at ya. You look—"

He paused when I squinted at him.

His eyes darted across my face. "Beautiful," he murmured in a low voice just for me.

"Mmhmm." I couldn't get rid of my damn grin as he stared down at me. I opened my mouth to say something, but Quinn leaned over and kissed me. Not chaste, but he didn't make it more, either. He held me there, his hand under my jaw, until I leaned into him.

"You don't look too bad yourself," I whispered when he let me go. Holy shit, I'd said it before and I'd say it again: I was in trouble.

"How's your nephew?" Quinn asked.

That broke the spell. Right. Other things to worry about. I winced and stood up straight instead of leaning into him. "Awake, alert, and not too grumpy. Wanting answers from the doctors—wait, that's me. They're talking about surgery."

Quinn hissed. "Heart surgery? Like a bypass?"

"Yeah. How's Seamus adjusting to France? Where is he, actually?" I looked behind him, just realizing Seamus hadn't walked out of the elevator with him. Seamus would look adorable in a young princely outfit. Quinn never made his son dress fancy in Seattle—jeans and t-shirts were fine, but Quinn's royal family wouldn't accept him, even if Seamus could never rule due to his "halfling" status.

The pair had been inseparable since we'd rescued three-year-old Seamus from Aswryn's cult. The trauma left them both fragile. Quinn couldn't fully relax on our dates, always anticipating Seamus' potential meltdowns, which had happened twice with other caregivers. Only after gradual playdates with our group had Seamus settled, though he still struggled around other fae except his aunt, Queen Orlaith.

Quinn took a shuddering breath. "He's with Orie. Charlie is planning to bring Ray over"—he checked his watch—"in the morning for a playdate."

After a moment, I picked my jaw up and tried to find something to say. "Was he...is he...I'm so sorry, Quinn." If this hadn't happened, Quinn would've been home with his traumatized son.

"This is a good thing. It was time. We talked on the phone as he got ready for bed, and I read him a story." Quinn pulled me in and kissed my forehead.

I rested my head against his collarbone and closed my eyes. Somehow, I'd make this up to him.

Not long enough afterward, Quinn released a deep sigh. "My parents want to have dinner tomorrow."

I moved away so I could look him in the eye comfortably. "Okay. Would you possibly take us down in your fancy jet?" They weren't just the ruling family of France, but *Céandalamh*—what they call the Motherland of the fae, encompassed most of France down to Crete, and to Eastern Europe somewhere.

"We won't need to. They're finishing up a few things, and then they'll be in Paris in the morning. Quinn cupped the side of my face and brushed my chin with his thumb. "It's okay. They come here often. My father has business here and my mother loves our Paris house. Um, except, they don't know about us."

"Yeah, I know." The only ones who knew were my friends and family, not even Queen Orlaith knew. We'd agreed to take our relationship slow. Seamus wasn't ready to share his dad with anyone. All the mourning time plus *enda* and fairy relationships kept Quinn hesitant. The fae hated *endai*. Video conferences with other fae nations made this obvious. Breathing wrong tightened the tension in those meetings.

Quinn's eyes glanced away, out the window. "I'm sorry, you do know." Quinn pulled me closer and played with my hair, twisting it around his index finger. "Hiding has been your thing for a century." He kissed me lightly on the lips.

A door clicked shut, distracting me from Quinn's gentle tugs on my hair. Quinn turned around to look as well. Nol walked toward us, rubbing his hands. Not too bad. His eyes darted to Quinn, then to me.

"Go to him, Hally." Quinn nudged me forward.

But nothing was wrong with Nol. I checked Quinn. What did he see that I couldn't? He gave me a nod. I looked back at Nol, who was already walking toward me, eyes nowhere else. Okay, then, not so good. I hurried over to my *muranildo,* and before I even reached him, Nol had his arms out. He pulled me in and squeezed, resting his chin on my head. He let out all the air in his lungs and paused. Not breathing or moving, he just held me.

"Nol? What—"

"I'm fine," he whispered into my hair.

I clenched my teeth, tired of his go-to word. I pushed off him, and he held me there, but let go after a moment. "What did he tell you? I told—"

"It's between him and me." His chin lifted and focused behind me. "Quinn."

Nol guided me to his side to face Quinn as he walked to us. Held out his hand and Nol took it, clasping his forearm then wrapped his free arm around him for a hug. Not as tight of a hug or for as long as mine, but a fierce one.

"My friend. Tell me." Quinn rested his forehead against Nol's, in the *endaen* custom. "Do you need a moment? Anything?"

"I'm fine."

Liar. Léon had said something that upset him. I wrapped my arm around Nol, and he lifted his arm so I could tuck myself against his side. I opened the bond, offering him some comfort, which he took.

I looked up from under Nol's arm and met his eyes. "I need to go talk to Léon. He wasn't supposed to upset you."

"No, Hallë. What was said needed to be said. Quinn, what news do you have?"

I pursed my lips, but we did need to talk about Quinn's news. We'd talk later, though.

I scooted out from under Nol's arm and stood so they were both in front of me, making a triangle. "We have to meet his parents tomorrow for dinner."

Nol rolled his shoulders back, a habit of wearing his uniform. "Understandable to prioritize the initial meeting."

Quinn pressed his hands together, almost pleading. "There's a catch, though. You are company, and company equals formal. Evening dresses and tuxedos. I'm assuming you didn't pack any of those?"

"My uniform wouldn't—eh—suffice?"

"Afraid not, my friend. Unless you have dress formals?"

"Dress?" Nol rested his arms behind his back.

"A fancy uniform instead of your daily one."

"Not here, no."

Zayuri had formal uniforms? Why hadn't I ever considered that? "I can't picture you in fancy uniforms with swords, jumping in and out of shadows."

He sighed at my teasing, then continued with his conversation. "Unless we're stationed in the capital, they stay in our closets."

"Why is the capital an exception? What do you use them for there?" I asked.

"We use them for formal ceremonies and holidays." Nol looked at Quinn. "And all the important dress-up days, much like your formal dinners."

Quinn scoffed. "Sounds about right."

Nol perked up happy he had someone who understood.

Quinn spread his hands out, then clasped them together again. "So, back to the main topic. Nolan, a tuxedo. We can go get you one while Hally is with Léon today. I know you're tired, but it's for the best if you stay awake to get used to the time zone you're in. Then, Hally, I was thinking..."

"What?" I drawled out, a warning against too much mischief.

"What if"—Quinn's lips curved up, promising that mischief—"after visiting hours, I take you dress shopping and make a night of it? What do you say?"

"Taking my boyfriend dress shopping?" I winced, unable to imagine it. "Are you going to hold my purse or something?"

"If that's what it takes, sure." Quinn tugged on a lock of my curls just above my shoulder and let it spring up. "We can eat dinner afterward."

"It is a great plan. Hallë?" Nol looked almost hopeful. "What do you say?"

I chewed on my lip and hooked my lip ring. "Sure, I guess that's what it takes," I said, echoing Quinn's answer. But what it took for what? An adult night out? Getting ready to meet his parents? All the above and more.

Quinn stepped in close and nuzzled my ear. "Perfect." The rumble of his voice sent a shiver of anticipation through me. Shit.

"Ready?" Nol interjected, startling us. Quinn straightened, and we turned to Nol, standing in front of us.

"Really?" I set my hands on my hips and glared.

Nol rolled his eyes. "Come on, Quinn. I need a shower, and then you need to show me this *Bibliothèque Nationale de France* I read about."

Quinn snorted. "Clothes before tourism, Nolan." He leaned in and pecked me on the lips. "I'll be back at seven. Enjoy your time with your family. And Hally? You really are beautiful, freckles and all."

I narrowed my eyes at his grin before he hurried after Nol, who'd already pressed the elevator button. Of course, he was excited about a damn library. I watched Quinn walk to Nol, and it reminded me of our close friendship with Gil. The three of us against the world. A small part of my mind froze. No one could replace Gil. Nothing would. Ever. The Mother just sent us someone to help us heal from his loss. Still, would Gil have believed that?

I took a deep breath and cleared my mind of everything fae and *enda* related. Léon was the important thing now. And his Yahtzee game.

6

Léon grunted and leaned back on the bed as he tried to get more comfortable. He was getting antsy, staying cooped up in this small room with no answers. Barely a soul came to explain anything. Even with the break in monotony with Nicole's company all afternoon, I was getting antsy, too. Hospitals never brought out the best in me, and I'd been in one all day. Léon, while his dislike of hospitals was near mine, didn't have a phobia. The only way I was getting through this was because I wasn't the patient.

"You're getting fidgety again." Léon scolded me.

"And you're not? It would just be nice to get some answers. Not one doctor has been in here. All these nurses do is poke you. For what? They take blood and put liquids in you but never tell you what it's for. I miss your father. Léon told patients what was going on. And he gave them the truth, every time. Your father was the best doctor in the world. It is a colder place without your parents in it." I rarely talked about the senior Léon anymore. Or Emma. Reminiscing wasn't me, but hospitals brought it out in me.

"Hélène…"

I rubbed my bracelet. "Sorry. I'm worried, is all."

"So am I."

"I'm making it worse. That wasn't my intention," I said.

"You've done incredibly well all day."

I scowled. "Don't give me platitudes. I can't stand that."

"You've also barely slept. That prince of yours better take you to dinner before getting you a dress, or you might bite his head off."

"I won't...but I agree with the dinner part." I pushed the lock button on my phone to make it glow and checked the time. Six fifty-seven.

"You should wait for him downstairs."

"He'll call when he gets here." He'd called earlier, too, when he'd taken Nol to a pub, after the tux fitting and the library. They'd enjoyed an afternoon of ale—male bonding. More Nol than Quinn. That Quinn got him to relax warmed my heart. Again, he wasn't replacing Gil. Quinn was building his own relationship with us.

"Hélène, you know I love you. You're my favorite aunt. But my hints are not working. I'm tired, you're cranky, and you'll see me tomorrow. And please, for the love of god, sleep in. Relax. The hospital will call if there's an emergency. We've made sure you are on the list, haven't we?"

"Yes," I grumbled. I had gotten the hints, but that didn't mean I was obeying them. "Mornings suit me here."

"The hell they do. You may get up earlier here, but that doesn't mean you're pleasant."

I grumbled in my seat. "I haven't slept yet. I'll be peppier in the morning."

"You better not." Léon made a sour face, his enormous nose and wrinkles bunching until I couldn't see his brown eyes. "I couldn't stand you. Tatie? Wait for your prince downstairs. Let me rest, woman."

With a groan, I stood and kissed Léon on the temple. "I love you, and I'm not ready for you to leave me."

"Who is ever ready for that?" The grief of losing his wife a decade ago hung like a shadow over him. They'd had sixty years of marriage.

I brushed the wispy hairs around his ears and neck. "If I could, you know I'd save you from all of it."

Léon raised his hand to touch my face. "I know. That is why you can't stay here. You give too much of yourself to me, to us. Promise me, after I'm gone, you'll free yourself of this burden."

I pinched his cheek and made sure he looked into my eyes. "You are not a burden. None of you are."

"You've kept your promise to my mother."

I bit my lip instead of arguing. My phone chirped. I pulled it out and checked my message: *Quinn just left me at your apartment. He's got your clothes. If you come back tonight, I'm kicking you out.*

As if he could stop me. My apartment was five minutes from the hospital. I settled my thoughts. Was this a scheme between Quinn and Nol?

"Tatie?"

"All right, Lee. I'll see you tomorrow. Late morning, okay?"

"Bring some coffee. Theirs is crap."

"Now that's a grave offense to humanity. I'll bring croissants, too."

Léon huffed. I kissed his forehead again and left the room. "Open or closed?"

"Open a bit." He held his hand out, pinching the air.

Blowing him a kiss, I left the door open a crack. The clouds still held some light, but the halls were deserted and the nurse at the station was on her phone. The elevator opened and a younger-looking doctor a few inches taller than me stood in the corner. Her eyes widened and she hitched her courier bag higher on her shoulder.

"Hello."

"Uh, *bonjour*." I responded automatically.

I looked her up and down. She was a doctor. This was a French hospital. Did I look American in these clothes? Maybe a little, my outfit—the one Mateo picked out—wasn't too out of sorts with Paris. I was getting ahead of myself. Maybe she was a visiting doctor from the States.

She caught me looking at her and smiled like we were friends or something.

"Are you American?" I asked.

"No." Nothing wavered, but she looked different. New grass-green eyes and wispy, light blond hair. Her high cheekbones were narrow and her chin was sharp. Oh crap. "Are you the elf? I heard you were visiting Paris."

"Um...how?"

She held her hand out, and what the fuck could I do besides shake it? "I'm Doctor O'Dae, Celine O'Dae. I never expected to meet you, and definitely not at the hospital. Are you visiting someone here?"

"How many know I'm in Paris?" I asked instead of answering her.

She giggled a childlike giggle. "Lots. Uh...don't worry, most will take it as a rumor anyway."

The elevator dinged and she raised her glamor. The door opened. Lo and behold, Quinn was at the elevator under the same glamor as this morning. "Hally? I was just going to surprise you."

Doctor O'Dae didn't move, and neither did I. Quinn grabbed the door as it closed.

"Is everything all right?"

I stepped over, yanked him in and pressed the top-floor button. "This is Doctor Celine O'Dae. She says lots of people know I'm here."

Quinn's face went from slightly surprised and mildly amused to "what the fuck?" and "you must die." Quinn dropped his glamor and glared. "Celine O'Dae, drop your glamor."

"Your Highness, I wasn't...I didn't mean..." The doctor bowed to Quinn and didn't look up.

"Doctor O'Dae, none of that. Rise. How do 'lots' of people know?"

"Erm, I heard she was coming to Paris from a few friends. How can this *not* be talked about? I mean, she's the elf! Like I told...the e—I mean, Ambassador Inara, most people will consider it gossip. I did, until she walked into the elevator, I mean."

"What do you know of the Ambassador's visit?" Quinn was not amused.

"Oh, um, not much. Honestly, I can't believe you're here. Who'd have thought, at my work? Wait, are you..." O'Dae covered her mouth. "I won't say anything about seeing you. Discretion and, yeah, I am a doctor. I'd never—oh my god, you think I'm some weirdo. I promise—" She pressed a hand to her forehead. "I'm embarrassing myself. I'm so sorry."

"Details, if you will, Doctor O'Dae. There was obviously more said than *the elf is coming to Paris.*"

"Oh-oh, right. Well...I swear, I'm smart. We were out barhopping and my friend heard—oh, it was in the bathroom!"

Of course it was the bathroom.

"They said—and yes, there were only fae—the Seattle elf is flying to Paris. You do know gossip always start with the servants, right, Your Highness? I'm not trying to get them in trouble. It's just a given," she said with a shrug.

"So, that's all that was said?" I asked. Nothing about Nol.

"Yeah. People want to know why, but that's just people being people, fae or otherwise."

The elevator door opened. Quinn pressed the bottom floor and the close door buttons. "Tell no one."

"No. I'm all about discretion, but Your Highness, unless, um...I'm sorry, how do you say your name, Ambassador? Everyone says it differently. Helen-Ava?"

Her question told me all I needed to know. They didn't know who I was as a "human," and they didn't know about Nol.

"Ambassador Hallanevaë Inara."

"Well, unless you raise your glamor, people will recognize you, especially the older fae."

Raise my glamor? Fae thought I had glamor. Again, good information to know. "Are there pictures of me somewhere?"

She'd said she was smart, but just because she was a doctor didn't make her wise. She couldn't have been that old. No one could chatter like this and not realize how much information she was giving away.

The doctor went to say no but paused. "Not that I know of, but I mean, you can tell you're an elf, and since you're the only one on Earth, it's kinda hard to mistake you for someone else."

"You have been very informative tonight, Doctor O'Dae."

"It's been my honor, Your Highness."

The elevator dinged again. "Good evening. And remember, tell no one."

"I wouldn't dream of it."

Quinn offered me his arm. "Ambassador Inara? If you would come with me?"

"Yes, Your Highness."

On the escalator, I glanced back. "She's—"

"Not here," Quinn muttered. "Wait." We walked fast, straight to the door, and then everyone was gone.

"Crap." I released Quinn's arm to take in the quiet. This was his magic. Off the pedestrian bridge and on either side, there was mist. Nothing else existed. I turned around, the hospital was still there. The lights were on, but no one was inside. A tug at my hand caught my attention.

Face tight, Quinn jerked his head toward the car lot. "Come on."

"What a fucking dimwit. She would not shut up."

"Because she couldn't. I'm not sure if you know this, but not all fae can lie. The royal families can, but not their subjects. Celine O'Dae is not of royal blood. I wasn't going to make her lay out all her secrets, but she gave me enough. Come, let's get to the car."

"If only those with royal blood can lie, is Drake of royal blood?"

Quinn paused, his mind clearly on the present and not about the fairy who'd tried to kill me. Who'd helped Aswryn take his son. "Yes. He is the tenth son of King Gomhar."

Gomhar? "I don't recall the name. Has he been in the video chats?"

"No. There is no way he'll agree to have anything to do with the elves. Come, Hally. Let's talk about them at another time."

7

Quinn stared out the front window of his brand new Porsche into the bush in front of us, either deep in thought or trying to purge the last ten minutes from his memory.

"We don't have to go," I offered. A growing part of me was already not up to this endeavor. It wasn't like Paris was new to me and he could show me all the sights. "If this is going to stress you out."

Quinn shook his head and brought his attention to me in the passenger seat. "Are you kidding? Wait, are you having second thoughts?"

"No," I lied. I hadn't had first thoughts. "I know we have to do the dress thing." This was our first time away from any obligations. Why was I trying to get out of it, then? I looked ahead at the same bush. Apparently, it was a very interesting bush to look at. "And I need something to eat before the fitting. I thought I could wait, but I haven't eaten since the plane."

He shot up in his seat. "The plane? Fuck, why didn't you say something?" He pushed the ignition button and checked the parking lot before pulling out.

"Because we were going out."

"Which we'll be doing now. I just..."

"What?" I urged as he gave me a sheepish look.

Quinn pulled into traffic. "I was gonna cook for you."

I did like his cooking. Charlie cooked well, but Quinn's meals were more...everything. My lips twisted as I weighed the choices: endure another few hours of hunger or find something quick.

"Can we stop at a café and get a little bite to eat before the appointment? Then we'll go to your place." Hopefully, he wouldn't be offended for ruining our date night.

The tension in his shoulders eased. He swallowed and turned on his blinker. "You'd be fine not going out on a date? The first night without kids or friends interrupting us?"

I laughed. "I'm not young, Quinn. Spending time with you is better than any romantic adventure."

Quinn veered right, off the main road, and parked. Within a few heartbeats, Quinn had unbuckled both of our seat belts and had his lips on me. I squeaked when he pulled me over the shifter and onto his lap without breaking the kiss. Okay, maybe he'd had some help from me with that.

I slipped my hands around his shoulders, and pressed my body tight against his. Quinn slid his hands under my short sweater. He pinched my bra and got two hooks undone, but the third one gave him trouble. His lips slowed as he had to put more concentration into it. I started to pull away, but Quinn moaned in the negative. My stomach fluttered, and my body responded with its own moan.

"Just a sec," I rasped. I let go of him completely and let him hold me while I grabbed my damn bra to unhook it. Our eyes met as I found the bent thing—I'd forgotten about that. His eyes were black, utterly black, and his breath was ragged. He swallowed and his exhale warmed my lips and cheeks.

Once finished he lifted his head off the headrest and connected with my mouth again. The bra loosened, hanging on by my arms, irritating the hell out of me. But stripping my shirt off to get the bra off was too far for a make-out session in a car, right? How far would we take this?

His hands found their way back under my sweater. My focus wavered from the kiss as his soft fingers inched their way higher up my ribcage. I squirmed on his lap as it tickled, and something firm pressed against me. I moaned as his thumb swiped the side of my breast and at the feel of him beneath me.

A warm current of energy swept through me to my core. It felt like his fingertips under my sweater, but the intimacy ran deeper to the core of my magic. I pushed away, panting, and stared into his wide, surprised eyes. "What was that?" I couldn't manage more than a whisper.

He looked around and outside the tinted windows as cars whizzed by. "What was what? Is this too soon? I'm pushing. It's just, you haven't reached out, and I thought I'd try it. I'm sorry. If you don't want to share energies, that's okay."

I took another deep breath so I could talk right. "Share energies?" Was this what Nol had been talking about at the house?

Quinn blinked. Ten seconds...twenty seconds. Shit. I'd ruined the moment. I would not cry, damn it! "It's just...I've only ever had sex with humans."

That unstuck him. His eyes closed, and he dropped his head back on the headrest. "Oh, fuck. I am such a fucking asshole. You don't even know what that is."

"I've ruined everything." I covered my face so I didn't have to see his horrified expression. I sat there on Quinn's lap, shaky and mortified, with my damn bra loose and uncomfortable as hell. "How ridiculous is it to panic over something as stupid as this?"

"Don't say that. It's not your fault."

He was just being nice to the ditz freaking out over sex. What mature French woman panicked during a make-out session in her boyfriend's brand new Porsche? The thought brought tears to my eyes. *Don't you fucking dare, Hally!*

"I should have thought about you and your needs. God, I'm an idiot. Look at me, please." He touched my hands and tried to pull them away from my face. That wasn't going to happen. If I could have vanished like Aswryn was able to, I already would have. "This shouldn't have happened."

"But I let it! I wanted it."

"Duh. Of course, you did!" He chuckled, making light of my embarrassment.

My breath caught in my throat and my body shuddered. *Damn it, he was making it worse!*

"Okay." He rubbed my arms and kept talking. "That was not appropriate. What do I need to do to help you? Do you want me to take you back to your apartment?"

I shook my head. His hands moving up and down my arms were helping. My breath was normalizing, my body wasn't shaking. This was working for me, but I could feel the tension in his whole body. He couldn't relax. He thought he'd violated me.

"I'll be okay...in a minute." I forced myself to lower my hands, but I couldn't find it in me to raise my eyes to his. "I'm sorry. I've never panicked like this with anyone."

Quinn stopped moving his hands and dropped them to his sides. He quit moving all together. "Please, don't apologize. You were unprepared, I gave you no warning. Do you want to talk to Nolan?"

That brought my eyes up. For a moment I thought he'd found out about the incident with Nol last night. Then I remembered Nol had told me to talk about this with him.

"Actually...maybe we should reschedule that fitting."

Quinn deflated, thinking I'd ask him to take me to my apartment and back to Nol. Making a decision, he nodded and looked back at me. "Fair. I can do that."

"I'd like to um...talk about it. Will you explain the energies thing?"

He cocked his head to the side. "Are you sure? I mean..."

Dropping my eyes back to his chest, I played with a button on his dress shirt as I chewed my lip. "I don't have any *endaë* or fae girl friends to talk about this with." I scrunched my nose as I, watched my fingers. "And if I'm going to have a sex talk, I'd rather have it with..." My eyes rolled up meet his mercury ones and I curled the corners of my mouth up. "My partner." As I tugged the button, his breath hitched.

Quinn's eyebrows shot up in surprise. "We-we could do that. It's just I already scared the life out of you."

"You didn't scare me." I played with the button again and his chest muscles relaxed. "I was surprised and I'm embarrassed—and disappointed in myself for not having this talk sooner. You're just..." My incisor hooked my lip ring.

"Watch it," he growled as I paused, waiting for me to remind him that he was thousands of years older than me.

"Experienced. And I'm not used to being the inexperienced one. I'm still getting used to the fact that there are people older than me here."

"You're doing a pretty damn good job at being experienced now."

"*Eh bien, je suis une femme française.*" *Well, I am French.*

That dropped the tension in his body. Quinn lifted a hand to tug on one of my curls, rubbing the soft hair between his fingers before letting it bounce. It was his turn not to meet my eyes. "Energy sharing is just what it sounds like. We send energy to the core of our magic and...lower. A type of magical foreplay. My energy will build inside you, and after a while, you'll send the energy back into me. It's natural, instinctive like sex." And with the last word he met my eyes like I had. The little devil.

I chewed on my bottom lip some more and I searched for anything that didn't make sense. My paper thin confidence was tearing. "My magic isn't normal. What if I can't?"

He pressed a finger to my lips. "You can. If there is a magical cell in your body"—he dropped his hand to rest between us and leaned in to press his forehead to mine—"Which I know there is, than you can share energies."

"Can we try again?" My request even caught me off guard. One minute I'm freaking out and the next I'm asking for it? What was wrong with me?

Quinn froze, his face so close to mine, shocked at my boldness. Either he wasn't sure I meant it, or he wasn't interested anymore. So I decided for him. Leaning in, I pressed my lips against his and snaked my arms around him. When he stayed frozen I broke the kiss, drew my eyes up and pouted. He got the hint and pulled me close. His lips touched mine and we were back to square one. Hands on my ribcage, fingers at my bra line, driving me insane. I tried to scoot in, wiggling, but nothing. Sure he was playing the part, but nothing happened below and his fingers wouldn't move! *Damn it.*

"Slow down," he whispered against my mouth. But he wasn't even doing anything.

I lowered my hands from behind his neck and went to open his shirt, but he covered my fingers to stop me. He wasn't comfortable with this. But then he slid my hands down between us and proved me wrong.

"Show me," I whispered.

Again, I felt a current of magic flow into my core. My breathing sped up as the energy built. He pushed more into me, and kissed my jaw to the base of my ear and down to my collarbone. His hands inched higher, until his thumbs were at the lower curve of my breasts. The ecstasy built and suddenly released. Energy sharing wasn't just foreplay, it was a different pleasure entirely.

"You try," he whispered against my neck.

I wanted to ask how, but I didn't want to ruin things again.

"You don't need to be nervous."

Concentrating, I searched inside myself. It was natural, instinctive, I was supposed to know how to do this. I let go of my doubts and apprehension and just did what I felt was right.

"I think I'm ready."

"Then go ahead. Send it to me."

I turned and kissed him as I reached out. Imagining a wave, I began pouring my magic into him. Quinn's hand tensed, holding my hips a little too tightly. His head flew back, and he stopped breathing. Oh shit! I was killing him.

"Quinn!" I pulled my energy back.

"No!" he panted, grabbing my hips and pulling me against his belly. "Oh my fucking god, do not stop. Please, keep going. All of it."

And even as the slave band started siphoning energy, I gave Quinn more. He'd give it back in a moment anyway. As my magic transferred to him and trickled into the slave band my head grew heavy until I could barely lift it. Except, as I gave him "all of it" like he'd asked, I realized I might have gone a little too far.

I slumped forward and rested against his shoulder. "Quinn, now, or I'm going to pass out. Please."

"Shit. Not that much!" His lips touched my neck and he kissed my jaw line as he sent energy into me and I struggled to keep still. I tightened my arms around him, enjoying it.

Then, all at once he slowed then stopped, and the anticipation from what I'd given him fell flat.

"You stopped!" I pointed out the obvious.

"You depleted all of your energy. If that happened again tonight, I'm not sure I could get you to Faerie fast enough. Replenish your energy. Restore your core. You could've died." Quinn grabbed my shoulders and squeezed, giving me a gentle push backward.

"If you give it back, what's the harm?"

"The energy our bodies take in is absorbed into our systems and changes. If I'd given you any more of my energy without you having your own base energy, your body would have rejected it. You'd have gotten sick—or worse. We can't do it again tonight. I'm sorry, darling. Promise me." Quinn slid his hand under my chin. My body shivered, but not with passion. "Promise you'll never share that much energy again."

I nodded with a pout. Quinn chuckled and pulled me close. We stayed that way for a little while, me on his lap with my head against his shoulder, him rubbing the back of my head. "Hally?"

"Hmm?"

"I still need to cancel that appointment. After that, I can take you wherever you want."

"'Kay." I climbed off and around his shifter. The world teetered, and my vision blurred. I was gonna be sick. "Quinn. I can't see straight." I fumbled for the passenger-side handle, barely touching the door. "I'm gonna throw up."

"Oh, shit. Energy depletion." The interior lights came on, blinding me. Cold air hit my back, replaced with silence. My door opened and Quinn wrapped his arms around my waist and pulled me out. The motion threw me off-kilter, and I about lost it.

"Down, now!"

I almost didn't make it out of his arms. He held my hair back as I threw up what little I'd eaten today. My hand found the bumper of his Porsche, and I groaned. I tried to open my eyes, but everything was blurry and the lights were too bright. I closed them before I threw up again.

"Hold on a sec." He set my hair down, making sure it didn't fall into my face. The car door opened and shut again a few moments later. "Here." Quinn placed a wet wipe in my hand. "Come on, let's get you in the car, and I'll take you home."

"Do *not* take me back to my apartment. I don't want to see him."

"Oh, hell no. He'd kill me if I brought you home like this. I'm taking you to my place."

He helped me into the car. I buckled up, fumbling with the belt. Then he helped lay the seat back before he closed my door. Without another word, he started to drive. Cars whizzed past, lights changed colors, and still we didn't talk. It wasn't long before Quinn was opening my door again.

"Okay, up you go."

"What are people going to say if they see you carrying me from your car?"

"They won't see anything. Not on the street or in the building. Let's go." I didn't pay much attention to the world around me, as I was just trying not to let my head drop off his arm. Or vomit on his impeccable suit. Keys jingled. A door creaked. My eyes didn't want to adjust to the dark apartment. It didn't smell like his Seattle condo, but then again, I didn't know how long he'd had this place. All I knew was I couldn't lift my head. "I'll get you to the shower and grab your clothes out of the car. You still with me, Hally?"

"Tired."

"I know, darling." He set me down on something cushy, but hard. My back rested on a cold surface.

Curious, I squinted to see where we were. I was on a bathroom mat against his cabinet. I heard a drawer open and plastic wrap rustle. "I've got a toothbrush if you're ready."

He made sure I could grasp the toothbrush and hold it in my mouth, before he left me to do who knew what, walking past the bathroom twice. A *thunk*, steps, and he was back in.

He set something on a towel shelf and crouched in front of me. "We've got a problem. You can't stand let alone wash yourself. I'm gonna have to help you in the shower. Are you okay with that?"

I lifted my chin and opened my eyes wide. "Look at me." His bright silver eyes focused on me, full of fear and worry. "Stop being a gentleman and suck it up. We almost had sex—well sort of did. That's intimate enough for me."

Quinn snorted, his head dropped as he laughed at himself. "You're right. It's just—" He looked at the floor. "Maybe I should call your niece."

"I'll pass out before she gets here."

"Fair point." He sat on the floor with me and reached for my hands. "I'm gonna try one more thing, first. It's been around fifteen minutes, so if I share a little energy with you, your body might not reject it."

"That might give me enough—" That was all I could say. Jeez, I was thirsty.

He placed his hands on my face. His breath was feather soft against my nose and lips. "I'll go slow and try not to give you a reaction." Yeah, foreplay didn't sound appealing at the moment. He closed his eyes, and I waited. His energy trickled in, but it didn't spark my libido.

"Tell me if I need to stop," Quinn whispered.

After a minute, my body accepted his energy, and my head cleared up. "Stop. I'm not dizzy." He helped me to stand and proved to him and myself I wasn't lying when he let go of me.

"I'll get everything ready. Can you undress yourself? Get in?"

I nodded.

"I'll be right on the other side of the door. All you have to do is call my name."

"And you'll be there?" I sang to him.

"Ha-ha, smart ass." But it got him to smile. "Christ. I know you're feeling better now."

Once he'd left, I got undressed, bummed that everything had gone so badly. I mean come on, he had to hold my hair back while I threw up, for Pete's sake.

I drank water from the shower, washed my hair—screw the conditioner—and scrubbed until I felt clean. Magically exhausted or not, I took the time I needed.

"Quinn," I called ten minutes later as I stood in his bathroom. My hair was still wet and the towel was on the floor. Sure enough, he came running, chest heaving. But he found me in his dress shirt and decent. Except, I couldn't push the last of the buttons through.

My chin trembled. "I've done everything, but I can't get these three buttons. Why did you pick a dress shirt? Don't you have any t-shirts?"

"No."

Come to think of it, I couldn't think of a time I'd seen him in one. "Undershirts?"

"Yeah…" He hesitated.

"What's wrong with one of those?"

"It was either this or…a white undershirt. They're a lot more see-through."

My fingers stilled. That made sense. This wasn't much better. "You just had to choose white, huh?"

He hummed. I looked up and he lifted his hands. "I'm a guy."

Giving him a glare, I tried pushing another button through. He sidled up to me and pushed my hands out of the way. His finger slid between two buttons and he tugged on the lowest closed one. A jolt went through me, all the way down. There was no way I had enough energy for more.

He leaned over, and his lips nuzzled my neck. "What's a guy to do when he has the best girlfriend in the world over at his house without any pajamas? Can you blame me?"

I tilted my head until I could see his face. "Yes, yes I can."

But I caught his lips with mine. His hands slid under the shirt and placed them on my hips. We were adults. Adults do adult things.

He was wonderful; his words were always kind. I loved that he called me beautiful. Darling always sent my tummy aquiver. He held my hair when I threw up. And he was so fucking sexy…and damn, those Converse were so adorable on him!

He pulled away. "Keep the buttons undone. For me. Please?" he whispered against my ear.

Kissing his jawline, I swallowed before I could speak. "No sex. I don't have the energy—"

"I know." But he lifted me, and pulled my legs around his waist. We bumped into the bathroom doorframe. After that, he managed to carry me to bed.

He read to me Gaelic in his very comfy bed, with very soft sheets. The smell of his cologne sent me deeper into my comfy place and made me dizzy in a good way. I wasn't sure if he noticed how much I liked it, but he kept tracing circles on the small of my back until I couldn't fight it any longer and fell asleep next to him.

8

ANOTHER TEST. THAT'S WHAT Léon's doctors had said about the last test, which we still hadn't gotten the results from. I didn't understand why they didn't wait for the results of one test before taking another. What if they found the answer in the test before? They would never know unless they waited. Plus, Léon missed his lunch because the last test had taken so long.

My phone vibrated in my pocket. I checked the caller ID before lifting it to my ear. "Charlie, *mon amour, bonjour,*" *Charlie, love, hello.* "I'm so glad—"

A sniffle came from the other end. "*Bonjour,* Hally."

Oh, no. "You sound congested." Movement out of the corner of my eye, accompanied by a *thunk,* brought my head around, but it was only a nurse's aide with a cart...staring straight at me. "*Bonjour,*" I said softly to him. He didn't respond, but half asleep and probably overworked hospital staff weren't my priority. Still quite rude of a Frenchman.

I kept the conversation in English for privacy. "And since you were healthy when I left, I'm assuming you haven't developed a cold in the last...two days." Ish.

"I don't want to go in today."

"What's going on?" Charlie, who was full of life and excitement, but panicked easily, didn't cry easily.

She sniffled again. "I'm taking Ray in to play with Seamus again. They really like it, but Collin is such a jerk."

"Collin? The doctor guy? He's been so nice to you." I looked back at the aide. He still hadn't moved. Maybe I was in the way. "Just a sec, love." I cleared my throat to get the aide's attention. "*Pardon, monsieur,* I can move if you need to clean here."

That got him out of his state. He shook his head, came forward, and started tidying around Léon's bed.

"Okay, keep going," I continued with Charlie. "What's with Collin?"

"He's a doctor, yes, but right now he's researching with me. More like babysitting me and he obviously thinks he's better than me. He said my work is sloppy. My work isn't sloppy!"

Sloppy was never a word to describe Charlie, especially when it came to her life's work. "Why did he say it's sloppy?"

"Because of the last group of tests I set up. The data and meds they have are great, but they're not responding to Aswryn's virus. I mean—" She blew her nose away from the phone. "He could have said something earlier. They weren't pointless tests, and it wasn't because my notes were sloppy that they didn't respond." It was only from decades of consoling my sister's female descendants—hell, her, too—that I understood Charlie's woes through her sobbing.

After some time to make sure she was done and then some extra time to come up with a good answer that didn't sound like I was taking Collin's side, I tried to console her. "Have you said anything to Collin since he said that?" I really hoped she hadn't.

"Initially, I told him to go screw himself. Then he told me I was getting too emotional and I needed to step back for a while."

Oh, boy.

"That he would take over my work so I could get some rest. My work, Tatie! Can you believe his audacity?"

"This was yesterday?"

"Yes! I took everything home with me. It's my work, not his!"

"Right, not his. He's only assisting you."

"And the side remarks all the fae give me. Like being a halfling is a dirty thing. I don't like being called a halfling. I'm human. To hell with whichever ancestor gave me these wretched fairy genes. If I hear another whisper about how I can't do magic, I will lose it on all of them."

"Collin said that, too?" That actually came as a surprise, as Collin seemed to be one of the most forward-thinking doctors in the lab.

"No." Charlie sniffled again.

The nurse's aide tucked over the top blanket on Léon's bed and marked something on a clipboard. He checked around the bed for who knew what...plates, garbage? When would this guy be done?

"No. He yelled at the other fairies when he heard it. But my techniques aren't sloppy, and their attitudes aren't affecting my work."

Ah. "Collin said they were affecting your work?"

"What?" Charlie came up short, her breath held back. "He didn't...yes, sort of."

Sort of? It sounded more and more like Collin had tried to get her out of the lab when the asshole fairies were acting like jerks. "What if you call Collin and invite him to see your lab? Your lab isn't sloppy."

"This lab? At home?" She snorted. "God, no. He'd pick it apart. Or worse, laugh at it. Not that this isn't a good lab. It's just, compared to theirs? No." She paused, then groaned. "Collin's calling. Fuck."

"Is he a morning person like you?"

"I don't know."

"You should answer it, love. Maybe he's calling to apologize."

Charlie scoffed. "Sure, and those fairies' heads will shrink to normal size. Just a sec." The line went silent.

The aide sure was being thorough. Léon's room wasn't dirty, and he didn't leave crap laying around. But the aide seemed determined to find something. Rolling my eyes, I got up. Even if he'd said I didn't need to move, the guy was creeping me out, like one of those weird orderlies in the movies.

"Tatie?" Charlie whispered. "He's here."

"What?"

"Collin. He brought Seamus. Here."

I stopped in my tracks, six feet from the door.

"I gotta go. Holy shit, this house isn't clean enough for company. Oh my god, what am I wearing? I have no makeup on! Shit."

Not a crisis then. My muscles relaxed. "Let him wait in the car. Take your time."

"Ray! Fuck, she's at the door." The phone picked up Charlie's stomps down the steps as her voice echoed through the stairwell in the house. "Ray, do not open that door."

She began hyperventilating. Ray said something away from the phone. Then a deeper voice asked if Charlie was all right, but Charlie was busy scolding her daughter.

"Never open this door without Mommy saying you can! Do you understand me? Anyone could be there! You know you can't do that!"

"But Mommy, it's Seamus," Ray mumbled. "And Collin."

A clattering and something brushed against the phone.

"Hello?" a man, who I assumed was Collin, asked.

"Collin?"

"Um, yeah?"

"It's Hally."

"Hi. Uh, I think, I think I scared Charlie."

"Not you. Ray tends to answer the door and scare her mom."

Collin forced a chuckle. "I see that. Can't blame 'er really, can ya? For bein' so scared that is. Bein' as what happened earlier this year?"

Charlie had a soft spot for British and Irish accents. That he knew this about Ray and Charlie meant she'd told him about Ray's kidnapping. Most fae only knew about the fae kidnappings. We hadn't made it well known that Nol and Ray had been taken just a few days after Aswryn had taken Seamus. Meaning, Charlie trusted this person. A lot. The freak-out before Ray opened the door and the not wanting to see him was starting to make sense now.

Charlie was consoling a crying Ray, scared to death by her mother. Whatever worked. "I'm glad you understand the situation."

"Aye. Maybe it wasn't a good idea to come. Kinda felt bad, 'bout yesterday."

"How about I leave you to it, then? Tell her 'she's got this' for me?"

"That I can do. Any tips you might have for a guy?"

A guy? Oh, this was going to be fun. "Smile and nod. Tell her that her lab looks fantastic. And never say her work is sloppy again."

"She told you 'bout that, eh?"

"Have a good day, Collin. Good luck."

Collin did that nervous chuckle again. I hung up as I grabbed the door handle, but something slipped around my shoulder, then clenched around my neck. By the time I realized the who, where, and what of the situation, my throat was completely closed off. All the self-defense techniques in all those freaking classes I'd taken went out the window. The lollygagging, creepy "orderly" yanked me back. My arms cartwheeled, but the floor never came.

The room disappeared or perhaps was never there. Except I recognized the place...but everything held a sheen, as if giving off its own glow. Above me, I saw a dark wood and green—something. Perhaps a ceiling? But I swore I could see sunlight, too. I didn't understand any of it.

I heard a soft murmuring voice, perhaps with an Irish lilt? Had I hung up with Collin? My phone wasn't in my hand anymore. The lilt, when I focused more, wasn't an accent but a language. Gaelic?

Were we still in Quinn's apartment? I shook my head to clear it as the language brought up thoughts of Quinn. No, we weren't in his apartment. We'd left it to find a dress this morning. It was blue with chiffon. Then what? He'd dropped me at the hospital. I was at the hospital! Had Quinn come back in?

"Qu—" Something was lodged in my throat and got in the way when I tried to swallow. My fingertips touched the hollow of my throat. All smooth skin, but what was the tightening feeling? "Q—" My mouth formed the word, but nothing came out.

Something flickered around the ceiling that wasn't a ceiling...a purple or a blue spark. Then a yellow one. A green one. They fluttered across my line of vision. I couldn't move my head. The light was dimming, and I couldn't swallow. I couldn't breathe. Why couldn't I breathe? And why was I seeing Faerie fireflies in...

Where was I again?

Léon's hospital room? But it looked like Faerie...

Neither looked right. Not at all. How could I be in Faerie and in Léon's room? Where was the aide? I closed my eyes and tried to think, but the soft not-Gaelic in my ear kept my mind floating and flickering like the fireflies. If the only constant was the words, I had to focus on those to ground myself. But where were they coming from? Certainly, it couldn't be from all directions. I blocked out the loud thud of my heart.

My left ear.

The orderly, who wasn't an orderly, was on my left side. A fairy. I anchored myself and focused. I felt his hand gripping my arm, the other was fisted at the back of my head, holding something around my throat. If I didn't do something soon, I was going to black out. What could I do though? I knew where his hands were, which ear he was singing to me in, he couldn't ensnare me. Denying ever instinct to fight, I sagged in his arms, making myself dead weight.

Black specks had replaced the fireflies, the green and brown ceiling flickered. Focusing on his hands, I sent tendrils of energy up his arms in his shoulders and then into his lungs. I soaked every air sac I could sense with my energy, then squeezed. Hard.

Once upon a last February, Aswryn had tried the same thing, but hadn't gotten as far. Maybe. This time it felt different. His not-Gaelic faltered, and the room came into focus. My heart slowed, with pauses between beats now. His chanting, was gone, his spell interrupted. No magic and no hazy, confusing illusion. His chest shuddered and unfortunately he dropped my arm and not my neck. More concerned with my crushed windpipe than holding onto my spell, I released my hold on his lungs.

Once I'd released him, he wrapped his arm around upper body and tightened the thing around my neck. He coughed, gasped and coughed again while I dangled in front of him. *"Sale chatte elfique,"* *Filthy elven cunt*. Oh, now we were speaking French, huh? And naughty words I didn't appreciate.

Done with playing dead, I raised both hands, I grabbed both arms and sent one of those zaps that Nol and I messed with, except I was going to put every ounce of power I had—no, I'd promised Quinn I'd be more careful. Even though this was nothing like last night, I needed to be more cautious of how much energy I used.

Paying attention to more than just my actions, I sent raw energy straight into him. If a zap to Nol was a 9-volt battery, this was Yumi's electric Rav-4—I don't know how many volts that was, but I knew it was a lot.

One moment the fairy was holding me by the neck, the next I'd fallen to the floor in a heap with him on top of me. Not cool.

The thing he used to choke me hung loose around my neck. I pushed at his dead weight, and even though he'd tried to kill me, and this was self-defense I prayed I hadn't killed him.

I gasped and tried to focus instead of gulping in as much air as possible. My breath made a noise, and the rasp hitched whenever I inhaled. As I fought to inflate my lungs around my nearly crushed windpipe, I crawled to the door and grabbed the handle to pull myself up. The handle lowered, and I leaned back, but the door wouldn't move.

My knee was in the way, so I scooted over to the wall and tried again. The latch didn't even click. Fine. I made a fist and banged on the damn thing. Silence. No matter how hard I pounded I couldn't hear my own knocking. What the fuck? I had to think around the sting of cool air as I struggled to breathe. The prick had warded the inside of the room. The irony was, I knew I hadn't killed him, because his spell was still it place.

Clenching my teeth, I glared at the unconscious aide, then set my palms on the door. But then I thought about it logically. If I blew the door open, humans would come in and see him. They'd try to wake him up, and then what? Human cops would be called. He would be processed, and I didn't know what else.

I needed help, but not the human kind. Did I call Quinn or Nol? Nol was out with Amelia sightseeing. I didn't want her involved in this. Just Quinn, then. Oh, Nol was going to be pissed at me.

It took a few moments for my hand to stop shaking enough for me to shove it into my pocket to grab my phone, then even more time to punch in the code to unlock it because my fingers were shaking too much for the fingerprint reader to work. There was no way I could talk.

The Messenger app opened with ease, though. Thankfully.

911. Hospital. I pressed send. After reading over my message, I realized I'd misspelled hospital and the app had autocorrected it to hipster. Fuck.

My phone rang. Of course it did. "Hally?" Quinn's worried, slightly high voice came through the tiny speaker. "Are you all right?"

It hurt to swallow or clear my throat, and the mucus or spit or whatever prevented me from saying anything without a gurgling noise.

"Quinn," I tried to say, but it came out as a grunt that didn't sound remotely close to his name.

"Hally, I can't hear you. Did you mean to text me?"

I nodded even though he couldn't see me. Didn't my silence or very odd grunts tell him something was amiss?

"Hally? Are you there?"

I tried to touch the keypad icon to try punching in numbers, but I didn't even know if that worked on a cellphone. This wasn't working.

"You're worrying me. I'll be there soon."

Thank the Mother. I laid down on the cold tile, and watched the fairy's unconscious body. I had to stay awake in case he woke up. My eyelids grew heavy.

Someone pounded on the door and shouted. Perhaps a female voice...yep, female. Crap, the fairy doctor. Quinn must have called her to check on me. A pressure throughout the room pushed until I thought my eardrums would explode, and then the ward the aide had set up in the room broke with a "pop."

"Ambassador?" She gasped. "It's me Celine. Can you hear me? Can you talk?" Her icy hands touched my shoulder and shook me.

Not that I didn't want to respond, but at that point, I couldn't.

"Who is this?" Celine whispered as she reached the unconscious fairy. She shook him less forcefully than she had me. Or maybe it just felt like she'd been harsher with me. The doctor checked my attacker's pulse. When she started to turn my way, I closed my eyes. "Don't worry, Ambassador, I can help." She touched my neck and the feel of her magic seeped into me. Until her phone rang.

The phone clattered to the floor. "Crap. Your Highness?" She paused as Quinn said something. "I found her, yes. It's bad. No. She's alive. Sorry, not that kind of bad. I found her on the floor, unconscious next to another fae. I'm working on her now, but please hurry. There's only so much I can do to keep this from the humans."

Oh fun. It seemed like I'd been saved after all.

9

QUINN HAD BEEN SO sure no one would touch us, even after Doctor O'Dae told us people knew. Nol was pissed—not at me, but at the fae and himself for letting his guard down. Their anger wasn't nearly as high as mine, though. I was the one attacked—in my nephew's room. But most of all, I wanted answers. And I was intending to get one now, or at least when we got up to King Domhnall's office.

That was, King Domhnall, Quinn's father. The one we were going to talk to about my attack. The royal armored vehicle car jerked to a stop in an almost empty parking garage. Only ten cars were parked here. Two fancy BMWs, an armored car like the Mercedes-Benz we were in now, a Lamborghini, and a few I didn't recognize. The other armored was a given, but who owned the other cars? The guards who were standing around waiting for us to get out? Or were we walking into an ambush?

Nol undid his seatbelt and went to open the door in one movement, but Quinn reached over and grasped Nol's arm closest to him, holding him back as he took off his own seatbelt. Nol didn't move away from the door, but waited for Quinn's explanation instead of pulling on the handle in his hand.

"We have to follow protocol; they'll open the door after they confirm it's safe." He glanced at the fairies outside our car, but looked back at Nol. "And, I beg you do not, under any circumstances, unsheathe your sword here."

Celine squeaked beside me. I glanced over to find the doctor gripping the armrest between us. She stared at Nol with wide eyes, her chest shaking from her shallow breathing, a deer-in-headlights reaction.

"Yes, you've been wronged and Hally was threatened, but they will consider you a threat to the royal family once that sword is out. It would be detrimental to Hally's work to bring peace between our peoples."

The moment Quinn said it, Nol understood. I could tell by the way his shoulders hunched. But that didn't mean he liked it. Nol leaned back in his seat as he watched the fae in the garage, his face was already set in his emotionless mask that the *Zayuri* trained all of their warriors to master.

Forget the sword, just staring at them he looked threatening. I leaned forward in my seat and placed my hand on Nol's knee. "You have to show some emotion. Don't hide behind your mask." He knew he scared me when he went full on *Zayuri*.

He still didn't take his eyes off the guards. "*Sye eavalem setar imortani,*" *I don't trust these people.*

"*Sitam, falen...*" *I know, but...*I glanced at Quinn and Celine, who didn't understand *Aemirin*, but I wouldn't switch to French or English. "We have to trust Quinn." Quinn perked up when he heard his name, but I didn't give an explanation. "You might be angry with them all, as am I, but he's the only one we can rely on."

Nol glanced at Quinn. "If Hallë is threatened again—"

"She won't be."

"Your fae assassin proved there is no guarantee of that today." Nol's emotionless tone gave us no clue whether he'd meant it accusingly or not, but Quinn seemed to take it that way.

Quinn leaned forward so he could look Nol square in the eye beside him. "He's not—"

The door on Quinn's side opened and a guard poked his head in. "Your Highness, all is clear."

Quinn blew out a slow breath and looked back at Nol. "Please?"

No one moved; Celine didn't breathe as we waited for Nol to respond. Finally, Nol gave Quinn a curt nod and opened his door. As I scooted out of my seat and stood, Nol stayed in front of the door to keep me behind him. As the guards positioned themselves around us, Nol moved over, staying an arm's length away from me. He glanced down at me, and I realized he had me in his peripheral vision as we walked.

Under any other circumstances I'd tell him he was overreacting, but until *Aemina* and Queen Orlaith came to an agreement on a suitable permanent ambassador, all of *Endae* was relying on me. Assassinating me would lead to a major diplomatic crisis and could escalate tensions, resulting in possible retaliatory actions—right from the playbook. And we'd be back at square one, trying to prevent a war between the fae and *enda*.

We followed the yellow-painted pedestrian path through the garage and to the elevators. I'd expected something similar to Orlaith's place: a terra-cotta manor in the foothills of the Cascades overlooking an expansive vineyard that had no business in the Washington mountain climate. Or at least something magical. But everything, from the elevator to the gray and black high-gloss tiles to the eighties gaudy furnishings, was mundane, not a spark of magic. Or at least on the surface; I had no way of telling if glamor covered the entire building.

The guard with lavender hair that was almost as short as me, fidgeted on Nol's other side after we made our way to the last door on the west side on the fifteenth floor. Why was it always the last door? After a moment, a muffled voice responded, and the lead guard opened the door.

The inside of the room was much brighter than the hall, with floor-to-ceiling windows letting in the dull white light of another overcast day in Paris' *La Défense* district. The guards fanned out around the edges of the room while we followed Quinn all the way to the high-end carpet. A couch, chair and coffee table were positioned near a fake fireplace, as if the view of the city wasn't good enough, they had to cover it up with a rolling orange light. Quinn stopped us before reaching the carpet. Nol stayed ahead of me, almost even with Quinn, while I stayed next to Celine.

"Father?" Quinn dipped his head as he called out to what appeared to be an apartment-sized empty office. "I've come with Ambassador Inara, *Hinam* Madorean, and Doctor Celine O'Dae."

A movement near the window made me jump. Beside me, Celine dropped to one knee and looked at the floor. A fairy as tall as Quinn, in a fitted black suit, stood close to the window, staring down at the people and cars going about their business. He stayed where he was with his hands held in front of him as if he hadn't heard his son.

King Domhnall's height was where the similarities to his son ended. Where Quinn's hair was slate gray and hung to his chin, his father's was golden blonde, cut in a trim, no-nonsense style. Quinn's skin was as pale as mine, and Domhnall's was a sun-kissed tan, a few shades lighter than Nol's.

A knock on another door broke the silence that had followed Quinn's words.

"Enter." The king didn't raise his voice, and it didn't fill the room, but somehow we all heard it, even the tall fairy with dark green hair that opened the door. Quinn had introduced him as Sergeant Cairan when he came into Léon's hospital room earlier.

The sergeant who'd arrested my attacker took five steps into the office, swished his long hair back over his shoulder, and bowed. "Your Majesty," he spoke to the floor.

His Majesty waited another minute to move, too enthralled by the goings-on of the people below. Must have been one riveting scene. Domhnall inhaled and turned until he faced Sergeant Cairan.

"What have you ascertained?" he asked in French. From his dull, bored tone of voice, I wasn't sure if the king was irritated or indifferent. It was almost as good as Nol's masked emotions.

The sergeant stood and faced his king. "Not much, Your Majesty. He is still incoherent from the ambassador's spell—"

King Domhnall held up his hand. "I was informed that you found him on the floor next to the ambassador?"

"Doctor O'Dae did, Your Majesty. She was first on the scene."

Celine and I had had to keep my attacker down while we were alone and she was working on my throat. I let the guy breathe, but other than that, I wouldn't let the prick twitch an eyelid.

All the fae were very polite when they were in Léon's room, but I wouldn't let Sergeant Cairan remove the fae who'd tried to kill me until Nol got there. None of the fairies understood why until Nol had stormed in, scanned the small room and walked straight to me. Not one word, he dropped in front of me, looked at my throat, which Celine had healed, then rose and stalked to the fae they'd bound on the other side of the room. He didn't touch him, didn't say a word, but I swear the coward wet himself before Nol asked me to release him and let the fae drag him out.

"Doctor Celine O'Dae?" Quinn's father turned in his lazy way to face the four of us. He studied us as if he were determining which lobster to pick for dinner. In every one of our meetings, Quinn's father had been the least talkative, only saying an occasional word or two, while his wife asked the questions and made the decisions.

He took a minute—literally—to study our group, settling the longest on Nol, who he'd only seen once in our meetings. The king walked across the room, his black wingtip Oxfords shushing on the plush carpet as he came to stand in front of us all. "Celine O'Dae, tell me, what was your assessment upon entering the room?"

Celine stayed on one knee staring at the floor as she answered her king with a nervous quiver in her voice. "Your Majesty, upon breaking the fae ward and entering the room, I found both of them on the floor. The ambassador was conscious but too impaired to answer me. Her attacker was unconscious on the floor across from her."

"Fae ward? Interesting. What were their positions? Who was closer to the door?"

Celine paused, as if she had been trying to remember, then continued in her trembling voice. "The ambassador was on her side, and he was on his back farther from the door. He had no apparent markings or abrasions. However, the ambassador had injuries to her throat, indicative of a strangling. Even after I healed it, the red abrasions circling her neck are visible."

"Rise, Celine, and look me in the eye."

The doctor rose, fidgeting and shaking, her eyes rolled up to King Domhnall, only a few inches taller than herself.

The king's shoes slid on the tiles as he stepped close and circled her, almost brushing me as he made his way around her. "You knew of the ambassador's travel plans, did you not?"

"Um...I wouldn't say...I'd heard that the elven ambassador was coming to Paris."

"Who told you this?" He completed his circle and stood in front of Celine.

Celine glanced at Quinn, who'd turned to face Celine and me, along with Nol.

"Do not look at my son. I am asking the questions. Did you think he wouldn't tell me?"

"No. I mean, that's not—" Celine cussed under her breath. She squared her shoulders, raised her eyes to her king and grew a pair. "Your Majesty, yes, I heard two nights ago at a nightclub that the ambassador was traveling to Paris. He-henam"—giving up on Nol's title, she pointed at Nol. "He wasn't mentioned."

"Who told you Ambassador Inara was traveling to Paris, and which nightclub were you in, Celine O'Dae?"

"Marcie Flynn, a maid in your service, told me and my friends at *Éclipse*. She didn't say who told her"— Celine dropped to her knees— "I'm sorry, Your Majesty. When His Highness asked last night, I called my friend to make sure I was remembering correctly. You see, I'd had a few drinks and—"

"Did you mention to your friend that you saw the ambassador?"

"Um...no, but she asked me why I wanted to know. I didn't give her an answer." The doctor paused, shaking her head. "I didn't tell her."

"Give me the name of this friend you spoke to on the phone."

"Diana..." Celine gasped, and her answer came in a sob. "Diana Martin. Please, Your Majesty, she's my friend."

"Does she hold any animosity toward elves?" Quinn asked quickly.

The king turned to his son with a scowl on his face. With a sigh and a slight eye-roll, he let it go. It was a good question, but Celine didn't answer, as if she only needed to answer the king's questions.

"Well? My son asked you a question. Answer it."

"I don't know. She's never... Wait, she might hold some. Diana is only seventy, but her grandparents fought and died in the war. Please forgive me. I didn't tell her."

"Sergeant Cairan, find Diana Martin and the maid, Marcie Flynn. Celine you will accompany my sergeant to locate your friend and all those involved at *Éclipse*."

"But my job—"

"This is bigger than your hospital work. You almost created an international, inter-realm crisis."

Almost? I still had to report to *Endae* about the incident, and I didn't know how they'd take it. Celine looked at each of us individually, only now understanding the full repercussions of her "not telling her friend" about me. Sorry wasn't going to cut it.

"Your Majesty, I didn't mean to."

Sergeant Cairan reached over for Celine's hand to guide her out of the room as she sobbed and asked for forgiveness, but the king ignored her. Instead, he turned to the three of us, his golden-blond eyebrows arched high. He nodded like the problem had been settled.

"Ambassador, *Hinam*. The fairy who harmed you is Thomas Guild. As my sergeant said, he's unable to answer any questions. I'm curious. what was the spell that you cast?"

The nerve of this guy! This was not how politics was done. No formal welcome, not even a greeting. No interest in my wellbeing or a fucking apology? And now he was interrogating me?

I just blinked at Quinn's father. No way in hell was I going to admit anything to this guy. No doubt he'd turn it against me. I'd already had that happen to me once. No fucking way.

I must have taken too long, because he leaned forward, raising his eyebrows to encourage me to answer him. Absolutely not. He was not my king. Where was his wife? No wonder he didn't talk at meetings. He'd screw everything up whenever he opened his mouth.

"Ambassador?" Domhnall spoke in English this time. "Perhaps you've spent too long in America? Is your French faulty? I urge you to answer the question. What did you do to Thomas Guild? I heard he was unable to move until you released him after *Hinam* Madorean assessed him. I've heard your magic is different from other elves. If it's different, tell me how your...er...attack, for lack of a better word, was different than how other elves would do it."

Oh, I called that bullshit a mile away. I was not admitting a damn thing. "After he almost killed me, you mean? Your Majesty?" I added at the end after a pause for emphasis. In impeccable French, making sure my accent was flawless. My mother would have been proud. "I'm not certain what he did, actually. At first, I was walking to the door of my nephew's hospital room, then something was around my neck, choking me. He began to speak Gaelic, that ancient Gaelic that I've heard the fae speak. I remember falling backwards and the room wasn't there, but I saw...I'm not sure, exactly, but the Faerie fireflies were there. They are lovely, I must say."

"Ms. Ambassador, I asked you what you did to him, not a full account."

"I felt I needed to give you the full story, Your Majesty. This will also be how I report it to all the nations of *Endae*. It's only right, I believe, for you to know. I will also be giving a full written statement soon after this." I gave him a sweet, innocent smile. And as fake as shit. "Oh! Where are my manners?" I pressed my hand to my chest. "May I say, Your Majesty..." I bowed a short head dip. "As I didn't have the chance to earlier, it is an honor to meet you. I was looking forward to meeting you tonight, and not under these disturbing circumstances. It was quite traumatizing for me."

Domhnall clenched his jaw and stared at me. Then a switch flipped, his shoulders loosened and his expression softened. "Yes, Ambassador, I'm sure it was quite traumatic. Doctor O'Dae said she healed it? May I?" The king looked down at my neck as if that explained his intention.

"May you..." Touch, see, ask? I wasn't a freaking psychic.

"May I see the abrasion?"

He continued to stare, expecting me to submit to his rude behavior. What was his problem? Was he trying to piss me off? I stopped short mentally. He *was* trying to piss me off to see how far he could push me. A test, as an *endaë* of a hostile nation, from the exile who'd broken the fae treaty. Fuck, I had to play along.

"Is something wrong?" The king's expression dared me to react.

"Pardon me, I thought things would be more formal at our first meeting. As you know, I am new to this and from what I've read, all the nations are about formalities." I almost told him his behavior disturbed me, but Quinn's little head quirk stopped me.

"And what exactly did you expect to happen?"

"A handshake, at least. A 'good day' or 'pleased to make your acquaintance' would be nice." Quinn started fidgeting behind his father, trying to get my attention. It seemed that he'd come to the same conclusion as I. Yes, I was poking the bear, but I wouldn't stop. I refused to be pushed around. I wasn't a damn lab rat, and I wouldn't fail *Endae*.

He turned to face Quinn. "She's an elf. I thought you said she was different."

Quinn gave him an exasperated look. "Father, there's a difference between self-imposed superiority and standing up for one's self. She knows your game." Holy shit. He'd called his father out. Would there be repercussions for that? And for fuck's sake, could we get on with Thomas Guild?

"Fine," the king grumbled before turning to face me. He dipped his head a fraction. "Madam Ambassador, welcome to *Céandalamh*, the Motherland of the fae. So nice to meet you in person. Our video meetings do not do your beauty justice."

I was unsure how to take his turnabout and the unexpected flattery. I was drowning, and how did I respond without thanking him? Okay... "What a very nice compliment. I must say, you rarely say anything in those meetings, so it is good to actually speak with you."

He threw his head back and laughed. I took the moment when his eyes were off me to give Quinn a "what the fuck" look. No help would come from him, just an annoyed sigh and sagging shoulders. Annoyed at whom, though? Me for being unprepared for this act of...what the hell did I even call this?

"Your Majesty." This had gone far enough, and my patience was wearing thin. "Thomas Guild, what will be done?"

His eyes hardened, and his posture stiffened. "We already talked about that."

"We talked about Celine O'Dae's possible involvement. I'm happy that you've found out his name, but I must know what will happen to him? Are you going to release him? When should I expect the trial? I would like to include a path of repercussions for his attack in my report." He'd already admitted to Celine how serious this was so he couldn't deny it. "I'm sure we can find a way to keep this from being blown out of proportion. If this fairy was a fanatic acting on his own, I need to know. My people need to know this won't happen again in your kingdom. Please give me something more to tell them than their ambassador was almost assassinated today."

The more serious, authoritative side of him finally came out after my little speech, but he hadn't just been assaulted. I had every right to be insulted and angry.

"Tell me about your wound."

"The doctor did a wonderful job of healing my throat enough for me to breathe. But my neck is still tender, and I have a headache the size of New York City. Other than that...I'm irritated that this took me away from my nephew—the reason for my visit."

"Ah, that. Which is a topic that needs to be addressed."

"And is supposed to be addressed later tonight after hospital visiting hours."

"Please permit me to examine your neck." He wouldn't even acknowledge the need to address this issue! I'd expected an apology, a word of sympathy, and concern for my wellbeing. But my family, that they'd knowingly harbored an *endaë* for the last century, needed to be addressed. Not that none of us had any idea that fairies actually existed. No!

But, instead of throwing more of a hissy fit, I took the high road and slipped my jacket off my shoulders.

"Do you know what he used to strangle you?"

"A scarf of some sort. I pulled it off my neck and dropped it at some point."

The king clicked his tongue, and without warning or permission, he sent a spell through me to check for magical signatures. The king's magic soaked into my skin, slippery and itchy, first at my shoulders and chest. Then, like a cloth being pulled out from under me, his spell inspected the rest of my neck and head. He stepped back, his jaw muscles working as he glared at me. He couldn't possibly be angry at me for this.

"Quinn. Come. Now." He turned away without another word and stalked off to the door the sergeant had come through.

Quinn stood still for a moment, his eyes darting from his father and back to me, unsure what to make of this odd behavior.

"Cuán, now!" Oh shit, his birth name? That must have been middle-name offenses with the fae. The king examined my neck, why was Quinn getting in trouble for it?

With that demand, Quinn's eyes widened as they met mine. He dropped his head back and closed his eyes. "Fuck," he whispered before he sped out of the room.

I glanced at Nol, who was as clueless about this display as I was for a second. "*C'yo*, Hallë." Nol had almost the same look as Quinn.

"*Ma?*" *What?* How come he always figured everything out before me? Before anyone—okay, in this instance, Quinn had figured out the problem first. Still, the king wanted to talk to Quinn, not Nol.

"He just checked for *imolegin*," he said in *Aemirin* so none of the guards understood.

"Yeah, so?" I shrugged, finding no problem with this if it helped prove Guild's guilt.

"*Malela...*" *Last night...* He smirked at me. "Had some fun, didn't you?"

I gasped. "*Sye tätaca cina*," *That is not fair.* Not only had the king sensed Thomas Guild's signature, but Quinn's as well. "We..." I pointed at my pain in the ass *muranildo* and continued in *Aemirin*. There was no way Nol and I would let this leak. "*Sae joducen mina, tusulira,*" *No teasing me, you shit.* "Do you think he's in big trouble?"

"*Ja,*" *Yes.* "I expect so." He was still laughing.

"Fuck," I muttered under my breath, and to that the little shit laughed even harder.

"Ambassador Inara, *Hinam* Madorean, come this way," a thick-armed, green-skinned fae with bumps all over his body walked in through the same door we'd come through. Quinn and his father were nowhere in sight. The serviceman—fae, whatever—waited until we'd followed him through the door before explaining further. "His Majesty and His Royal Highness send their sincerest apologies. However, they are indisposed and do not wish to take up any more of your time. The royal family looks forward to seeing you tonight at dinner."

With a nod, the service person handed us off to the same guards who had brought us here. He was still watching us as we got into the elevator. We didn't say anything, not a whisper, as the elevator brought us down to the garage. Tonight couldn't come soon enough, but first I had to give Léon some sort of explanation for why I wasn't there when he got back from his test.

10

"Wow." There were no other words for it.

Nol looked suave and sleek in his tuxedo. He fidgeted in the narrow space between my salon and dining room. The curtains were closed and the dated living room lamp gave off a warm yellow glow. The moment he got to my apartment yesterday, Nol had cast a sweep spell to air out the place. Sure, I'd had a maid clean periodically, but no one had lived here in over a decade. There was a difference.

He pressed his hand against his tux jacket. "Are you sure it's not too much?" He brushed at nonexistent lint.

"You look great, Nol, promise." Did I think it was too much? Yes, but not his tuxedo. The whole idea of a formal dinner with fancy clothes just to meet us for the first time was too much. We'd already met Quinn's father, so what was the point of swishing around in fancy clothes?

"I feel silly with the bow. Ray wears these in her hair. And I don't wear gray. This is too much." Maybe Nol felt odd going to formally meet the royal family without his uniform on. If he'd brought his dress formals, he could have, but whatever. He looked outstanding in the dark gray and blue, and I found my mind drifting, envisioning him in the all-black tuxedo he'd have to wear for Sam and Mateo's wedding.

"Hallë?" Nol waved his hand in front of my face. He'd walked across the room to where I was perched on the couch arm against the wall opposite him, staring at nothing.

"Sorry. Lost in thought." When his look turned playful, I rolled my eyes and searched for something else to talk about besides what he wore. "This could go very wrong. What if they're so mad that Quinn is dating me that they refuse to let us stay? Or something worse?"

Nol deflated as my worries turned from the party to politics. "If Quinn could delay his marriage to Katie for centuries, he can settle this. Besides, we don't know for certain that was the reason the king took Quinn away."

"Fine. Let's not dwell on it, right?" I inhaled a deep breath and blew it out, checking his tuxedo again. "The tux is nice. Don't take this the wrong way, but you look gorgeous in gray and blue. It brings out the blue in your eyes and makes your skin glow." Like hell would I say anything more. That was as high of a compliment as I'd give him. But it was true. "I only wonder about the vest."

"What about it?" Nol pushed his jacket back and pressed on the deep blue vest. My dress was blue as well but not as dark. The official color of *Aemina* was a shade of blue I had yet to find in this realm. But it made sense to dress us both in blue.

"The buttons are angled. Not that it's a bad thing, just...not exactly traditional." The splash of color on the vest notwithstanding.

Nol looked away, but I caught the rebelliousness in the smile he'd tried to hide.

"What?" I poked him in the ribs when he refused to answer. "Tell me what that smile was about. What does this mean?" I tugged on his vest.

"Quinn wasn't going for traditional. I mean, look at your dress."

Taken aback, I clutched my chest and almost fell off the couch. "What about my dress?"

"This looks nothing like the fancy clothes I saw online."

I jutted out my chin and narrowed my eyes. "Oh, like where on-line?"

He hadn't said one damn word about my dress until now. Not that I'd expected a compliment or even a comment, but I had given him a nice compliment. Nol pulled his phone out of his pocket, his fingers tapping away at his screen. "See?" The website was a news article about the previous year's White House State Dinner. Most of the women were either older, rich, or models.

"I'm not wearing beads and sequins, and like hell I'd ever wear that." The woman I'd referred to wore a lace corset with satin fabric hanging from the bottom to make it a floor-length "gown."

"Which one?" Nol pulled it back and looked, then scoffed. "*C'yo*, you could never pull that off."

"Are you trying to piss me off?"

"No! Look at the other ones. They're not...this." He gestured at mine.

"This? Quinn helped pick it out. He would have said something if it wasn't appropriate." The dresses those women wore were either traditional to their customs, like an elegant long kurta, or sparkly, shiny dresses that would look horrible on me. "Most of these women are in their thirties or higher. I look like I'm twenty. My gown is fine. Besides, almost all of them showed my scars."

"I never said I liked theirs, but I had expected something like this." He shook his phone. "Because it seemed standard for your role."

"You need to stop talking." I pushed him away, slid off my couch and went to check on my hair or do anything other than listen to my *muranildo* criticize my clothes.

"Hallë, I'm not saying you look bad. They—"

"You're digging yourself deeper."

Nol grumbled something under his breath in *Aemirin* as I shut my bedroom door in his face. Leaning against the door, I looked down at the blue gown. I guess there were tiny sequins, but not like sequins that looked like fish scales.

This was pretty, right? "Not what he expected. Ass."

What if I called Charlie about it? She was young. I patted down my skirts, looking for my phone to send her a picture for her opinion. There were no pockets, and none of my clutches were blue like the gown, but I felt naked without it by my side. Perhaps a cream clutch would work. Or a black one. I pushed off the door to head to my closet. My phone was going with me, damn it.

"Hallë!" Nol gave the door a few solid knocks.

"Leave me alone, Nol."

"Our driver is here."

"You're serious?" Because, as I always said, he was a pain in my ass.

"Yes. I swear."

"Say one more word about my dress and I'll punch your lights out."

Nol groaned like the brat he was. "Fine." Nol muttered, stomping away.

I dashed into my closet. It'd been a while since I'd come here, and my bags weren't where I'd expected them. Had Amelia or the maid moved them? Or—the drawer! That's right.

"Hallë, the driver is waiting!"

"And they can wait a little longer. I swear if you nitpick me the entire night, I will..."

"What?" Nol had poked his head in to ask.

"That was locked."

His eyes widened. "And?"

I grabbed the first black clutch I saw—with sequins, unfortunately. "Now I know how An'di felt!" I shoved my phone in the bag and stomped to the door. He wouldn't move, so I shoved him out of my bedroom, hand on his chest while he grinned.

"You can't be that mad. Come on."

Ignoring him, I grabbed my best long coat. Even while ignoring him, I held it out. He had just insulted me and he was trying to make up for it.

"What?" He blinked at me, clueless of what I was expecting.

I scoffed at myself for my expectation and slipped it on myself. He didn't know human etiquette, but my human parents raised me in a time where it was expected for a man to help a lady into her coat. He wasn't human, he didn't open doors, or help ladies out of cars, or into their coats, not unless it held a purpose. He followed his observations and people didn't do that anymore. Why did I, even for a second, expect that from him? Because I had a formal dress on and it took me back to that bygone era? Yes, I had.

The driver stood at the apartment stoop in an all-black chauffeur uniform with her hands in front of her, staring straight ahead. Nol followed me out, and I had to shoo him over so I could lock the door.

I almost asked Nol where his coat was, but at the last minute, I remembered I was ignoring him. "We're ready," I informed our driver.

The chauffeur made eye contact with me and nodded. We had to go around and through the apartment complex's outdoor courtyard to get out, complete with gardens and a fountain. As we turned the corner into the space, Nol tucked my arm under his. When I went to pull it out, he tightened it. He knew I was mad, and if I didn't want to make a big deal out of it, I couldn't fight him on this.

"I'm sorry for teasing you about your dress."

Narrowing my eyes, I glanced over, because he did sound sincere. He didn't look it, though, with the goofy grin he gave when he caught me looking. The chauffeur held the heavy wooden front door of the private apartment complex. Nol let go of me so I could go through first.

He was back by my side, scooping my arm up two steps later. "You can't stay mad forever. You're my *muranildë.*"

We'd see about that.

"Your dress is—"

My sharp look shut him up, and he stayed silent until we reached the car.

"Madam Ambassador?" The chauffeur held open the door to another armored Mercedes-Benz. I stopped and held my hand out for Nol to go in first. After a brief pause, he followed my silent instruction and got in. Like the other car, the interior was a creamy leather with brown trim, but it had one forward-facing bench seat. I liked the other one better with its captain chairs and armrests.

As we secured our seat belts, Nol's motions told me something was bothering him. He pouted and watched Paris go by while I brushed my dress and settled the layers, trying to ignore him.

"What is this?" I couldn't stand it any longer as we made it to the A1 autoroute going east out of Paris. I waved my hand in a circle to indicate him and his attitude. "You're pouting." And he'd got me to fold. Damn it!

He kept silent for a while. "They attacked you, Hallë. Getting in first means I leave you alone out there."

"*That*? It's protocol. An ambassador enters last so they can get out first. I've told you this. You've read it. Besides, the chauffeur was there."

"Their own people attacked you. I don't trust them to keep us safe."

"I let you get out first in the garage." He'd been scary as shit in the garage, too.

He continued to pout. Yes, the visit had been odd to say the least. We hadn't heard from Quinn, any fae after that. And it was eating me up. How much trouble had I gotten Quinn into?

I looked out my window. "Quinn's father is..."

"Odd? Strategic?" he supplied in *Aemirin*, getting frustrated with—how did he put it? His limited English vocabulary lacked the full meaning he intended to convey. I just "dumbed down" his translations for the average human. Mother help us. "Mad, certainly, but with a construct beneath it. He was testing you and in my opinion you passed."

"Gee, thanks." I rolled my eyes. Yeah, nobody believed me when I said he could be a condescending jerk. To be fair, not knowing the words that I'd want to use instead of an elementary synonym would annoy me every once in a while. "You don't think he'd punish his son for...fraternizing with the enemy?"

"Enemy? Do you truly believe they still regard us as such?" he continued in *Aemirin*. "They enacted a treaty, Hallë—an alliance that ended the war. But I harbor no illusions about their intent. I do not trust them to protect us from the zealotry still festering among the fae population. I believe Thomas Guild is one such zealot—a fairy driven by inherited hatred. And I hold no doubt that others remain, still clinging to the notion that two young *endai* are to blame for a war of their forebears."

"Yes, but I broke the treaty. I'm just scared Quinn is going to get in trouble."

The brush of calloused fingers slid over the top of my right hand. The feel of his magic called to me. Nol opened our link and waited for me to respond, if I wanted it. What I wanted to do was lean over and curl up under his arm, pull my legs in, and let his magical energy surround me, calm me. Nol even lifted his arm to offer it. That was what I always did when we needed to balance our energies. Or recharge, as Gil used to put it.

I shook my head no. "My makeup will rub against your tuxedo if I lean in."

Nol shrugged. "*Nanas*," *no biggie*, he said. A moment later, Nol's head was in my lap, and I was petting his hair. It wasn't like he'd done a one-eighty and changed his attitude. His irritation was still under the surface, but the tension in his shoulders eased as I played with his hair. He'd needed the comfort, too. Nol reached for my free hand, and I gave it to him. He played with my knuckles, rubbing each one between his thumb and forefinger like he knew I liked. I opened my side of our link and closed my eyes so I wouldn't see through his eyes as well as mine. My heart slowed, my breathing evened out, and my thoughts settled.

"*Estum*," *I swear*, "we'll get through this." Nol promised.

I sure hoped so. Sighing, I eased farther into the seat.

QUINN STOOD ALONE IN front of a shell of a ruined castle in a small field in the middle of nowhere, waiting for us as our car turned into the driveway. The golden light of the early evening touched the top stones and a tower with an intact blue turret. Was this a joke? I was getting *A Midsummer Night's Dream* vibes, and I'd never liked Shakespeare.

I chewed on my lip as we came around to park in front of Quinn in his impeccable black tuxedo. Tall and sexy and... "Does he look irritated?"

Nol leaned over until his face was almost pressed against the window. "No. Maybe a little nervous."

"Really? Why? Okay, maybe the meeting will be crazy, but—"

Nol sat back in his seat, an eyebrow raised. "The meeting? I'm sure they've had other things to argue about this afternoon. *C'yo*, his parents just discovered their heir is sleeping with an elf."

"We're not *sleeping* together," I grumbled, but then realized what I'd said and to whom I'd said it. Crap. I was going to get so much shit for this!

"No?" Nol blinked slowly, making sure there was enough time for me to say just kidding. "What about last night?"

"That's none of your business." Did he really think that?

"You slept there, did you not?"

"That's not—"

"What in the realms did you do, then? His signature is on you like—"

I smacked him on the shoulder. Like any of that was his business. And when the hell had he checked me for signatures? Rude.

My door opened. We'd been bickering so much that I hadn't noticed the car had stopped.

"Ambassador?" Without thinking, I jumped out first before Nol had a chance to complain.

Quinn offered his hand just after I'd climbed out of the car. "You look beautiful." Quinn's fingers curled around mine, and he leaned forward for air kisses as if this afternoon hadn't happened. "Welcome to my mother's Paris chateau."

I squinted at him. "Hardly. It's fifty kilometers outside of Paris."

"My mother hates the city, but it's close enough to get there when needed."

Nol came out right behind me and stepped to my side so he and Quinn could clasp forearms. After their small greeting, Nol moved so he was on Quinn's other side.

"Come. Ambassador Inara, *Hinam* Madorean, the party awaits."

"Party?" At a dilapidated castle? There had to be more. "I thought it was a formal dinner."

"It is." Quinn winced. "With a few more guests." With the not-so-happy fake smile forced on his face, I knew we had issues.

His lame attempt at subverting the issue with compliments wouldn't get past me. "Is everything..."

"Not as bad as they could be, but not well." That told me absolutely nothing, but he hadn't treated me any differently from Nol, except for the cheek kisses. If his parents were going to make him break up with me, they wouldn't have let him meet us out here.

We had to clear the air. My stomach was in knots, and I just needed answers. Hopefully, I'd get at least one. "What's going on? What happened today? Am I in trouble? Did you get more information on Thomas Guild or Celine's friends?"

"It will be discussed later. Don't give me that look. There are other concerns on the agenda tonight." He hung his head. "We've got company. Come, we're falling behind."

Nol turned away, his back to the setting sun, his hair a halo of auburn. "More than us." He made it a statement in an unemotional tone. "*Majut*," Nol cussed. "A political move? Is Hallë safe? My sword is—"

Quinn stopped and placed his hand on Nol's arm. "My friend, your sword is where it belongs tonight."

He let go of Nol and got us walking toward the dilapidated castle. Quinn knew what he was doing. He'd been balancing the peace between three different countries for longer than I'd been alive. If he thought we needed to present a united front, we'd do so. Quinn offered his arm, then pulled me in close. He nodded at Nol. "We've got this." Quinn's encouragement didn't banish all my worries, but he was our only ally here.

Three steps closer and Quinn waved his hand, and the veil to Faerie wavered, then fell, revealing another castle, similar to the mundane one on the grounds. The day's last rays were dimmer, thanks to the much larger surrounding forest. This place, while not ominous, was darker. The trees were larger, the forest was thicker, and I imagined this was how Europe had looked before the land was torn to shreds and covered with ivy and blackberries and progress. We walked on Quinn's arms together into Faerie. I looked back after several steps to find the car and all the mundane buildings gone.

The only unnatural things left were the castle and us. The marble steps of the new castle led up to the enormous portico with four thick stone pillars. On either side of the doors were tall, narrow windows that emitted a golden glow, like beacons of light in the deep, scary darkness.

Quinn let me set the pace, which gave me some time to squeeze information out of him. "Tell me who's here. I should know who I'm meeting. There are protocols for—"

"For using an emergency visit to spring political agendas on an ambassador to a realm that my people consider hostile? Agreed, but it also saves everyone a trip, which is the excuse you'll hear my parents use."

A screech from the dark forest broke the silence. Then a guttural growl followed.

I shivered. Not daring to disrupt the silence that had returned, I pulled on Quinn and rose onto my tiptoes to whisper in his ear, "What is that?"

Quinn tilted his head, then shrugged. "It could be any number of things, but they wouldn't dare harm us." Quinn nudged me after a moment of silence. "What?"

"Tell me, whose mind do I need to change? Who do I need to focus on so your parents—your country—will give me a little trust? It would help if someone would tell me what happened."

"I know." Quinn patted my arm. "Lady Úna is the oldest fae, probably as old as Gavin. You should focus on her. They'll follow her opinion."

"And the others?"

"Marchioness Mirren is younger than me by a thousand years, but don't assume she's willing to cooperate. Her father's a prejudiced bigot."

"Is he here as well?"

"Good god, no. My parents aren't stupid."

Two steps after, Quinn paused. I squeezed his arm. "What's wrong?"

Quinn stared straight ahead as if the ground had offended him. "Many are not happy that I'm friends with either of you. Marchioness Mirren's father, Marquess Eoghan, is the guardian of the southern seas and lives on the border of our land. Mirren often comes in his place."

"Treat Mirren like I'm talking to her father, got it. Do I need to watch out for her?"

"No, that's Rory and Rose. They're twins and dreadfully cunning. Loki incarnate, I swear. Along with my sister, Rayne, they make up the three R's: Ruairí, Roisin, and Rionoch. They like to think they're triplets, but it's just the twins and my sister."

"Was that on purpose?" I asked. "The three R's?"

"By Anu's design. Rayne, my sister, isn't here, and pray you never meet them together. Their mischief is legendary. Many human wars were started because of their antics."

"Tell me about Úna. Why her? Just because she's ancient?"

"No. She has a way about her, and she is calm and reasonable. She has questions about—"

Quinn stopped talking as the ten-foot-high oak doors opened without a whisper of sound, and sunset yellow light rolled out to brighten the large circular entrance. "You'll see."

"Here we go," I muttered under my breath.

11

AFTER MY EYES ADJUSTED to the brightness, I took in the grand entrance as Quinn led me up the stone steps and between the pillars. White granite covered the floor throughout the entrance and vestibule, drawing the eye to the dark grand staircase that was set farther back in the entrance. The area was bigger than my living room, dining room, and kitchen combined. As we walked closer, I could make out the large paintings on the left wall.

"Your coat, *mademoiselle*?" A fae, popped out of no where thin as a rail, and pitch black. He smiled a black-mouthed, black-toothed smile and held his arms out. Yet, another species of fae I'd never heard about. His voice was rough yet high, like a child with strep throat. Did fae get strep throat? Focus, Hally.

Quinn helped me out of my coat, and handed it to the servant, not because I needed it, but because he was being a gentleman. He looped my arm in his again. "You okay?"

Besides my nephew being in the hospital, a fae attacking me, and the fact I was dating the heir to the The Motherland of the Fae, oh—and that they thought Quinn and I were sleeping together. "Yeah, I'm good."

Quinn guided us into the castle's extravagant great hall. The room had vaulted ceilings, ornate trim and nature scenes of Faerie painted on the walls. I recognized my favorite multicolored fairy fireflies. A fireplace that Nol could walk into occupied the middle of the inside wall. Large modern, cottage-style furniture was spread out around it, making a large square with room between all four walls and each piece. A long table against the far wall held an assortment of wine, sparkling water, and fruits.

Two fairy women were already in the room. One sat on a fainting chair, her back to me. The other stood closer to the middle windows. I'd expected to see Quinn's parents and the twins. Between the fae women Quinn described, I'd bet my best hat these were Úna and Mirren.

I'd imagined Úna as an old, large woman, but fae didn't age, and neither of these ladies was large. The one standing had her hair pulled back to better show off her tattoos. Spiral designs started at her chin and spilled down her neck, continuing past the collar of her elegant silk-and-lace gown. The other fairy turned as we stepped through the threshold. Her stark-white lace dress accentuated her dark brown skin and pupil-black eyes. She wore her white hair in tiny cornrow-like braids piled atop her head.

A fae, I swear, faded into existence before we made it three steps. "Announcing His Royal Highness, Prince Cuán," the herald announced in French, right in my ear. "*Endae* Ambassador Hallanevaë Inara, and *Zayuri*, *Hinam* Twynolan Madorean." Then he leaned in and used his inside voice. "Their Majesties, Queen Brigid and King Domhnall, will arrive momentarily. Please, make yourself comfortable. Refreshments are on the far side." As if we couldn't assess all of that ourselves.

"Allow me to make introductions, Madam Ambassador, *Hinam* Twynolan," Quinn said in French. Now I was really glad I'd given Nol the ability to speak French. Translating this entire evening would have been exhausting.

"Oh, Your Highness you're playing Orlaith's ambassador duties quite convincingly." The fairy on the couch rose from her seat, a self-important flare in her movements as she batted her eyes at Quinn. "*Comme c'est adorable*," *how adorable.*

"And this is the Marchioness of *Tir na Mara Dheas*, Lady Mirren." Quinn gestured toward the one who'd stood from the couch.

He reached for my hand to escort me over, and Mirren hissed through her teeth.

"Your Highness, please, you are above playing with commoners. Is this really part of your foreign duties?"

"On the contrary, Marchioness Mirren." I dipped my head and leaned over. Not a bow. "The Inara family has served as royal advisors in the *Amura Ore* since the first era."

Mirren stopped batting her eyes at Quinn as she turned a scathing look upon me.

"In our co-regency-oligarchy system"—I paused for dramatic effect—"I outrank you."

She didn't even sputter. Mirren just stood there in front of the fireplace, frozen, like I'd broken her. Laughter shattered the tension in the room. "Your Highness, this one's a keeper. Good for you, little one. Good for you," she said, her voice low and husky.

Quinn's eyes were wide with shock when I looked, but a broad smile soon crinkled them. "Duchess of *Lusitana*, Lady Úna." He gestured toward Úna, who had stopped laughing but still had a smile.

"Way to play nice, Hallë," Nol muttered to me in *Aemirin*.

"*Dunar'aë*," *She started it,* I muttered right back. Besides, I'd won Úna over with it.

Quinn encouraged Nol to follow us. "Lady Úna, please allow me to introduce you to Ambassador Inara and *Hinam* Madorean."

"Yes, intriguing." Úna held her hand out for me to shake. "May I say, Madam Ambassador, you come from a longer line than you know. Your family has been in politics much earlier than the transition to *Endae*. Your great-grandparents helped write the treaty, in fact."

I leaned away, taken aback. "I'd say it's a few more than two generations between them and me, but that *is* interesting." It got my mind spinning on the who's who of my family. "I'm not surprised. The council likes to keep us close. Troublemakers, the lot of us."

"*Hinam* Madorean—" Úna tilted her head toward Nol—"It is wonderful to have another *Zayuri* in this realm. That your honorable families were required to leave as well saddened many. I heard Queen Orlaith granted *Zayuri* to come and go. Is that true?"

Nol bowed. "It is, Lady Úna."

Mirren approached, scrutinizing Nol. "What's so special about a *Zayuri*?"

"Many things, Lady Mirren," Úna said, and I got the distinct feeling they didn't like each other. "Yet I don't believe we have the time to delve that deep tonight."

"Quinn?" someone with a high, nasally voice called, not from the entrance we'd come in from, but from the far side of the fireplace.

Quinn tensed. "Rayne, I didn't know you were coming."

Rayne? His sister, the third of the trio of R's that he'd hoped we'd never meet together. Rayne was almost as tall as Quinn, and her platinum blond hair, with tips of bright blue, spilled down her shoulders.

"When Mother and Domhnall informed the twins about this, I felt compelled to come. The triple R's stick together, after all."

"How could I have imagined otherwise?" Quinn leaned over and kissed his sister on the cheeks. "Mother told me you weren't in the country."

"Faerie gave me a boost. You know it loves me."

Interesting. Could she be that bad if Quinn had said she was a great big sister and Faerie approved of her?

"Speaking of...where are your counterparts?" Quinn surveyed the room.

"They stayed in the kitchen. You know Rory. He never stops eating."

That sounded familiar. I glanced at Nol.

"Let me get a good look at these elves you've been spending your time with." Hands on her knees, Rayne hunched over, coming eye to eye with me. "She's smaller than I imagined elves to be. Are all females short like her?"

"Rayne—"

"I thought their eyes were lighter." She moved on to Nol. "This one, now, he looks more like it. Is she...stunted?"

I choked on my spit. Talk about no filter. "Good evening, Your Royal Highness, Princess Rionoch." I curtsied. "What a lovely surprise to meet you. Prince Quinn informs me you are a wonderful big sister."

Rayne turned to her brother. "An apt title. Rory and Rose will be delighted to meet you." She squinted, and I thought she might try to pinch my cheek. "I find it peculiar that your country chose an exile to represent them. Is that normal? Part of a redemption program?"

I had to laugh. "For now, I represent all countries of *Endae* until each country choses their own representatives. And yes, *Aemina* exiled me a century ago, and there is no redemption program."

"Yet they trust you to represent them. It must be an elf thing. You lived undetected in our country. Kind of a rude thing to do...but then, if you're breaking a treaty, that would be counterintuitive. We would either have killed you on the spot or gone to war with your people. I'd have killed you, if, as you say, they exiled you."

"Your honesty is refreshing, Your Highness. Regardless of the repercussions, I probably would have found you and introduced my-self had I known of your existence. Not only was I a child, but I spoke no human languages, and frankly, I had no clue what the hell I was doing."

Rayne threw back her head and laughed. I noticed Úna chuckling, too.

"What about you?" Rayne turned to Nol. "Are you some kind of warrior? That's what the rumors say."

"Rumors? Are there many of them, or does that mean it is a far-reaching rumor? I am uncertain which you intended. If there are...multiple rumors, I cannot confirm them all at once, Your High-ness." Nol non-answered, leaning on his *Aeminan* accent more than usual.

Rayne paused and searched his face before turning away to head over to the refreshment table. "There are several rumors about the two of you. There's a new one on the wind, that you and the ambassador are fucking my brother. If that one is true"—she grabbed a flute of champagne and turned to face the rest of us—"we'd definitely want in." She purred the last, then popped a strawberry into her mouth, the entire time looking at me, not Nol.

No one in the room knew what to say.

Rayne smirked, looked at her brother, and rose an eyebrow. "Is it true? Are you fucking them both, brother?"

"Don't be absurd. I am honored to call them my friends, and Ambassador Inara, Hally, is a colleague, as well."

"But you're fucking her. The wind picked up the conversation with your father today."

She kept mentioning the wind. I wondered if that was her magical talent.

"Stop stirring, Rayne."

"Your Highness?" Mirren asked in a wispy way, full of shock and horror. "She's an elf! How dare she fornicate with you."

"Mirren, don't. This is getting out of hand. Rayne, settle this," Quinn snapped at his sister.

"I want to hear the truth from them." Rayne sipped her wine again. She lifted an eyebrow and looked Nol up and down. "Are you?"

"Which?" Nol asked, a little snooty to play along. "A warrior? In part. A lover? No, not that it's any of your business. Was that meant to offend Lady Mirren? To gain control of her emotions. Or is that play?" Nol turned to Mirren and nodded. "I am certain Lady Mirren is above such petty attempts as believing rumors you hear on the...wind and, as Prince Quinn put it, stirring."

Instead of Rayne, my attention remained on Mirren as she settled, realizing, as Nol had observed, what was happening.

"How dare you call me petty!" But Rayne didn't have as much conviction as Mirren had had earlier when I'd called her out.

Nol shrugged. "Do you deny it?"

She lifted her chin, pleased with Nol. "No. You're fun. We should get to know each other."

"Prince Quinn and I are friends, and he talks positively of you. While you are more blunt, I think we could become friends, too. I, for one, would enjoy total honesty without fear of...repercussions."

Two fairies emerged from the wall where Rayne had entered. So it was a hidden passage. I couldn't blame them for taking that way instead of having the herald yell in their ears.

"Quinn, it's been forever!" The male fairy, no doubt Rory, called out as the two came closer. "Hello, Mirren. Miss Úna, you're here, too? How exciting." He opened his arms wide and gave Úna a hug. We were informal now, huh?

Rory had fiery red hair that may have gone down to his shoulders, but it was such a wild mess, it seemed to defy gravity, sticking out every which way. Rose, on the other hand, had black, well-behaved curls and sapphire blue eyes.

"Rory! Rose!" Rayne lifted her flute of champagne. "Come quickly and meet the elves."

"Why?" Rory asked. "Will they scatter and hide if we don't hurry?"

Rose slapped her brother on the arm for his comment and made it to Rayne's side in front of us before her brother. She grabbed Rayne's arm and leaned against her, giggling.

"Did you see?" she whispered to Rayne. "Mirrie's look?" To which Rayne said something even quieter that made Rose giggle again.

I glanced at Mirren, but couldn't tell what the ladies were referring to. Pursed lips, her nose as high as she could make it, and intently staring off into the distance. Maybe Rose and Mirren had dated once at some point.

"Prince Rory," Quinn nodded to the fairy who'd stepped in front of us. "Princess Rose. This is Ambassador Inara and *Hinam* Madorean. Ambassador, *Hinam*, these are the royal twins of *Scáilmara Báite*, Princess Rose and Prince Rory."

"Ambassador Inara? Rory leaned forward like he was going to bow, but looked up at the last minute until his eyes were level with mine. "So you're the stowaway. How on earth did you stay under our radar?"

I swallowed as he scrutinized me like he'd throw me into the shark infested waters for sneaking on to his ship. Rory's eyes clouded over with the colors of the fiercest hurricane. The feel of the wind tickled the nape of my neck and I jumped back. He laughed, reached over and squeezed Quinn's shoulder. "Good to see you, mate."

"You are such an ass," Quinn told him.

"Hey, at least I didn't ask if you were sleeping with them when I walked in." Rory winked.

Quinn dropped his head and shook it. "I am so sorry for their behavior, Hally and Nolan. I did warn you of their antics."

"Really though, no one ever said anything? You don't look as exotic as us, but no comments at all?" Rose asked.

"Why would they?" I asked Rose. "Humans don't know we exist. I got accused of being Jewish for a a brief period." No one breathed for a moment. They knew what moment in time that meant. "Many people stood up for my family heritage and it was thrown out before anything came of it."

"The halflings who took you in, you mean? My father said their only talent is sensing our signatures. Fascinating that they found you before one of us did!" Rory chuckled. "Or should I say lucky. My father would have sliced your delicate neck and have been done with it. No one wants another war like that."

Rose responded before I could find words to respond to Rory. "Oh please, brother, that is not all he would have done."

Her brother leaned toward his much smaller sister. "You're right, Rose, he would have squeezed all the answers out of her that he could first."

"They look so lovely!" Rose giggled again. "Is that an elven thing, or..." She paused as her eyes rolled up until she met Nol's and licked her lips. "Can we play with them, too?"

Rayne shrugged the shoulder that Rose was still leaning against. "Oh, I asked. They're not fucking him."

Rose whined and glanced at Quinn. "I'll get you one day, my prince." Now this was interesting. Rose and Merrin. Now Rose wanting Quinn. I had to know more about the three R's.

Quinn scoffed and shook his head. "Rose—"

A gentle strike of a gong filled the expansive room. Our group perked up. The herald lifted his chin, looking important. He had the most important job, after all. "Announcing Their Majesties, Queen Brigid and King Domhnall of *Céandalamh*."

Queen Brigid walked into sight first, a heartbeat after the announcement. King Domhnall followed her in with an unfocused, bored look. They stood together, almost the exact same height. Brigid had pale brown skin and white hair with gold stripes in it.

Even now, as with every video meeting, Queen Brigid kept her face trained with a thin-lipped, almost pleasant smile. It looked fake, but she was never rude, unlike some of the others.

Brigid roamed the room, her amethyst eyes bright, wide, and cunning. Her smile softened as she locked eyes on Quinn, but it widened just enough for me to notice when she saw Rayne. "Welcome Ambassador Inara, *Hinam* Madorean. It is a pleasure to have you here."

I curtsied. "We are honored by your welcome, Your Majesties."

"*Esamia*, Your Majesties," Nol greeted them with the *Aeminan* greeting.

The royals paused, but their expressions never changed.

"Welcome, all of you." The queen lifted her hand, and with a graceful sweep of her arm she encompassed all of us in her greeting. "We will move to the dining hall momentarily. I trust you've had a few moments to mingle."

A trill echoed like the gong's sound had. I couldn't find the origin. Faerie magic?

"Your Majesties, dinner is served." The herald announced.

"Mina," King Domhnall said, addressing the herald. "An unexpected guest is present. Lady Rionoch is home. Set a place for her."

Mina clapped once, swirled his hand in the air, and bowed. "It is so, Your Majesty."

As a group, we walked out of the elegant receiving room and followed the king and queen through the vestibule. We passed the grand staircase, and the light shifted on the floor from above. High above us, the large Faerie moon shone down through a round skylight, even though it hadn't been out before. Faerie did what Faerie wanted. Clouds soared past, white from the moon's rays. It took my breath away.

"What's the matter? You've never seen Faerie's side of the moon before?" Mirren's barb washed right over me.

"It is beautiful," Nol commented from behind me.

When I looked around again, all the fairies stood together, watching us admire the moon, except Mirren with her sneer. It took a moment for me to catch my breath. "Your home is beautiful."

Brigid nodded. "I'm happy you like it. Come, you can see her from the garden."

Mirren rolled her eyes. "But will she stop gawking at it long enough to eat? Pathetic."

"How is it pathetic for them to admire the moon of the elven goddess?" Úna asked.

My heart leapt at Úna's words. The fae worshiped Anu and the *Tuath Dé Dannan,* not Anara.

"What did you say?" Nol asked.

"Your Mother, Anara. The elves still know her, yes?"

Hand to my chest, I almost fell forward at Úna's words. Our Mother had a place here. Why did our ancestors never acknowledge the fae deities? Was that part of the conflict?

"I didn't know about her," Quinn said. "I assumed it was their word for Anu."

"You wouldn't know, Prince Quinn," Úna said. "She's not in our books because she is not a descendant of Anu. She is her sister. And I'm assuming no one in *Endae* has heard of the *Tuath Dé Dannan?*"

I shook my head, unable to speak.

Nol placed his hand on my shoulder and squeezed. "No, we only know of Anara. We feared she was another lie that whoever erased our true history made up."

Úna stepped forward until she was standing right in front of us. "Dear children, of course she's real. If she wasn't, you wouldn't be here."

The Mother had made our *Muranilde* bond, but the reason why would always be a mystery. Úna grabbed Nol's arm. "Come, children, we will discuss this at length another time."

We followed the fairies across a ballroom that was the entire back of the castle, three times the size of the great hall. We walked through one of the four double French doors that opened into the castle gardens bathed in moonlight. Burbling water echoed from somewhere. My guess was near the large boulders on the left.

Between the gardens, off the patio, and wherever flowers didn't grow, moss grew like a living carpet, with miniature night-blooming flowers. Quinn offered his hand as we stepped off the patio stones and onto the springy moss that cushioned my feet.

In the distance, past the expansive garden was the dark forest, where any fae imaginable could walk right up to the castle doors. Again, I thought about the screech earlier and shivered.

"Are you all right?" Quinn asked under his breath.

I nodded and looked up at the large Faerie moon, feeling Mother Anara's presence.

The king and queen led us to a long dining table set under a pergola in the middle of the large plaza to the right of the gardens. The legs of the table grew out of the ground, supporting an oblong, flat tree trunk. As we walked closer, roots grew out of the ground, stretching to reset the table for another guest. Brigid and Domhnall chose two chairs from the narrower side. Quinn sat close to his parents. The twins picked their seats at the end of the table, while Rayne sat across from her brother.

"You seem surprised, Madam Ambassador," Brigid said. "Do elves not have magic like this?"

"We do have something like it, but it takes longer." Nol and I found our seats midway down the table. "Our magic encourages nature to shape itself as it grows without quickening the growth."

"Your world is mundane?" Rory sneered. His sister elbowed him.

I ignored the attitude, especially since his sister was telling him to play nice. "It's not alive like Faerie, no."

Obviously, Faerie was responding to what the king and queen wanted, which got me thinking.

"Your Majesties, I've noticed that Faerie responds to you. Perhaps you might know more than Queen Orlaith does about a situation of mine. You see, in March, when I entered to find the children Drake had stolen, Faerie asked me what I was doing there. When I explained, it asked me if I was staying. I assured it that I was only there to find the children, but its question stuck with me. Perhaps you have more insight?"

Domhnall shot up straight, but when Brigid touched his arm, he mellowed out. "You must be mistaken. Faerie wouldn't speak to you."

"Does Faerie often speak to fae in Seattle, Prince Quinn?" Úna asked from across the table.

"It is known to do so. That part of Faerie is wilder than here, more unpredictable where Orlaith hasn't shaped it. Ambassador Inara was on her own. I believe Faerie felt her distress and sensed her intent. She found and saved ten children that Drake had taken, tortured, and experimented on for years. Some for decades. So please, Father, if Faerie spoke to her, it had good reason to."

Domhnall grumbled but didn't have a retort to that sensible answer. I grimaced at Quinn and mouthed "I'm sorry." I needed to keep my big mouth shut. Less talking, more listening. Where were my ambassador manners?

"King Domhnall?" Úna asked. "Pardon my boldness, but what did you mean when you said Faerie wouldn't speak to Ambassador Inara?"

"Faerie is for the fae. We know this."

"Leaving this realm didn't take away their lineage," Úna said. "They are fae."

"That is ridiculous!" Mirren pounded her fists on the table then stood. "The elves are not fae. My father and I are tired of this. They must go home. To *Endae*. Queen Orlaith has been patient with these children while they clean up the mess that the insane elf created in the first place. I demand for this facade to be over."

"Lady Mirren, you will sit and be silent," Brigid demanded calmly.

"They don't belong here. The other countries will include any fae nation that harbors an elf as an enemy when they declare war. You are putting all of us in danger." Mirren lifted her arm.

When they declare war? What did that mean?

"Mirrie, no!" Quinn yelled.

As Quinn started those words, Nol grabbed me and pulled me away from the table. Something flashed blue, and my heart sank. Nol had snuck his sword in here. Another flash of blue shot through the courtyard. No, this wasn't the black-blue of *Zayuri* magic. Oh no.

I scrambled up, staying behind Nol like he wanted. Nothing made sense. The living table lay on its side, the top facing away from us, roots bare and torn. Nol stood with one arm out—no sword, thank the Mother. Another flash of blue revealed why Nol looked frozen with his arm in the air. A third flash exploded and hit Nol's ward.

"Lady Mirren, stop!" Rayne yelled.

A dark mist swirled around the entire side where the king and queen had sat moments ago. Quinn was protecting them. I searched for the triplets. Rayne held her hands in the air, sweeping them in a spiral pattern.

No one besides Rayne and Mirren was visible. Mirren's pretty dress whipped all around, her braids out of the bundle and flying like ropes from her head. Why wasn't anyone doing anything?

"Rayne, here!" Rory called from some hidden place.

Rayne caught something that fit in her palm and yelled, "Lady Úna!"

Úna stepped out from the mist and caught the small thing. A second later, a twisted wooden staff was in Úna's hands, giving off a faint green glow.

"I warned you, Mirren," Úna's deep voice rumbled. She lifted her staff, and when it touched the courtyard's spongy floor, the earth shook. The pergola swayed. Rayne's arms stopped swirling the air, and Mirren stumbled and fell on her knees. The blue glow from her hands died. She gasped and lifted her hands again. Magic sparked in her palms, and then it was gone. So was Quinn's barrier. The king and queen stood behind Quinn, furious. After a moment, I realized Nol's ward was the only magic still working.

Rory stormed out from under the castle's terrace, murder in his eyes. He went right up to Mirren, grabbed her arms, and hauled her to her feet. She squeaked as he shoved her against the toppled table.

"Lord Ruairí, rein in your anger. We don't need chunks of Mirren scattered over my courtyard. It took ages for us to clean up your last mess."

Rory turned to the king. I could just make out the seething glare he gave Domhnall. "Your Majesty, she threatened all our lives. Please allow me to punish her."

"No. She must sit and bear witness. *Zayuri,* please let down your ward. No other threat will come to you or the ambassador," Domhnall promised.

"How was his magic not muted with ours Lady Úna?" Rose asked.

Perhaps Lady Úna's talent was to nullify magic. Rayne's was controlling air currents and something about rumors. But the twins' powers were still a mystery, if I didn't count the chunks comment.

"Twice in one day, attackers have assaulted Hallë since coming here. What certainties can you provide that she will remain safe?" Nol demanded.

"Only *Zayuri* magic will work until I lift my staff," Úna said. "As you saw, Lady Mirren couldn't gather her magic, and you still have yours."

"Nol, it's okay." I patted his arm. "Let's get out."

He dropped his arm and then his ward. "This is unacceptable." His face was blank, his voice devoid of any emotion as he stared at the fae under the moon. Nol took a step toward the table but stuck out his arm when I went to walk around him. "Hallë has done nothing to deserve this. We cannot control who our ancestors are, but our actions speak to our integrity. Hers"—Nol jabbed a finger at Mirren, who held one arm and looked miserable—"is lacking. Hallë is here to see her sick nephew. She will do so without further abuse or you will face consequences. That is a promise, not a threat." He was going to take us through the shadows. Oh fuck, he was furious.

"Wait!" Queen Brigid's voice echoed through the Faerie night.

I paused, my hand right above Nol's.

"You're right. This never should have occurred. We..." She paused and waited for her husband's nod. "We wanted to let you meet some of us and show you we are open to progress. Lady Mirren, for all her faults, was supposed to listen and consider a way to bring her father around for a discussion with your people. With *Endae.*"

"We wanted to propose a meeting with the elves." Domhnall laid his hand on Brigid's shoulder. "Once we spoke to you about it, we were going to suggest it to the other nations."

"Our hope was for you to discuss it with your councils," the queen added.

"They want answers," I said before I could stop myself. "You're not giving me any. I also require information about my attack. When you're ready to discuss that, I'll consider your proposal." I stopped and almost didn't continue, but damn it, Nol and I were both angry. "And Quinn? We need to talk."

"Tomorrow. I'll meet you at the hospital."

"I'll come to your apartment after I've spent quality time with my family." I grabbed Nol's hand and felt the cold seep into me. Damn it, my coat was inside.

"Hally?" Quinn called out before Nol could draw the shadows around us completely. We waited. "I'm sorry. We're all sorry."

Nol didn't give me a chance to respond, even if I'd wanted to. He wrapped his arms around me. The surrounding light vanished and, along with it, any kind of warmth the sun had ever promised this world.

My skin prickled, starting at my elbows and neck. We had to leave the shadows before I got frostbite. I drew in a breath, warmed only by Nol's body heat. Otherwise, I might have frozen my lungs. I tapped on his chest. *Please be over. Please.*

At last, Nol let me go. The ground below me crackled as my dress shoes ground the pebbles and sand into the cement of wherever we were. The air smelled like exhaust, fried food, and urine.

"Let's get inside," Nol whispered beside me.

I cleared my throat to get words around my frozen throat. "We left everything at the castle. My keys, my coat, my..."

"Oh, Hallë. We don't need keys."

I turned my glare on him, because I knew he didn't have the same problem. "No, but I want my phone."

He winced. "That's unfortunate."

12

THE MOMENT I OPENED the door to Léon's hospital room the next morning, I knew it'd be busy. Inside were two doctors and three extra Bercots. Nicole and Amelia sat next to the bed, with Gerald behind them. Checking out the doctors, I could see Léon was right. While they were clearly adults, both of them looked too young to have a medical degree. How did these kids get out of medical school so fast? Were they teaching them in secondary school? All eyes came to me as the door clicked shut behind me. It was a bit creepy having six sets of eyes move almost at once. Which horror movie was that? Yikes.

"*Bonjour.*" I waved a tiny wave when no one said anything. "What's going on?"

"Hally, come tell my grandkids going home is a good thing."

This made sense now. "Ah. Did the tests come back with good results, then?"

The dark-haired doctor lifted her chin and frowned at me. "Who are you?"

"Oh, Hally Dubois. Léon is my uncle," I said, lying through my teeth. "You're releasing him? When?" I blinked oh-so-innocent eyes at the hospital staff.

"Now."

Stunned at the quick answer and even quicker decision to kick him out, it took me a moment to respond. "No bypass thingy? I thought that was necessary."

"Your uncle misunderstood the situation," the black-haired male doctor said. "There was a possibility of a bypass, not an inevitability, since tests had not all been completed yet."

This right here showed two of the problems I had with hospitals. They were always right, and the patient never knew what their own bodies needed. "Right. Did Gerald and Nicole misunderstand the explanation as well? In the first twenty-four hours, Léon wasn't alone at all, was he? So that explanation would have been given to more than one person." I waved my hand and laughed at myself. "What am I saying? It must have been they who misunderstood."

"*Mademoiselle* Dubois—"

"Silly us," I said, interrupting the male doctor. "What do we know? Only three people were listening to you while you explained the plan. I'm sure you know better." I gave the two doctors a few long blinks. Then I dropped my smile and pushed my shoulders back. "Could it possibly be that *you* made the mistake? I have a pet peeve when it comes to others telling me how I feel and what I think, and that applies to my family as well. When three people hear your conversation differently from how you remember it, perhaps you should take some responsibility, learn a little humility, and apologize. My family will not be belittled and pushed around. Is that clear?"

"Yes, Madam Dubois. It is possible that-that the error was on my end. You're right."

"Thank you, Doctor"—I looked at his name tag—"Davidson. Please go do what you do when people are being discharged. I'm sure my uncle will be ready to leave by then. I'd like some quality family time with my aunties and uncles."

They couldn't move fast enough to get their asses out the door. Amelia reached me first with air kisses. With her light pink dress pants, dark gray blouse, and bouncy hair, I could tell she'd hurried over from her office for this.

"A bit much?" My face had scrunched up before I realized it. "Was that the issue, or was there something else?" I reached Gerald and pulled the big brute in for a hug.

"Who said there was an issue?" Gerald asked when he'd let go of me. He still wore his three-piece suit from the office, light and dark browns with a striped white-on-white button-up. The man detested jeans, and last time I checked, he'd never worn a hoodie, which was what I was wearing, hence the assessing look he gave me.

"I read the room. Eyes wide and terror-stricken. Oh wait, those were the doctors'. Léon, I see what you mean. How young are they?"

Léon laughed, the happiest one in the room. For sure because he got to go home. Well, he wouldn't like what I had to say, then. I hugged Nicole, the sweetest woman I'd ever met. She looked like she'd come from home—black trousers, a camisole, and a cardigan, with her pretty brown hair in an updo.

"What's going on? You both seem a bit rushed." I pointed at the two siblings.

"That was my fault," Nicole said. "I called them here when I got confused with the doctors. When they start with medical stuff, I just can't follow them, and it seemed like they wanted to send Léon home at that moment. They said 'now,' and I assumed now means now. It turns out it was just me being"—Nicole hung her head—"me."

"It meant *this morning* in doctor language." Amelia leaned against Nicole and rubbed her arm. "Imagine that. You did nothing wrong, Nicole. These kinds of conversations need to include everyone and not just be dropped on your shoulders."

Nicole tried to smile, but I could tell it still bothered her. "Doctor language or not, I'm happy you're all here!" I said. "This whole emergency has been on my mind as I've been dealing with fairy drama, ugh, and I'd like to bring up a suggestion."

The three of them stepped back. Nicole crossed her arms and curved her shoulders in, reminding me of the phone call from the airport. I walked over to Léon and sat near his feet to include him in this discussion.

"A heart attack is a huge ordeal. We all got scared and needed support, and I hope you feel the same. I know you all are happy with the arrangement you have at the house. But what if we get Léon a nurse to check on him daily? Make sure he's actually taking his medicine." I glared at Léon.

Nicole hunched in further, and Gerald stood taller.

"Hélène, we're still capable of it."

"Oh! That's not what I meant, Gerald. I apologize for making it sound that way. Yes, you all are doing a remarkable job of taking care of Léon. You don't need the help, except for times like these. For instance, Nicole couldn't give Léon CPR. She just physically cannot push his chest down hard enough."

"A nurse could help out if they put him on a more complicated medication regime. They could be there to take his blood pressure. Remember, he had a heart attack. He'll need more monitoring. They can yell at him, instead of you two, when he doesn't eat his spinach. If there is an emergency, you will have professional support. They wouldn't take over, I promise."

"Can I have a pretty one?" Léon asked.

I think we all had the same unamused look in our eyes. "You're getting a male one," I told him.

Léon scoffed. "No fun."

Nicole giggled at our banter.

I made eye contact with each one of them. "It's just something to think about. You can never have enough support."

"He does get pretty testy about his vegetables," Nicole teased, but I saw the relief in her body language. Gerald expected her to help Léon the majority of the time. It was never my place, and I had never told them what to do, but I'd asked before if they'd ever thought of getting help. Gerald had been against it, saying they didn't need it. Yeah, well, *she* needed it.

"I like it, if I can send them out for more ice cream. You never bring enough home, Gerald," Léon said.

Again we got a giggle from Nicole. I tried to silently plead with Amelia to help. We needed to present a united front to convince the proud fifty-eight-year-old man.

"Gerald, stop being so stubborn. Contrary to your opinion, accepting help does not make you look weak."

Wonderful, Amelia.

Gerald opened his mouth to argue with his sister, but Nicole surprised me. "I want to get one. I never want to walk in on your father lying on the kitchen floor, or anywhere else, for that matter. Get him a pretty one. I don't care."

Gerald looked down at his wife and her uncharacteristically assertive stance. "Well, if that's what you want, my love, we can do that." He kissed the top of her head and didn't know what to do with himself after that. It seemed simple enough. He could do the legwork and get his sweet wife some help with his father. Thank the Mother he had listened this time.

Nicole lifted her chin, her cheeks red under her makeup. "It is."

"Hally? You said fairy drama. What have they been doing with you?" Amelia brought up the subject I'd loved to have avoided the entire visit. "You were gone on an errand when Nicole and I came in yesterday. That had to be fairy-speak, right?"

"You're right. It hasn't been fun, I'll clue you. My errand yesterday was meeting King Domhnall after I was attacked in this room." I gave them a shortened version of yesterday, and their faces froze when I got to Mirren's attack.

"That's two assassination attempts in one day," Nicole said.

"And when I get back to Seattle, I'll have to report it to *Endae*. I'm already not looking forward to their response."

"I hate to say this," Gerald said. "But thank God you had Nolan with you last night."

"Speaking of, where is he?" Amelia asked.

I looked to the door. The same door that had been warded shut yesterday. "In the hall, playing guard."

"Get him in here. Introduce him to Gerald and Nicole."

"That would negate the point of having a guard, Amelia," Gerald said.

"You just don't want to meet him," Amelia shot back.

They still bickered, even in their fifties. Nicole and I smiled at the sibling rivalry. I closed my eyes as I heard it start to turn personal.

"Enough, you two. Léon will be out of here in a few minutes and your argument will be moot. Amelia, stop provoking your brother. Gerald, you'll have to meet him at some point. He's stuck here until this slave band is off me, anyway. The real debate should—"

Lightheadedness swept my words away. I took a breath and tried to assess myself. This wasn't right. The next sweep wasn't so gentle. I gripped the end of Léon's bed as the entire world shifted. What the fuck? The back of my neck tingled. The feeling traveled to the top of my head, then out to my extremities. Shit, I knew what this was. My grandmother was using *Olauvë* to contact me. Then a big wave washed through me because I was ignoring her, and apparently, three seconds wasn't fast enough. My entire world shifted, and I teetered sideways.

"What's going on?" Amelia asked.

Not wanting to scare them, I tried to push the nausea down. *"I'm coming, Yalu!"* I tried to impress on my grandmother so she'd knock it off. Something was wrong. I swallowed hard. This would get worse if she didn't stop pushing. "Amelia, would you get Nol, please?"

Amelia's ballerina shoes hurried away, but I didn't dare lift my eyes. Nol came to my side moments later. He grabbed my upper arms while the world righted itself again. I reached for Nol's arm as another dizzy spell washed over me. "Yalu needs something. She won't leave me alone."

Nol pursed his lips, and with a nod, he picked me up. "Gerald, will that seat go back? I need you to push it back."

"What's wrong with her?" Amelia's voice shook.

"Nothing, love," I tried to explain. "My grandmother needs me, and I need to speak with her before she makes me pass out to force me there. This is urgent."

"I have you, Hallë. Lie back." Someone handed him a blanket, and he covered me. His brow furrowed, and the crease between his eyes deepened.

"Explain to them that I'm okay. That I'm not dead—"

"You don't look dead when you're in that state. You look like you're sleeping." I tried to look at the kids, but Nol pressed a hand to the top of my head to keep me still. "Just go. I've got you."

Because my grandmother had come to me and because I was getting used to it, the transition to the astral plane was a quick shift of my mind. Any absent council member could join any meeting at the capital using *Olauvë* as if they were there, able to "sit" in their seat in the assembly room. My grandmother had seen our entire conversation and still, she'd pushed until I couldn't stand.

I found my grandmother beside me, yet she didn't even look like her physical self, just an impression of her energy. This was too important to bother with appearing like our physical selves.

"What's happening, Yalu?"

"The Trees of Connection's root system is failing."

Okay, that was pretty serious and had warranted this. Not that it made any sense. The system couldn't just go down. It was a natural occurrence, like water going down streams or air currents on the wind. "What does that mean?"

"An explosion in the capital destroyed the Assembly of *Aemina*. The royal family is being held hostage in the Starborn Palace. And no one can leave *Aetyru*."

She needed to slow down and give me some context. "Yalu, stop talking and let me listen. Share your memories with me." This way, she could show me everything that had happened. In the next moment, her memories came to me as if they were my own.

The last five hours had been a shit show for her. Tolwe was called out of their home on an emergency. My grandmother couldn't go back to sleep, so she went down to make tea and relax in her small garden connected to the kitchen. As she was settling down, she heard the front door slam, followed by heavy footsteps. They faded as Tolwe walked farther into their home, toward their bedroom. His footsteps paused then came her way again.

"In here, Tolwe!"

Nol's uncle poked his head out the door and did a sweep of the garden. The moment he met her eyes, his features softened, the wrinkles around his eyes and forehead relaxing. Tolwe walked over to her. "There's a problem."

My grandmother was already expecting some problem or another, an almost daily occurrence in *Jinatrau*.

"This will be a shock." He knelt in front of her, took her tea from her, and set it down. He took her hands and placed them in her lap. "My love, the capital was attacked just hours ago."

She jerked, but Tolwe was there, prepared for her reaction. She waited for more, instead of asking questions like I would have.

"One of my soldiers came from the capital this morning. The Assembly of *Aemina* was bombed. There is another explosive at the Starborn Palace, and if demands aren't fulfilled, it is set to go off."

I felt my grandmother's distress and her panic. She thought of all her council friends, her brother, and my grandfather, but then stopped herself. She focused on the future, her duties, and how to protect the royal family in their palace. "How long do we have?"

Tolwe shook his head, frustrating her to no end, but she waited with patience.

"The message sent with the bombs demands that the *Zayuri* who murdered Aswryn come to the capital."

"Nolan?" She wiggled to get her arms free, but Tolwe kept her hands pinned. He knew her well. I could feel her need to stand and take action. "But that's impossible."

"If we can't convince the council to agree to get Hally here, it is. I don't know the Assembly's casualties, but you need to contact all the delegations in the districts and get Hallanevaë's exile temporarily lifted so Nolan can get back here."

"But—"

"This is an emergency, Zella. I don't give a damn about their fucking politics, policies, or whatever the fuck it is. For the sake of the royal family, she must come." Tolwe looked torn, and guilty. "I'm sorry for snapping." He rose and placed a kiss on her temple. Something in her memory fluttered back to another time. I felt the hurt caused by that anger; it had driven them apart. He touched her cheek, knowing where her thoughts had taken her.

"Now, for reasons I can't fathom, the Trees of Connection are shutting down. They're sure it has something to do with the bomb. The

Tree in *Aetyru* shut down right after the explosion and the radius is expanding. Even *Jinatrau* is shut down. Tell the delegates it's a political emergency ceasefire. A temporary truce. I don't care. I am leaving to find a working connection to tell Nolan and Hally."

"You'll take a *meril*," My grandmother commanded. "I'm not letting you leave without a way to connect with me from over there. From what you and Hally have told me, it's awfully chaotic."

Tolwe nodded in agreement to the *meril*. He pulled out some folded paper from the hidden pocket of his uniform shirt. He tapped it once on his knee and handed it to Zella. "I don't know what this means. My soldier gave it to me when he arrived from the capital."

My grandmother laid the paper on the palm of her hands and read the front. "Nolan," not *Hinam* Twynolan or Twynolan Madorean, just Nolan. It had come from someone he knew. My grandmother extended her magic to search for any *imolegin*. She felt a seal around the paper. It was for Nolan's eyes only. Nothing more, except for the most important thing ever.

My grandmother gasped. "Gileal!"

I ended her memory sharing at once. "Yalu! Is it really him?"

"Yes."

"How? Aswryn said she left him to die."

"But he wasn't dead, just dying."

The letter...his signature couldn't be faked, could it? I prayed to the Mother and would have to hold on to hope like there was no tomorrow. Exiled or not, with or without permission, I was coming to find Gileal. He had to be there. The Mother wouldn't be that cruel, would she?

Then a major problem came to me. "We aren't home. It would take us almost an entire day to get back."

"Even better. Tolwe went to Earth to tell Nolan and now he's stuck on your side of the Trees of Connection, like he feared. Perhaps you still have time before the connection closes where you are."

"How long do we have until the bomb detonates?" I was already trying to figure out if we had enough time to get where we *might* be able to cross over. It took six hours to get to Nice by car.

"Four days."

"Why four days? That doesn't make a damn bit of sense. Choosing some arbitrary number out of their asses."

"Nevie, what is today?"

Nothing came to mind. Here, it was April twenty-eighth, and both realms were right in the middle of spring, which was *Zaris* in *Endae*. Now that I wasn't there, I never paid attention to the days in *Endae*. By *Aemina's* calendar, we counted days and months by the season. I had no fucking clue.

"The fortieth day of *Zaris*."

That didn't help.

"Zaris Wyuendell," Spring mid-season celebration.

The midseason celebrations weren't too big a deal anywhere besides *Aetyru*. The royal family stepped out onto the main balcony of Starborn Palace and waved at their subjects. There was a banquet for the council on the ground floor, with the royals on their mezzanine balcony. Questions, concerns, and comments could be exchanged through the three highest council members. I thought it was a huge pain in the ass and needed to be streamlined. Things needed to change. The royals needed to be more involved. If the Mother could talk to us, so could the Starborn family. But it took a long time, or a threat like a bomb in our capital, to change our society. A *Wyuendell* was the perfect time to do that.

"Yalu, I must get back. We must go before the connection closes. I love you." I couldn't wait for her goodbye. I was already drifting back to reality.

Nol was pacing the room, his hands clenching and unclenching. My family was behind him, huddled together. Had Nol not told them *anything*?

"Nol!" I moved the chair to a sitting position.

"I know."

"How much did Tolwe tell you?"

"Everything—I think. Did Zella say more?"

I thought back. Had she found anything out after Tolwe had left? My grandmother would have shared that. Plus, she would have told him through their communication *meril*. "I don't think so. Why are you pacing?"

"The connection to the Trees was lost in Seattle already. Tolwe has no way back. We have no way there."

"Nol, hold on."

He stopped immediately.

"We can travel from the tree I came through."

Nol jolted. "That's genius. I'll give Tolwe the news." Tolwe couldn't help *Aemina* or us. I couldn't imagine how helpless he felt.

"The only problem is the location." I paused, and Nol's shoulders jerked with impatience. "I'm not certain of the exact place. It was over a century ago, and I was freezing, terrified, and...damn it, Nol, I wasn't in a good place mentally or physically either. Hypothermia was setting in, and I was starving and recovering from blocking my magic."

"Why bring it up if you can't find it?"

"I *will* find it," I assured him. "It just might take some time. How much time do we have?"

He looked at the floor, lost in thought and calculations. "Tolwe is east of Seattle...judging by the distance and time of the explosion versus the time of—"

"Just tell me."

Nol pursed his lips with annoyance. "Ten hours, at the very most. Is there enough time to get to this place?"

"Um, yes." If we left now. I looked away and at my terrified family. "Come here." At once, my family came, except for Léon. I flipped the footrest down and stood to embrace them.

"Hallë," Nol warned, because I still hadn't given him a real answer.

"Nol—" I spun around. "Give me a few minutes to explain."

My family stayed still, listening to us bicker or discuss the situation, whichever way they perceived it. I hated leaving them and that they didn't understand. I went back to them and walked to Léon. "There's been a terrorist attack in *Aemina*." I explained what I'd seen through my grandmother's memories. "And we have to get to Nice and find—"

"You're right. Go." Léon squeezed his blanket until his knuckles went white. "You're wasting time here."

Nodding, I leaned in and hugged him tightly. "I'm so sorry. I came to visit you, but I've brought more fae drama than anything." And now *endai* were taking me away from them.

"Don't let that council near her." With Gerald's comment, I released Léon, ready to defend Nol once again, but he was shaking Nol's hand.

I kissed Léon's forehead a few times and hugged the rest of them. "I love you, my babies." Grabbing Amelia last, I couldn't let go. So many things could happen. "Be good while I'm gone, and get Léon a nurse that he won't sexually harass, please."

Amelia laughed but cried at the same time. "Please, be careful."

"Always."

Nol grabbed my hand and squeezed. "I'm sorry, Hallë, but the map says Nice is six hours away. We must go now."

That was all the time we had for sappy goodbyes. It really was. Nol nodded at my family as he opened the door and I realized a very possible opportunity. "My parents."

Nol frowned, not following for a moment, until he studied my face. He shook his head. "Your dad is infected."

I walked through the door and tried to convince him while we moved down the hall. "I'll be with you, and *Zayuri* are immune. It will protect me. It protected Gil."

"It's too dangerous."

Hands together, I literally begged him. "I won't get close, just close enough to see them. Please, Nol. I will never get another chance."

"You don't know that." But he did. His mind had already calculated the chances.

"The odds of me coming back are almost zero. Please, Nol. Please!"

He stopped in the hall, hunched over, and sighed. "A brief visit. From a distance. I mean it. Stop looking for ways around it. I know you are."

I shook my head hard. "No, I'm not. I'll keep my distance."

"A distance *I* set, not what you think is far enough."

I jumped over and hugged him with all my strength, then backed up, grabbed his hand, and tugged him down the hall. At the elevator, watching the light rise and stop at a floor, I wondered if the stairs would have been faster. Speaking of faster, transit was not the fastest. Planes were out, too. Getting in and out of the airport would take hours.

"We need to call Quinn. He can get us to Nice the fastest."

"I'm on it." Nol pulled his phone out, flicking his thumb across the screen to search for Quinn's number. The elevator dinged as the phone rang.

"You might lose service."

But he ignored me with his phone to his ear. "What will you do if the council says no?"

My jaw clenched as I thought about the council refusing to let me in. "Let them try to pull something. We're finding Gileal."

The phone went to voicemail. With a scowl, Nol pulled the phone away from his ear. I felt the doubt in Nol's core, the very center of him, through our link. "It's not impossible to trick your grandmother."

By the look my grandmother had given me, I had no doubt, because she had no doubt. "That possibility is minuscule, Nol. We have to believe with all our hearts, without a doubt of hope."

"I don't think my heart can take it."

Then I'd hold on to that hope for the both of us.

The phone rang, startling us both. Nol pressed the answer button and put it on speaker.

"Quinn?"

"Hey, I got your text." Quinn's voice came through the tiny speaker. Nol squeezed my hand. "What's going on now? What's in Nice?"

"We've got an *endaen* problem," Nol paused. He acted so calm and Quinn just waited for more. "We must get to the tree Hallë exited when she first came. We must get to *Endae*, and it must be now."

There was silence, except for a thump of a car door and an engine turning. "What a coincidence, I'm leaving my parents' place now. Tell me everything."

13

WE HAD THIRTY MINUTES before Quinn made it to Paris, which gave me time to pack. I grabbed a backpack from my apartment and stuffed it with essentials: underwear, toothbrush, a few flannels, leggings, and comfortable t-shirts perfect for *Endae* in the spring.

Unlike rainy Paris, *Rudairn* would be drier, though I packed hiking gear for the Southern Alps where we'd find the tree from my exile. Nol reminded me we were also heading to cooler *Atryeu*, so I threw in a warm coat.

An hour later, I found myself sitting next to Lady Úna in Quinn's private jet, flying to Nice. She'd demanded that she come along. How had she known? Rayne heard it on the wind and Lady Úna made Quinn turn around and get her. So now the entire fae royal family knew what was going on at home. And the rest of the fae would probably know by tomorrow.

Úna and I were disagreeing—not arguing. No, I wouldn't argue with a lady older than dirt, even though she didn't look a day older than me. So odd.

"It couldn't have been *Breil-sur-Roya*," Úna said. "The grove is right above this commune." Úna tapped the screen.

"I remember seeing a mountain above me. Like this." I pointed to a mountain peak close to it without trees on top. But it was nowhere near any cities, villages, or communes. It'd taken Marie's husband, Jean, and I all night to get to their mountain village. I'd agreed that the city had no doubt grown since then, so I wasn't basing the location on the size of the town. I was adamant about the bridge, though. "It's just not high enough. Plus, it's in Italy."

"It's higher, and that area changed from Italy to France countless times through the ages. Did you *see* a French map? How sure are you that it was in France? Look." Úna tapped the side of the map and brought up the elevations. "The grove is here. I swear. You said you came at night?"

"Yes, but I didn't start moving until the next morning. I know what I saw. Above me was a clear mountain peak with snow and no trees. It took me *all day* to get to the road." Her place just didn't work. Sure, it had a bridge in this one, but the drive to Nice was wrong. "And the way to Nice from there is down to the Mediterranean. We went inland."

Úna's eyebrows rose, and she muttered under her breath.

"We didn't go through the Mediterranean." I stared at the map, comparing both towns. "How certain are you of this grove's location? It could be anywhere."

"Certain, as I knew the fairy who found you."

Nol and Quinn stopped their quiet conversation. I stared at the calm, falsely young fae, unsure what to say. There was no way she knew. Marie wasn't even full fae, unless she'd been using glamor. Was Úna trying to trick me into giving up information about her? Marie did not want to be found. She'd been quite clear about keeping silent. I hadn't even given the fae any information on Marie, including where I'd met her. Although, looking at a digital map on a plane about to set down in Nice, it was pretty obvious where I'd seen her. Still, the world was big. Marie could have moved on from that place.

"You don't know her."

"I do. She's the guard of the grove. She must have sensed you before you blocked your magic."

"I was here less than ten minutes before I blocked it."

"That spell would have sent off some pretty powerful energy. I heard getting it back was what alerted the fae to your presence in Seattle?"

I would neither confirm nor deny her attempt at fishing for information. "She thought I was magicless." Not that I knew that for certain.

Úna rested her chin on her palm and leaned on the table between our seats. "Then how did you find Hally, Nolan? I never understood that. If we couldn't sense her, how did you find her?"

"Her cuff." Nol pointed to the thin little cuff hugging my right ear, usually hidden within my favorite dragon ear cuffs. "The moment I came into this realm, I knew where she was, because I designed it that way." He sounded so proud I almost called him out. When we were little, he'd lost me in the woods. His uncle had helped him design the ear cuff so that he'd never lose me again after that. To an extent at least. But we found out, since my blocking spell broke, my cuff hadn't worked. He kept saying he wanted to try invoking the spell again, but I hadn't let him yet.

Quinn bumped my shoulder as he leaned in to look at the tablet. He hissed. "So, will there be hiking involved in this?"

For a moment, I didn't know what to say to his disgusted look. My boyfriend didn't like hiking? "You're a fairy. Nature is, like, your thing."

"Nope, not this one. Do you think we can take a helicopter in?" He grabbed the tablet, *tsk*ing. "Maybe I'll stay with the plane."

I gawked at him. "You're serious?"

"Yeah. Well, not about the plane thing—I'll go, but I do not like hiking. Oh shit." Quinn lifted his eyes, deer in the headlights. "That's not a deal-breaker, is it?"

"I mean...no, but you're gonna have to deal every once in a while. I thought you liked skiing."

"Oh, that. Yeah. That involves lifts. No snowshoeing or cross-coun-try stuff. Is that all you mean? Skiing?"

"No! We go hiking on occasion."

Quinn looked aghast. "Lewis goes hiking?"

What did that mean? Sure, Lewis was big, but that didn't mean he couldn't enjoy the outdoors. "A little. Mostly he stays at camp. But he loves going camping."

His eyes bugged out. "Camping?"

Oh boy. "We'll talk when I get back." I was only half serious. Sort of.

"So, about that helicopter..."

AN HOUR AND FORTY minutes later, Quinn took the last hairpin curve, and we got our first look at the village. I had to admit, the small roads and mini walls, which wouldn't do a damn thing to keep us on the road if we happened to misstep, reminded me of the journey to Nice so long ago.

By the time we came to the village, perhaps twenty minutes later, Nol was green and Úna and I weren't talking much. The bridge Marie's husband had driven over a century ago wasn't here and the wall near the village hadn't been there. Quinn drove right through. Some people, mostly elderly, walked around, carrying bags or pushing those small carts many elderly people used.

"Quinn, turn down this road," Úna said. We took a left, and I could see out into the mountains. The sun would make all the buildings orange in the sunrise. I happened to turn and look out the left window as we drove past a bright red door.

"Stop!" I yelled a bit too loudly.

But it did the trick. Quinn stomped on the brakes. The moment the car stopped, I was out and running back. The red door. Jean had helped me out of the wagon and carried me to this door because my body had been so cold it had felt like spikes were stabbing my legs when I stood.

"Do you remember anything about the ride down? Possibly where Jean picked you up?"

Jean? She knew his name? I started shaking, realizing what this meant. Úna knew what Marie had done. I heard Úna's shoes. Her hiking boots had a little squeak in them that I'm sure irritated her.

Marie had been so kind to me, and it would be my fault if they hurt her. "She was only helping me, because...because..." I'd never asked.

She hadn't wanted me to speak. "I didn't have magic, and she'd wanted to help. Do you know if they hurt her?"

"They haven't done anything. *Tu as été très courageuse, petite elfe,*" *You have been very brave, little elf,* Úna said in French, too similar to the words Marie had told me. "No one else knows because you kept your promise."

I blinked as I stared straight ahead, not believing my ears. This couldn't be...I turned to Úna, standing beside me.

"Or perhaps it's because you've forgotten most of it?" But this wasn't the Úna I'd met a day ago. I knew her as someone else. As I watched Úna's glamor wave into existence, she became the woman I thought I'd never see again.

"I didn't forget anything." Jean had picked me up on the side of a dirt road, right time, right place. Her family had been so kind to me. Marie had taught me to hide among humans and a few French phrases. She'd given me some human clothes. Then Jean and their son, André, had taken me down to the orphanage in Nice the next morning.

"You were so brave," Úna, under the glamor of Marie, explained. "You were my reason for coming here, I realized, that day. I never would have guessed what Anu had in store for you, but you are perfect for the job ahead of you."

"I think I can follow the situation, but do you mind if we could do this on the go? While we might have six hours left, if my estimations are correct, I don't want to risk it." Nol looked at his phone. "That estimation is based on someone else's estimation. We'll have time when we get back."

Úna glared at Nol for several seconds, then turned the glare on Quinn. "Your Highness, please pardon my outburst."

"On the go," Nol snapped at us a few times. "All of this can be done while driving."

I groaned.

"Gileal is alive."

Oh, he was playing *that* card. "Fine. We have six hours. You know you're never wrong."

"But my uncle is, and my math is only as good as the accuracy of the data."

But I was already getting in the car. Úna and Quinn followed suit before Nol was even in the damn car. "Let's go!"

"Your Highness, the grove is past the village. And yes, there is hiking involved." She didn't sound the least bit remorseful. "Hally, hand me the tablet, and I will pin the location of the grove."

"But you already said—"

"I lied." Úna chuckled. "I wanted to make sure you were true. That you weren't the elves of old and I could trust you." There was nothing funny about it. "It's on this side. Jean said he picked you up about here, and the grove is here." She tapped the spot and set a pin.

"Oh, that makes much more sense," I said.

About an hour later, and after lots of hairpin turns and narrow roads, Úna told Quinn to stop the car. "Does this look familiar?" She stood on a flat surface on the ravine side of the road where we could see the valley below. But that didn't mean it was the same view.

"Lady Úna, this all looks the same to me. The season is different, and it's been a century."

She nodded, set her hands on her hips, and turned to the trees behind us. We'd have to climb a small dirt wall to get to them. Looking at Quinn's resignation at the prospect of climbing, I stepped back and searched for a shorter wall. Nothing. It wouldn't be that invasive to make a little trail, would it? I could always cover it back up once we were up.

"All right, stand back for a second." Then I envisioned the steps I wanted to create.

"What are you doing?" Úna grabbed my arms and shook me. "You don't change the landscape to make your way easier. Humans do use this road, too."

"I was going to put it back."

"Ask before throwing your magic out, girl!" She let me go with a tiny shove, her tattooed face flushed. "We don't have to go far. You can all endure a brief walk in the woods."

Hopefully, her idea of *brief* wasn't too far. To Quinn's credit, he didn't complain and even offered his hand after he'd made it to the top before me. He pulled me in for a hug. Did he think I was pouting after my scolding?

"You okay?" Yep, the scolding thing.

"Everything's good. I get her point."

Pine trees sprawled up around us. With only our trees to compare them to when I'd first seen them, I'd thought they were so thin back then. Some of them were small enough to wrap my arms all the way around, but some older ones were twice—and even three times—that size.

Thirty feet in and several stumbles later was another steep incline. This one looked kind of familiar. The rock face was solid stone and towered several feet above Nol's head. The angled layers of orange and gray deposits gave no real footholds to climb up.

"Here we are," Úna announced.

Nol came up to stand beside Úna, gazing at the top. "Where's here? It looks the same as every other inch of this wall."

"The grove starts above this cliff."

"The entire grove is interconnected? So, we should be able to touch the first tree and use it?"

"That's right. We just need to get you up there."

"How do you suggest we do that if we can't use magic to alter it?"

Úna interlaced her hands and mimed boosting someone up. "This is where we say goodbye and good luck."

She was serious. They weren't going any farther. I'd thought they'd walk right up to the trees with us. Now that we were here, my shoulders started to tense as doubt settled in. What if Nol's *meril* didn't work? He'd never tried that one and I didn't know who made it.

I turned to Quinn, my chest heavy, but I didn't know what to say.

Quinn kissed me gently. "You have to go, Hally."

"I know. I'll be back soon." But I had no control over the outcome of this trip.

If Nol walked into the capital, the bomb could go off and kill him. I wouldn't die right away. The time in Faerie where our link had been open was an odd fluke. With our link closed, it would take me years to die. I'd slowly get weaker until there was nothing left of me. A crap-tastic way to die, but I'd die with my friends around me.

Quinn grabbed one of my curls and tugged on it. "Make sure you do. Bring that sorry excuse of a *muranildo* of yours back with you, too."

"I heard that." Nol came up beside me and reached out his arm. "I'll bring her back to you, old man."

"She has many people here who need her, my friend—and you, as well. Bring each other back, do you hear?" Quinn clasped Nol's outstretched arm and pulled him in for a one-armed hug. "Be careful." He let go of Nol and turned to me.

I jumped toward him and hugged him as hard as I could. He kept hold of me for a while, and when we parted, I saw a look that concerned me. "We'll be back."

"I know." He leaned in and kissed me for the last time for who knew how long and spun me around to face the wall. "Ready?"

We were doing this. Where was Nol? I looked up and found his cinnamon-red hair fluttering in the wind. He reached an arm down for me to grab. Shit, shit, shit. Quinn leaned over and interlaced his hands, ready to give me a boost. I hadn't said goodbye to Úna yet.

"Úna?" I sounded about as confident as a first-time skydiver about to jump out at thirty-thousand feet. Or however far up they went.

She was there next to me, smiling. "Be brave," she whispered. "You'll do just fine if you're brave."

I nodded, and without another word, I stepped on Quinn's hand. After only a few feet, Nol grabbed my forearm and pulled me up.

"Did you really walk all the way down from there?" He pointed up the steep incline.

"Yep, and jumped down that, too." I pointed at our mini cliff. "To be honest, a ton of snow was covering the ground, and I thought the ground was closer." But I had turned and slid on my belly to be safe. "Let's do this." I grabbed Nol's hand and squeezed.

We didn't choose the first tree or even the second. A few more feet in and Nol pointed to a larger one ahead. He squeezed my hand before letting go and pulled out his strand of *merili*. His fingers found the yellow *meril*, the second one on his left. With a twist and an activation word, we were ready. So simple compared to other *endaen* spells.

"You first," Nol said as he placed his hand on the tree. As I touched the tree below Nol's hand, I felt Earth pull on me, like it didn't want me to leave. I took the first step out of the human realm and into a space that wasn't a space. Roots tangled and fused, reached high into the air and down into the soil, all together in a misty in-between place of being. I considered the likelihood of being stuck here, but before I could contemplate it further, Nol pushed on my back and I stepped into *Endae*.

The hush of the inside of the Tree of Connection was vast, the sting of tree sap tickled my nose, refreshing and...home.

14

Nol bumped into me, making me stumble. I caught myself and looked around the utter darkness. An orb blinked into existence across from us as Nol conjured a sconce to ignite. Soft, yellow light revealed the small, empty corridor of the underside of this ancient *Coyana* tree. *Endae* was a few hours ahead of Earth. Everyone was home or visiting others, eating their dinners, and who knew what else—just not here. I took a deep breath of the wood-and-sap aroma. These massive trees had the same scent as their relatives, the giant redwoods in California. The trees grew so vast that my entire house could fit in one, the two houses on either side of mine, too. It was a hard concept to fathom for a human who'd never witnessed such a size.

We used the Trees of Connection to travel to different places across the realm. Local lawmaking work and government assembly meetings were done within this tree. I was sentenced and exiled here because the local council had already determined the outcome. It did not bring back happy memories.

Still, I was home. The thought of being back hadn't sunk in. After a hundred and nineteen years, I stood in the same spot from which I'd left this realm. But I'd be able to see my parents. Just see them, from a safe distance, without the risk of exposure. That had to be enough.

"Let's get going." I hurled myself ahead, terrified, nervous, and ecstatic to see my parents.

"Wait. I need to contact the *Zayuri*. The sooner I check in, the sooner we can get to the capital and find Gileal. Mother, please, please let it be true. Let us find him alive."

I prayed the same thing. He had to be alive. My grandmother had felt his signature. "Once we get to your parents' house, I can contact Yalu," I said.

Nol scoffed. "You might as well do it here. My parents won't leave you alone once we're home. They'll be just as excited as yours. Can you do it here? I'll keep you safe."

Why couldn't he get this? Yes, I was vulnerable, but that wasn't all of it. "Nol, I have to be comfortable enough to drift into that state. I'm not comfortable here. I can use An'di's or your room once we get there."

"If we go to my parents' house first, do you really think they'll give you time alone to do that? No. We can go to your grandmother's house. No one is there."

That was so *not* happening. "That takes us closer to town. No. When you contact someone in *Jinatrau*, tell them to contact Yalu. I'll visit her in her dreams tonight."

The crease between his eyes deepened again as he contemplated that. "Fine, but I'm contacting the *Zayuri* here."

"Just hurry up about it." I tapped my foot while I waited.

He pulled out his dagger, a miniature black metal blade like his sword. I'd used that thing to stab the fairy who'd helped steal the fae and *endaen* children six weeks ago—and almost died from the magic I shouldn't have been able to wield. Nol placed the blade on the palm of his hand. I had no idea who he was trying to contact since his uncle was stuck on Earth.

A minute passed as he stood there with his head bowed, the black-blue glow reflecting on his face. He slid his dagger into his boot sheath. The movement was slow and the crease between Nol's eyes was still there.

"What's wrong?"

He stilled after the dagger was gone. "The radius has spread faster than I estimated."

"How fast?"

"A minute longer and we wouldn't have been able to travel. Three more *Zayuri* villages have been cut off." We were stuck in *Endae* until they figured this out. "Sanae is very eager to get to me, and I'm worried she will overdo it. If she's too exhausted when she arrives, we'll have to wait for her to recover. She's not listening to me."

He was arguing with his dragon? I refrained from giving him a smart-ass remark. Barely. I had no doubt she'd missed him after seven months of absence. "How long until she gets here?"

"About six hours." He rubbed his eyes and leaned back against the tree. Then we'd leave for *Aetyru*, where Nol might be walking to his death. But what else could we do? Abandon our sovereigns? Not happening.

"*C'yo*, we need to get there sooner."

I reached for Nol's hand and opened our link, offering him comfort.

He breathed deeply, and his shoulders loosened. "What if I don't make it in time?"

"There's no way to know, but we have to try." Life would go on. That part was certain. "We can't let the worry consume us."

"I contacted my commander." Instead of agreeing, he changed the subject.

"Great. Where are we going first, then? Your parents' house or just hit my house first?"

"Hallë—"

I shook my finger at him. "You agreed." In my mind, I listed what things I wanted to talk to my parents about, but then it would just be nice to see them and hear their voices. "All I mean is you can go knock on the door and I'll stay at the edge of the road. Easy-peasy."

He pursed his lips, and I thought he'd break his promise. "Fine. Let's go before I change my fucking mind."

Nol cast orbs for the sconces on the wall of the tree to light our path. We didn't run into anyone as we walked through the halls under the humongous tree. As we came close to the entrance, the afternoon sunlight refracted off the tiny white iridescent pearl tiles on the roof and sides of the hall of the underside of the tree. These tiles were the same as in the main hall in the famous tunnel leading to the assembly hall in *Aemina*.

The clean, untainted air of *Endae*, filled with the scents of ancient trees and salt water from the harbor past the center of the city, not only filled my lungs as we stood at the entrance, but also brought back memories. I closed my eyes and shoved away all the bad ones as best I could.

Nol stood beside me, giving me a moment to breathe in the scents of my childhood. "Are you doing all right?"

Nodding, I gave myself a few more seconds before I opened my eyes. Change was harder for us than humans because our memories were so long. We had more of a "change isn't always better" type of mentality. Humans always wanted to improve, even the shit that didn't need to be improved upon. It had taken me a while to get used to that; now it surprised me that *Rudairn* hadn't changed.

I'd been banished in the winter, but now spring flowers and green grasses brightened the ground. The trunk of the Tree of Connection was a lighter brown because it wasn't wet. I turned and looked up at the massive tree. The bark's crevices were so big that a person could fit in one.

"Let's go," I whispered, not wanting to break the peaceful sound of the leaves in the wind.

We walked down the narrow road that led to the thirty-foot-high, brown-leafed *greslyn* tree. Here the road broke off into three directions. Bushy domesticated trees lined the sides of each road. The tree was also Nol's, Gil's, and my meeting spot. Gil lived south of this point at the moon temple. His father was the cleric of Anara's Sacred Moon. Similar to Catholics, they worshiped our goddess, Anara, but venerated Her sacred cosmos aspects. My family didn't follow their path but deeply respected Gil's family and their beliefs. Across from us, to the west, was the road to the city spiral with all the main halls, like the Hall of Knowledge and Hall of Justice, and the market. Nol's and my homes were in the northern direction, as well as our favorite tree close to the wild forest.

Nol and I headed north, but paused when two girls ran out of the tree line on the road to the city center. They skidded to a halt, looked at Nol, screamed like little girls do, and ran back the way they came.

"Don't they recognize you?"

Nol shook his head. "I don't come here often enough."

Poor kids. I knew how they felt, being afraid of a big, bad *Zayuri*. Squinting, my jaw dropped. "When was the last time you came?"

"I don't remember." Without another word, he continued on his way like nothing had happened.

"How do you *not* recall how long it was since the last time you came home?"

"Between hunting Aswryn and other missions, I just haven't found the time."

I got moving and caught up with him. "You're telling me you haven't visited either of our parents in so long that you can't recall the last time you were here? How the hell do you know how my dad really is then?"

He stopped and heaved an annoyed sigh. "Tolwe visits and gives me updates. Please stop pestering me about it."

"Nolan, Nevie—" a frantic voice called from behind us.

We turned to see two female *endai* hurrying from the same direction as the girls. The girls must have alerted them. They knew our names, but I didn't recognize them. One had strawberry-blonde hair and the other had honey-brown hair.

"Your moms are just behind us," the blonde one said.

My stomach flipped. I'd see my mom sooner than I expected. She was here without my dad, which meant I could be close to her, hug her. My feet were moving before I realized it.

"Nevie, no!" The brown haired *endaë* stepped in my way. "Wennië says you have to get off the path and hide."

That didn't make sense. "Why would she say that?" I backed up before she could touch me. Who was she?

"Tiaë isn't—it wouldn't be good for her health. She's fragile. I'm sorry, Nevie," the blonde *endaë* said.

"I can't imagine how that feels," the one brown haired *endaë* said, placating me. "But Tiaë can't handle surprises." I was going to punch her if she came any closer.

"*Micsi moticon juetera täta?*" *Why would you say that*? I realized my breathing was becoming erratic.

"Nevie?" a familiar voice called from behind the two *endai*.

Both *endaë* winced. One closed her eyes and the other cussed under her breath. Their joke was uncalled for and cruel. If I wasn't so excited to see my mom I would have shoved them both to the ground. The *endaëi* backpedaled, then ran down the southern road and out of sight while my mom and I stared at each other.

Both of our moms held baskets; I saw something green and leafy poking out of Wennië's. My mom stood a mere ten yards away from me, her eyes wide with surprise, but looking as healthy as the day I'd left.

I began walking slowly toward my mom. "*Murë*?" *Mom*? She hadn't moved since she'd called my name.

My mom gasped and dropped her basket to run toward me. We hadn't gotten to say goodbye before I'd been banished. There was no way I wasn't going to hug her this time.

"Tiaë, no!" Wennië yelled, dropped her own basket and grabbed my mother around the waist. "Nevie, stop! Twynolan, what in the realms do you two think you're doing? Get Nevie away from here!"

Stumbling, I flinched at Wennië's harsh tone. Why would she say that? My mother twisted against her best friend.

"*Murë*, *we* have permission," Nol assured his mom. He turned to me, as clueless as I was about Wennië's sharp tone.

"This isn't good, Nolan."

Speechless, I glared at him. "Why wouldn't it be good?" I snapped at him in English.

"You said she isn't infected! Is she?"

Wennië looked from him to me, lips pressed tightly. My mother was *right in front of me*. Wennië didn't want me to see her.

"No." Nol's eyes dropped to me. "I don't know." How would he? He didn't visit enough to know about our parents.

Nol reached for my hand and tugged me to his side. "Murë, what's wrong? What would it hurt to let them at least talk? Orin isn't here."

Talking I could do. I eased up on my fight to get away. I could stay back.

"Take her to our house, now."

No. I pulled on Nol's arms. If he was going to listen to his mother instead of keeping his promise, I'd fight with all I had. Nol grabbed my other arm and held them both to my sides. This was bullshit.

An endao ran up from the south road. The two female *endai* who'd tried to keep me away from my mom trailed behind him. I immediately recognized the older *endao* with his sandy-blond hair and stocky figure. Gil's father, Balin, ran to my mom just as she broke free from Wennië.

"Tiaë, no. I'm sorry," Balin told her while staring at me. "Both of you, we're all sorry, but you can't be near Nevie."

When my mother's knees buckled, he swept her into his arms. "She's fine," he assured me. "She's exhausted. I'll see her home safe and check on Orin. I'm sorry, Nevie. Truly."

Exhausted? From taking care of my dad? She was fine walking with Wennië and running just fine a moment ago. But why had she collapsed? They were keeping something from me. Wennië was storming past them toward us, fury in her eyes. She stood six feet away from her son, seven inches shorter than him. She pointed at Nol. "Jespine and Fena told you to get off the path. Now Tiaë is upset." She pointed at my mom and Balin, who were walking off.

Nol wouldn't let go of me as my mom was being carried away! I struggled against his grasp. Unless I wanted to use my magic to harm him, Nol's hands were going to stay clenched to my arms.

"Nevie, hear me. *I* am immune. Your mom is always home with your dad, but I take her to town once a week. I am the only one who stays near her. Like with any other illness, the virus could be on her hands. It would easily infect you. I'm not risking your lives for that. I'm sorry."

Nol pulled me against him when I struggled once more. "Murë, please, I promised her she could see them if she kept a safe distance."

"Both of them?" Wennië's eyes bulged. "That's impossible. Orin never leaves his room!"

Nol sputtered, and I knew he was looking for a solution. "There has to be a way."

Wennië crossed her arms and stared us down. "Think about how she's feeling. What would you do if it were Cam? Could you hold back?"

Nol froze, his arms going rigid. "That's not fair."

Balin and my mom weren't visible anymore. They'd gone around a bend and hidden by the trees lining the road. If I could just see them. Nol's hands dug into my biceps as I continued to struggle against him. If I could follow them. Why couldn't I just talk to her? What harm would that cause?

Another moment passed, and Nol rested his head on top of my head. "I'm sorry, Hallë."

"You promised." I pushed and pushed, but Nol kept telling me no.

"It breaks my heart to keep you from them, but please stop this." Sure, he meant he was sorry, but he didn't understand. He hadn't lost his parents, then his foster parents. He could hug his parents. I wanted my mom!

"Come home and you both can eat something." Wennië touched Nol's hand. "You must keep her safe, Nolan. No matter how hard it is for you. I'm sorry, Nevie." We started walking the same way as Balin. We'd see them when the road straightened out again.

"She prefers Hally, Murë."

Wennië huffed and didn't reply for a while. Ten steps later, she gave me her opinion. "I like it." Her eyebrow rose as she considered it. "I think it suits you. Hally. A little like Hallë, but strong and bold. Just like you."

That didn't mean I forgave her. I refused to look at her. "What about Balin? Is he not worried about getting infected?"

"Balin already has it. It affects everyone differently. He is functional, but he has his bad days. Somehow Tiaë hasn't contracted it, but lately, she has become forgetful, fragile, and confused during times of great stress. If we had a healer, we could know, but"—Wennië shuddered—"we don't."

"How recently?" *Endai* thought of recently differently than a human. "I'm not a kid anymore, Wennië. I can deal with hard truths. It might be my fault that Murë is slowly dying."

Wennië frowned and squinted at me. Fuck, like Tolwe and Gil, she struggled to understand me. Nol said he'd gotten used to my "accent." I was doing something wrong and I couldn't figure it out! Nol repeated my words, Wennië thought about it for a moment and nodded a quick movement of her head.

"After your father contracted the curse, I believe. Almost a decade ago."

I glared at her, then at Nol. He was just as guilty, agreeing not to let me see her. "Fine."

I crossed my arms tightly and walked beside them. Wennië let out a relieved breath, and Nol loosened his hold on my arms. I waited until Balin and my mom came back into sight before I tried anything. Three more steps, five, and he relaxed. That's when I tried to bolt. I didn't get far. Nol had sensed it, his damn *Zayuri* senses, and scooped me up in his arms.

"Nice try."

"I hate you right now." And I meant it.

Nol met my eyes, saw the truth in them, and looked away. "I didn't know they'd be out in town. If only it had happened differently."

"Don't you two try sneaking out tonight either," Wennië warned. "If she hasn't forgotten already, Tiaë will have done so by this evening. Keeping a safe distance, as you said, Nolan, would never have worked. Tiaë wouldn't have stayed at the door, and Hally cannot see Orin. You both know the truth in that. If I could see An'di one more time...I'd risk anything to wrap her in my arms."

Nol mumbled something, and I lifted my head to see his jaw moving as he ground his teeth but agreeing to it all the same. "We won't go over." He looked down at me, his blue eyes pleading with me to forgive him. "I'm sorry, Hallë," Nol whispered to me.

But sorry would never be enough.

My eyes stayed trained ahead, watching Balin's back. How could he have the curse and be strong enough to carry my mom all this way? Nol stopped and I glanced around to see why. We'd made it to his parents' house, but he wasn't following Wennië.

"Nolan."

"Give her this, Murë. Just this."

My parents' door opened, from Balin's spell, perhaps? He pushed the door the rest of the way open with his shoulder, tapped his feet to shake any loose dirt from his shoes, hooked the door with his foot, and closed it. She was gone. Wennië couldn't know for sure my mom couldn't handle it, but I was certain of it.

A shaky creak, like a pin grinding against metal with a divot in it, brought my attention back to Nol's place. The familiar sound was from their front door as Wennië opened it. Nol's dad, Edvic, liked the noise. He said it alerted him if his kids snuck out. It never worked. We'd just snuck out the window.

As Nol carried me through their front door, the smell of Wennië's dyes and Edvic's orange blossom wine hit me next. The air held the aroma of their dinner in the kitchen, not that I recognized it, but their cooking was always fantastic. I couldn't breathe right, and all at once, I was thankful Nol was carrying me. This was just as much my home as my parents' house.

"Can I put you down yet?" Nol murmured just above my face.

Absolutely not, but not for the reason he thought. Besides, I was still pissed at him, so I kept my eyes trained on his neck, ignoring him.

"Wennië." Edvic's voice came from down the hall, likely from his study, judging by how muffled it sounded. "What is this noise? Nolan? What are you doing here?"

"You've been studying too much, Edvic. The council members told us earlier today that Nolan and Hally would be here."

"Hally? Wait, Nevie?" They were quiet, and I almost looked to see what they *weren't* verbally saying. But that meant Nol and Wennië would win, and like hell I'd do that. Edvic gasped, and his solid steps thumped closer to us. "Is she hurt? What did you do, Nolan?"

"What do you think he did, Edvic? Your crazy son was going to take her to see Tiaë and Orin. Nolan. Go. Sit. Now."

Nol obeyed, his parents followed, whispering close behind as Nol brought me into the hearth room.

"Tiaë saw her daughter as we were walking home. You can imagine what happened next."

Edvic *tsk*ed. "That isn't good for her health right now. Son, what were you thinking?"

Wennië let out a bark of laughter. "He wasn't!"

Nol hitched me up higher and sat next to the fire. "I know, I'm an idiot."

"You are not an idiot, my boy," Edvic said. "Just blind when it comes to your *muranildë*. Set her down and let her cover up."

"She'll try running again!" Wennië called out from where I estimated was the kitchen. "Hold her still, and I'll get her something warm to drink."

"Let me talk to her," Edvic suggested.

I felt someone brush my hair away from my neck, letting it fall down behind me.

"Nevie? Would you look at me?" Edvic shook my hair a little. "This is an odd turn of events, isn't it? Like I always say, we can see a good thing in every situation, can't we? This attack has brought you here first and you brought Nolan, too! He never visits anymore, so thank you for that."

"*Laro,*" *Dad*. I could almost hear Nol's eyes rolling.

"What?" He stilled his hand on top of my head as he talked back to Nol. "Tolwe told us the sixty-third day last winter that you followed Aswryn to *Rosava*. And you've been there since before Autumn *Wyuendell*. You travel for work, yes, but it wouldn't hurt to come home and see us sometimes."

Nol's dad was a worrywart, it came with the territory of teaching alongside someone who handled current politics. I understood why Nol hadn't told them about Earth; following Aswryn to Earth was a split-second decision. He'd tracked where Aswryn went, gotten council permission, and left. No time for family chats.

But that didn't excuse Tolwe. He could have told them sooner.
So why hadn't he?

"Hallë doesn't need to know all the drama." Nol snapped at his dad.

Edvic began brushing his fingers through my hair. "It was painful,
Hally, I know, but you did see your mother, didn't you? It hurt, didn't
it? No matter where you had seen her, it would have hurt regardless."

"Edvic, make yourself useful instead of bothering the girl. Go get
some firewood. The harbor cleared while we were at the market this
afternoon, the temperature is already dropping."

Edvic grunted as his knees creaked. "Yes, my love. Make myself
useful, ha!" He patted my shoulder as he left. "I gave her two children.
What do you have there, Wennië?" There was another pause. "Eck,
don't give her *that*! First time she's here in a century and you give her
that tea?"

"It will calm her down. Medicine isn't supposed to taste good.
Otherwise, they'd want it all the time. Go get the firewood, husband."

I smirked into Nol's upper arm at their banter. I missed that a lot.

"Murë, he's right. Hallë hates that. What about lavender honey in
some hot water?"

"I suppose I could put more of that in there."

"None of the tea, all of the honey."

"Fine!" Her voice faded as she left the room. "No tea!"

"Be warned, Hallë," Nol whispered. "Murë will try to cover up the
root tea to make you sleepy. The honey doesn't work."

Typical of Wennië and unavoidable. Still angry with both of them,
I didn't comment.

"Here we are…" Wennië came back in before Edvic returned. "Hallanevaë, sit up and take this." She paused when I ignored her. "Stop
being childish and sit up. Nolan, let go of her legs and put her up in
your lap."

Nol did what he was told, except he sat me beside him. Once I had
to sit up, I refused to take the drink or even look up at her. Instead, I
stared at the fireplace to our right. Since most of our buildings were
living trees, fireplaces couldn't sit in walls. Instead, they resembled
small backyard fire pits, partially covered by a thin half-dome to shield

the wall from sparks. Magic kept the surrounding stones cool to the touch.

Wennië let out an exasperated groan. "Hally—"

"Murë, leave her be for now and give her some time to decompress. We'll have time to sleep." Nol rubbed my arm as he tried to convince me to cooperate. "Sanae will need to rest and eat before we leave for *Lairenya*."

"*Lairenya*? Why that way?" Wennië asked, still holding the tea. Nol was right. I could smell the root from here.

"Sanae is taking two passengers. This way we can see how she does with the extra weight."

He stopped rubbing my arm when Wennië touched me, or rather, she touched the slave band. "So, it's true. Has there been any progress in finding a solution to get this horrible thing off?"

"I need a phrase to release it." He rested his head on my head and took several deep breaths.

A clatter from the back room saved us from answering Wennië's question. Edvic made all the noise as he came through the house, carrying an armload of firewood, his nose and cheeks red from the cooling air outside.

"Ah, good, she's sitting up." But the spark of mischief that he'd passed down to his son dulled as he caught my eyes. "I thought I'd bring something a little better for a troubled spirit." Edvic lifted a bottle of his homemade orange blossom wine he held in his other hand before setting his armload of wood next to the fireplace.

"She doesn't need alcohol, Edvic!"

My hand shot out, and he gave me the brown bottle. My fingers brushed the emblem on the neck, and I pulled out the cork. "Alcohol sounds like a very good solution, Edvic."

"Perfect. My lovely wife." He kissed her. "Would you ma—" Wennië raised an eyebrow, waiting for him to finish that sentence. "—be a dear and get some glasses while I put the firewood away?"

"Good save, Laro," Nol mumbled.

"Nolan, give Hally some space," Edvic said to his son.

"She'll run."

"No, I don't think so. Not right now, at least." Edvic winked at me.

Nol let go of me so I could stand and pour Edvic and myself some wine. Nol could get his own.

Wennië came back in with three glasses. "I don't recommend alcohol right now, but if you insist, here." She shoved the glasses at me.

A hard knock sounded at the front door, and everyone jumped.

"That better not be who I think it is," Wennië snapped.

"I'll get it, Murë, in case it's them." Nol stood, rolled his shoulders back, and brushed his jacket down. They knocked again. That's when I got a distinct suspicion about who *they* meant.

Lo and behold, Nol took his time. I set the bottle and glasses down on the table near the chairs. Edvic stayed close behind me while Wennië hurried to follow Nol. There was a third knock before Nol grabbed the handle. From this angle, I only saw Nol's back and the door. "*Aore* Junae, to what do we owe this pleasure?"

There was a pause, because even though Nol had said it in *Aemirin*, the phrase didn't line up well.

"That means greetings and why are you here in a human language," Nol informed him.

"*Hinam* Twynolan—"

"We don't need to be formal here, Junae."

The local senior council member, one of three who had banished me one hundred and nineteen years ago, paused. People were supposed to respect the council members, not mock them. "It has come to our attention that you've brought *Savilë* Hallanevaë with you."

"Your sources are correct. State what your concern is."

"While her presence was authorized, she is required to stay at the Hall of Justice until you are ready to leave. When is your dragon arriving?"

"*Aore* Zella said nothing about her detainment."

"Regardless…it is true. Here." There was a rustle of paper and another pause.

"It requires supervision, not detainment at the Hall of Justice. I am responsible for her. That will be sufficient."

"For the safety of the citizens of *Aemina*, *Savilë* Hallanevaë needs to come with me." Junae hesitated. "Per the authorized agreement."

"No. It is what you want, not what was agreed upon per this paper. That will be all." Nol slammed the door in his face.

Nol spun and found the three of us staring at him in disbelief. "What?" He blinked at us as if it were perfectly normal to defy a council member.

"The agreement!" *Aore* Junae pounded on the door.

Nol opened the door a crack. "I'm keeping this copy, Junae. You know as well as I do that we are supposed to have one anyway. It's time for you to leave."

"*Hinam* Twynolan!"

"Yes, it is *Hinam* to you now, and as you are aware, I do not answer to you. I am on official Starborn Royal duty. Hallanevaë is my responsibility at all times. Leave or I can detain you."

I choked at those words. Could Nol really do that? *Zayuri* were the only officials that could arrest council members, but what would be the official reason? Being snooty pricks was kind of their thing. Admittedly, my grandparents could be just as stubborn at times. Nol closed the door again, locked it with a spell, and walked by us into the living room.

"You just..." Words. I could find them! "Won't you get in trouble?"

"Oh, you're talking to me now? You know the answer, just as Junae does. I have no respect for him, and I know how they twist the truth to meet their wants. He can't do that with *Zayuri*. Are you going to have some wine or not?"

"I..." There was no lying to myself. I knew I had to talk to Nol and Wennië eventually, at least to tell her goodbye. "Screw it, why the hell not?"

Split between the four of us, Edvic's wine didn't go far. Wennië had taken two sips before she passed out, while I was still nursing my first cup. Nol and his father were on their third cup and down to the dregs of the bottle with all the clove pieces. Yuck. Worse than coffee grounds.

"To have you both here is a blessing. I will get another bottle." Edvic turned to move Wennië, who was leaning against him.

"No!" Nol and I said together.

"Laro, we'll be flying in less than five hours. I don't want to be hungover on Sanae's back. Hallë either."

Hungover, my ass. He'd still be drunk.

"There's a solution for that." Both *endao* blinked their red-rimmed eyes at me. "I could stay here."

"Out of the question," Nol said in English, then waved his hand in the air as if that was how to switch languages in his head. "*Sae,*" *no.* "There are multiple reasons you must go. In order of most to least important: The slave band. Just like Seattle to France, we're not risking the distance. Second, I'm responsible for you and I take that duty seriously. Third, the temptation to see your parents will grow the longer you're here." Nol's ice-blue eyes rolled to the left, searching for something. "I forget my fourth one. Laro, I'm cutting myself off."

"Hally? One more?"

I held my hands up, reached out for their cups, and took them into the kitchen. Nol was responsible for me, yet I was still going to see them. This was my only chance to tell them goodbye, to tell them I loved them.

"Don't try it." Nol's voice startled me, and I would have dropped the cups if they hadn't already been in the sink.

I grabbed the edge of the sink and tried to discombobulate my thoughts. We were too damn drunk to have this conversation. "What?"

Nol watched me for a moment, collecting his thoughts or preparing himself to speak without slurring his words. "The look in your eyes. I already know what you're planning to do. Don't make me set a ward to keep you in."

If he managed to cast anything, being as drunk as he was. Not that I'd challenge him. He could have proved me wrong, and then I'd have been screwed.

"I'm not planning to go; it's that I want to see them. I won't go."

"Bullshit. Write them a letter. You can tell them everything that way. In fact, it would give them something of you to hold on to, especially Tiaë. With her memory challenges right now."

But what would it do for me? Grinding my teeth, I turned back to the dishes, coaxed the soap out of the wooden container, and turned on the water. I had the dishes clean in seconds flat without even touching them.

"That's the Hallë I remember. It is nice to see you using basic magic."

"It's different on Earth, and you know it." Finished cleaning, I turned to face him.

He leaned a shoulder against the doorframe and shoved his hands into his pockets. "I am sorry. We would have gone, if Murë hadn't pointed out the obvious."

I crossed my arms and leaned against the counter, settling in for a talk. "I don't hate you, but I hate that..." He hadn't lied, just given me hope. Then he stole it. "I let my hopes get so high. Having families sucks! You draw them close to you and then...you lose them."

"It's not fair that you can't see your parents after you lost your foster ones. And I'm prepared for you to hate me for keeping you safe, but I must insist that you stay here tonight."

My eyes dropped to the floor, and I played with my bracelet for a while, searching for something to convince him that I agreed. "Your idea isn't that bad, actually. About a letter. Maybe one for each of them."

Nol perked up, always pleased to hear he was right, no matter what. "Great! I'll get you the paper—"

"Unless your parents moved Edvic's study, I'm capable of getting it on my own. Go get some sleep, and I'll stay down here and write those letters."

"You won't...take them over yourself, will you?"

I winced, caught again. "Why would I do that?"

Nol watched me until I squirmed under his scrutiny. "Look at me and tell me you won't go."

Unable to give him what he wanted, I kept my eyes trained to the floor, where I watched my toes wiggle. I fidgeted against the sink while Nol gave me time to decide to do what was right in his eyes. The bad part about knowing each other so well was that I couldn't hide a damn thing from him if he was paying attention. He, on the other hand, had learned to be mysterious, and I found it hard to read him.

"*C'yo*, Hallë," Nol cussed after a full minute of watching me. "I am sorry for this, but I can't trust you." The next moment, Nol was less than a foot in front of me, no room to move. With a few quick movements and without touching me, he cast an intricate spell far beyond my rudimentary knowledge of traditional spells. "*Sayete*," Nol whispered the invoking word of whatever spell he'd just cast. I felt his magic settle around us. He stayed where he was, took a deep shuddering breath, and wouldn't meet my eyes. "You can't leave the house without me now. I am sorry, but I can't risk your safety."

My eyes widened as his words sank in. He hadn't meant a ward on the house, but a ward on me. He'd literally detained me in the house. Still reeling from the freedom he'd taken from me, he leaned over and kissed my forehead. "Good night. Please get some sleep before we leave."

I sincerely doubted I would sleep, now that I was a prisoner and angrier than before. If I knew he wouldn't dodge it, I'd have punched him right in the face. Nol closed his eyes, almost said something, but chose the better option and walked out of the kitchen before I could yell, scream, or beg him to release me. It wasn't fair. They were right there!

I stormed after him, out of the kitchen, took the first left, and ran up the steps, but came face to face with Edvic at the top. "Good evening, lovely girl. Are things well?"

"No. Your son warded me in here. He just...he...I don't even know what that was. I can't leave the house."

Edvic glanced over his shoulder and shrugged. "I don't blame him for keeping you safe." He reached out and patted my shoulder. "My, you're almost as tall as Tiaë. Walk with me." My second father gestured to the stairs, expecting me to walk down ahead of him.

I pursed my lips and looked past him down at Nol's room on the left. Edvic moved so he was in my way again. He smiled and I noticed the rim of red around his eyes. Was it from drinking or had he been crying? I looked toward Wennië's and his room. He must have just helped

Wennië to bed, in her few sips of wine drunken stupor. I'd forgotten what a lightweight she was. So why had she done it?

"Edvic? Are you okay? You and Wennië? My presence must remind you of An'di."

"It does, but they are such fond memories. Don't regret visiting. We're happy to have seen you. Now…" He hunched down so he was closer to my level. While not nearly as tall as Nol, there wasn't a single *enda* besides my grandmother who was as short as I was. "Nolan said something about letters?"

I groaned. "What a sneaky shit," I muttered. Of course, they'd met in the hall and designed this intervention together.

He threw his head back and laughed a full belly laugh, breaking the silence in the house. "Hallanevaë, I never thought I'd witness you as an adult, foul language and all. My son is a sneaky shit, isn't he? I suppose it goes with the territory. Come down and we'll find you supplies."

I stomped down the stairs in front of Edvic and followed him to his study, pouting the whole way. He entered his large study first, a cluttered place with papers, books, and a few *merili* in a bowl. While it was none of my business, I immediately wanted to know what the *merili* were for.

Instead of a desk, Edvic had made a counter that wrapped around three walls of the room. Above it were two shelves built into the wall, full of books. Below the counter were several columns of drawers and shelves holding various things that I'd imagined he'd need as a teacher.

He pulled out papers, a pen and a black inkwell. He shoved the bundle of stuff into my arms. "Don't be angry with him too long. He truly has good intentions. I'll make you some room here, and you can get started."

Looking at the writing supplies I was holding, I realized one big flaw in the plan. "Actually…"

Edvic stopped moving things, his delight wilted to disappointed.

"Would you help me?" I shifted from foot to foot as my face got warmer and warmer. "As you can see, my *Aemirin* isn't the greatest. But it's even worse than that. I realized I've forgotten how to read it. Please help me write the letters?"

Edvic's mouth dropped open. My incisor hooked my lip ring as I waited for his response. How embarrassing, admitting my illiteracy to the *endao* who'd taught me in the first place.

I squeezed my eyes shut, tugging at the ring as I waited. The look of horror on his face was too much to keep silent. "It's ridiculous, I know. I speak and write in twelve human languages. I can remember enough *Aemirin* to talk to you, and a little *Mellorian* and *Pequwynian*. But I can't even read in my first language. It's pathetic—"

"I'll do it. I'll write a twenty-page letter, I don't care. There's no reason to be embarrassed. When would you have practiced?" He placed one hand on my shoulder and cupped my cheek with the other. "The good news is that you'll pick it up quickly because you learned it already." He pulled the paper out of my arms. "Now sit and tell me what you want to say."

"Please, don't tell Nol."

"It's our secret." He winked. "But Hally? When have you ever been able to keep things from him?"

I wasn't going to delve into that topic with Nol's father. Edvic didn't need to know our issues. "I'd just rather not see the look on his face that you just gave me. It's worse coming from him."

He wrote three letters for me that night. A general one, giving my parents updates, explaining everything. Edvic just kept writing. The other two were personal for each of them, and hopefully, they'd feel my hugs through the paper. That was all I could do.

15

ABSO-FUCKING-LUTELY NOT. SANAE WAS huge. Like, bigger than the orcas in Puget Sound—no, like humpbacks in Hawaii big. I was not getting on a humpback-whale-sized dragon.

"Come on, Hallë. You're embarrassing yourself."

"Like I give a shit. I am *not* getting on that thing." I should have realized why we'd been waiting until she arrived. I'd been laser focused on my parents to ask why we'd waited. This made sense, but not with me. I was willing to test the distance limitation of the band.

"She's not a thing and riding her is safer than riding in a car."

"She can flip whenever she wants, and down, down, down I go to my death. At least a car has a roof and seat belts!"

"Not your motorcycle."

I stomped my foot and set my hands on my hips. "That's different. Bikes are small, they stay on the ground, and I have gear to protect me. She breathes fire and has five claws on each hand the size of your sword. No fucking way." I pointed at him when he failed to hide his grin. "This is not funny!"

Sanae had to rest for almost two hours. She'd practically crashed and didn't want to leave the yard without seeing Nol. I thought *Zayuri* dragons were all black. Due to her youth—in her fifth century—her belly was black and her back was a dark red color with a few spots of brighter red at the base of her tail. Instead of a muzzle like I'd imagined she'd have, her head was shaped more like a cat's: small nose, large eyes, and tiny pointed ears. One ear was dark red and the other was black, an endearing quality that gave a few points in her favor. I still wasn't riding on her. Why wasn't there a riding saddle? That would've been nicer.

"You can't fall off her. Her magic is in harmony with mine, and it protects us from air pressure, wind speed, and *falling down, down, down to your death.*"

"We'll freeze."

"Her body heat keeps us warm. *Zayuri* have been riding dragons for as long as we've known, and maybe they even brought them here to *Endae.*"

"What do you mean, 'brought them here', Nolan?" Wennië asked, as she handed me a strong tea with a light nutty flavor. I never liked it as a kid, but things change. Steam rolled off it in the cold morning air. It didn't taste like coffee, but it was smooth and had a good pick-me-up. I'd forgotten that she and my mother drank it almost every morning.

"Murë! Don't give her more tea." Nol closed the bag attached to Sanae's neck, with all of our crap in it, and patted her under her chin. "I'm trying to get her on Sanae, not keep her off."

"It'll give her more courage. Plus, you've had more than her."

"Because I was up earlier," he whined. "Nothing was stopping her from getting up when I did."

He'd even tried waking me up—that hadn't gone over well. The *endao* was digging his hole so damn deep with me that I wasn't sure he'd find his way out.

"Sanae promises to protect you, just like she protects me. We have to go, Hallë."

"We're still waiting on Edvic!" I sipped my tea, nice and slowly. Nol groaned, exasperated with me and his parents. "So impatient," I whispered to Wennië. It served him so damn right. Broken promises, not trusting me—even though I had planned to sneak out—waking me up before the day even began.

"Nolan and Sanae are a great pair, but that doesn't mean there weren't struggles. It took them a while to adjust." She snaked an arm around my shoulders.

"That's not helping, Murë," Nol yelled to his mother from Sanae's side at the edge of the meadow.

Sanae had landed and napped the night before ,on the side of the house that faced away from the city and the Tree of Connection. The neighboring house was past a small meadow, the perfect size for *Zayuri* dragon landings. Wennië and I stood in the front of their house, sipping our tea, forty feet away from Nol's dragon. My parents' house was to our left, behind the large *Hassop* tree that split the road.

We weren't leaving right away, but I hadn't even gone near Sanae and Nol wanted me to acclimate to her. Don't get me wrong, I liked dragons, but never had I considered getting near one, let alone riding one. I'd take my chances here.

"You go. I'll stay here."

"Don't make me drag you."

I paused with my cup almost to my mouth. "You're not touching me."

"I'm serious. I can't leave you here and you know it."

"I'll walk."

Nol gave me a flat look.

"You needn't worry, partner of my Nolan. No harm will come to you on my back."

My breath billowed around me as I looked around for the owner of the female voice, because it could not be who my brain thought it was.

"What's wrong?" Wennië asked after she'd taken another sip.

"Um...nothing wrong exactly."

"My Nolan says time is short." I couldn't deny it any longer. Sanae, Nol's dragon, was talking to me. *"I understand your hesitance, but he tells me you are very brave, and if anyone can overcome their fears, it's you. My heart was full of anger when the Zayuri told me Nolan had stayed with you. But now I see why. My Nolan has a light where once there was darkness in his heart. He can stay with you if you bring his light out more. Will you do that?"*

I was stunned. Wennië had said something a while ago, but I hadn't caught it. After Sanae finished, I realized Nol had come to stand in front of me. Had he said something, too?

"*Why haven't you seen that light before?*" I thought to Sanae.

"*Sad things. Love left him, but he always was sad, because you are his light and you were gone. I see now. We will ride and help my Nolan's Zayuri.*"

Only *Zayuri* that were linked to a dragon could do this. It was part of their magic, and I hadn't been born with it. "*How is this possible?*"

"*You are his light, the other part of him, so I decided to try. And I was right!*"

Nol grabbed my shoulders and shook me, spilling tea all down my shirt. "Hallë! Answer me," he said in *Aemirin*.

"Ow, Nol!"

I called the tea to the surface, or at least the water out of my clothes, and released it into the air. Now my clothes smelled like tea. I had half a mind to throw the rest at him.

"Look what you did!" Not thinking, I snapped at him in English. "Give me a fucking minute. Did she not tell you?"

"Who told me what?"

Gathering my thoughts, I went back to *Aemirin*. It was going to be a challenge to think in one damn language. I kept jumping between French, English, and *Aemirin*. At least he knew all three. "Sanae...she says she won't let me fall."

"She talked to you?" Wennië and Nol said together.

I threw up my free hand. "It's because of our bond, she says. Something about light."

Nol's eyes darted away, thinking. Then he turned to Sanae. "True, but a little forewarning would have been nice."

I swore she was considering roasting him right then and there.

He shoved his shoulders back. "That's just..."

Wennië and I continued to sip our tea. I leaned over to her and muttered, "Do they do this often?"

"Wouldn't know. He never comes around anymore. It's hard for him to be back."

Our families seemed to know about the issues Nol was dealing with, the shit he didn't want to tell me. He said he was scared I'd think of him differently. This shit was coming to a head, and I was about to sit him down for a heart-to-heart. I was his *muranildë*, and he was supposed to be able to tell me anything. To make it even more one-sided, he knew more about me, and I'd given him space.

Nol's argument with his dragon interrupted my thoughts. "She does not. And no, that isn't what that means."

I stopped listening to Nol argue with his dragon and looked at Wennië. "I'm still mad at you."

She brought her cup to her chest for warmth. "But you understand?"

With her smug little attitude, I almost didn't hug her. But that would have been petty. There was a very strong possibility I might never see her again. I pulled her in for a one-arm hug. "What matters is that I still love you."

"I'm so grateful I got to see you all grown up." She patted my hair and let me go. "You look so much like your murë and your yalu. Will you let me make you another vest? Is that something they wear there?"

My grandmother, Nol, Tolwe, and now Wennië, had told me I was a mix of my mother and my grandmother. If I ever had the chance, I was going to stand in front of the mirror with my mother to see where they were getting this from. I pulled myself out of my thoughts and focused on Wennië. "That would be lovely."

"Blue or green? Both would look stunning on you."

I loved her blue dye, but she'd created a hue of green to match my eyes and loved using it for my clothes.

"Blue. We'll do blue first," Wennië determined before I could pick. "The *Aemina* blue. You need something to signify our country. I can make you a few other things, too. We're never letting you go again. Here or there, it doesn't matter. We're all so very proud. Ambassador of our entire realm."

"Hally!" Edvic called as he rounded the corner of their house after delivering my letters. By the time he reached us, he was out of breath, and my heart was in my throat. "They love the letters. Here, Orin wants you to have this."

Edvic held out his hand, his fist closed around something from my dad.

I held my hand out, but then retracted it. They'd kept me away from my parents and now it was okay to touch…whatever Edvic had?

"I've cleaned it and myself thoroughly," Edvic assured me.

"But yesterday—"

"Touching Tiaë is more extensive than a tiny present. There's more risk of infection if your mom hugged you."

"My mom knows that." Not that she didn't love me, but we were never as close as my dad and me. "It was just a reaction. If she's prepared for it, she'll stay back."

"No dear, she wouldn't. Given the chance, if we saw An'di again we would never be satisfied standing at a distance."

"But she knows I'm here and she isn't pounding at the door, demanding to see me. If she can do that, she won't come too close."

"Hally, it's hard to explain without seeing it, but Taië gets confused and forgets things easily now. We don't know why. Seeing you briefly isn't long enough for her to register that you're really here. You can't go over there."

I looked over Edvic's shoulder, at the tree that split the road in two. Two minutes away, tops.

"Sweetie, take the present." Edvic lifted his hand again. "Your dad wants you to have it. Please?"

My hands trembled as I waited. His fingers brushed my palm as he opened his hand. I'd thought it would be one of the toggles that my father liked to make. They were my favorite. A small wooden ring laid in the middle of my palm. Delicate night star trillium flowers twined around the outside, weaving in and out like a flower chain. Not only had he etched the three petals of the flowers, but the three leaves, too, and if I brought it close enough to my face, I could make out the three sepals of each flower. Only magical tools could have carved them.

"He's pretty sure it will fit," he explained as I looked at them. "He asks if you'll visit your murë in her dreams, he thinks it would be good for her."

"When did he do this?" I knew my father's work, the tools, infused with magic to create the intricate details, but this? It would have taken much longer than a few hours. And I sensed much more than just the presence of this *imolegin* from his tools.

"He said he made it years ago, intending to make it a *meril*."

"And this..." The things he handed me were even smaller, and I knew right away what they were. All the ear cuffs *Aore* Junae had taken from me the day I was banished. So, he had given them back to my family, like he'd promised. Then I noticed a new one. A wooden one with even smaller flowers. "I'm glad to see you're still wearing the cuff Nolan made you."

Nol preened a little. "I couldn't have found her without it."

I turned the small cuff my father made as I explained how I'd held on to Nol's. "Junae hid it in my pocket. He told Rassel he was looking for something else. I found it later when I was washing my clothes." If it hadn't caught the light at the right moment, I'd have missed the tiny black thing at the bottom of the washtub.

"Getting lost in the woods paid off, didn't it?"

The three of us gave Edvic a flat glare for the silver-lining excuses he always used. The incident as a kid was scary and wasn't talked about much. Nol got in a lot of trouble for encouraging me to go with him on a "wilderness adventure," and it turned out to be a night alone in a hole I'd fallen into.

Edvic's hands waved defensively. "Everything has a reason. It can just take a while and sometimes heartbreak to see our Mother's reasons. If Nolan had never asked Tolwe to make your ear cuff afterward, then he never would have found you in *Rosava*."

What he said was kind of the same thing my grandmother had meant when she'd told Nol it was a twisted fate that had sent me to Earth. If I'd stayed, I'd have died. If I'd stayed, I wouldn't have met the human family I had. Perhaps if Charlie found a cure, our entire people would be saved. But that made it sound too prophecy-ish. And there was no way it had all happened for a reason. The Mother couldn't be that cruel, could she?

"Sure, Edvic," I muttered.

"Here, can I help?" Wennië asked.

When I gave all the cuffs to her, she handed her cup to Edvic. My second mother placed each one on the appropriate ear, and I about cried. Nol slid his hand into mine and squeezed, offering comfort so I didn't get all emotional. There'd been enough of that.

"Your father asked if I could put the new one next to Nolan's, if you don't mind?"

Unable to talk, I nodded. Wennië handed Edvic the little wooden cuff and kissed my cheek. "We'll see you again. And you'll see your parents. I know it. I just do."

Wennië and Edvic gave us both several hugs, before Nol and I walked up to Sanae. Next to her, I felt her heat radiating, like a living furnace. Carefully, I reached out to touch her, and she shifted, startling me. *There is nothing to be scared of*, I chanted to myself as I tried again. The smoothness of her skin surprised me.

I stroked her back and wished my skin was that silky. "I thought dragons had scales."

"They do. They're just very, very small. Be careful if you touch her face. They're more delicate there. And don't put your feet on her *vese*," he said in *Aemirin*.

"Her what?"

He carefully touched the place where her back leg touched her lower belly. "Here."

"Haunches. Horses don't like that either. Not that you're anything like a horse." Nol and I shook our heads, even though Sanae couldn't see it. But she could read our thoughts and saw the animal in my mind.

She huffed anyway, but she was only pretending to be miffed.

"Are you ready? It's like riding a bike. Hold on to me."

I nodded. Nol got up and reached out to help me up. I just touched his fingertips. Nol groaned in annoyance.

"I'm so sorry I'm short. I'll work on improving my stature to make your life easier."

He rolled his eyes. "Jump."

"Sanae, I'm sorry if I step on you!" I backed up and prepared to make a running jump. With a boost of magic at the last second instead of using Sanae as a stool, I shot up. I didn't consider how smooth

Sanae's scales were and almost slipped off her other side, but I grabbed Nol's waist just as Nol grabbed my arms. "Sorry! I thought I'd help."

"*C'yo*, Hallë. You're light, but damn that momentum makes you heavier than a—"

"Finish that sentence. I dare you."

He shut up, I settled in, and Sanae jumped into the air. Gravity played by the rules, and I felt myself slip back. I screamed.

"You're fine," Nol hollered, his voice barely audible in the wind.

Her scales were too silky. "No, I am not. I'm going to slide right off. I want off. Like hell I'm going now. Go down." I felt his body shake with laughter as I panicked. "This isn't funny, Nol!"

"It is, actually. You're not going to fall. Just calm down."

Sanae settled in the air, her wings whooshing twice, and I wasn't slipping anymore. This wasn't so bad. I could do this. I looked down to find we weren't higher than the tree line. We'd have to go up more. She'd slowed her ascent for me.

"*Ready to go higher?*" Sanae thought to me.

"*Sae!*" *No!* I yelled, but she ignored me. This time, though, she flew up at a more gradual incline. It was still scary, but I realized my body only felt like it was sliding back, and her magic kept me in place.

"You wanna loosen your grip?" Nol asked.

"Um…"

He patted my arm. "It's okay. Maybe in a little bit, then."

"You both need to stop laughing at me," I grumbled, glued to Nol's back.

"I HAVE TO PEE!" And I was hungry and freezing. I wasn't sure how Nol knew which way to go, but the sky stayed dark, except for the faint dusky glow in the east of the constant pre-dawn. The wind made it impossible to have any lengthy conversation, but I knew Nol had made this trip before and I trusted him.

"Can you hold on a little longer? We're almost there."

"How long is *almost there*?"

Nol didn't answer right away, but I knew he knew.

"Nol?" I drew out his name in warning.

"Two human hours-ish," Nol yelled back.

"I don't care which side the *ish* it's on, I can't wait. Sanae's tired, too."

"She did not tell you that."

"No, but her wing beats have become more erratic. Just a little rest, please, Nol?"

Silence for a moment. "Fine. You both together are insufferable."

"Us girls gotta stick together. Down. Now." But Sanae was already making her descent. I just wanted to bug Nol.

As Sanae landed, I didn't feel like I was falling off, but I scrunched my eyes shut as she touched down.

"Do you want to get off first?" Nol asked once Sanae stopped moving. "I can hold your arm and help you slide down."

The ground wasn't as close when she was standing and I couldn't use her leg as a stool. Sanae was much larger than a horse, but I could use the same principle to get down.

I scooted back, leaned forward and swung my right leg over until I was on my belly. A moment later I started slipping and there was no saddle to grab. Nol grabbed my wrist before I fell. A bolt of fear shot through me, just for a moment. The position was too similar to the nightmares I constantly had. The faceless creature almost always held some part of me above the Starless Abyss. With Nol's face mostly in shadow, looked just like it.

I tucked my feet under me to help me pull away. Falling was better than being near it. "Let go!" I tugged, but it didn't.

It began to pull me up. "Hey! It's me. I've got you." I swallowed and tried to think. Nol was pulling me up. But when I looked up again, all I saw was the faceless creature. I wouldn't let it take me.

I yanked and bucked trying to get away. Still it wouldn't let go. I screamed, but again, I noticed, there was sound. There was never sound in my nightmares, my screams were always silent. The noise gave me pause and then I felt it: Nol's calming energy as he opened the link and offered me comfort.

"I'm sorry." I panted, not looking at him. If I looked up, I feared my mind would go back to my nightmares. "I'm—"

Nol pulled me up, this time into his lap. "I've told you, never apologize for your night terrors. It's not your fault."

"But I wasn't asleep. I shouldn't have panicked." He had looked so much like the being that haunted my dreams. No eyes, no nose, but he didn't have a mouth full of black, needle thin teeth. I tucked my head under his chin until my heart slowed, my thoughts wandering to all the shitty things my mind made up while I was sleeping. But I was awake now. "I'm awake. I'm awake." I swallowed—my throat was too dry. "Nol, tell me I'm awake."

"You're awake." He didn't chuckle and he didn't have an amused tone in his voice. "You're awake," he whispered.

"Tell me one more time."

He squeezed me tight and pressed his face to the top of my head. "You're awake." We stayed like that for a few more seconds. "Maybe I should get down first."

I nodded. "That might be better."

Nol kissed the top of my head and then helped me settle on Sanae's back before swinging around and jumping off. If I pointed my foot, I could touch the top of Nol's head. Not that far. Not the Starless Abyss.

When he lifted his arms, his fingers came to my knees. "Roll over and slide down on your stomach," Nol called up. "Ready?"

I swallowed and looked down at him. His face was still in shadow, but instead of panicking again, I conjured a light orb and floated it above our heads. "Yep." I did what he said, his hands curled under my arms as I dropped, and before I knew it, I was down.

Even after my feet were firmly on the ground, Nol's hands stayed under my arms. "Do you need another hug?"

"No, but thank you." Only he'd understand why I'd panicked, as he could see and change my nightmares. "I actually really need to pee."

Nol chuckled and let go. "I'll start collecting firewood then. You're frozen solid."

Nol was arranging a pile of wood when I got back, as Sanae sat on her haunches watching him. They both perked up and looked over as I came out of the trees. I'd seemed to have interrupted their mental conversation. The bag that held all our stuff was on the ground near him and open. Wennië had packed the provisions, and knowing her, it was probably all healthy stuff.

"Did she give us anything except vegetables?" I asked, but Nol's only response was a grunt. Which meant no.

He cracked a branch in two, sat on the ground against a log that he'd clearly pulled over, and picked up something that he'd laid on his jacket. Had he found sweets? I hurried over before he could steal all of them. A quick look through the sack of food Wennië had packed for us and found nothing of the kind.

"Hey!" I let the sack drop back in the bag. "Did you take all—"

Nol held one pastry out for me. A small bag was on his other side and it looked full of more goodies. Edvic baked the best sweets. "What else did your dad sneak in there?"

"I don't know what you're talking about. These were the only two I found."

"Liar." I was hoping for sticky rolls, but Nol wouldn't have hidden those from me. "What else?"

"Just a few more of these. Anything else would have gotten everything messy."

I took a bite of the crunchy, round pastry. Cinnamon and honey baked inside without the stickiness.

Nol lifted his head, looked at Sanae and pointed at the fire. The mental conversations would take some getting used to.

Sanae stood up and took the few steps needed to stand near the wood pile. Without any warning, a bright light filled her mouth, and a basketball-sized fireball hit Nol's pile of wood. I dropped my pastry and scrambled over the log Nol was leaning against. The force of the fireball flung the smoking sticks in all directions.

Just when I was getting comfortable being near a dragon! I knew they could spit fire, but seeing it up close and five feet in front of me? No fucking way.

A deep thudding sound, almost like helicopter blades whomping, came from Sanae's chest. Only after Nol burst out laughing did I realize Sanae was laughing at my reaction.

"That's not funny!" But they didn't stop laughing. "You could have warned me."

"Then it wouldn't have been as amusing." But his laughter had calmed and Sanae's whoops had stopped.

"This entire ride has been scary for me, and you two had the gall to purposely scare me. Shame on the both of you."

"It wasn't on purpose, but it was welcome relief. Come sit and share some food. Murë packed *etyin* rolls, and I saved your pastry."

Another whoop of a laugh from Sanae. "*I would never harm you. My Nolan speaks truth, we didn't mean to scare you. We are both sorry.*"

How could I stay mad when a dragon apologized to me? "From now on, don't do anything that *might* scare me about you and we'll call it even."

"*That is fair. I will find my meal now.*" I got an image of a river that she'd noticed as she thought of the taste of fish.

I crawled back over the log and retrieved my pastry. Sanae walked far enough away that the gust of air from her take off didn't blow out the fire. After a moment of pouting, I sat beside Nol. He handed me one of Wennië rolls, not as in bread rolls, but more like sushi rolls without the rice and fish. Thin layers of nutritious and filling vegetables, a nut spread between them, all wrapped up in dried seaweed. A flash of despair hit me, knowing that my parents would have done something similar.

"She made us enough for the whole trip. I know they're not your favorite, but they'll last us and—"

"Stop. It's fine." They were Nol's and his sister's favorite. More of a staple at their house. My dad didn't like them either.

"What are you smiling at?"

I hadn't realized I was. "Did you know my dad and I would sneak these over to An'di when Wennië brought them to picnics?"

"What? You didn't."

"Mmhm." As I chewed my first bite, I realized why I'd never liked them. She didn't add salt to the nut spread. I swallowed the bite, but handed the rest to Nol. "True. She never found out either. Tell her and I'll tattoo a penis on your forehead."

"As if you could hold me down long enough."

"I have my ways. Don't test me." I reached for the sack of food and found some dried fruit and nuts. "This will do."

"You'll have to eat it at some point. It's the most filling thing we have."

"I'm not like you, Nol. I can live off...these." I shook my hand with the nuts in it. "Besides, she also packed *dyamas* sticks." I grabbed one and bit the end of the crunchy veggie. These were almost as nutritious as the rolls and Wennië liked to cut them into sticks like carrots. Nol liked to dip them in the nut spread—yuck. I always preferred mine plain.

Endai weren't vegetarians—well, not as a whole—and neither was Nol's family, but Wennië did push veggies and fruits before meat, sweets, and dairy. That, and they'd last us for the four days we'd be traveling. "Is *Lairenya* really two hours away from here?" I took another bite of *dyamas*.

"That's a rough estimate." Nol grabbed a stick and tossed it on the fire. "We're going much slower than Sanae and I are used to."

"Because of the extra weight or because I can't stay in the shadows longer?"

"Mostly the shadows. We can normally make the trip in two days, but then, we don't make the detour to *Lairenya* either."

"How do you know where we're going? *Zayuri* spells?"

"A *Zayuri* spell, shadow traveling, and mathematics." He leaned over and pointed into the sky. "See *Balesca*? The bright blue star? I'll use that once we leave *Lairenya* to navigate our way to *Aemina*. We'll sleep for a few hours in *Lairenya*, but then we have to stay awake most of the way."

"For four days? That's impossible."

"We have to."

"Nol, I'm not trained to stay awake for long lengths of time like you. What if I fall asleep? Will I fall off Sanae? And be serious this time."

"I've never fallen asleep on her, so I don't know. We might find out if you can't keep your eyes open."

"You better not let me fall, Twynolan. If so, the moment I'm old enough in the next life I will thrash you."

"Stop worrying, I won't let you fall." He rummaged around the sack, then pulled out the tin of tea leaves, two cups, and the bladder of water. "Tea?"

I grabbed my cup and jutted out my chin at him as I grumbled about my possible demise.

Nol poured me some water and I took a large pinch of the tea—the same morning tea that Wennië had given me. Warming the water with a thought, I hunched over it and looked into the fire. "Do you think *Lairenya* is close enough to leave me so you can get to *Aemina* faster?"

Nol didn't answer right away. "No. *Lairenya* is about as far as...England? I'm not sure, the map on the plane's screen wasn't very accurate. Plus, we're on land, and our flight to France was over the sea. Either way, it's still too far." He stuck his finger in the water, pushing down the leaf bits. "Even if it was close enough, I wouldn't leave you there." His eyes caught mine and he lifted an eyebrow. "We can't find Gil together if you're in *Lairenya*."

"Are you sure it's not because I'm your responsibility and you can't let me out of your sight?"

"And that." He smirked as he messed with me, or was he? "Sanae should be back by the time we're finished with our tea and then I want to leave."

Sanae was late getting back, and so I got an extra twenty minutes of ground time. I made sure to thank her for it, too.

ACCORDING TO NOL, WE'D traveled for six hours total from *Rudairn* to the northern *Zayuri* outpost of *Lairenya*, an empty snow-covered land which seemed to have only one building a hundred yards away, a grove of stunted, sad-looking trees in the distance, and nothingness everywhere. With the sunrise now hours behind us, the only light we had were our light globes above us. He'd cast two globes, but I cast five more. The void around us made me twitch. Nol grunted as he threw his leg over and slid down Sanae's side first.

"Good." He patted Sanae's neck, nodding like they'd agreed on something. "Sanae is comfortable with four hours of rest."

"Just four? I thought we'd have more time."

He squinted and shoved his hands into his pockets, waiting for me to follow him. "Our other stops were too long, so hurry and get down here. You need to eat and nap. I don't want to hear you bitching when we leave, either."

"All right then, *Dad*. You've sure gotten bossy since leaving your parents' house."

Not a twitch of an expression on his face as he stared up, waiting. "Technically, didn't I get bossy when I restricted you to the house last night?"

I ground my teeth and tried to get my limbs moving. "I wasn't going to go."

Nol grabbed my ankle and shook it. "Do you think I didn't see right through your facade? Suddenly talking to us like there was nothing wrong? No, you were going to wait until we were passed out to jump from An'di's window like you always used to. Stop messing around."

"I'm not, I just can't move well." Holding my breath, I swung my left leg over—or tried to. It didn't want to move. With a mighty effort, I wrapped my arms around my thigh and pulled. It wasn't fair that his *Zayuri* magic and Sanae's magic, combined kept them warm. If only he could share it. Instead, their body heat was all they could provide. I'd need to find a better way to keep warm for the rest of the trip.

He let out a deliberately long sigh. "Do you want help again?"

At last, my legs obeyed me. "No." Like before, I rolled over onto my belly to slide off. But I'd leaned over too far as I rolled and with a squeak, I slid down sideways.

"*Tullaca*!" Nol cussed as I fell on him. "Ow."

Lying in the snow, on top of Nol and staring up into the utter darkness of space, I couldn't help but laugh. *Ow.* I mean, after everything I'd seen him do, falling on him was 'Ow'? "I'm sorry! I didn't realize how close to the edge I was."

Nol shoved me over so he could get out from under me. I was still lying in the snow when he sat up, one leg propped up as he probably looked for the loose screw in my head. But what was funny—not funny—was the bloody nose. Not severe, but I had no doubt it hurt.

"What is your problem?" he asked, all huffy and serious as he stanched the bleeding.

"I tapped your nose!"

It took him a minute to get it. He stared at me as I laughed and rolled away toward Sanae. Something hit my ear, cold and hard. Another smack to my shoulder. I rolled back toward Nol in time to catch him throwing a third snowball at me.

"Hey!" I ducked my head and snow hit my neck. "Come on. It's not like I meant to fall." That seemed to be it. "Done?" No answer.

With my hair in my face, I rolled onto my back and sat up. Had he left? My fingers were so numb that I couldn't tuck my hair behind my ears and I couldn't check to make sure I still had all my ear cuffs.

Sanae moved from her spot. Now that we weren't on her back, she was going to rest like Nol had suggested. I rolled my eyes. He wasn't our boss. To that thought, I got, "*He is my Nolan.*" Did that mean something more than I thought?

"Can you stand?" Nol's voice came from above and behind me.

I tipped my head back. Nol stared down at me, nose no longer bleeding. "Huh?" He'd asked something... "Oh! Gimme a second to warm up and I can walk."

Nol scoffed. "*Etwa*," *whatever*. He reached down and picked our bag up out of the snow—when had he taken that off of Sanae?

The magical energy I'd begun to build in my palms started to tingle, then sting, as the heat warmed my hands. I backed off, and tried to level the temperature so I wouldn't burn my legs before transferring that heat. Sharp pinpricks stung under my skin as I rubbed down my thighs to my ankles. My legs began to shiver. I hadn't realized I'd been *that* cold.

"We're going to have to think of something to keep me warm."

He squatted down in front of me, took in my now shivering body and cussed under his breath. "Agreed." He puffed out his cheeks and watched me as I warmed up. "We've already reduced the amount of time in the shadows."

I tried not to feel guilty about that. My lungs and body couldn't handle longer times spent without heat and oxygen.

"Don't." Nol placed his hand on my knee. "It's not your fault. You're not *Zayuri* and you're actually doing well with the jumps we've already taken."

"Don't coddle me. You'd be there in a few more hours if I weren't with you."

"True. But we'll never get there if we reduce the time in the shadows." His eyebrows shot up and his head tilted as he thought of something. "You could use my jacket."

I gave him the flat look that his idea deserved. "Your *Zayuri* jacket, with your sword on it? Isn't that against the rules or something?" Plus, it'd be huge on me.

Nol shrugged. "Do you have another solution?"

He knew I didn't, not a good one anyway. I squinted at him.

"Let's go, the heat of the lodge will warm you more efficiently."

He was right, but getting a little more feeling would help me walk better. "My method is working. You can go ahead if you want."

"If you are too proud to let me carry you, you can lean on my arm."

"I'm not too proud—"

Oh, the look he gave me shut me right up. "I'm not weak, Nol."

He pinched the hair that I couldn't move due to my numb fingers, and tucked it behind my ears. "You aren't weak." He touched an ear cuff and then another. "A pain in the ass, yes, but never weak."

He offered his hand. I accepted the help to stand and the offer to lean. He let me hobble along beside him to the building—I refused to call the tiny thing a lodge. But it was big enough that we could get food, stay warm, and get at least an hour of sleep.

16

We'd traveled thousands of miles east on the back of a dragon. The sun had been behind us the entire way. Sometimes it had winked at us over the horizon, but when it did, Nol pushed Sanae faster to get ahead of it. If we didn't, he couldn't use the shadows to travel.

At times, I cast my own magic to warm myself, but like in running, I could only go for so long without exhausting myself. Luckily, my band hadn't siphoned any of my energy while in the air. I kept waiting for it, but nothing happened.

"We have to ride hard for the rest of the way." The breath from Nol's soft words drifted past me as we watched the sunrise light the tips of the mountain range. We sat atop a big boulder at the edge of a mountainside clearing, reminding me of the *Sound of Music*. Sanae was curled up on the other side of a cooling campfire she'd helped make two hours ago.

"How much longer?" I warmed my tea again and sipped. Not too fast, as this was the last cup I'd get and it was keeping my fingertips warm.

"I hope to get there at about midday." Nol grabbed my cup and took another sip. The butt couldn't get his own because he'd broken his.

"So, seven more hours?"

"We will stay lower, and it will be during the day. The sun should keep you warmer." He gave me back my tea, and I pulled the cup into his jacket, which I'd wrapped myself in, legs and all. "Can you handle that?" He held his breath. Waiting for my complaint, perhaps? His shoulder bumped into mine, and he leaned over, his head resting on mine. "Hallë?"

"Hmm?"

"Did you fall asleep sitting up?"

"No." Another sip, more so to keep it close to warm my lips—and guard it. "There's no choice, so it's a rhetorical question."

He reached for my cup again, and I lowered it. He wouldn't dare reach in there. "You can keep my *Zayuri* jacket the whole way."

I'd refused to give it back to him at this stop. "I might not give it back at all. No wonder why you wear it all the time." Even if it was several sizes too big, and the sword was heavy, it was so comfortable.

He chuckled. "You've done so well. I'm proud of you."

I rolled my eyes up. "Gee, thanks." I ducked, knowing what was coming even before I'd said it. Sure enough, he reached in to tap my nose. I giggled as he tried to move my arms and the jacket enough to get to my face, but he gave up after a few moments.

He'd never said he was proud of me before. Kids don't say that kind of shit to each other; we were all just trying to make it to the next stage. So I'd never expected such a compliment from him. Within these past two months, I'd been more than proud of him. He didn't do well with change, but he'd adapted on Earth easily enough. Yet, decades ago, he'd embraced the *Zayuri* path—and that was a huge, life-altering change.

He sat back up but kept close to keep warm. "*Quturode racar omeya'a,*" *You're a pain in my ass.*

Forcing myself to stop smiling, I rested my forearms back on my knees. "Not as much as you are in mine."

"When the sun has risen twice its distance, we'll leave and head southeast."

"That's an hour." We'd already rested for two.

"I don't have the heart to wake Sanae yet. You should take a nap, too."

"What about you? And don't give me the 'I'm too cool to sleep because the *Zayuri* trained me' bullshit. You still gotta sleep, and you haven't done much of that."

Nol shifted, and a few pebbles crunched under his shoe. "I can't. Every time I try, I picture *Aetyru* destroyed or Gil lifeless on the ground. It takes everything in me not to push you both even harder."

"Put that way..." I muttered. "Truth? I can't sleep either, not since that first night."

"*Sitam,*" *I know.* "I've watched you try." Weren't we a know-it-all, then?

"You need to stop being so nosy and pay attention to yourself." The jacket started slipping back again, and I set my cup in my lap to adjust it. "Once we're done, we can both sleep."

Neither of us mentioned the alternative. All we knew was that the terrorists had demanded Nol come tomorrow morning. We didn't know what would happen after that.

Nol leaned in and whispered, "Sanae is stirring."

"If she wants to start earlier, I'm up for it."

"I want to see the blue pallor of your skin gone before we go up in the air."

I shook my bright red fingertips at him. Not blue.

"All over." He hadn't said it in a teasing or sexual manner, but it sure was funny when his brain had caught up with his mouth. A heartbeat later, he leaned away. "That is not what I meant."

I tried to keep the laugh in. I really did. I normally felt awkward from his teasing, but he'd never been *that* forward. He pushed me away, making a show of his indignation.

He got on his feet and crouched beside me. "We leave in an hour, you pain in the ass. If you weren't so cold, I'd take back my jacket." Then he left me to watch the rest of the sunrise and chuckle over his embarrassment.

EVEN WITH THE REST this morning, Sanae was pushing herself hard to stay in the air. By late morning, we were flying over the foothills of the mountains we'd seen the sun glow up earlier. The Valley of *Aetyru* was on the other side. My stomach fluttered at the thought of seeing it, not only for the first time, but at a bird's-eye view.

Sanae banked right and caught air. We flew up with the current, then soared down.

"Hallë, look." Nol sat up all the way, letting go with both hands and scaring the shit out of me, because I was holding on to him to stay on the dragon. He twisted until I could see ahead of him. "Look!" He pointed left.

This was what I'd missed. Ancient forest from mountain to horizon. The Valley of *Aetyru* lay below us. I scanned the horizon for a particular color, but there was nothing besides green in sight.

Nol knew what I was looking for, the place I'd expected my fate to take me as a kid. "We're not close enough to see the *Aetyru* spires."

He gave me a few more moments to look at the sea of trees before he settled back down. I tightened my grip around him and rested my cheek on his back again. We coasted down the mountains into the valley, the sun at our backs, the clouds above, and the beautiful forest below.

Sanae's words filled my thoughts. *When we are done, I will fly you over the capital if you would like?*

That would be lovely, Sanae.

BY MIDAFTERNOON, SANAE BANKED left for the last time. The capital was just ahead. Hints of darker blues, teals, and greens of moonstone on the Starborn Palace shimmered in the sunlight. I didn't see the moonstone spire of the Assembly of *Aemina*, though. A chill went through me. Both the palace and the Assembly of *Aemina* were built with onyx and flint and separated by a courtyard, they were next to each other in the city spiral. Or supposed to be.

Nol's yell startled me from my thoughts. "Hallë, there! The outpost is those five buildings away from the road."

"You mean by the huge meadow? Yeah." The largest building was as big as my house in Seattle, but the trees that encompassed them kept them well hidden from the road.

"We made it." Nol leaned over and patted Sanae on the shoulder. "You did it."

Thank the Mother.

Sanae aimed for the grass and flower meadow, her speed increasing. Sanae's descent faltered, and her wings fluttered twice. She adjusted and continued. With a whip that rang in my ears, Sanae's wings collapsed. There was no time to scream or think.

"*Tuck down!*" Sanae thought in my head. I obeyed, tucking my head in as close to her as possible. The world seemed to stop, and moments later, we slammed into the ground. Sanae's body toppled to the right, and her wing bent at an unnatural angle.

As she rolled, Nol twisted, grabbed me, and leapt off. It felt like we were abandoning her. Squeezing my eyes shut and not giving a shit about the slave band, I pictured our trajectories. If I did this quick enough, I could save all three of us.

My magic wrapped around Sanae to pull her toward us while I forced us to slow. I'd be her anchor, slowing us both down. This all *had* to work. The surrounding air thickened to a gel-like the density to cushion our fall and stop Sanae. Like a rubber band, Sanae snapped back, but the thick air I'd created slowed her slide. Nol and I hit the ground next, our contact only as hard as falling on Ray's trampoline.

My mind let go of the complicated combination of magic all at once. I gasped in the thinner, breathable air. My lungs inflated a moment later, but I threw myself forward, scrambling to make sure Sanae was all right. It might've taken Nol a minute to realize his bones weren't broken.

"Sanae!" I screamed, sprinting back to the dragon I'd been terrified of three days ago. The tall grass whipped at my thighs, stinging even through my pants. I almost fell on the uneven ground but righted myself and kept going. Sanae wasn't moving. Had I screwed up and suffocated her? Or had the hard fall and slide killed her? I reached out with my thoughts but got no reply.

Nol yelled my name, but I knew he was fine. We weren't the ones who had slammed into the ground at some hundred miles per hour or more. Reaching Sanae, I touched her soft, warm back and dragged my hand along as I hurried up her body to her head. After a few moments, my heart and breathing slowed enough that I could feel air flowing in and out of her dinner-plate-sized nose.

Nol halted beside me and dropped to his knees. Chest heaving, he placed one hand on Sanae and one on the ground. He rested his forehead on her head.

"She's just unconscious." Nol gulped in more air. "I'm sorry, Sanae."

Voices—people yelling Nol's name. Muffled thumps of feet hit the ground as multiple *Zayuri* warriors ran over to us. All of it, I pushed aside. I was worn out. Not just from days without sleep, but also from the massive use of magic, and I wasn't at my peak strength. It took me a while to realize I was shaking, but I gave myself points for not passing out. My arm tingled as the slave band settled back to neutral after siphoning magical energy off me as I'd cast.

"*Hinam*, are you hurt?" a male *Zayuri* asked. "Check them for injuries."

I'd made sure we hadn't been injured in the fall. Unless Nol had bitten his tongue or something. Someone touched me, and I jerked back. "I'm fine!" I snapped in English, swallowed, and switched to *Aemirin*. "*Husoni Sanae*," help, Sanae.

They let go immediately but argued, "Hallanevaë, I must make sure—"

"*Nol ie mina epenecar*," Nol and I are fine. "It's Sanae who I failed."

"Listen to her," Nol ordered. "She knows her magic. Check Sanae's wings."

Everyone went to work, bustling around us, and then I heard a familiar voice. "Hally, it's me, Jenne. Let me help you up, please. They need to examine Sanae."

I nodded and opened my eyes. I hadn't realized they were closed. Relieved to have someone I knew besides Nol there, I let her help me move away about twenty yards in the tall grass while they folded

Sanae's wing under to inspect the one she'd fallen on. Jenne had come to Earth with Tolwe in March. She'd helped find the fae and *endaen* children, and carried me to a river in Faerie to save me from the *Zayuri* magic of Nol's dagger.

"Will she be okay?" I asked after my breathing had evened out.

Jenne tilted her head and thought for a moment, deciphering my horrible *Aemirin*. "A *Zayuri* outside saw you and came to get everyone. We heard Sanae's crash and ran out."

Shaking my head, I could only stare as a dozen *Zayuri* worked together to move and inspect the humpback whale-sized dragon. Nol stood just out of reach of her, talking with a fellow warrior. His buddy glanced back at me, then continued on with their conversation.

"What will they do if she's really hurt? Do you have dragon healers?"

Jenne watched the working *Zayuri* for a while before answering. "We have two dragons coming over to her. They have their own ways of healing. Would you let me walk you inside? I'm sure using all that power was draining."

"I want to stay." What if Sanae was severely injured and never woke up? Losing her, even if we found Gil, would devastate Nol.

"*Hinam* Nolan told me to walk you inside." Jenne pointed to the group of buildings.

I looked away from Sanae to glare at her. "When?"

"Before I came to you." Her brow furrowed with worry as she checked me all over. "Are you sure you're okay?"

Like hell would I be dismissed. "I'm tired, but I won't collapse." I scrubbed my eyes and shoved my hair back as I watched everyone. "Why didn't I notice sooner? Or start reacting before she hit the ground."

"What you did was...unbelievable, and if it weren't for you, it would have been much worse."

I scoffed. "I'm not a child, Jenne. You don't need to..." I paused, searching for the word.

But Jene got my meaning. "I'm serious."

"You've seen my grandmother do things, too. I'm sure she'd have thought of something better." She'd have thought of something quicker, too.

Jenne didn't argue, but she did find a small mound to sit on.

"What are you doing?" Wouldn't someone yell at her for slacking?

She huffed a short burst of laughter. "I will *not* be the one who leaves *Hinam* Nolan's *muranildë* alone."

Great, he'd found a substitute babysitter. Wouldn't want to let the *savilë* loose on the population. Then I reminded myself Nol was taking his responsibility seriously, not because he didn't trust me, but so he could honestly say I'd been in his, or at least *Zayuri* custody, if someone on the council asked. 'She knows her magic,' he'd said. *Nol trusts me.*

I sat down beside Jenne where the wild grasses and flowers had yet to bloom. After a moment, Jenne pulled her jacket off and laid it next to her. I still had Nol's on, and I wondered briefly if he'd get in trouble for letting me wear it. We had bigger things to deal with than a scolding from his superiors.

No one left Sanae's side, even after two pure black *Zayuri* dragons landed and inspected her. The people backed up and watched. My throat was tight as we waited for an answer. One dragon touched Sanae under her chin. Its deadly sharp claws touching such a sensitive part made me shudder.

"What's wrong?" Jenne whispered.

"Those dragons are fucking scary."

Jenne's giggle took my attention away from the three dragons. "Sorry, it's just...I shouldn't make fun."

I rolled my eyes, remembering when Gileal and Nol had made fun of me for my "attempt" at cussing in *Aemirin*. "Shut up." But when she laughed again, I couldn't help but laugh with her. Call it exhaustion, stress, or a girl thing, but it helped relieve some tension.

She leaned over and bumped her shoulder to mine. "If we find time, we'll work on your *Aemirin*."

"Nol cusses all the time. I should be an expert by now." His was a combination of English and *Aemirin* or muttering in annoyance. Not the best example to follow. "Maybe you can visit me in Seattle. You can try coffee and meet Charlie."

"Really?" Jenne perked up, her gray eyes shining in the sun. "I'd like that."

A deep blue light brought our attention back to the serious emergency in front of us. The light glowed from Sanae's chin for another moment before her body absorbed it, spreading the blue light through her body. The second black dragon placed its paw at the base of her tail, and another glow ignited. The lights expanded until her entire body was glowing like a *Zayuri* sword. After what seemed like forever, her tail moved, pushing the dirt disturbed by our crash. Her head tilted, then her back leg moved.

I jumped, startled and excited. "Did she open her eyes?"

"You'd know. They'll be glowing blue when she does."

I found Jenne's arm and squeezed, praying for that blue glow to come. Sanae's wing moved, first a shudder, then a full shake. Her eyes flew open, like deep sapphire gems glowing. I gasped and was on my feet without even realizing it.

"That means they healed her, right?" I bounced on my toes, too excited to stay as still as Jenne. "She moved her wing. It's not broken."

Jenne shrugged, her eyes glued to the dragons. "We'll find out soon."

We didn't have to wait much longer. The light in her body dimmed, first extinguishing where the two dragons were still touching her, then dimming throughout her body like water flowing down the drain. Once the light only remained in her eyes, Sanae's whole body shuddered, her head lifted, and she tried to roll onto her belly. With a little help from the dragon at her tail, she was on her feet, blinking those amazing sapphire eyes.

She looked around at all the *Zayuri* and only stopped when she saw Nol. He ran up and touched her face. At last, the two broke apart, she shook again, and the two black dragons guided her away.

"Where are they going?" I whispered, as if any loud sound would break the spell and Sanae would be dying again.

"They have their own grounds around the grove over there. Perches and nests. She probably won't be flying for a while."

"Not with how hard we pushed her to get here," I muttered, pulling a grass stalk out of the ground and folding it.

She studied the others. "I think they're headed in."

"Hmm." My eyes wandered to the road past the meadow that led to *Aetyru.* "It's peculiar, you know?"

"What?" Jenne dropped her hand and scanned the clearing.

"When I was a kid, I longed for the day I'd see *Aetyru.*"

She pulled some of her pale hair out of her face and tucked it behind her ear. Her eyes widened as she listened. "I got my first glimpse of the roofs today, reflecting the sky, and I felt"—I dropped the stalk—"disappointed."

Her head stopped nodding, and her eyes darted away as she thought. "By the colors? You know they're really not blue, right? They're pearl." She couldn't have been older than me, not by much, but why did I feel older?

"*Sitam,*" *I know.* I hummed and closed my eyes, the wind playing with my lashes. The heads of field grass rustled like waves against the shore.

"We should go, Hally. Preferably before *Hinam* Nolan finds us missing from the lodge."

Scowling, I dusted myself off and started walking. "He's got more important things to worry about than my location." I shielded my eyes and squinted. "I don't see him."

Had he gone after Sanae without me seeing him?

"*Oiy.*" Nol touched my shoulder from Jenne's other side. "Try not to give Jenne too much grief."

"Where the hell did you come from?"

"I came up through there." He pointed to where everyone else was. Where he hadn't been two seconds ago. "I saw you staring down the road."

"*Hinam,* I'm sorry—"

"Forgiven, *Avrel* Jenne. I should have anticipated her unwillingness to listen to you."

I set my hands on my hips and glared at Nol. "Jenne did a great job babysitting me, and if I'd chosen to run off, she would've been perfectly capable of tackling me to the ground and pinning me down."

Nol's lips twisted, either fighting a smile or a frown. "*Avrel* Jenne, you are free to go."

Jenne straightened and saluted Nol, pressing her right arm to her heart, her hand in a fist. "Yes, sir!" She gave me a quick hand wave from waist high as she hurried past me.

"Thanks for staying with me, Jenne!"

She didn't look back, not even for an acknowledgment.

"She wasn't told to *stay* with you. Jenne was supposed to take you to the lodge," Nol grumbled.

"Yeah, well, I wanted to make sure Sanae was okay." I poked him in the chest. "You should have considered that before giving her an order."

Nol grunted and tugged on me until we were walking. "How much did the band siphon?"

I tucked myself under his arm, and we followed the group. "Not sure. But my arm was tingling after I got to Sanae."

"Tingling? Is that good or bad?"

I shrugged. "I dunno. Maybe it's almost at capacity and won't take any more energy until you can figure out how to empty it."

"Funny. The tingling, did it hurt? What kind of *tingling* was it?"

"I don't know how to explain it. My focus was on Sanae, so I barely felt any of it until everything was over."

"Where did you think to do that?"

"Do what?"

Nol studied me, then looked back up at the lodge where everyone was meeting. "You solidified the air—the actual air—to stop us from moving."

"Oh, that part. Um...I don't really know. Can we not use the word *solidify* again, though? It sounds like I was trying to harden us into something, like Jabba the Hutt and Han Solo. I was going for more of a Jell-O consistency to cushion our fall, not freeze us in carbonite."

"Jell-O is a solid." He ignored the movie reference, not because I hadn't introduced him to it, but because I'd once compared his sword to a lightsaber. Come on, it hid itself *and* it glowed.

"Is it, though? Those Jell-O shots you tried to make beg to differ."

Nol snorted and wrapped his arm around my neck. "Thank the Mother you thought so quickly." To my relief, he didn't harp on me about what had happened. For once, he didn't treat me like a kid.

We were nearing the others, and I couldn't wait any longer to ask. "Is Sanae gonna be okay?" I twisted my wooden ring, trying to be nonchalant about asking.

He glanced over my head toward where the dragons had gone. "After some rest. She wasn't sure what happened after she fell, so I shared it with her. We're both grateful."

"And the others?" I squinted up at him.

"Is this about sending Jenne with you?"

"Kinda. I noticed a few others glancing back. Maybe they thought I'd blow up."

Nol stopped. "Blow up?"

"You know, a ticking time bomb? What I just did and what happened before?"

"You're safe here. The ones who came to Earth weren't there to find me. They were there to protect you from the council."

"Yalu sent Tolwe over with some *Zayuri*. That doesn't mean they'd do it on their own." Not all the *Zayuri* who had come over trusted my magic. One *Zayuri* in particular had voiced his concerns in front of me. "They follow you and Tolwe. They don't know me."

Our time alone was gone, as we'd caught up with the rest of the fifteen or so *Zayuri*. Nol straightened, standing at attention to address the rest of the gathered *Zayuri* who'd come to see him off to his possible death. Nol didn't hesitate or fidget or reveal any type of expression.

"*Esamia.*" Nol raised his voice so everyone could hear him. "Before we progress in the matters of our mission, there is a matter I want to make clear. All of you know who I have brought with me. If you speak to her, I expect you to be respectful. You will address her as Hally." Nol looked at me for confirmation. I nodded. Hallë was Nol's name for me, not anyone else's. "Under no circumstances will you address her as *Hallë*." Some *Zayuri* looked away. "No one shall pester her about past events. Like *Aore* Zella, she is in full control of her magic. Act appropriately. This is your only warning."

Almost in unison, the group confirmed Nol's command with a quick "Yes, sir."

"Dismissed." The group broke up, many of them walking away, giving me uneasy side glances. Nol's command didn't mean they'd change their minds about me. Five *Zayuri*, all with dark blue, gold, or silver ear cuffs, came over and grasped Nol's forearm in the formal *endaen* greeting.

An *endao* with white hair clasped at the nape of his neck came up first. Not only did he wear a gold ear cuff, but also matching metal loops in the collar of his leather jacket.

"What are your orders, *Sudome* Tamden?" Nol pressed his right arm to his chest in salute to his commander.

"*Esamia, Hinam* Nolan. We are relieved you made it."

Nol nodded once in acknowledgment but didn't elaborate. Obviously, their concerns weren't warranted, no comments needed. My *muranildo,* an *endao* of little words—at least around these guys.

"We need to discuss..." *Sudome* Tamden started using words I didn't recognize, but I got the meaning. Meetings, discussions, plans, and updates. All very important, immediate information. We had fourteen hours before we had to be at the site of the bomb. I imagined how it would go. Perhaps Nol had to touch the device to stop the countdown. My mind kept picturing bombs in human movies with timers and colored wires. This wouldn't be like those, but I couldn't picture anything different.

They led us through the doors of the largest *endaen* structure within the largest tree. Two twelve-inch-thick branches rose on either side, creating a peaked frame. Once inside, we turned left and came upon a wide staircase large enough for three adults to walk abreast.

Nol discussed directives and mission-related stuff with Tamden and the four other officers while I trailed behind and stared around the living building.

The staircase we began to ascend naturally grew out of the living wall. Branches created a railing from the bottom of the stairs across the loft-type second floor. It reminded me of a large, more open version of my house—minus the tree. *Zayuri* were walking to and fro, doing whatever *Zayuri* did when they weren't fighting bad guys or saving citizens. Paperwork and bureaucracy crap, no doubt.

"Forgive me, *Sudome*." Nol's words interrupted my thoughts. "I was under the impression the royal family was out of the building."

Wait...what?

"The active threat is holding the family hostage," Tamden explained. "If they try to leave, the bomb will explode. However, we have the family staying on the south side of the courtyard to keep them as far away as possible."

"How bad was the *Amura Ore* hall explosion?" I asked. "I noticed the absence of the spire."

We all stopped, three and four steps up. The *Zayuri* officers' eyes crept over and down to me on the step behind Nol, as if this was the first time they'd noticed me. As if I hadn't made a pretty big introduction. Tamden looked around the main room. After a few more moments of silence I began to think they hadn't understood me.

Sudome Tamden's attention came back to me and he lifted his chin.

"Were any of my family members injured or killed?"

One of them flinched. For interrupting, or for the reminder that I had family on the council? I couldn't decide.

We don't have those details at the moment. Right now, the royal family is our objective. When the guard announces a safety report we'll let you know. *Hinam* Nolan, we need to conduct this meeting."

"I understand, sir. If you'll excuse me while I explain things to my *muranildë*."

"Meet us in East Hollow."

"Yes, sir. Thank you."

"And Hally?" Tamden called my name and turned back to the stairs. "Welcome. It is an honor to meet you."

A smile played at my lips, and broke free a second later. This wasn't something I'd expected from a commander. "Thank you, *Sudome*."

Nol puffed out his cheeks and looked around the room. "I know you're exhausted. Would you like to find a secluded area until I can find you somewhere to sleep? They'll assign me a room for the night later."

"We have, at most, thirteen hours before we have to be in the capital. I can't sleep."

"Hmm, yes, but if you don't rest before then, you'll be a zombie."

"What about you?"

"I'm trained to work—"

"Yeah, yeah, *Zayuri* don't like to sleep. Got it. What if I wait around here? I'll pick one of these." I pointed to a group of chairs with one occupant reading a stack of papers. "You don't need to hold my hand. I'm a big girl."

"Do not sneak upstairs. They'll know."

"Damn." I hadn't thought of that. "Nah, go have your meeting, then tell me everything they said later."

Nol snorted, but something behind me piqued his interest. "*Avril* Jenne?"

Jenne had come in from outside. She waved and hurried over. The girl just couldn't get away from him. I hoped she wasn't the one who'd broken his heart. Punching her in the face after she'd saved my life felt tacky.

"Sir?" Jenne stopped in front of us.

"We have a meeting and—"

"You don't need to say more, *Hinam*. Hally can't go inside. I'd love to spend time with her."

"I appreciate that, *Avrel*." Nol touched my arm and pulled on his jacket. "I will find you as soon as I can," he said in English as he slipped it off me and over himself. Damn. "Be good."

"No promises."

Nol gave Jenne a pointed look. "Perhaps find her something to eat..."

I rolled my eyes. "I'm not a child, go away!" I shooed him and watched until he'd turned the corner upstairs. I wondered where "East Hollow" was. "You know...I don't think Nol gave you an order."

"What's that?"

"You don't have to babysit me. Oh, and I made sure he knows it wasn't your fault that I stayed. He grumbled, but like he always says, I'm a pain in his ass. No doubt, I'm a pain to others, too."

Jenne blinked at me.

"Did I say all that right? I don't want to sleep, but damn, I am tired. My *Aemirin*—"

"Is fine. Honestly, it's just your pitches and pauses—oh, and your choice of cuss words is odd." Her smile and soft tone set me at ease. "Come, we'll get you something to eat."

"Once again, Nol is right. Food would be great."

Jenne headed toward the door on the right, quick steps that made me hurry to keep up. "Did you mean it? About visiting? When this chaotic situation is under control, I mean."

"For coffee and Charlie? Absolutely. She'd love you. Everyone would."

"It wouldn't be inappropriate? *Hinam* is a higher rank and—"

I waved it off, and she smiled. Now I got it. "You've known Nol a long time?"

"Since I joined, yeah." She rolled up onto her toes and looked around the mostly empty room. "He was my first commanding officer."

"You can't be more than a decade apart. How was he an officer before you joined?"

"He's Twynolan..."

"And?"

She glanced up the stairs. "*Hinam* Nolan is a legend. Everyone says he will make commander before a century."

"That makes sense. Nol hates to fail and will work until he masters the subject." I wondered if he found *Zayuri* secret stuff more challenging than classic education.

"I wouldn't call it mastery, but he worked hard to get where he is. We all respect him deeply."

"I see that you do." I bit my lip before I mentioned that once upon a time he'd vowed never to become a *Zayuri*. I searched for something to say to end the longer-than-comfortable silence. "So how much farther to this food you spoke of?"

"Into the back. We call them the Glades. With everything going on, there won't be many people, and it's not like anyone is stationed here. Lana—our cook—arrived with me this morning. There was some confusion on where you two would go, but thankfully everything was confirmed this morning."

"This morning?" I asked as I followed her around another curve. "Nol contacted someone when we first arrived."

"I don't know all the facts. The important part is, you're here in time and everyone now knows where you are. Now, the glade—" Jenne opened a wide door and leaned against it so I could see the room "—Is where rowdy lower ranks meet there after shifts."

I'd imagined this glade to be a cafeteria or some dorm common room—and while it was a little of both, it was also welcoming.

"Now, in *Jinatrau* or another village, this would be much larger and more active, but this is it."

The glade was a large room, filled with much cushier chairs and a lower ceiling, giving it a laidback and comfortable feeling. Two people sat at a table in the back, holding cups in their hands. A group of three *Zayuri* stood at a table around a box. One reached in, touched something, and yanked his hand back with a laugh. A game or a dare? His friend beside him tried next. I made a note to check it out.

"Hey Jenne!" The *endao* from the back held up a cup. "Bring her over here. We'll get her a drink."

"Now we're talking." I grabbed Jenne's arm and dragged her back to the handsome brown-haired *endao*.

17

Jenne got to enjoy extended downtime babysitting me. For what felt like twelve hours, but was more like an hour, we hung out in their common room. Her boyfriend, Bren, offered me a taste of his drink— A pick-me-up drink. Caffeinated? Yes. Alcoholic? Probably. It was a little bitter with a hint of sweetness at the end, but it didn't taste bad. In fact, I liked it enough that Lana, the nice older *Zayuri* who enjoyed cooking, made me one of my own.

These people shattered my idea of the stoic, mysterious *Zayuri* warrior. Their laughter was contagious, their compassion was unbounded, and their loyalty to one another was uncompromising.

I found a comfortable seat that faced the back of the room where five people were playing a bar game. Jenne and Bren were at a nearby table with enough space to pretend it was private, while technically still babysitting me. The equivalent of my babysitter watching television after she'd put me to bed.

The crowd had waxed and waned, but at the moment, Lana was prepping for those who were supposed to come in soon. She fed me soon after my arrival, so I could watch and observe this rowdy species of lower-ranking *Zayuri*. But my mind was elsewhere, wanting to know what they were talking to Nol about, how much longer until we had to leave, and why wouldn't the *sudome* answer me about my relatives?

"Not the best view of the room." Nol walked around my large, comfy chair, blocking my view of the cute *Zayuri* who'd kept winning at the *jontay* game. No fun.

"No, but it hid me enough." I moved to sit up straighter.

Nol looked over at Jenne and Bren. "You're in full view of Jenne." Other *Zayuri* around the game table started to notice Nol talking to me. One slapped her buddy on the arm to get him to stop talking. Not that we were speaking *Aemirin,* but they could understand our tones and hear that Nol was being serious but not intimidating.

"My babysitter, you mean?" This seat wasn't the best in which to have a conversation with a standing person. I'd manage, though.

"If you'd like to call it that. Would you rather I had left you at the steps alone?"

It seemed while all these people respected him and were willing to come to this little outpost in support of this plan of theirs, none of them could say they liked or disliked him. They didn't know enough about him to get an opinion.

"I'd have found my way back here." I leaned back and crossed my arms.

He looked up at the ceiling—praying for patience, perhaps? I knew how he felt.

"Sit down here and talk to me. Jenne said they were rowdy. This is a tomb compared to Cinder's on a Saturday."

"We don't have time to sit and chat, Hallë. Come, it is time to go."

My eyes shot open, payback torture forgotten for a second. "It's only been an hour, an hour and a half, tops."

"We need to talk. In private." Nol held his hand out to me.

Instead of taking it, I snuggled in deeper and pointed at him. "I learned something about you today."

"Oh?" Nol shifted, a hint of a worried expression before he hid it. Nol had noticed the attention we were gathering. Even if I paid for this later, oh, it'd be worth it for my broody, pouting *muranildo.*

"No one believes Jenne."

Nol frowned and looked away. "Okay, I do not see how that is about me, but we will go with it. Carry on."

"She told her friends she saw you smile. On Earth, after our dip in the river."

He quirked his head and narrowed his eyes. Instead of relieving stress like I thought it would, he seemed more uncomfortable. "I smiled?"

"Yep. That's the thing I learned. That no one has seen you smile. And you know what else?"

"Are you drunk?"

"No. Caffeinated as hell."

Nol lifted an arm and waved at someone behind me. "Lana? What'd you give her?"

"*Tanadlyn*. Sorry, *Hinam*. She tried some of Bren's, and well, she's an adult—"

He held his hand out to stop Lana. "*Wana nanas*," *say no more.* Nol looked back at me, eyes hard and wary. "How many cups did you have?"

"Why? Am I going to get in trouble? I'm not a child, Nol. I can drink whatever I want."

He shoved his hair back and clenched his jaw. "*C'yo*, I am aware you're not a child. I want to know if you're able to walk to the room."

I swatted my hand at him. "Psh. Just the one, and the rest of Bren's." I gave him a huge smile. "I like it."

"Most do. It has a higher alcohol content than my father's wine."

"They said it has a stimulant to keep me awake." But I had suspected the alcohol.

"It has that, too. Do you think you can walk?"

"Of course I can, but we're not going anywhere yet."

He crossed his arms and refused to sit down. My ploy wasn't working, and my neck was paying the consequence.

"Yet?" He arched an eyebrow.

"I'll go with you if you smile. Prove to everyone it's possible for you to do so."

"Hallë, this is not funny."

"Nuh-uh. Jenne says you'll probably make commander before your tercentenary. Bren says you never stop working. You're apparently a legend. But you've never thanked them. Not once."

His eyes darted around, as if he was looking for someone to yell at for tattling to me. "Come on, Nol, smile. Oh, and thank them for babysitting me. And Lana for her wonderful drinks and cooking. And you get to drink something. Probably not the *Tadlyn*—"

"*Tanadlyn*." Nol groaned as he closed his eyes.

"Sure, that one. I'll go with you when you"—I counted them off with my fingers—"smile, use your manners, and take a shot."

"We don't have shots."

I waved his excuse off. "The small cups. Close enough for me. Now get on with it."

"I am not playing."

"Neither am I." Okay, yes I was, but it didn't matter. "How long before we leave for *Aetyru*?"

His jaw moved as he ground his teeth. "Within ten hours."

"Plenty of time, then." Not really, if we wanted to get some sleep. It still felt like a sprint to me, but here, as the *Zayuri* had sat around for days actually *doing* things to prepare, they were running a marathon.

"You are embarrassing the both of us."

I grinned at him. "You can only be embarrassed if you give them permission."

He didn't have a word to say to that.

"You train with them. You trust them. Many of them, I found out, live in *Jinatrau*, so you live near them, too. Yet you've never smiled. That's crazy. I can't think of a day I haven't seen you smile. You've got a gorgeous smile, and you use it all the time. They don't believe that either."

"I use my *gorgeous* smile all the time?"

"Yes, to get your way. Oh, and you like seeing people's reactions to you. Like with the flight attendant—yes, I noticed. Don't worry, I didn't tell anyone that."

"This is done," he muttered and moved to grab me.

I slapped at him and he stopped. "As soon as you do what I say."

"I am their superior. I do not fraternize with them."

Okay, then drinking might have been too far. I gave in a little. "Fine. No drink. Manners, at least. With a smile."

Nol pressed his fingers to his forehead, squeezing his eyes shut. "I do not act like that here. I am not *that* here."

"You're not that person here?" I asked softly. "You can still be a badass and say thank you."

A light blue eye peeked open, and a hint of a smile showed on his lips, hidden by his hand.

"Tell you what. I'll *say* you're a badass *Zayuri*." I rolled my eyes. "If you tell them thank you for babysitting me. They did a great job. And I didn't drink *that* much."

"We have a crisis. How can you be so chipper?"

"Oh, how the tables have turned."

Nol dropped his hand and glared at me. Yep, he got it. He had done the same damn thing to me when he found me in Seattle. Sure, I'd taken him to a café to talk, that way he couldn't make a scene. I paid for it as he gave me shit the entire time.

"Payback, bitch," I emphasized the ch for the fun of it. Okay maybe I was more drunk than I thought. "And I get overtime."

"I hate you so much right now," Nol growled. "Fine. No drink, agreed?"

"Agreed."

"*Ai*, I don't need this right now," he muttered in *Aemirin*, too low for most to hear him. He looked around at the *Zayuri* in the room. "As I have just been informed by Hallë, none of you believe *Avrel*—"

"Just Jenne, you're not working," I said in *Aemirin* and got a chuckle from someone.

"—Jenne when she tells you she saw me smile in *Rosava*. I assure you, she is not lying. Every *enda* with the musculature to do so is capable of using them, if uninjured." He sighed, huge and long. "Under duress, I have been instructed to smile." He gave me an oh-so-fake grin that did *not* look good on him.

"*Sait! Vuma hezict, Twynolan,*" *No! An actual smile,* I demanded from my seat. "Come on, Nol. You can do better," I added in English without a hint of teasing or attitude. He was getting off so easily and only because we were in a crisis. Otherwise, I wouldn't have cared one lick about his stoic reputation.

Nol jutted out his chin. "You have to *admit* I'm a badass to everyone at home. And I don't want to hear you say anything about Agent Thomas when you admit it, either."

"He's the one who started it!"

Nol squinted. He wouldn't do what I said if I continued to argue. "Fine," I grumbled. "I'll say that you're a badass and tell everyone at home."

Agent Zack Thomas, the asshole of a DEA agent who'd harassed me for years, claimed Nol was the "badass" I'd told him about when he found us the night Aswryn had died.

I clapped twice and nodded. "Okay, here we go. You can do it. Think happy thoughts. Ice cream and mochas. Shopping with Mateo..." My teasing drifted off. I had no idea what he liked to do over here—except... "Flying with Sanae. You love that."

Nol shook his head. "You are such a pain in my ass."

I gave him the broadest smile. "I know."

That did it. He even laughed a little. I rarely ever skipped our tradition, but this was worth it. I stretched my hand out so he could help me up but retreated when I realized I'd forgotten a term. He, being far quicker and cunning, realized this, too, and snatched my hand.

"You still have to say thank you."

"That was before you were standing." With that, he pulled me farther away from the chair, and I let out a yip of surprise. He guided me in front of him, where he placed a hand on my shoulder to whisper, "I'm getting some of Lana's cooking before we leave. And I always thank her."

"It is really good, isn't it?"

He walked behind me all the way to the high, long table where Lana was setting plates of food whenever she came back in from the kitchen. "Never tell my mother this, but Lana's is better." He pulled a plate off the table. "Almost as good as yours."

I just about died laughing. All the while, Nol kept staring at me, blankly. This coming from the *endao* who'd refused to believe my cooking wouldn't kill him two months ago. His concerns had been warranted, however. As a kid, I wasn't a good cook. To this day, I didn't know how I'd ruined the last meal my mother had allowed me to cook. I loved my mother and Wennië, but my foster mother deserved all the credit for my talent in the kitchen.

I grabbed his arm holding the plate. "Come on, you're at least telling Jenne thank you."

Nol groaned. "I still haven't heard a single syllable of admittance from you."

"Oh, that's because you reneged on our deal first."

Nol stopped, his expression open for everyone to see his surprise. "It's okay. I know you think I'm a badass. You have to think it before you can offer to admit it." I'd said *admit*? I thought I'd said *say*. Damn.

We were already at Jenne's table, and we needed to speak *Aemirin*. I was enjoying this, our own language thing.

"Sir?" Jenne stood next to Bren, their hands at their sides, waiting to be inspected.

"Hallë is right. We aren't on duty."

"Yes, sir. I apologize."

"Jenne, there's no apology necessary. By no means would I expect you to keep quiet about your experiences in *Rosava*. I came over to thank you. For looking after Hallë."

"I'm honored that you trust me with her."

Okay. That was it. "We don't need to go that far. I'm not his child, Jenne. He may treat me like one, way more often than he should, but I promise, I grew up, too."

Jenne looked at us. Who did she address about that one?

"I hope to see you in Seattle after this is over. We can make a day of it."

Her whole face lit up. "I look forward to it." She glanced at Nol. "If you're comfortable with it, *Hinam*?"

"Am I supposed to be there on this 'day of it' in Seattle?"

Jenne paused in her automatic no.

"No, Nol won't be there. And if we see him, no *Zayuri* etiquette will take place. Is that understood?" I shook my finger at him.

Nol gave the room his second smile of the day when Jenne looked too confused to respond. "I think she will, after Hallë's badass *muranildo* is gone," Nol said in English.

I groaned. Never living it down. Ever. It was like a teenager pointing out they were taller than me every minute of every day. I knew the kids would eventually grow out of it, but I couldn't think of an excuse for Nol.

NOL PUSHED OPEN THE door of his room wider and went around me to set our bag on a chair, pouting the whole way because I'd made him smile at everyone. Darn.

The room wasn't huge, but I wouldn't call it a barrack room, because the beds weren't visible—in fact, between the sitting area place for two and the tiny table next to it, was an open walkway. That had to be the way to the rooms.

"It's small, but adorable. Look there's even a bookshelf. It'll hold what, two books?" I pointed to the shelves set into the far wall between the chairs.

Nol snorted as he set his plate on the table.

"Small? It's as big as your bedroom closet. These are the...uh, apartments for the soldiers. I think they're called something else in English." He stopped and looked around the room. Really looked.

"It has a rug. My closet doesn't have a rug. And unless they expect us to sleep in chairs, there are bedrooms."

"There are no two bedroom apartments here. This isn't a village, just another outpost. When the capital begins to get too much, but it's close enough to walk. I think the dragons use it more than anyone."

"So...dibs on the bed."

Nol rolled his eyes and looked at the chair. "No. It's not like we haven't shared a bed before, suck it up. How are you feeling, by the way?" Nol opened a drawer under the tiny table. "*Tanadlyn* is unpredictable."

"Tired, but not bad. Jenne will have to bring some of that over when she visits."

Nol's eyes lit up as he found was he was hunting for—a spoon. "Do we need to start a trading route between realms? I can imagine your grandmother enjoying coffee instead of tea. Our milk would be a hit with the...which ones go without meat? They both begin with *ve* so I get them confused."

"Both. Vegans go without any animal products and vegetarians just don't eat meat—it's also vague, because some vegetarians won't eat—."

"I get it." Nol gave me an exasperated look. How dare I go into detail.

I waved my hand, dismissing him. "Go eat your food. I'm checking out the bedroom—it better be a big bed or I'll kick you out in your sleep."

Nothing came from the peanut gallery. I was already moving and conjuring a light globe to come face to face with a set of narrow stairs over the sitting area. Another closet room? This wasn't going to work.

Fifteen steep steps later, a largish bed with a blah natural blanket and a side table/cabinet for clothes—or their daggers—maybe both. Natural-colored sheets, with a dark blanket. I sent my globe to the sconce on the far wall above the table, lighting up the whole room. Nothing fun or unexpected. Some sort of decoration would have been nice. Paint. A twisty twig, a dead leaf to match the blanket. Something.

I hopped back down the steps, fighting against the sleep my mind was trying to force on me. Nol sat at the table on a narrow chair. He swallowed a mouthful and tilted the dish to scoop some more out. We hadn't brought much on our journey. And Nol ate a lot.

The table and drawers distracted me before I could pester him. Intricate carvings were etched on the sides of the drawers under the table. It made me think of my father, and I lifted my ring to inspect it again. I played with it every time we landed. It kept my mind calm whenever I pictured what could happen in the morning. I squeezed my eyes shut but forced them open when I felt dizzy. I would not fall asleep standing up.

"Why are we waiting so long to go into the capital?" I asked. "Is it timed or something?"

"We are waiting for three other *Zayuri*. At the very earliest I don't see us leaving for another six hours." He cussed and complained in *Aemirin* under his breath, mumbling something about Tamden and I might have heard Gil in there, then scooped up another bite.

"What about Tamden and Gil?"

"Nothing." He swallowed. "I'm tired and frustrated." He played with the spoon on his plate. I waited—as patiently as I could. "When we got to *Endae* I told *Sudome* Tamden I had to take the northern route. *Zayuri* communication is not like *Olauvë*. One person at a time, every time. No words either, all thoughts, like how it is with us. Whether *Sudome* didn't understand or...something else, the communication was out of my hands after that."

Why was he being so vague about this? It wasn't like I would blab *Zayuri* secrets. "Okay, so which way did he *think* you were going?"

"Most *Zayuri* expected me to come to *Hylise*."

"What's *Hylise*? Why not *Jinatrau* or here?"

Nol stared at me, warring with what to tell me. The *Zayuri* were secretive about everything, but I always got him to tell me. Besides my family knew more than the average *enda* because of how close we were. Living together for a decade would do that. But it was the only way Nol survived his childhood. Nol set his elbows on the table and rested his chin on this hands, watching me across the table. "Hallë?"

I pinched my mouth closed and waved for him to continue.

"Since they cannot get in without me," he continued after a pause to make sure I wouldn't interrupt again. "They were waiting for us in *Hylise*. So now we must wait for everyone to converge here. They will report once they arrive and then we will leave."

He could have just *said* that without me having to pull it out of him. I leaned forward, my chin on my hands, mirroring him. And still he was keeping things from me. More recent things. More pertinent to *us* things and it scared me.

"And what about Gil?"

Nol leaned back, puffing his cheeks out. "They had Gil's letter in *Hylise*."

"Oh come on! Will we get to read it before it's time to go?"

"*Pesset* Drezalen is bringing it as we speak."

"*Pesset* sounds like pissant." *Pesset* was similar to a sergeant.

Nol choked, smiled, and choked again. "Warn me next time. *Tulla*. That was a good one. Thank you, I needed a laugh."

I shrugged a shoulder. The news hadn't been as bad as I had imagined.

Nol squinted at me. "You're as tired as I am. How are you so energetic?"

"I think it's the *tanadlyn*. I'm tired, and I know this is all very serious. But it's a weird, carefree feeling."

"You do need more of that, then. You're always grumpy at home."

"Am not. I've gotten better."

Nol touched my elbow. "Much better. Charlie says she hasn't seen you like this." He swallowed. "I just hope it's the release of your magic and not me."

I looked down at the counter and chewed my lip. If it was his nearness, then I'd get worse when he went home permanently. Nol's thumb brushed my arm, just below my slave band. "We haven't had any time to talk, but we need to have that conversation. I've been telling you since March and you've avoided it."

"We've gotten better." My eyes got heavy, and I should have told him to stop, but it felt good.

"I don't want to break your heart."

"Charlie says that, not me. You're gonna feel just as bad. The facts remain, it's gonna hurt us both when you go back" —I looked around us—"Here."

"No," he said in a harsh, grumpy whisper between his teeth.

A *no* meant a lot of things.

"We won't have to say goodbye. I'm not going back until we get this shit sorted—not counting this fucking thing." He touched the band. A shock went up my arm, and I jumped way the hell back.

Breathing uneven and heart hammering, I stared from the band to him. "Did you feel that?"

Nol nodded. "Lean over. Let me try again."

Hell no was he touching it again. It *hurt*. "Screw that. Touch it again and die."

Nol scoffed, waving his fingers, trying to get me to lean over again. "Don't be a baby. If something happens, that means we're closer to figuring this thing out and getting it off you." He reached over farther than I thought he could, grabbed my arm above my elbow, and pulled me until my entire torso was on the table.

"A bit excessive!"

"This way you won't fall back. Stop whining." He took a breath. "Okay." His fingertips touched my skin gently, and he traced a line up my arm.

My eyes got heavy. Holy shit, I was tired. His fingers brushed the band. Nothing.

"*C'yo,*" he growled and let me go. Nol shoved his hair back and walked away.

"Maybe it was something you said when you touched it." But he ignored me. "Nol?"

"There *is* a way. There has to be." Nol paced the room, his hands clenching and unclenching. On the last pace, I expected him to come close to the table again, not hit the wall near the door. Not once, but three times.

I ran over after my initial shock and barged into his side to stop him. We fell over in a heap.

"What are you doing?" I couldn't keep the terrified waver out of my voice. My hands were shaking as I grabbed his fist. Bloody and raw. Not broken, thank the Mother. I'd never seen him express so much anger like this.

"*C'yo!* I'm sorry." Chin to his chest, he pressed a thumb to one of the knuckles. "Why don't I think when I'm mad?" he growled.

I leaned forward and rested my forehead against his. My face scrunched up, and my throat tightened. "Why?"

He swallowed hard, his breathing ragged. "It's a problem I've got."

I lifted my head to look at him, but he kept looking at our hands. This wasn't funny. "Really? A problem? Since when? You've never—"

"Why do you think I leave the room when I get mad?" he asked. "We're a very angry bunch. Puberty kinda hits us with an angry streak. Those of us who get the gene."

"*Zayuri,* you mean?"

He nodded. "I was showing signs of it before you left. My murë saw it. That's why she kept pushing. Tolwe, I guess, got pretty bad fits, too. That's why we have to control our emotions."

He had to be joking. "You bottle them all in and won't let anyone see? That's not very healthy."

"It's not like that." He paused and closed his eyes. "We go through emotion management. It's why I can't...I can't talk about a few things yet. They hurt too much."

"Well, when you can...will you tell me?"

He shook his head and reopened his eyes. "I don't know. I'm afraid you'll—"

I frowned. It wasn't that I was insensitive to his feelings, but Nol knew me. Knew that I wouldn't be that petty. Especially, since I knew it was so hard for him to talk about. "Think differently about you? You've said that before."

Nol pulled me close and took a few deep breaths. "But you've helped me in so many ways already." We stayed there for a while until Nol stirred. "We've gotta get up. *Majut.* I have to get back."

"Back?" I crawled so our feet weren't tangled and he could get up, but he didn't move, just pulled a knee in and paused. "I thought the meeting was over."

Nol sighed, long and tired, if sighs could be tired. "We took a break. *Hinam* Myall will be arriving any moment." He turned his head, rested his temple on his knee and watched me, slowly blinking. "She is bringing information about the device that was used. I'll tell you what they said in the first meeting when I get back. Please try and get some sleep. And I'm sorry for scaring you. I feel helpless and…" He squeezed his eyes shut and clenched his fists.

"We both have issues. Do you know what's good about issues?" I poked him.

His eyes opened genuinely curious. "What?"

"They can be solved."

Nol smiled, one of his rare unguarded smiles that were way nicer than when he knew people were watching. "Watch it. My father is rubbing off on you."

We both smiled. Edvic and his silver linings. "Whatever. Get to your meeting."

18

THIS ROOM HAD NOTHING to eat or drink, and I didn't want to go out to the common room to find something. I didn't know how long it had been, but my body wasn't set to *Endae,* and clocks weren't a thing here—not like Earth's system anyway. Nol had said it wouldn't be long, but I was thirsty and getting hungry.

On the inside wall, the closed cupboards looked promising, but I couldn't see in them to know what was in them. Everything was built for tall people. With a groan, I pulled a chair over to the wall and climbed on top. Nol would've laughed his ass off if I fell. If I hurt myself, I wouldn't be able to go to the capital.

Then I realized my next problem. I was too close to open the cupboard. Groaning, I climbed back down and moved the chair back and got back up. A squeak caught my attention and I looked over as Nol opened the front door and conjured a globe to the sconce in the sitting room. I'd kept the light low, and he hadn't noticed that he hadn't needed it.

"Hey."

Startled—a very un*Zayuri*-like move—he first looked over at the stairs then did a double take when he saw the low light in the eating area.

"What are you doing?" He came over and looked in the cupboard.

"Can't see the top shelves. I'm hungry, and I was hoping to find food."

"There's no food here. Mice."

Even magical elves had rodent problems. I scrunched my nose and dragged the chair back.

Nol slipped his jacket off and draped it over his chair The way he held his shoulders, I knew there was something either on his mind or something he knew I wouldn't like.

"How long has it been?"

He sat down. "Two hours."

I about fell. "Two hours?"

"There was a lot to say." A long, slow blink and a pause interrupted his words. "A lot to argue over."

"Why were they arguing?" I scrubbed my face and shoved my hair back. My palms touched my new/old ear cuffs. "Nol, we're too tired for twenty questions. Tell me, then get some sleep."

"Can't. *Pesset* Drezalen should be here soon with Gil's letter. I want to have it before I go into the capital." He swallowed as he studied me. "They want to know, too. The commander thinks he snuck out some information about the attack. It makes sense, if his captors were already delivering something." He rested his elbow on the table. "I don't know, words aren't coming out right. I have something else on my mind at the moment."

"The argument?"

He jerked, his hand moving away from his face, blinking the sleep away. "Yes. No one was on my side."

"*You* argued with them? Aren't you low man on the totem pole with those guys?"

He thought about that for a second. "I don't know what that means. But I'm the one who has to go in. They want several people to go in with me." With one straight finger, he tapped the table in a slow beat. "And some they don't want going."

"I'm going with you."

"That's what I said. But...you're not trained for situations like this."

"And you are?" I rushed to add the last lest he thought I doubted him. "How many hostage situations have you negotiated? How many bombs have you deactivated? Is this a regular weekday for you all?"

"Okay, I get that, but you don't have the control for this. We've trained for—"

It was my childhood all over again. They all thought I didn't have enough control of my magic for anything. I thought they trusted me. I thought he believed in me. "I can control my magic." Tears stung my eyes.

"That's not why." He reached across the table and grabbed my hands. "They saw what you did and believe in you. The *Zayuri* want to protect you. They're the only ones keeping you safe right now."

"What does that mean? The council approved my travel here." Nol even had a copy of the document. "Besides, aren't they a little busy with, oh, I don't know, finding bodies in the rubble? Counting survivors? They were bombed they have bigger things to worry about than me."

"Listen." He squeezed my hands and rubbed the knuckles between his thumbs and fingers. "If things go bad and the bomb detonates it could kill me and the other officers coming in with me. I would not be surprised if the council took you then. We don't trust them to keep you safe. Jenne, Bren, and three other *Zayuri* are staying with you and Sanae. *If* the worst does happen Sanae will fly you to *Jinatrau*. *If* the Trees of Connection start working, they'll get you back to Seattle. But if the portals remain closed, Sanae will fly you to *Pequwyn*. They'll find you a way back. If I'm gone, I want you to swear to me you'll live your last days with the people you love and be as happy as you can be."

"Those are a lot of ifs." A lot of focus and planning about me and my safety instead of the royal family's. "I don't want you making contingency plans for me. If you die, I'm not going to wait ten years."

"Please."

"I'm not going to wither and die like our last life. That's why it took me so long to meet you here, in this life. I'm not doing that to you again. I want to come with you. If they kill me..." I shrugged. "I'll be with you."

"You'll leave your family? Never say goodbye to them? We come back in our next life and what? The curse has destroyed all of *Aemina*. We live in *Pequwyn*."

"We don't know anything about the future. I'm not staying here."

We stared at each other, neither of us wavering until his shoulders dropped and he retracted his hands. "Okay. I'll tell them."

By *here*, I'd meant *alive*. But he'd meant here, as in the post. We'd go with that. "You said it was decided."

"It is, but you're not our prisoner, and we can't keep you here. If you follow us, that's your choice."

Was he doing that reverse psychology thing? "Okay…"

"We can't guarantee your guard's safety, either. Sanae, Jenne, and the rest might follow you into the capital, and if it goes bad, they'd be in danger, too."

"I'll consider it."

Nol got up, his shoulders hunched, his body drained. He grabbed his jacket and dragged himself back to the door. Was he exaggerating to make me feel guilty? It was working.

"Nol? You don't need to tell them. I can wait up for this guy and wake you when he brings Gil's letter. Go sleep a bit."

He shook his head. "Later." And he walked out the door. I'd have followed if I hadn't been in Wennië's nightshirt.

Growling, I balled my hands into fists and stomped up the stairs. I'd have to get dressed and go find him and maybe yell some sense into the other badass *Zayuri*. My *muranildo* needed sleep. Upstairs, I yanked my bag onto the bed with me and chose the first outfit I saw. Gray shirt, black pants. Good enough for me. It'd keep me hidden in the night, too, if I ended up sneaking out ahead of them.

"What are you going to do, Hally?" I asked myself with my clothes in my hand. They wouldn't listen to me, just like any other *enda*. I couldn't stay in this room, though. I'd find something to drink and wait for the letter.

My mind went through the possibilities of what it might say. It could be a sorrowful warning that we had to choose to save him or the capital. Or he'd sent the letter at the cost of his life to tell Nol not to go. But if we could find him somehow. Somehow? I could try. This was as safe a place as any, around a bunch of *Zayuri*.

I tossed my clothes on the bed, lay down, and let my consciousness drift away. In my mind's eye, I rose above myself and out into *Endae*. I sensed my grandmother to the southwest. My consciousness turned west to *Aetyru*, where *we* would be in less than eight hours.

I rose higher and pushed my magic out wide, like I had the very first time I'd gone through the realms to find my grandmother and tell her that Gil was dead and Nol couldn't go back. *Endae's* magic, the natural energy of the land, pulsed, and I sensed the *imolegin* of every *enda* around me. All the *Zayuri* here. I felt Nol's where the East Hollow room had to be, with five other *Zayuri*.

I reached out, searching for Gileal's *imolegin*. All around, the curse still dulled the energy of many people, eating away at their *imolegin*. I needed to focus on Gil. I pushed everything away, intent on finding him.

There, to the north, a gentle feeling against my mind pulled me. Gileal's *imolegin*. And it wasn't far. Gil's *imolegin* was at the very northern part of the mountain range we'd flown over yesterday. In a thought, I was closer to him.

I sensed other *imolegini*—more people. The *imolegini* grew stronger and more refined as I closed in. Five people, including Gil. His trail loosely followed a large river. Then, on the mountainside, three-quarters of the way up, next to the waterfall that divided the mountains from the valley, was a fortress built in the mountain.

Gil's *imolegin*, was strong, healthy, and uninfected somewhere in that thing. I pulled back. We had eight hours before the start of the day. If we hurried, if Nol and the other *Zayuri* believed me, we could get there before morning. Getting back depended on how hard it would be to overtake Gil's captors and fly him back. But there was a chance, and I would fight like hell to take it.

SCRAMBLING TO THE END of the bed, once I'd come out of the *Olauvë* state, I grabbed the clothes I had picked. Why hadn't I gotten dressed before I'd done this? Stupid questions. My mind was reeling, trying to remember the location in order to convince Nol and the others to go get Gil now. My pants wouldn't go on, and I fell off the damn bed. I shoved my boots on and was out the door, running through the hall and straight to the lodge, with its large door that peaked at the top.

A *Zayuri* soldier coming outside almost ran into me as I skidded to a stop and turned up the stairs. My legs were burning by the time I made it to the East Hollow room. I paused at the door before knocking. One of the officers opened the door, looked around over my head and I cleared my throat to get her attention.

"You can talk to *Hinam* Nolan when we're done." She began to close the door, but I stuck my foot out to keep it from closing.

"No, I know where Gil is.""

She paused, but frowned. "After we're done—"

This wasn't working and the window was closing to accomplish both missions. Who knew if Gil's captors would punish him after the *Zayuri* thwarted the terrorists precious plan? They weren't getting Nol and they for damn sure weren't keeping Gil. That was, if we got to him before they killed him.

"Nol! I found Gil." I yelled in *Aemirin* instead of arguing with the officer in front of me. "Let me show you where he is."

The others were at the door in two seconds. Nol pushed to the front, grabbed my arm and walked me to the opposite wall. Nol's brow furrowed as he leaned over so I didn't have to crane my neck. "What do you mean you found him?" he asked in English.

"I found his *imolegin*. He's alive and there's no doubt in my mind that we can get there tonight.We have enough time for both."

Nol stared down at me for a beat, thinking it through, then looked at the other officers. He wanted to get Gil as much as me, but his duty was to the Starborn family.

"Just let me show you. We're wasting time!"

Nol stood straight, grabbed my hand, and pulled me through the group of confused, frustrated, and annoyed *Zayuri* officers and into the East Hollow room. I got it, I really did, but if they cared for Gil like I was certain they did, then they would hear me out.

"What is going on, *Hinam*?" Tamden demanded as we walked past him, the last one blocking my view of the room. A large, heavy looking table was in the middle of the room and spread across it was a metal box, or what was once one, now one of its sides was mangled and bent. Shards of metal and glass, tattered leather and splinters splayed about it, like it had belched it out. Was that the bomb? Were they studying it? I shook my head. We didn't have the time, besides what did it matter to me?

"Hallë is going to show us where they are keeping Gil," Nol informed them as if he were the highest ranking officer in the room.

"Impossible. How would she know?" another officer asked.

"We don't even know who has him or *if* someone has him," the one in the far back said.

"We don't have time for this," a fourth one commented.

I ignored them. "I need something to draw with."

One of them scoffed—the one who'd doubted me. I didn't give two shits.

Nol handed me a pen then hurried over to the large cupboard and riffled through until he found a bottle of black ink. This stuff really stained, but if I was careful, it might work. My mother's workshop flashed through my mind and all the paint she'd made me scrape off the floor as punishment. A part of me smiled, she'd have killed me for this. I uncorked the bottle and threw it on the floor to everyone's astonishment. Before it hit the wood it froze as I pictured the landscape of the Valley of *Aetyru*. The ink flowed and moved like a live thing as it obeyed my thoughts.

"That's *Aetyru*," one of the officers pointed out as the ink matched the image in my mind. "And the *Aetyru* river."

But the mountains were the most important part and I had a problem. "I need more room. Someone please back the table up."

It took three people to push the table against the wall with no other questions.

"I felt Gil's *imolegin* this way." I swept my hand up the tiny ink river I'd made. "I followed the river—"

"What are you talking about?" The doubtful *Zayuri* yelled. I looked up, it didn't take long to find the brawny, copper haired endao with his scathing look. Did he treat my grandmother this way, too? Probably, or at least when Tolwe and Nol weren't in the room. "How, by the Stars could you have done that?"

"Have you been trained to use *Olauvë*, sir?"

"Don't be ridiculous, of course I haven't, and—"

"My grandmother trained me since I was seventy-five. It's not something you easily forget. Or do you doubt *Aore* Evazella's abilities." I waited, giving him time to comment. He crossed his arms and hunkered in on himself. "So yes, I followed the *Aetyru* river valley to this waterfall."

The ink flowed to make a detailed model of the mountainside, waterfall, and the ground below. "I sensed five *imolegini*. All are strong and uninfected. But the fortress is here." I pointed to its location. "It's dark and hard to see and very high up."

"You're saying you went there in the astral plane," the *endai* who'd opened the door asked, with hesitant skepticism.

"Yes. What do—" I shook my head and my retort away. It would do no good to argue with them.

One of the *Zayuri* reached to touch the ink in the air.

"Don't touch the ink!"

He pulled his hand back. Dumbass.

"Hally, did you see any roads or trails to get up there?" Tamden asked.

"It was too dark. I only had the moon for guidance."

"Incredible." Tamden knelt to bring himself at eye level with the ink fortress. "Why don't we know about this? It's next to *Metaela* Falls."

"It's not visible from below," I explained. "So if you don't know what you're looking for, you'll never see it."

Tamden stood. "Impressive, Hallanevaë. You can put the ink away now."

I held out the little bottle and willed the ink inside. Like a movie reel in reverse, it sucked right back in. I let go of the cork, and it followed the ink back on, just because I could.

I handed Nol the bottle back and faced the room. "Well? Getting there wouldn't take long at all. We could be there and back well before morning."

Tamden placed his hand on my shoulder. "You're not going with us into the capital. We don't trust the council."

"If Nol dies," I searched for my words, *Aemirin* was damn hard when I was tired. "There really isn't much point in me going on. I'll die within a decade. If the council takes me and kills me for whatever reason they can conjure,...they'll only be...quickening the death," I finished weakly. I waited, but they responded with silence.

"It's my choice."

The *Zayuri* from the door raised her hand. "We could send two groups. There's enough of us—"

"We don't know what awaits us there, except there are four mysterious *endai* to fight. We don't know Gileal's state. It's too big of a risk."

The tallest *Zayuri* crossed his arms and glowered at the floor. "I don't like it. We focus on the capital first. Then we will all go find Gileal."

I chewed on my lip, my mind spun as I tried come up with a solution. If something happened to Nol, would they even try to save Gil?

"We aren't dismissing you, child," Tamden said. "We *will* find him."

Swallowing, I looked at Nol. He let his emotions show through the crease between his eyes and his deep frown, like he wanted to speak out. He looked torn. Gil was his best friend. I was his *muranildë*, but Gil was closer to him in more ways. They'd spent the entire time I'd been gone together. They were brothers, and it was killing him not to go. My begging and defiance were hurting him. There was a chance Nol would never see Gil again. He'd never be sure that we found him.

Nol came up behind me and turned me around. "I will come find you after this," he said in English. "We'll have time to say goodbye before I leave."

"Will you read me Gil's letter?" *If it ever gets here!*

"If that's what you want, sure."

Giving them all pointed looks, I walked to the door. But I couldn't leave. They'd kept him here—with the detonated bomb. I briefly wondered if I could scan the thing for spells or *imolegin*, but that'd take time and they were already ushering me out the door.

19

I STOMPED DOWN THE stairs, pissed as hell. They weren't the council, but they might as well have been with their own damn politics and ranks.

"*Oyi*!" someone called out from across the room. I stopped my descent and looked around. "Hally! Over here." Bren waved, Jenne under an arm. Maybe they'd help me find something to release this anger.

"I thought you were sleeping." Mischief danced in Jenne's eyes. "Were you spying?"

"No. I know where Gil is, and they don't want to save him. Yet," I added when I saw their eyes go hard. Yeah, Tamden hadn't lied. They all liked Gil. "They said *after* the capital. So, if shit hits the fan and they die, Nol will never see Gil again. And I might not either if they make you take me to *Jinatrau* right away."

"*Sercae cumo*," Jenne swore under her breath. Her look of pure anger reminded me of when Nol hit the wall.

Bren's jaw was clenched so tight I heard his teeth creaking.

"Got a good way to release some anger?" I asked.

"*Voida ja majut mina*," *Fuck yes, I do*, Bren growled.

My breath caught. *Zayuri* were still scary, and I was really glad they were on my side.

"Without killing anything, if you wouldn't mind."

His eyes flashed to me. "Who the fuck could I kill out here? Don't take this offensively, but it pisses me off even more that I cannot go rescue Gil myself, as I volunteered to protect you."

"No offense taken. It's nice to know how much you care about him." My words seemed to calm them, and all I wanted to do was sneak out with them and go. They all had dragons. One of them should be willing to let me tag along.

"Come on." Jenne didn't wait for either of us as she stormed out the door.

Behind the buildings was a covered small training ground, open on one side, facing the forest. Training swords and daggers were held in a closet, along with padded protective clothes. A few of the open rooms held mats for hand-to-hand training. Bren and Jenne picked an outside circular area for sword practice. They gave me a training sword to whack against a post while they got to hit each other. Not that I complained. Going head-to-head with a *Zayuri*? Not on my life. Still, a wooden sword with nothing to do? Never give me nothing to do. Walking away from them toward the forest, I found a large pole in the ground with chunks hacked out of it. It looked like people whacked their swords into it.

I looked down at my wooden sword, then back at my two new *Zayuri* friends. I shrugged and spread my magic over the wood to harden the training sword, similar to the sealing I'd done to Nol's jacket. The wood shouldn't break. Maybe. My first swing didn't do much. Even though the power reverberated up my arms, it wasn't enough to trigger the band. First, the band had allowed me to save Sanae with only a numbing tingle, and now it wasn't siphoning energy? I added more magic, and still nothing happened. Was it asleep? I'd find out in a second.

I imagined my magical energy soaking into the sword, not just for protection but for strength. At the last moment, I made a note to also protect the pole and buildings around me, so that if the energy fanned out, it wouldn't go too far. Centering myself as I stared down at that piece of wood in my arms, I pulled the stick back, then checked to see if Bren and Jenne were still in the ring. Focusing all my intent on the pole, I threw everything I had into the swing.

Maybe it was a bit too much. The slave band reacted, except slower than normal.

The power *did* protect what I wanted it to, but not the giant trees behind us. I flinched when the tree straight ahead creaked and bent from the base of the trunk. The large tree touched the trees behind it and the trees behind them bent as well. For a moment, I thought they were going to all snap, but the roots stayed in the ground. I covered my face with one hand, squeezing my eyes closed, listening to the trees creak and moan as they bent back.

"What the fuck!" Bren yelled.

I whipped around to check on them. For a moment, I thought my magic had somehow reached them and the buildings behind us, hurting everyone. Nothing looked out of order. Jenne and Bren were safe, but they were running toward me.

"What was that?" Jenne asked, even though it should have been obvious.

"They're gonna spring back!" Bren yelled as the two *Zayuri* came up to me. "*Mujut.* It's going to come our way." He cussed a little more colorfully in words that had no English equivalent. Sure enough, the trees—not just the biggest one, but all of them—started bending back our way.

If I could swing power into it, I had to be able to stop it, even if the slave band would have a buffet on all the extra power. These trees were not going to reach us. I ran like I'd run to Sanae, full-out. My arm tingled, and I remembered my promise to Quinn. Keep my base protected. Great. Now I remembered.

I threw the same raw power I'd used to make this happen to stop the trees' forward momentum. Except, I wanted to stop them this time. Period. It would happen. With almost everything I had, I made those damn trees hold still. I wouldn't let it come back on us. I wouldn't let it go the other way. It. Would. Stop.

And it did. Even the leaves didn't rustle. I dropped to my knees in the grass, expecting to pass out, but I didn't. I let the band take my magic willingly. Kneeling there, I listened to the absolute silence of the forest beyond the hammering of my heart.

Bren and Jenne came up on either side of me and took a moment to catch their breath. I looked at Jenne, but the night hid her expression.

Jenne knelt beside me, staring at the trees. "*C'yo,* Hally. The whole place is silent. Are you still holding it?"

There wasn't enough magic in me to use, just enough to protect me—like I'd promised. Cutting it a little close, but at least I remembered. "No, the wind will pick the leaves up soon."

"How can you use that much and still be conscious? That was massive."

"I don't know." I looked up at Bren and then over at Jenne. "Would you guys mind helping me up? I'd like to go sit down for a little while. And maybe have some more of that *tanadlyn.*"

"That sounds like a good plan." Bren grabbed my hand and pulled.

There was so much we didn't know about the band, but I couldn't have done this two months ago. Regular magic use had built my endurance like physical training, delaying when the band would pull energy. But this level of improvement felt unbelievable. Perhaps it was being in *Endae,* where magical energy was everywhere. It made sense, and the only way to know for sure would be to test it out when and if I got home to Earth.

Nothing seemed out of place as we stepped back into the lodge. The three people we passed were going about their business. No one had sensed a thing.

I leaned over to Jenne after a *Zayuri* passed us. "Can we not mention that incident to anyone? What they don't know won't freak them out."

Bren snorted. "I think that might be a good idea for now."

JENNE PUT HER FEET up on the empty fourth chair around our table. "I cannot stand that they won't let us go." We all felt hurt and betrayed, but at least we'd blown off enough steam to be calmer.

"It's not the only way to go about it, but it makes sense," Bren said into his cup. "The only thing we know is that they've been able to keep Gil this whole time, and he's not a wimp. He's got some damn strong magic of his own."

I looked around the dark, empty room. We were the only ones here, so we'd only lit the sconce near us. "Did you guys know he can mask his features?"

They frowned at me. That must not have come out right. I waved at my face. "Change what he looks like. He made his eyes look more blue and his ears look round. Aswryn could do it, too. Do you think that means he'd found a way into her inner circle?"

Bren looked skeptical. "He would have mentioned that."

Jenne perked up and uncrossed her arms. "What if he did? To the high *Zayuri*. They could have kept it secret."

"Maybe." Bren licked his lips, pondering. "If it were common knowledge, it would have gotten back to Aswryn. She'd know Gil had told someone."

"He'd have been burned." Jenne stared into her cup of *tanadlyn*. "You don't think that's what happened when he brought *Hinam* Nolan back, do you?"

I was sipping my drink slowly, alternating with water. "Where exactly does my tree connect to? That's where Gil went through."

"Near the north side of the capital. I don't understand how Aswryn overwhelmed him."

I curled my lip. It wasn't my favorite topic. Aswryn had told me herself that she'd killed him. Well, she'd assumed he was dead.

"*C'yo.*" Bren leaned back in his chair. "He was so angry with Nolan when the council gave him permission to find you, but not Gil."

Jenne hummed in agreement. "When Nolan came back to get those samples you wanted, Gil wasn't going to be left behind again."

"He told me he wasn't coming back." Bren twisted his lips. "I didn't blame him."

"He told me that, too," I said. "He planned on coming back to me after he took Nol and Aswryn home. I hate to think how long Gil lay alone. There are so many questions I want answered. I won't go back until we get Gil, so don't even try to force me through a tree." I glared at them each in turn.

"He loves you so much, Hally." Jenne rolled her eyes, smiling. "It was always on his mind to get you back here. On *Hinam* Nolan's mind, too."

"I cannot believe you got him to smile and thank Jenne. I'd follow him to the Starless Abyss if he asked, but he's...he took the emotional training to his soul."

"He never lets up—" Jenne stared at the table and nodded, probably remembering something Nol had done. Did that mean he was an asshole? Sounded like it.

"But he is fair and never gets pissed," Bren added.

"Never. It's just no one wants to disappoint him. You get it?"

I tried to imagine Nol the way they described him. "I don't. No. I can't see him like that. He's been distant with you, and it's impossible to make him use his manners. I swear his mother taught him some. I was there, getting the same damn lessons from both our sets of parents." I chuckled at the memories. "Who you've described is just not my Nol. Mine loves books and learning, not fighting." I leaned on the table and rubbed my forehead. "I mean, I see it now; the part of him that is *Zayuri*. It scares me, how intense I've seen him. How fast he can move and how he can hide his emotions from me." I had to pause when it reminded me of his outburst in the room. "But how you describe him, it's another person. When I found out his uncle convinced him to become a *Zayuri,* I about died—"

Jenne held out her hand to stop me. "What do you mean Tolwe convinced him to be *Zayuri*? He took the pledge of the *Zayuri* path after An'di, Raj, and Camber died."

My heart stilled, and I stopped breathing. Nol had told me about An'di. I'd assumed Raj had died when Nol refused to say anything about her. She was my best friend. We'd been in the same year in school and had similar outlooks. Though she'd been so shy, we'd clicked.

Everyone thought being a seer meant she could see everyone's future and knew everything about them. Not true. The closer the connection to her, the less she could see. She'd always told me my future was tangled and twisted. It had given her a headache to even try seeing my future. And since Nol was so close to me, she couldn't see his either. He never believed me. It was a surprise that Raj and Nol *had* gotten close, or become friends at least. A good surprise, though. But who was Camber?

Bren's next words brought me out of my thoughts.

"No," Bren corrected. "Raj and Camber got infected while he was gone, after Aswryn took him and Gileal. He pledged after the *Zayuri* found him, so he could go after Aswryn to break the curse and save them."

What did they mean by pledging? Nol never talked to me about any pledges. The two kept talking, as if I weren't here, just shooting the shit like any old *Zayuri* conversation. As I listened, I found it hard to follow. Who was Camber? What did they mean?

"Oh." Jenne shrugged. "I hadn't pledged yet, so I'm only going off secondhand knowledge."

Bren turned his cup around on the table, staring at it instead of looking at either of us, lost in thought. "We made our pledge to the *Zayuri* together. He was different before they died, almost happy. Gil said after you left"—Bren lifted his head from the table and looked up at me—"he was never the same, but after they had Camber, Gil said he saw that spark in him. He'd come back to life. Nolan was so, so focused on getting Aswryn. I get it, right? Knowing that your kid and wife will die if—"

Things clicked the moment Bren said *they had Camber.* I couldn't hear anything else. My whole body shaking, I stopped Bren. "Kid and wife?"

They shut their mouths and snapped their heads up to stare at me, shock written all over them.

"Oh, fuck. You didn't know?" Jenne asked in a terrified whisper.

"Nolan never told you? How is that possible?" Bren didn't look as scared as Jenne, just shocked and confused. I was shocked, too, since my *muranildo* should've been able to tell me anything. Like the fact he had a *wife and kid*. That they'd died. From the curse. Two of my very best friends. Raj had had the biggest crush on him and would get too tongue-tied to string two words together around him.

"Camber is his *daughter*? He-he had a kid with my best friend." I was on my feet before I realized it. My cup fell, the clear drink running off the table onto the floor, dripping as things fell into place.

What Wennië had said to him in *Rudairn*, if it had been Cam. Cam had to be Camber. That hadn't been fair of her to use his dead daughter as a comparison. I wasn't dead, and his daughter was. My mind went back to that first night he came to Seattle, when Nol was venting. He'd mentioned a Cam. I'd thought it might have been An'di's daughter or someone close. Then every moment Nol spent with Ray, when he was happy...when he wasn't.

"I'm so sorry, Hally. I didn't know. Why—"

But I was already up and moving before Bren could finish the question that no one but Nol could answer.

"Hally, wait," Jenne called out.

"Leave me alone, Jenne. I will deal with this. Now." My hand shook as I touched the railing to the stairs. I'd climbed them before I realized it. The door to the East Hollow room was locked, but that didn't stop me.

The door slammed into the wall, and the six *Zayuri* stared in shock.

"*Hinam!*" It was Jenne behind me. "I'm sorry!"

"Why didn't you tell me about Raj and Camber? Why did I have to learn about your *child and wife* from someone other than my *muranildo*?" I spoke in English, but they must have heard Raj's and Camber's names because everybody moved. They left all their little toys and papers and cleared out while Nol stared at me in shock.

Someone shut the door, and that's when my patience wore off. He wasn't giving me an answer, and I wanted one.

"Tell me, Nol. She was my friend."

Nol looked down at the floor.

"And you didn't have the decency to tell me?" I didn't give a shit if the whole lodge heard me. If they could hear me in the capital. I didn't care. "I knew she died. I knew when you didn't mention her, like you didn't mention anyone else. I thought you couldn't talk about them."

He shook his head. "I can't."

"But Raj is different—more than them. She was your wife! Your wife. And you had a baby!"

He flinched. "I knew it would hurt you to know—"

"To know what? That my best friends actually found some resemblance of peace? That she could comfort you? I knew my banishment had hurt you. Gil, Yalu, Tolwe—they told me you weren't the same. That you got distant. But what you didn't have the balls to tell me was the thing I'd tried so hard to show you for years!" Hands in fists, I threw them in the air. "Years!"

His eyes shot up, surprise all over his face. "You—"

"Why do you think I pushed you so fucking hard to get to know her? Like hell she'd be able to tell you! She was so fucking shy, and you were such an *ass* to her. But she liked you regardless. Such a fucking ass. And you didn't tell me. Me, your *muranildë*. You're supposed to be able to tell me anything. You didn't trust me enough with that?"

"It's not that—"

But I wasn't done, and I yelled over his timid voice. "That's why you love playing with Ray. She reminds you of Camber, doesn't she? Every time I saw you play and watched you turn inward, watched the light in your eyes dim, I thought it was because of An'di. You missed your sister. But it was your own daughter you saw in her!"

"Ray is *not* Cam," he bit out, and I was happy he was standing up for both of them.

"Of course she isn't! But I saw you there, and I could have at least comforted you if I'd known. But you didn't trust me enough to tell me you had a daughter. Why? That-that is something *you* should have told me. Not Jenne and Bren, not Gil or-or anyone else. We need to talk? That's what you say. We need to talk about where our relationship is heading and our feelings, if they're changing? Well, we're not talking about that until we figure *this* out. This is more important. Far more important than what could be. Is this why you thought I would see you differently? Why?"

He'd never seen me this mad. In fact, I couldn't remember a time in my life when I'd ever been this angry.

"Why?" I yelled when he didn't answer me. "Why were you so afraid to tell me? You were given the wonderful blessing of finding something other than yourself to live for. Something beyond you. And you couldn't share that."

"Because I knew you loved me." Nol leaned forward but didn't come closer. "I didn't want to hurt you."

Yeah, that shut me up. What the fuck?

"We all knew. Everyone saw it. It's hard not to when you always wanted to be with me. It hurt Gil, but all he ever wanted was your happiness."

"Are you fucking serious?" Oh, the look on his face told me he was pretty damn serious and rearranging all his assumptions about our childhood. "The only thing I was thinking about was my future. I was a kid, and you are my *muranildo*. I wanted to be with you because I felt complete near you. I felt safe and calm. It quieted my mind. I was able to *think*. It was comforting.

"Of course I loved you, but did I want *that*? Hell the fuck no! I was dealing with the council, the teachers, the kids bullying me relentlessly. I was warring with myself over what *I* wanted to do with my life: taking the council's proposal, shoving it up their asses, and going to *Pequwyn*, or hoping they'd compromise on their shitty expectations for me to be their puppet, marry whoever they chose, and breed for them like they did to Yalu.

"Nowhere in my mind did I have the capacity to fathom being with anyone. You were the only one I knew who would be there, no matter what. I couldn't have any little girl ideas about love. Sure, I liked

Gil, loved him in a way, but not the way he loved me. There were no thoughts of playing house with either of you."

I shoved my hair back, my chest heaving. "I enjoyed trying to get Raj and you together to get my mind off all the shit I couldn't tell you about. If you or Gil or even my parents had known what the council wanted me to do, everyone would've lost their shit. Hanno, Yalu, and I decided to keep it between us. So no, it wouldn't have *hurt* me if you'd told me about finding someone to love and build a family with. The fact that I screwed up so badly that I never got to meet Camber or be her auntie, or see Raj as a mother, breaks my heart. But worse, what-what is breaking my heart right now is that you didn't tell me. I could have known her through you. Maybe I could have helped you talk about them without you hurting. I know it would've been hard. I understand that!

"You let me cry on your shoulder just days ago and didn't tell me once—not once—that you'd been through something worse. I don't have children of my own, Nol, but I've loved those kids like my own. When we lost Franny, the times Emma miscarried and her little one died two minutes after she was born, I broke when she broke. So many fucking times, I broke. And I stood beside her and helped her through it. It kills me to think about them all, but I do."

"You didn't tell me—"

"Because you didn't ask! I asked. I offered to be there for you. To comfort you. That is my job, and you didn't let me do it."

"Hallë, I'm sorry." Nol stepped forward, as if he could fix this with a hug and an apology.

"No. I can't be here right now. I am so livid with you. Tonight, of all nights, this had to happen. I hope you survive because I want to fucking *kill* you myself when you get back. Do not try to apologize and expect me to forgive you. This won't go away."

"Can we work through this? Could you forgive me eventually?"

What a fucking stupid thing to ask. "Of course we can work through this! We're *muranildi*. It's a requirement. But I can't be here right now."

I turned to the door. There was so much anger in me that I could barely see straight. I thought it was a figure of speech, something people just said. No, it was definitely a thing. I flung the door open to find an empty hallway—thank the Mother.

As I stormed away, Nol's words stopped me. "Are you coming back tonight?"

Shoving my hair back, I turned and wished I hadn't. He looked broken and lost, or maybe left behind. Raj and Camber, his sister, and Gil had left him, and now possibly me? It made sense. But then...

"You're leaving *me*! And I can't do anything to stop it. I'm tired of being told no. All the time, I never get to choose. Well, fuck that."

And I left. Right out the door and down the road. I needed to do something. Something *I* chose. Damn it!

***

I'd made it a mile down the road when I heard a familiar whoosh of air. The sound of really big wings. I looked up at the sky, searching for a dragon. Well, she wasn't exactly in the sky.

"Sanae? What are you doing?" I ran to her as she folded her wings in. "They told me you won't be flying for a while."

"*That's what the endai say,*" Sanae thought to me. "*Not what I say. I felt my Nolan's sorrow, and he said he's lost you. But I found you.*"

A very simple way of looking at it. "I found out about Raj and Camber. Did you know them?"

"*I did. He loved them very much. Are you leaving my Nolan? He is afraid you will.*"

"Did he ask you to come get me?"

"*No. He wanted to know where you were. I thought if I could find you, he might not lose his light.*"

"Sanae..." I closed my eyes and considered what I needed to say. "He's not losing me. I just need time away. I want to do something to help. To be useful."

"*I can take you away for a little while, but I don't know about being useful. You have made my Nolan happy. Isn't that useful?*"

Smiling at her and her straightforward solutions, I decided what that help could be. "Sanae? Would you take me to Gil? I know where he is."

"*This idea is good. We will bring Gil home and you will all be happy.*" If a dragon could preen, she was doing it now as she hopped from foot to foot, her huge body prancing. "*I sensed it when you told my Nolan that you'd found Gileal. It hurts him that he can't go. I will take you.*"

"Are you going to tell Nol?"

"*Uh...*" She paused. "*I didn't mean to tell him. He sensed it just now. If you want to go, we should go before they can follow us.*"

"They?"

"*A few others...Jenne and her mate, Bren. And the others who will stay with us when my Nolan goes to the endaen city. My Nolan seems very concerned about your safety. We should hurry.*"

I looked down at myself. No coat. Otherwise, I was ready to sneak off, with my plan being to follow Nol into the city. I looked back at the lodge.

"Fuck it. Let's go."

Sanae lay on her belly and moved her back leg forward so I could use it as a step. Something we'd come up with after all those days of flying. Reaching around her neck, I pulled myself up and straddled her.

"*Stay down and I will keep you warm as best I can.*" Her natural magic enveloped me as I settled at the base of her neck. She unfolded her large black wings, and with two giant whooshing flaps, we were in the sky. "*Show me where to go.*"

I pictured the direction we needed to travel. Such an easy way of communicating. No need to find the right words to understand each other.

"*You are mad at our Nolan,*" Sanae stated after we'd leveled out and were past *Aetyru*.

"*I am,*" I thought back to her. There was no need to yell into the wind.

"*He was afraid you would be angry, but you don't feel that angry. You feel sad. And something else.*"

"*He's a fucking idiot about the reason I would be mad.*"

"I'm confused. There is more than one way to be angry?"

"There're lots of ways, Sanae. Many. He thought I was in love with him when we were kids."

"But you were not. I feel what you say in both of you."

"I wanted Nol to be with Raj. He kept that a secret. That hurts."

"If he had told you that he fell in love with Rajamë and they had a child, and then that he had lost them, would you not have been angry?"

How would she come to that conclusion? *"No. My heart is broken by this, but now I know why he's hurting. But also, I'm happy, because for a tiny amount of time, he found happiness. He got to be a father. I wanted that for him and for Raj to be a mother. I'm sure they were great parents. But he was so selfish. How could he? This whole time, I never knew what was going on. How much he was hurting. How could he keep this from me?"*

Sanae didn't say anything. She knew I knew the straightforward answer.

"Hally?" Sanae thought to me after we'd flown so far that the capital was a little white dot. We'd be there soon. *"I think I have an answer, but it's hard for me to understand."*

"Okay..."

"He loves Raj and Camber. Still loves them so much it hurts to think about them and their deaths."

"Nol doesn't want to admit they're gone?"

"Sometimes, he wants to not think about them. When it is too hurtful for him, he turns away from them."

What Sanae said reminded me of something Nol had told me a few times in different ways. He wanted to be here and not think. He wanted to play ponies with Ray and pretend he wasn't there to assassinate Aswryn—or had he meant who he was doing it for? Being there with me helped him not think about *it*. He missed them so much, he'd said, crying on my shoulder.

"Sanae? I think he did tell me, without telling me." I let her see all those times Nol was with me and my family and what Nol had told me.

"Without telling you, yes. He sought your comfort when he thought about them, but you didn't know what he needed that comfort for. You are very smart, Hally. Do you forgive him?"

"No— I don't know. I'm still angry with him."

"That's fine. I'm glad you've forgiven him. You can be angry, as long as you don't leave him."

"I didn't say I forgave him."

"You didn't have to." I felt her smugness over seeing through my anger, at least thinking she did. I still wasn't sure myself. *"Hally? I see the waterfall. We're almost there."*

20

SANAE SOARED AROUND THE waterfall on the opposite side of the fortress. We'd looked at it from all angles, flying past like any normal dragon would, should they come out here. The problem was, *Zayuri* dragons were distinctive in size and color. We had the night to help hide us but still tried to be as careful as possible. Twice, I thought we might have crossed into *Mellori* territory, but what they didn't know...

"*I will have to climb the rocks below,*" Sanae thought to me, showing me in my mind where she was talking about.

"*I can climb there if you perch over to the left.*" I showed her where I meant in my own mind. "*What do you think?*" The walls of this monstrosity had to be twenty feet high. For sure it was much longer than it was deep. The fortress didn't protrude far off the side; instead, they'd found the widest part of the trail, built a stabilizing platform below, and carved into the side of the mountain to make the castle. The only way Sanae and I could find to get in was the wide-open front gate, as ominous as it was welcoming.

"*Not stable. I'll crawl up to the edge of their path. You climb over my head, and I will wait for you to come out with him. Are you certain you can do this?*"

I huffed a short laugh. "*No,*" I thought to her. "*Not at all. But I will try.*" Cloaking myself in my magic should be simple...even if I didn't have a lot of energy.

Sanae felt my hesitation. "*If you are taken, I will find Jenne and Bren. I think they would like to do something as well. We didn't like the idea of being left behind either.*"

"*Fine. Deal.*"

With that, Sanae dove almost to the ground under the fortress—a bit too much like the crash earlier, but I survived. She grabbed the side of the cliff and hopped up, using her wings to push herself up the mountain. Grasp, jump, whoosh, and grasp. The noise of the waterfall muted the sound of her climb.

"*I didn't realize you'd be climbing the mountain from this far down.*"

"*I have to.*" Sanae paused her thoughts as she made another jump. "*We will not fall. If we slip, I can fly off.*" She jumped again. "*Don't fear.*"

"*I'm not afraid,*" I lied.

"*I can sense your mind, Hally. You can't lie to me.*"

Ten feet under the wide trail in front of the gate, Sanae stopped jumping and climbed. She slipped once, but she was confident we wouldn't fall, and I believed her.

Once below the trail, I climbed up her neck, and she boosted me up with her nose. Saying this was a trail was a bit of an understatement. A semitrailer would fit easily. But I thought *trail* because we were on a mountainside and it wasn't smooth. Rocks, dips, and roots of the straggly little trees grew out of the side of the mountain.

Either way, the giant trail led up to the entrance, unmanned and open. Why would they care to close it, anyway? No one knew about this place. Who would climb a mountain and happen upon it? No one but me.

"*What are you waiting for?*" Sanae thought to me. "*Be quick so my Nolan can see him sooner.*"

"*Yeah, yeah.*" I rubbed my hands together and blew into them. Shit, it was cold. Taking a deep breath, I thought about all the practicing Nol and I had done, and quickly ignored my broken heart. Maybe Gil could help us work through this?

"*Good thinking. Gileal is good with those sorts of feelings,*" Sanae agreed, not like I'd shared my thoughts with her.

My wards still weren't very strong, but I wasn't going to make a ward. I was going to tweak what Nol had explained to me and make my own version. I suspected *Zayuri* had a similar spell. I let all thoughts out with my air, until the one single idea of going unnoticed remained.

"*You're still visible. I can see you.*"

"That's because I'm not done. And you talking in my head doesn't help me," I said out loud.

She'd just been trying to help. I felt her apology.

"*It's okay. I know you're trying.*"

Why did we have limitations and call them wards or shields? What if I thought of it like a tent, a bubble, or a blanket? I liked the idea of a blanket. Call it stupid, I didn't care. I sent my magic out around me, coating me like a blanket. When it was covering all of me, I pictured it protecting me. Protecting me from eyes that didn't know me. That way, Gil could see me. That would make sense. Sanae couldn't tell me if it was working, though. I had to believe in myself to do it. And if I could knock down a whole forest and then still every leaf, I could keep myself protected, damn it.

With the substantial amount of energy I'd used in the last twelve hours, I only had enough to cast small stuff, like globes and wards. Plus, I couldn't expect the slave band to continue being generous. So I had to work fast and smart. A second longer to ponder if this was working and I was off.

As I entered the grounds, I quickly moved to the right side and was soon under the lip of the mountain cliff. The lack of wind kept the chill out of my bones. It took me a moment to realize why my nerves were on edge. The pounding sound of the waterfall was almost gone. When I couldn't see my fingers in the dark, I stopped. How deep did this thing go? Shuddering at the thought of all that rock above dropping on me, I pressed my back to the fortress wall and waited until my breathing evened out.

These people were self-sufficient. Inside the outer walls, a garden covered over an acre of land. The building was at the back, built from the rock. I had no way to tell how far into the mountain it went. I released my magical security blanket and listened. If I could hear everything, then anyone could hear me, but they'd have to use an orb to see because they wouldn't be sneaking in; they'd be out in the garden finding a midnight snack! *Keep it together, Hally.*

Using an orb of my own would alert anyone looking out the window or from above on the wall, so I backed up until I could make out the crops. Security blanket back in place, I stepped off the wall and stopped after four steps. My boots echoed far into the black abyss of the mountain. Fuck.

Boots hanging around my neck by their laces, I tried again. The rocks didn't feel like a massage, I'll clue ya, but I didn't hiss. I tried to step lightly. By the time I touched the cool wall of the castle, my feet were screaming at me. I shoved my socks and boots back on, making absolutely sure there were no pebbles embedded into my feet. Now to find a door...

My security blanket needed to stay up now that I was inside the walls. It wouldn't do if that person getting a snack opened the door to find me standing there. I couldn't trust the slave band to work with me forever, but I was grateful it was letting me keep more magic in *Endae.* As I walked down the side of the castle without its familiar pull, my theory about the slave band in *Endae* solidified in my mind, which sucked because I couldn't stay here.

The rough texture of the stone grazed my fingers, but then something cold and smooth made me jump. Metal. I realized as I'd been lost in my thoughts that I'd walked into the darkness again. When I couldn't find a handle on either side, high or low, I paused. Why would someone put a rectangular sheet of metal—nevermind, I found the hinges. So it did open. Then there had to be a handle, but for the life of me, I couldn't feel one. Then I got it and almost slapped my forehead. *Endai* and magic. If all the doors required magic to open them, I was screwed. One hundred percent, they'd have a ward to detect something like that. Did I risk it? The more I contemplated, the more time I wasted.

"*Oiy!*" A male voice echoed around the vast fortress walls. Maybe he wasn't talking to me. Fat chance. I couldn't see a damn thing, and the echoes made it impossible to tell me his location. A moment later, I found out. A large hand grabbed my shirt and yanked me off my feet. "I said, *oiy.*" His breath smelled like pickles and beer. "What is a pretty little thing like you doing out here? I think I know…" His hand covered my face, a spell washed over me, and I was out.

FORTRESSES WERE SUPPOSED TO have dungeons with cells and maybe a few shackles. Gil would have been in one beside mine. They were supposed to have bricks I could wiggle free or holes I could make bigger somehow and crawl out of. This had none of that. My younger self would have said "Boring." They had me in a closet-sized room with no windows and one door without a handle. I didn't call it a closet because they'd managed to get a lumpy mattress made of…lumpy crap in here. It could have been wood shavings. It poked and prodded me when I woke up and moved around, so maybe more like chunks of wood.

Now I was pacing the narrow room. Three steps in either direction. I'd fiddled with their door spell hours ago, only to have someone pound on it and tell me to knock it off. I was pretty sure it was Pickles who'd said it. That was the only reaction I'd gotten. What if he was the only one who knew I was here and that's why he wanted me to stop? The others would detect me if I kept at it.

How long had I been out? I had nothing to gauge the time with since I couldn't connect to Sanae. The one thing I knew with absolute certainty was that Nol wasn't dead. I'd have felt his loss. Had he read Gil's letter yet? Were they on their way to the capital? I hadn't come back…I'd left him behind. Every few paces, my mind would go back to that, and I'd stumble. Oh, how fucked up was this? Nol had left me once. Did he think I'd done the same to him? Left him out of revenge? That I'd chosen Gil over him because Gil had stayed? This wasn't like that, but one could look at it that way. It sure as hell felt that way right now. That's not what I wanted Nol to think when he went into the capital, if he wasn't already there. I would get Gil and take him to Nol to show him I hadn't left him.

So first...this damn door lock. "Here goes nothing."

At first, I felt inside the door, seeking out the magic that made it lock. My magic brushed over it, looking for any weak spots. Nothing was perfect, and if the caster had had any hesitation in the intent they had used to make it, any shake in the hand as they'd drawn out the sign, I would find it. Fuck their intent, and fuck their hand placement. Traditional spells. Even if they'd cast it in their heads, they still had to know the correct hand placements and incantation. The deformities in this spell were minute ones, but that's what I had to work with. I picked one of the few soft spots and poked it. A bang on the door startled me, and my mind let go.

"Try it again and you'll regret it," Pickles hollered at me.

Oh, if that was all it took. I shoved my magic in there as hard as I fucking wanted to, and it...fell. The door cracked open, Pickles hit it again, and the door flung into the wall. The metal shook and hummed from the force. Luckily, I hadn't been sitting close enough for it to smack me. He caught me sitting on the floor, legs crossed like I was meditating. Well, in a way I had been. Fingers pressed together in front of me, I stared straight up at him as he righted himself. He didn't fall, points for him.

"Uh...I have to pee?"

He blinked, trying to figure that out. "Then why didn't you just knock and tell me?"

Oh, we were actually having a civil conversation? I thought it was going to be the bad guy storming in, roaring. Then I'd have slipped through his legs. Damn, I was zero for two here.

I spread my hands wide and shrugged. "You didn't seem too accommodating. You should really work on your people skills."

His sort of surprised, sort of interested expression closed off, and then he stormed in like I'd imagined. Time to go. Being lower gave me the advantage, as he had to lean over to get me. I grabbed his arms just as I swung my feet around, planted them at his knee joint, and forced his knee to bend at the wrong angle. Pickles toppled to the ground, and if I hadn't rolled away, he'd have landed on top of me.

I'd like to lie and say I sprung up in one fancy ninja move and ran out the door, but let's face it, I'm not Nol. Instead, I rolled until I thought I was out of Pickles' reach and sat up. He was on his side, shaking his head. He must have fallen on it. Damn. Been there, done that. He focused and saw me staring at him from the floor. He closed his mouth and sucked in air like he was going to yell. Nope. I dropped my light orb on him. Not that it had a lot of energy behind it, but it startled him.

"What the fuck?"

"Yeah, it's kinda my go-to. Not the most inventive, is it?" I conjured another one, fed it more energy, and threw it at him.

He didn't say anything after that. I made sure he was still breathing but didn't stay long. Between the head injury and my shock of energy to his system, he could be out for a while. If he was thickheaded, he could be up at any moment. That's when I scrambled to my feet and ran.

This was more like what I'd envisioned a castle looked like. Dark stone walls, dark stone floors, magical sconces on the walls, all giving off a soft glow. I could have intensified them and made it daylight bright, but I was already running around a corner. Stairs leading up! Eight steps up and I heard someone coming down. There was no place to hide. I bolted back around the corner.

"Hally?"

My body froze, so much so that I had to brace myself against the wall so I didn't fall. Breathing raggedly, I was afraid to turn around, that my mind had made this up. But I'd felt his *imolegin*. A stupid fear, but what if I was wrong?

"Hally?" Gil's voice was more certain now. "I felt your *imolegin*. You broke the door locks."

He had broken out, too or we could say I'd broken him out. I used the wall to help myself turn, less excited and more terrified that we'd be caught.

Gil stepped off the last step. He stopped, and I saw his beautiful, wide teal eyes, his chest heaving. I couldn't say or do anything except stare. They'd treated him well, at least. Let him shower and gave him clean clothes. No signs of torture or mistreatment. He moved, one foot forward, and my body was free. I ran. Before I knew it, my arms were around him, and I'd never let go. He was never allowed to leave us ever again. I'd drag him to Earth and Nol and I would keep him safe. They'd both stay safe with me. But we had to hurry.

"Gil?" I pulled away from him. "We have to go! Do you know a way out?"

He stared at me, probably not expecting my first words to be anything but happiness. I watched those eyes blink, the ones I thought I'd never see again, and I kissed him. Yes, I had Quinn as a boyfriend, but who could blame me? Gil hesitated at first. My reactions were a bit contradictory. *Let's run, but first, kiss me.*

He pulled away, his hand pushed my hair back, and he caught sight of my ear cuffs. "What are you doing here? You're exiled. The council is gonna kill you."

"No." He didn't know about any of it. His letter wasn't related to the bomb, then. "Yalu contacted me. They found your letter, so we came back. They gave me permission." And for other reasons, but we didn't have time for that now.

"But-but you came with him? Why would they allow you to come here? You're *not* supposed to be here, my love."

I touched the hair at the nape of his neck, rubbing the coarse strands between my fingers. He was here, really, really here. I wanted to see his crooked smile, but he was too concerned with shit he didn't need to worry about. "We can talk about that later. Sanae is waiting for us." I hoped. "We're taking you back."

"Sanae? Nolan's here, too?" His breathing grew rapid, and his eyes widened. He peeked over my head, as if expecting him to come out of hiding or something.

"It's just Sanae and me. A lot's gone on in the last few days. Can we talk about it on the way back?"

"Sanae let you fly her? Alone?"

"Yes—"

"Did he read my letter?"

"I'm sure he's read it by now, yeah."

Gil's arms tightened around me. "But you didn't?"

"No." I huffed out a laugh at his obvious question. I pressed my thumb against his blond eyebrow as my palm touched his face. "Gileal, listen." Why wasn't he listening to the most important part of this conversation? "We gotta go before Pickles wakes up or they find you out of your closet."

"What? Who?"

Oh, for the love of all things holy. "We need to leave!"

He gave me his smile. Not a big one, but enough that the one side twisted. "You're safe here. The council won't find you."

My arms loosened around him, but he wouldn't let me go. "What?"

"They wouldn't let me leave." He rolled his eyes like it was a preposterous idea.

"No. The council is fine—wait, what do you mean I'm safe here? We're being held captive. It's not like we're going to *ask* them. Why are you so calm?"

"Here, come and I'll show you." Gil let me go and grabbed my hand. We walked up the stairs. It opened up to a large, bright area with large windows on all sides. Daylight streamed in, lit up the whole place, from the cathedral-type ceilings to the light stone floor.

The day had already come. Sanae must have left to get the others. Nol was at the capital. That meant the bomb hadn't gone off. It had worked. If all went well, that meant there were probably many *Zayuri* on their way. And I hoped to be outside waiting for them. I had to knock this Stockholm syndrome out of Gil's mind. Fast.

Gil led me through the middle of the room. Our shoes squeaked on the polished floor. Four large tables were grouped together filled with different science supplies. I noticed familiar *endaen* equipment that would have fit right in our school's labs in *Rudairn*. The last time I was near anything like this, my friends had been on the floor dying from the spell I'd cast.

This wasn't that. We weren't there.

Movement across the open room made me jump behind Gil. People. Three of them. That meant all *endai* were accounted for.

"It's all right, Hally. You're safe here."

The others staring back at me didn't look too certain of that.

"Gileal, this isn't a good idea," a light-colored *endaë* with blue eyes said, echoing my thoughts. Her hair was white, and she was the palest *endai* I'd ever seen besides Yalu and me. Her mouth was puckered, but she waited without further comment.

"She'll understand, Leda."

Leda crossed her arms, disagreeing with Gil.

"Understand? Understand what?" I turned to Leda, then the other two. A brown haired *endao*, a little taller than Gil and another *endaë* with deep lavender eyes and brown hair plaited down her back. They didn't look evil. They felt,I hated to admit I thought this, but, nerdy. And the rest of the room didn't help detour those thoughts either. It looked like one of Charlie's labs at the Udub, complete with a wall of books behind their tables of testing equipment.

"It's nice to meet you, Hally." The *endaë* with lavender eyes searched me with a hesitant smile. "I'm Nyda."

Maybe Gil had found others like An'di and they were looking for a cure.

"Are you healers?" My voice came out in a whisper.

The *endao* shook his brown hair back, drawing me to him as he fidgeted, his hand covered his mouth as he hid a smile.

"No, Aswryn killed all of them," Leda said. "Gil, didn't you tell her this?"

"She knows, but come on, Leda. What would you think?" Gil sassed like he'd known her a while. This Leda person sneered at him. Understandable. His sass was a bit much sometimes.

"What's going on?" I asked when no one else said anything.

The *endao* looked away and over at their workspace. "We're—"

Gil raised his arm, and the *endao* halted with a sheepish downcast look. "Let me show her."

The three *endai* didn't seem to like that too much, but Gil wasn't paying attention. For some reason, he wanted me to see whatever these guys were working on.

"Come." Gil pulled me over to the first table.

Nyda walked over and grabbed his arm as a reached for a shoebox sized metal box on top of the table, near the sealed glass containers of white, and black materials. A larger sealed jug of water was on the other side. "Be careful."

"I'm well aware, Nyda."

"Gil—" she hissed.

"You know I would never risk her life. She's fine."

Lips pursed, Nyda didn't say any more, but she wouldn't leave my side. They seemed to know a lot about me. Did they know about the bomb? From what I could tell, these people were out here working on a cure to the curse, oblivious to the world. Did they even know what was happening in the capital? These people were geared toward science, research, and finding a cure, not hellbent on taking over the world.

Gil opened the metal box, inside were dozens of rectangular, amethyst colored bottles. "Hally, this is the cursed virus, *Pae-lesoda.*"

My eyes flew wide open and I looked around for confirmation. Was this a joke? The three *endai* strangers in the room did not seem to think so. They must have been working on either breaking the curse or curing the virus. He'd found people to help! But then why did he think they wouldn't let him leave? Gil reached for one of the small bottles, but stopped when Nyda, inhaled sharply.

Gil, shut the box and pulled me around to the table across from it. This one also had equipment set around it, organized for function. Measuring equipment and collection containers on a shelf under the table while larger equipment were on top of it. Gil opened another metal box to reveal small, sealed, green bottles.

"This is *serilesoda.*" He waited to see if I got whatever he was expecting me to figure out. None of them explained any further. We were wasting time.

"Gil, I don't get it. What's *serilesoda*? Should I know what that means?"

The brown-haired *endao* laughed. "How do you not know what *serilesoda* is?"

"Why do you think she wouldn't know, Savis. Sorry, Hally. Gil's told us, Savis is just being a jerk, again." Nyda gave Savis a glare, but he didn't seem too phased by it. "Gil, stop being mysterious to impress your girlfriend and just tell her."

Gil paused his tour of their research lab, because what else could this be if not research for a cure? Everything led up to that. He'd found others that could help. So why had he hid from us for so long? He looked around at these strangers, then settled on me and his shoulders slumped. "*Serilesoda* is the virus Aswryn cursed."

"Okay. That's good. Is this something you just discovered? Is that what the letter is about?"

"What letter?" Leda raised her chin and crossed her arms, giving Gil a glare that put his to shame. "Gil, we talked about this."

Gil was just opening his eyes when I looked back at him. Oops.

"You told him?" Savis asked, like it was a sin against nature.

Gil about broke, and it reminded me of Nol's look last night.

"What's the problem with telling Nol about what you've found? This is great. You've found people who can help—"

"*That's* not what he told him about," Nyda explained, the only one besides Gil who seemed to have any empathy. "An'di found out about the *serilesoda* connection thirty years ago."

"Then why is it such a big deal?"

"Because it's here. *Serilesoda* is an extinct virus that handicapped a person's magic. It didn't kill them. An *endao* named Serin found a cure for it over six thousand years ago. Since the *Zayuri* were already immune to *serilesoda*, Aswryn was trying to alter it so it would only infect the *Amura Ore*. Not to become a cursed pandemic for the *Aeminan* people."

Thank you, Nyda for being up front. Jeez. "Fantastic. And you're here researching all of it to find a cure."

Savis muttered something I didn't quite catch under his breath.

Gil's eyebrows furrowed, and his eyes darted away in frustration. "Guys, leave us be for ten minutes. Come on."

Nyda groaned, dropping her head back, but they listened and went away. Out of earshot, I couldn't say, but they did leave our line of sight.

Gil held my arm and guided me to the other side of the large room, farthest away from the windows, tables, and lab equipment. They'd set up the corner here as their break area of sorts. There were shelves of books and four chairs over a cushy rug. Probably a thinking corner to brainstorm ideas.

"You see, no one was supposed to die." Gil picked a chair and sat down. "We're searching for what Aswryn hid in the beginning. For the first few years, they thought it was a mistake she'd made. She promised to fix the problem before it got too far out of hand, but then she vanished. Now, we all know she was hiding in *Rosava*. Charlie can't kill the virus without *endaen* help. The curse anchors deep and tricks the virus into believing the curse is part of the *serilesoda* virus and they're stronger together."

"But you found Serin's work, didn't you? And the virus." I picked a chair close to him and sat as well and reached for his leg to squeeze. I was so proud of him. He would do it. He'd save everyone.

"Yes." His lips twisted as he thought, probably about how to explain more science stuff to me. "He found his cure in a small number of *Zayuri* who had become infected."

"But I thought they were immune?"

Gil reached over and tucked a stray lock of hair behind my ear. "Yes. Listen, my love. Immune systems are all different, just as everyone's *imolegin* is different. What Serin found was that the immune systems of the few infected *Zayuri* fought it off quickly.

"*Zayuri* immune systems changed the *serilesoda* virus to make it attack itself. One of these changed viruses could kill a colony of *serilesoda* within days. He found a way to use those changed viruses to kill the original *serilesoda* in others, ending the pandemic. Does that make sense?"

I looked away as I tried to find the catch. "It seems too easy. How would this work for everyone? And even if you somehow found that cure, didn't you say Aswryn's curse makes it stronger? Would this *Zayuri*-changed virus be able to...enter the cursed one?"

Gil sat up straighter, delighted that his explanation was getting through to me, sort of. "Not without help. The curse was very involved and multifaceted so that it merged with the virus. Each person had to work on a single section, and even that was complicated. With Serin's notes and Aswryn's work, we've finally developed something that works."

Now I saw what he was trying to point out. I glanced past the tables, uncertain if the other *endai* were within earshot. I leaned in and whispered as low as I could, "Are these the ones who hired Aswryn? Are they keeping you here?"

They must have picked Gil up after Aswryn had left him for dead. Gil knew so much about the cursed-virus, and they were using his expertise and outside perspective.

"That's what you told him, didn't you?" That was why Gil had said they wouldn't let him leave. *Amura Ore* would force Gil to tell them who they were.

Gil put his hands in his lap and looked at my chin. "Yeah." His smile didn't reach the spot where it made his lips crooked.

My stomach dropped. "Gil...you know you can't lie to me. I'm one of the only ones."

His face lost all hope, and his eyes brimmed with tears. "One of the reasons why I love you."

"Gil?" My voice wavered. "Look me in the eye and tell me with all honesty that you weren't one of them. That they found you after you took Nol and Aswryn back. Tell me they begged you to help them find a cure."

A tear rolled down his cheek. "I can't." He looked down at his lap. "I was so angry, Nevie. They took you away, my reason for living. We were all lost, and I wanted the *Amura Ore* to pay. We were all trying to find a loophole or make an appeal stick. The council denied everything and wouldn't even see our case. I was desperate. Then Aswryn offered a solution; possibility to hurt the *Amura Ore* like I was hurting.

"The council had hurt us all in our own ways." He encompassed the room to include his three buddies, and probably Pickles downstairs. A tear fell when he moved. "But we never wanted to kill them. Just hurt them, make them pay. The council doesn't care about anyone other than themselves. But not like this. Not like..." Gil shook his head, lost in his own thoughts and torment. "Aswryn tricked us. And then...there were a few of us who...weren't bothered by what she did. They sent the bombs to the capital, and I sent the letter to Nolan when I couldn't stop them. I begged him not to go. I don't understand why the council would give you permission to come here? Why did you come?"

It took me a while to realize he'd asked a question at the end of his monologue. There was no way to get my thoughts untangled enough to answer whatever he'd asked. He'd hired Aswryn. At the steam plant, while we were fighting, Aswryn admitted that someone had hired her to make the curse. No matter how many times I said it in my head, I couldn't believe it. These people had hired a psychopath with a vendetta to get revenge on the council, not considering the ramifications if things went wrong. And Gileal was one of those people.

"He trusted you."

Gil didn't respond.

"You stood beside him, watching him mourn the loss of his child and *wife*. My friend. All the while, you were responsible for their deaths."

"Ask me why I sent the letter." Gil's tone had changed from calm to unrepentant.

I shot to my feet. "Tell me you didn't send those bombs."

Gil looked up at me, all seriousness, honest down to his bones. "I didn't send the bombs, but...I did what I could to save lives. It was imperative to me that I send the letter to Nolan. If anyone could get to you at your house, he could." Gil glanced out past the tables.

Why had he specifically said my house?

"Nolan would be safe at your house." Because his buddies had found a way around the immunity, and with the Trees of Connection down, Nol couldn't come back and contract the curse. "Please, tell me what you meant when you said he didn't open the letter before you left? Is that a human thing? Why didn't he read it when I sent it to him? Why are you in *Endae*?"

It took me a full minute to decide whether to answer him. He didn't deserve answers. My father was dying because of him. *His* father was dying. This *endao*, who loved me and claimed to be such close friends with Nol, had betrayed him. Destroyed Nol's happiness.

"Did you infect Raj and Camber?"

Gil took in a deep breath, thinking about something. "No. I was with Nolan and Aswryn. I didn't know what was happening at home."

"Tell me what happened. Nol said Aswryn killed An'di and took you."

"True. An'di found what the virus was and started researching it." Gil squeezed his eyes shut. "We needed more time because we thought Aswryn was fixing the curse. An'di found the *serilesoda* inside the curse, and she was planning to go to a conference to share her work and get others involved." Gil dropped his head into his palms. "She was like a big sister to me, too. Aswryn killed her in front of me and dragged me away so I couldn't stanch the bleeding. We left her on the floor to die in her own office. Aswryn must have left clues behind for Nolan to follow. Her intent was to lure Nolan out. I know that now."

"And you helped Aswryn escape the capital guard."

He nodded, head still in his hands.

"Gil!" Leda came running over and grabbed Gil by the arm. "We need to go. Now. The *Zayuri* are here."

He looked up at me, shocked. No, I hadn't mentioned a damn thing. But if he'd pulled his head out of his ass, he'd have figured it out.

I swallowed and looked up at Leda. "You're not going anywhere."

21

GIL DIDN'T LOOK BETRAYED or shocked as he stared at me. Perhaps relieved, but mostly resigned to his fate. Leda yanked on Gil as he stared at me. Nyda and Savis came closer, wondering what the fuck was taking so long. Pickles still hadn't come up—I really needed to find out that guy's name. It was killing me.

Savis went to hit me.

"Savis, no!" Gil yelled, and Savis went flying. "I will kill you myself if you harm her in any way."

"She led them right to us, Gileal." Leda flung her hands in the air but stopped short of touching me. "We have to leave."

She didn't get it. They weren't going anywhere. I'd taken over the door lock spell, which meant I got to decide who came and went.

"It's over." Nyda sank to the floor, resigned as well. She looked up at me, reached for my knee, and made sure I was paying attention. "Thank you."

Gil jumped up and the others didn't dare get near him.

"Nevie." But instead of finishing whatever he wanted to say, he hurried to one of the tables he hadn't shown me. He yanked open a cupboard below and grabbed something. A few clinks of glass and he was hurrying toward me. "Listen to me. You know I love you with everything I am. Right?" Gil waited for my confirmation. He didn't deserve answers. "Do not let anyone open those vials I showed you. Do you understand? You know when I'm lying, and they are what I said they are." He slid something cold into my hands, a stone box as large as my hand but narrow. "Get these to Charlie. She'll know what to do. Can you do that?"

I still didn't answer him.

"Who's Charlie?" Savis asked and was ignored.

Gil twisted his lips, made a decision, and went back to the table, cussing under his breath as he pulled open cabinets and drawers. Nyda, Leda, and Savis watched Gil, but none offered any help. They knew they'd lost.

A tug in my mind—a gentle, familiar brush of thought. Nol. I couldn't use our communication *meril* without touching it, and they'd notice me reaching for my necklace. I let him feel how low my energy was, hoping it'd hurry him along. Then I let him see. Once my eyes, and his, had settled on Gil, I felt pure rage. I never wanted to be on the other side of that. It scared me so much that I shut down the link.

A metal door screeched open. Seconds later, someone yelled my name. "Found them!" Bren yelled, and his feet echoed through the large empty room. "Past tables. Back of the great room."

Bren in full *Zayuri* uniform, his *Zayuri* dagger visible for all to see, jogged past the tables until he was level with Gil. He grabbed Gil's arm with his non-sword hand and shoved him toward the rest of us. He looked around at the four of us, held his hand out, and my body stiffened. Bren had cast a *Zayuri* detainment spell on all of us.

"Sorry, Hally." Bren winced at me. "It's gotta be all of you until we get the all-clear. Nothing personal."

In March, when Nol and I were looking for the kidnapped fae children in a crappy house on Capitol Hill in Seattle, Nol had used the same spell to detain and control two fairies. They'd helped kidnap fae children and had held them hostage for years; a few of them were held for decades. Nol was able to make them walk and sit. He could have made them walk off a cliff. The five of us had no choice but to stay where we were.

Bren stared at Gil, emotions shoved down deep, but I could hear his teeth cracking from eight feet away. Jenne's light-haired head bobbed into sight. She looked at her boyfriend and realized the same thing I had.

"Bren," she warned. "Back away."

"I'm good, Jenne. *Basean* Tolwe is still with *Hinam?*"

"Yeah." Jenne moved around, staying out of the small space we were sitting in, but positioned herself so she could jump in front of Bren if he tried to lash out at Gil.

"Hally, you good? Safe? *Hinam* said you might be in trouble."

"She's too close to the others. Had to put her under." Bren searched me in a head-to-toe evaluation. "She's good—or looks to be."

Dozens of footsteps echoed through the great room, and other *Zayuri* found our cozy group. Bren assessed his fellow *Zayuri* before releasing his detainment spell.

Jenne ran up to me, checking everywhere. "Are you hurt? You look...well, you're always pale, but..." She leaned back on her heels and caught my eyes. "Hally? Talk to me. Are you hurt?"

Yes, but not in the way she needed to know. "Not hurt."

"Thank the Mother. She's all right..." Jenne looked around, then snapped at a *Zayuri* standing around. "Get Gileal in custody and out before *Hinam* Nolan sees him. I don't know if *Basean* Tolwe can keep him back much longer. And this *traitor* will get his day in court." She glared murder at Gil.

The *Zayuri* Jenne had snapped a Gil without a hesitation.

"Hally." Gil coughed once. "I'm not lying. Please believe me—"

I dropped my head and refused to listen to anything else Gil said. When I glanced up and found his space empty, my chest ached. Jenne laid her hand on my shoulder, made eye contact with me, and my world resettled. He'd betrayed us all.

One by one, Jenne and Bren shackled everyone and handed them off to other *Zayuri*. But Jenne and Bren stayed in here with me. As if they didn't want me to leave.

"What's—" My chest tightened, and I had to clear my throat a few times before I could speak.

Bren winced. "Sorry, that was from the spell to hold you still."

"What's going on?" I checked to make sure my fingers and toes were moving correctly.

"*Hinam*—" Jenne stopped talking as we heard distant yelling. We all listened and looked out into the empty great room. Our vision was limited in here, but something loud was going on.

"*C'yo*." Bren bolted.

It was Nol and Gil. I knew it. Gil wasn't safe, and he wouldn't get his day in court as Jenne had said. He'd betrayed everyone who'd planned on rescuing him. I tried to stand, to go out, to help, but Jenne placed a firm hand on my shoulder.

"It's not safe."

"I can handle myself, Jenne. You've seen that."

She looked out at the big room again, wincing. "*Hinam* told me your energy is almost at zero. We're going to stay in here until things settle down. *Basean* Tolwe will give the all-clear."

Tolwe? Why? She must have seen the confusion on my face.

"It's been a busy morning." No shit. The bomb obviously hadn't detonated. Tolwe was back, so the Trees of Connection were connected again. All that in one morning?

When more yelling came from outside, I grabbed Jenne's hand, still firmly on my shoulder.

"Nol can't kill him. He wouldn't be the same—"

"Hally, he's killed people before, more than Aswryn."

"But this is Gileal. You can't kill family, and he's the closest thing to a brother Nol's ever had. Tell me I'm wrong."

She dropped her hand, and we ran through the great room with its windows and glossy tiles. I followed Jenne to the hall on the right, out the front door, and into the sunlight. I hadn't expected to see Sanae pinning Gil to the ground in the middle of the vegetable garden. I also hadn't expected Nol to have his sword to Gil's throat. How had it gotten so far out of hand so fast? With Nol's sword out, everyone had backed away. Even the dragons, except Sanae.

Everything had been trampled, food, barrels, and who knew what that pile of wood used to be, but someone's dragon had demolished it. A dragon backed up every *Zayuri*, probably their own. All of the

Zayuri were frozen in indecision. Did they let the dragon and *Zayuri* slice the head off their enemy, or did they do the right thing and take him to the capital? Hard decision.

Across the grounds, Nyda's lavender eyes locked with mine. Her head shook in slow motion, a warning not to interfere? I didn't know and I didn't care. Gil's real friends were on their knees, in front of four *Zayuri*, but everyone's attention was on Gil and Nol. I grabbed Jenne's arm and stepped slowly down the steps. We couldn't take our eyes off the three living beings in front of us. Bren glanced at us, then back at the scene. He didn't know what to do either.

"I can feel Sanae's worry and anger. She wants to keep Nol safe but wishes to rip Gil's head off and eat it."

"You can sense her?"

"Yeah, she thinks it's a *Muranilde* thing." I peeked around Jenne to Bren. "Where's Tolwe?"

Bren shook his head. No one moved. Nol shifted his sword, and Sanae's claw followed. I had to be the one. Nol would do anything for me, and I'd do anything for him. And Gil was our best friend. The three of us against the world. It had to be me.

When I took the first step, Jenne grabbed my arm, but she saw what I'd already realized when she looked in my eyes. She let me go, worry and a warning not to die in her eyes. Right, I planned on not dying. I pushed my fear and panic aside, telling myself I was safe. None of them would ever hurt me.

Six steps in and Sanae's ear twitched. Ten steps and I saw Nol's head move a fraction. Fifteen steps and I felt Sanae's heat and saw Gil's face. His eyes were closed. He was ready to die. He wouldn't fight, and he wouldn't look Nol in the eye.

Another step and my hand reached for Nol's left shoulder. He was humming with power and rage. I swallowed and moved my hand up to his neck. The magic was more bearable here, but he still radiated deadly *Zayuri* energy. This was what they'd meant about the sword's song; the magic was much stronger than the dagger. My thumb brushed Nol's ear, and my fingers went into his silky hair at the base of his skull. I opened our link, but Nol had it shut down firmly. He wouldn't make that mistake again.

I licked my lips, uncertain of what to say. I traced little circles on his scalp, hoping to calm him, but he wouldn't even accept my comfort.

"*You are his light,*" Sanae thought to me. "*Guide him out of his darkness.*"

I scooted closer to him. We would've been standing abreast if Nol hadn't been leaning forward. Now his left shoulder was lower than his right, at about my chest level. What did I say when he didn't want me there?

"Nol?" I whispered above him.

Gil's eyes flew open, terror in his beautiful gaze as he looked from Nol to me. He did not make a noise, just pleaded with a single look. *Be careful.* I'd try.

"You are hurting, and he's to blame." I waited as Nol stood stone still. He hadn't moved his sword since he'd seen me at my tenth step. "He deserves to be punished, and death undoubtedly awaits him." I made more circles on his scalp in hopes to ease some of his tension. The power radiating off him intensified. I was losing him. "You can't do this."

Nol flinched, Gil hissed, and Sanae tightened the two claws closer together where Nol's sword was touching Gil's neck. The wound bled heavier than a cut that size should have been bleeding. Right, *Zayuri* could cause a wound to coagulate, or they could reverse it and cause a person to bleed out from a seemingly insignificant wound.

"Let him go, Nol."

"Don't—" Nol forced the word out between clenched teeth.

"I have to. I am asking. Please, Nol, release him."

His head twitched in a no.

"Nol, please? Please don't do this. Walk him into custody and glare at him in the cell until his day in court. It will be fast because these are the people who cast the curse. Once they're dead, the curse will end. Nol, it can't be you who kills Gileal. Please, come back to me. Put *Oturan* away and look at me. I need you to do that."

"Step back," Nol growled at me.

"Not without you."

"I need you to step back, or I can't sheath *Oturan*."

Oh, but could I trust him to put it away instead of slicing Gil's neck? Would he call it an accident?

"Promise me you will put it away and not kill him when I step back. Swear it."

I waited. I got a sigh when he gave in.

"I swear I won't harm him further. I swear I am merely going to sheathe my sword."

"Thank you." I stepped back but didn't take my eyes off any of them. He did as he had promised and swung the sword up and slipped it into the back scabbard.

The moment Nol's sword was out of his hand, the *Zayuri* swarmed us. Sanae lifted Gil up and away from Nol. Tolwe came over and grabbed his nephew's shoulders, pulling him into a fierce, long hug. I'd never known that Tolwe and Nol had a close, amazing relationship until Nol had come to Seattle.

I was afraid to come closer. Afraid Nol would reject me for what I'd made him do. That it would be too much for our bond that I'd taken away the chance to kill the person responsible for his child's death. Yeah, I would have reservations about me, too.

Tolwe let him go and patted his shoulder. He turned to me with almost the same blue eyes as his nephew, his weary expression telling me everything I needed to know. Nol didn't want me. He saw me take a step back and reached out to embrace me as well.

I couldn't recall a time Tolwe had hugged me, and though he and Nol were the same height, Nol was broader in the shoulders like his father. But the love was there, and I'd accept that.

"He needs time," Tolwe whispered. "You did the right thing. Just give him time to process. You can ride to the capital with me, okay?"

I about lost it right then and there. Throughout the whole ordeal, I'd kept my composure, joked with myself, and kept my fear and sorrow inside. But to be told I couldn't ride a dragon I'd been terrified to touch four days ago hurt the most. *How pathetic am I?*

"*Not pathetic at all. He still loves you,*" Sanae thought to me. I'd forgotten about the whole *reading my thoughts whenever she wanted to* thing. I'd take it. She was a pretty cool dragon, after all.

22

I UNCOILED MY BODY from the neck of Tolwe's dragon until I could stretch my legs and scoot down. The *Zayuri* had their own dragon stables in the city of *Aetyru*, between the Hall of Justice, the Starborn Palace, and the Assembly of *Aemina*. No one was there when we landed, except for the dragons in the three-story stable, complete with perches. After the capital guard lost Aswryn years ago, I doubted the *Zayuri* trusted the guard to keep the five prisoners detained. Besides, they didn't need permission or clearance to keep their prisoners, not when they'd threatened the royal family. Nol might get to sit and watch Gil up until his trial, like I'd suggested.

"Slide down and I'll catch you," Tolwe called to me. At first I thought he was joking. It wasn't like I hadn't ridden a dragon before. I looked down. Oh. While not twice as high as Sanae, the fall was higher than the big slide at a park—and straight down. I'd take the help.

As Tolwe walked me through the Starborn Palace, I looked for friendly faces, but there weren't many faces to search. None of them were *Zayuri*, and whenever they caught a glimpes at who was coming, they scurried away.

Tolwe walked two or so steps ahead of me, going faster than I was comfortable with. "Nolan said something about your energy being low. How are you doing?"

"I'll live. Thanks for asking." I hurried to catch up again.

The Assembly of *Aemina* and the Starborn Palace were bigger than they seemed, even with the spire in the front toppled over. Flying in, it had looked to be as big as the mountainside fortress, but then I took in the grounds, the stables...the path we were walking down. *Aemina* outdid herself in grandeur. Every detail had meaning. The wood decorations on the covered walkway we were on depicted the embodiment of our Mother Anara, the mood goddess, in the first ruling royals of the Starborn Family. The courtyard in the center mapped out the phases of the moon and planted within it were the sacred herbs associated with each phase.

"Hally?"

We'd stopped moving. Tolwe was waiting, staring down at me.

"Sorry. I think..." I caught a glance of the inside of the palace and its great hall. There were no words for its magnificence. Within these walls lay the history—the past six thousand years—of our country. "Where are we heading?"

"She is not staying here!" A high, self-important voice rang out from the other side of the moon phase courtyard. *Loret* Estwyn, who the council had appointed as Earth's ambassador way back in March, stormed through the large open space on our side of the gardens. "Get the *savilë* out!"

Tolwe didn't move, except for that vein in his temple—not really, but if there had been one, it would've been twitching. I held back my groan.

We both held issue with this irritating twat of a politician. Tolwe had had to escort the council-elected ambassador of Earth to discuss the Fae-*Endae* treaty that my presence on Earth violated with the Queen of the Fae of the Pacific Northwest. Queen Orlaith wasn't a fan of his either. She'd kicked him out of her manor and off of Earth after listening to him for ten minutes. She'd refused to speak with any other *endai* politician besides me since then.

"Get her out, Tolwe. She's not welcome here."

"Hallanevaë was given permission to be in the realm, *Loret* Estwyn. She's the reason we're still standing here."

"*She* isn't welcome, and if you don't take her, the capital guard will remove her for you." But Estwyn looked a bit too eager for that. He pulled the hem of his *Amura Ore* uniform down. Was it a habit, or was the shirt too small? I'd seen him do it before.

"Hally has first-person accounts of the accused," Tolwe argued.

"There's no way we can trust her."

"That's a you problem, Estwyn, not a we problem." Another *endao* came walking out the great room of the Hall of Justice. He wore the same color, the blue of the capital, but his uniform was more intricate, including a lighter-colored shirt with a sash and a deeper blue sleeveless robe that fluttered when he walked. The *endao* came straight over, cowing Estwyn to move. "Nevie. I'm so happy you're safe."

"*Esamia, Yaluro,*" greetings, Grandfather. I dipped my head in respect. *Aore* Onaeris, my grandma's ex-husband, stood before me. My dad was shorter than Onaeris, but they had many similarities. Both were a bit on the heavier side, with broad cheekbones and a small nose. They had the same smile. "*Aore* Onaeris, it's been so long. It appears *Loret* Estwyn was told I'm not welcome? Perhaps *Basean* Tolwe and I are the ones with missing information? I'm sure—"

"That *Loret* Estwyn is a whiner who got his position from licking *Aore* Tunis's balls? Yes. They do it every night."

Estwyn looked like he was going to explode from Onaeris's crass statement. His face grew darker as he held his breath, trying not to sputter.

"Tunis is a great person." My grandfather rubbed his temple. "I don't see what he sees in Estwyn. Alas, love is love. It offers no excuses." So, Onaeris was serious? I didn't know my grandfather well enough to gauge his sense of humor. "Either way, welcome, Nevie—no, Hally. Hally is what you call yourself now. I am working on remembering that. I see you, and it slips. Hally, you have been given permission to stay in *Endae*. It was requested that you stay under the supervision of an officer, be it *Zayuri* or capital guard, which you've done."

"She flew off—" Estwyn sputtered, but Onaeris stopped him with a look.

"*Zayuri* dragon Sanae took you on a flight around the Valley of *Aetyru,* I heard," my grandfather said. "It was unfortunate that the terrorists separated you from her, but the rest of the *Zayuri* found you safe, just where *Zayuri* Sanae had left you to find help. Being captured is not the victim's fault. Is it, *Loret* Estwyn?"

"She is no victim. You are playing favorites—"

"Now who is casting the potion?" Onaeris laughed. "By the Stars, Estwyn. You were outvoted. Hallanevaë, my granddaughter, *Endae Catia'ej Rosava,* follow me."

I never thought I'd hear another *enda* call me anything without using the *Savile* title. I should have corrected that and reminded him that our neighboring countries were searching for their own ambassadors. But no, I let it slide because I liked the way *Catia* Hallanevaë Inara sounded. It had a nice ring to it, no matter how temporary it was. And it was pissing Estwyn off.

Onaeris walked us across the great room. "We have to go through the Assembly of *Aemina* to get to the lower floor of the Hall of Justice since the spire collapsed." Onaeris folded his hands together in front of him and looked up and around. "The Assembly hasn't seen so many people at once."

As we charged through the Assembly of *Aemina*, I didn't get a chance to stop and drool over everything I'd read about in history books. We barreled straight through as Estwyn turned plum beside me. We went out one entrance and down the ramp to the next floor. For decades, I'd imagined myself here, and now we were hurrying through to get to the other *Zayuri* and watch them book Gil and his team. I didn't need to see this, but perhaps Tolwe and Onaeris thought I wanted to.

"She can't go in there," Estwyn muttered. "*Aore* Onaeris, this is uncalled for."

But Onaeris pushed a pair of double doors wide open into an empty assembly room. The entrance led us onto a balcony, so everyone who came in could see above the entire group. Entrances to the right and left led out and down to three rows of seats, one for each city of *Aemina*. At the very bottom and across from the balcony were the three elder council member seats. One had the voice of the royals, one had the voice of the people, and one had the voice of the council. Yeah, they were all biased as fuck and did what they wanted. Everyone knew that, but it sounded pretty and ligament. I'd always wanted to see this room.

"Where's *Rudairn's* seat, *Yaluro*?" I asked my grandfather.

Onaeris went to the edge of the railing and pointed close to the middle bottom. "Your grandmother's seat is in the first row, third in, I believe."

"Fourth in, *Aore*. It was changed when the village of *Sayderin* was given a seat." The one and only time Estwyn had said something without whining and it was to correct my grandfather. He had to be right. Someone fucking get him a country to advise. Please. Just not any on Earth.

"I thought you'd enjoy that." Onaeris pressed his hand to my cheek. There was so much he wanted to say. It was there, but he couldn't because he was on the council. He tucked my hair behind my ears. "They gave you your cuffs back? You need one for *Catia,* then, don't you?"

I snorted a laugh. "As soon as they make one for *Savile.*"

Neither of them laughed. "Hmm." Onaeris leaned in. "Is that your father's work? It's beautiful. Oh, at least he's talented. Tiaë was a perfect match, they're such talented artists."

Biting my cheek, I didn't remark on my grandfather's backhanded compliment. I closed my fists and hid the ring. He would not get the chance to comment on that, to make less of it, even if that wasn't his intent. Backing out of the double doors and onto the ramp, I untucked my hair to hide my ears again.

We followed my grandfather down and around the spiral ramp. All the *Zayuri* had congregated in the main area of the Hall of Justice, waiting on, like always, paperwork. And if it wasn't paperwork, it was bureaucracy.

A *Zayuri* officer I hadn't seen before came over and saluted Tolwe, then bowed to my grandfather and Estwyn.

"No one knows who any of these people are—"

Tolwe gave the officer the respect she deserved and kept his eyes on her.

I tried, but there was too much going on. "They know who Gileal is," I blurted before Tolwe could reply.

The officer glanced at me. "Yes, but not on paper. Somehow, their *imolegini* comes up as unidentified."

Unidentified? His *imolegin* felt the same as last night when I found him. They had a different *imolegin* recorded for his signature or something? Where was Gileal? I couldn't find his sandy blond hair in the ocean of browns and blues of *endaen* uniforms. Nobody had let Nol sneak out the back with him, had they? Gil still wasn't standing out. They needed to get these guys in before anything went bad. I had no doubt they were much stronger than they looked. "So book them as terrorists."

"Book them?" She looked to Tolwe for clarification. "Sir?"

He shrugged. She knew what I meant. I knew lawmaking, not arresting people. "What is the problem with processing them as noncitizens?"

"There isn't, except we have no proof of what they did. All we have is a letter from Gileal admitting what he did. Other than that, we yanked these peaceful people out of their commune on the side of a mountain between *Aemina* and *Mellori*."

"You can link their *imolegin* to the curse, can't you?" my grandfather asked. But that couldn't be done in the lobby of a jail. Why couldn't this be simpler?

"Like I said." She tilted her head and closed down her emotions. A creepy combination. "Their *imolegin* isn't identifying them. Even though they are the same in our eyes, the system shows them as separate people. We can't 'book' them."

Fucking-A. And Gil wouldn't admit to it. "Where is Gil?"

We all scanned the crowd. Four of them, Leda, Nyda, Savis, and Pickles were sitting on chairs against the wall.

"Where is Nol?" The moment I asked, I found him. A tall, red-haired *Zayuri* wasn't hard to point out. But if he didn't have Gileal, who did? Wasn't he planning on glaring at him until the end of Gil's life? No, that had been my suggestion.

"Um, we might be able to break one of them. The one with the lavender eyes." I pointed while I counted chairs. "Third one from the counter. Wheat-colored hair and sienna complexion. When I closed them in and waited for the *Zayuri* to find us, she thanked me. I think she wants it to be over. There's your weakest link."

Tolwe turned to me. "I'll see what I can do. *Catia* Hallanevaë, stay with *Aore* Onaeris and *Loret* Estwyn, please."

Once he was in the throng, I turned to the two council members. "Gil told me he's the one who released Aswryn years ago. If he knows of a way out, he could be leaving now."

Onaeris leaned in close and muttered, "Are you saying a full alert is needed?"

No way in hell would I claim responsibility for that. "I'm just passing on what Gileal told me."

Moments later, Tolwe came out from a room with a *Zayuri* and Gil. Estwyn chuckled. "Lavatory break."

Once Gil was settled next to Pickles, Tolwe found his way to Nol, who lifted his gaze over all the heads and met mine. He said something to his uncle, possibly "*Sae,*" *No.* But I couldn't be certain.

My attention turned back to Gil and his team. Gil had stood by Nol for thirty years, pretending to help save people while sabotaging and spying. Gil's ragtag group of vengeful scientists needed to pay for the sorrow they had caused. But the *Amura Ore* would merely sentence him to death. What could *Aemina* do otherwise? Exile them like me? Or leave them in cells for the rest of their lives like humans do? Be a drain on the economy sitting there? I should've had an answer, but I didn't.

"Onaeris? I know their fate is death. But will the *Amura Ore* try to go around the law and carry out their sentencing, or will they do it legally?" Which would take no less than three months.

"Legally, of course." Estwyn felt the need to cut in.

"*Loret* Estwyn, I was speaking to *Aore* Onaeris." I glared at him, daring him to say more. The fucking hypocrite. Only a month ago, he'd lied to other council members and used illegal paperwork to have me arrested. My grandmother had told me there was no recollection of the incident or any paperwork. "Onaeris? If you were in charge, what would you do?"

"What are you getting on about, Hally?"

My meaning had to get across fully; otherwise, the nosy junior council member would accuse me of helping them. "If we can find the cure to the virus before they're executed, they could see their failure."

"That's the same request you made for Aswryn," Onaeris said.

I stared straight ahead at the doomed five *endai* and had to hold my broken heart deep below the surface. "It is."

"There's no guarantee you'll find it anytime soon. Are you suggesting we keep them alive for however long it takes? Five, ten years?"

My hair tapped my shoulders as I shook my head. Jeez, I'd do just about anything for a shower. "My niece told me before we left that she and the fae had found a virus that is similar to the one Aswryn used in her curse."

"To the *serilesoda* virus?" Onaeris asked. "Did you know, our scientists, including our *curse expert*"—Onaeris narrowed his eyes at Gil lounging across the large room. He thought he was going to get off on technicalities—"calls the cursed *serilesoda* virus, *Pae-lesoda*, because he didn't want to associate it with the *endao* who discovered the virus."

"Yes, that's what Gil told me today. He also said it's extinct, but he found Serin's research and the original virus. He has samples of both the original and *Pae-lesoda* at the fortress"

"He-he found Serin's research?" Onaeris looked away, clearly taking a moment to process the news. "Our scientist will need to be updated. Their fortress must be inspected immediately."

I looked down at everyone waiting. Gil still sat lounging. He didn't even look remorseful for lying to the people he'd spent decades beside. Who was this *endao*? "If the council will trust me enough, I can give an account of my time there."

The likelihood of the council listening to me was slim and it might bite me in the ass one day, but I was loyal to *Aemina*. My country didn't betray me, the corrupt *Amore Ore* council that weighted its people down was the thing I didn't trust. The very thing I wanted to join was the thing I was against. It's complicated.

The three of us stood quietly above the *Zayuri* and the prisoners. Lost in my own thoughts, my mind kept turning to Nol's sword on Gil's neck. Nol's cold eyes as he stared emotionlessly at me after Sanae pulled Gil away. He wasn't mad at her, even though she'd been trying to prevent him from killing Gil.

"Do they know how similar their virus is to *serilesoda* through the *Pae-lesoda*?" my grandfather asked, interrupting my thoughts.

"That's what I thought that means. Maybe they're on the cusp of a cure. Could we ask for three months? Isn't that standard, anyway?"

Onaeris held his chin as he thought, just like my father did. "It is standard."

I leaned around my grandfather to check on Estwyn, who stood, considering, not sneering at the idea.

"*Aore* Onaeris, it might be worthwhile to learn more about this fae virus." Estwyn gave me a pointed look. "Make no mistake, *Savilë* Hallanevaë, you still do not have an ally in me. But I see possibilities for a solution."

"Is that as close to an apology as I'll get from you for accusing me of helping Aswryn?"

Estwyn went back to glaring over everything, his look sour and petty.

"If you're so open to solutions and research, why didn't you look for some with me? Why follow rumors blindly?"

Onaeris held his hand up, stopping me. "We won't get into this. The issue is over."

It took me a while to stop seething, but my grandfather outranked Estwyn, and if I were really *Catia,* then he outranked me as well. I'd assumed the role on Earth. I might as well take that responsibility here, too, even if some people didn't accept it.

"Council members? Ambassador?" Tolwe came up behind us, out of nowhere, just as Nol liked to do. "We have progress. Look."

The three of us searched the crowd for something new. A *Zayuri* took Savis into the back. Another *Zayuri* took Pickles.

"What are they doing?" I asked.

Tolwe came to stand behind me and put a hand on my shoulder. "They like your idea, Hally. They're going to attempt to break them." As we watched, others came and took Gil and his merry band of evil scientists away.

I tilted my head to look up at Nol's uncle. "This will work, Tolwe." It had to.

Tolwe leaned over and pressed his face against my ear to whisper so the others wouldn't hear, "I need to talk to you privately, please."

The anticipation made my heart race. Nol had something to tell me, I knew it.

OUT OF THE ROOM and past a set of doors, Tolwe stopped and waited, arms crossed over his chest.

"He isn't coming, is he?" My shoulders sagged, and I wanted to cry.

Tolwe shook his head. "He needs time. Nolan will see that you did the right thing, but he's full of rage right now."

"I don't blame him." I leaned against the wall and closed my eyes. Nol hadn't even acknowledged me at the fortress after I made him release Gil. He told Tolwe to give me a ride and left without saying goodbye. "Before I left with Sanae, I was yelling at him."

"Nolan has requested that he stay here until Gileal is sentenced, and he also wants to be there for his execution."

"You mean he's asking me if that's okay? Or he officially requested it without asking me?"

"Officially."

It could be months! And he hadn't even considered me or our friends. "Onaeris didn't say anything to me."

Tolwe dipped his chin. "Onaeris isn't part of the judiciary committee. Neither is Estwyn."

I squeezed my eyes shut, getting vibes of my own trial. "Please tell me it's not just three members."

"There are fifteen coming."

Ten less than the full judiciary committee, so there was a small chance the trial would be fairer.

"What do you want to do?"

At first, I wasn't sure if I'd heard him right. No one gave me a choice. Ever. And coming from Tolwe? I was speechless.

"Hally? Do you want to wait here? Do you want to see the sentencing and execution?"

Still speechless, I looked away from Tolwe to the wall in front of me, then to my feet. "It's just that...I've never been asked before. No one ever offers me a choice."

Tolwe's head tilted to the side. "No one might have asked you, but you had choices. Did you not *choose* to cast the prank? You *chose* to go after Aswryn by yourself. You *chose* to find the children. Did you not *choose* to go find Gileal?"

Jeez, he was relentless. "Okay, okay, I get it."

"No, I think you need to hear this. You didn't have to do any of that. There were times when others made choices that affected you, sometimes at great cost to you, but because you're a good person, you went along with it and saved so many in the process. You've sacrificed so much, but you've come through and you shine even brighter. The council will decide the outcome of Nolan's request, but you can make your own request. So, I ask you a third time, what do you want to do?"

23

THE COMMITTEE WAS IN session. My nerves were fried. I was beyond tired. But, I got a shower! And an *Aeminan* shower was so much better than any shower on Earth. It was a full eight-by-eight, sauna-style room with a waterfall shower pouring out of the ceiling on one side of the room. Best pressure, best temperature, the best place to fall asleep.

Clean, warm, comfortable, and with a spell to keep the water at the temperature I chose, I nudged my worries to the wayside. Being the last *endaë* to use it, I didn't have to worry about others waiting on me. I fell asleep on the sauna bench to the sound of water falling.

Jenne woke me three hours later. No nightmares, no restlessness. Maybe I needed to invest in a white noise machine at home. And a sauna. Why hadn't I ever thought of it before?

"Hey, you." Jenne crouched down to my level while also trying not to get wet. She'd turned the waterfall off, and it was getting cold. "We were getting worried. I know you're really tired, but we should find a better bed than this."

"Have you ever fallen asleep in one of these?"

With her mouth hanging open and a stunned look on her face, she looked away. "Um, no. I haven't."

"Here's a human phrase I like. Don't knock it 'til you try it," I said it in English first and then gave my best *Aemirin* equivalent. "There isn't a great translation, but you get the idea. Try it in your own shower."

Jenne's eyes sparkled as she crouched in front of me, smiling like I was crazy. Maybe I was. One friend had betrayed me and the other might hate me. And I was sleeping in the shower. Crazy would about cover it.

"Let's get you out of here."

Wrapping a large towel around me, I followed her out to the dewdrop chamber, a semi-wet area, where we dry off. With a quick thought, I expelled the water from my body and the towel. My clothes were safe from moisture in the drawer meant just for that.

"Oh, *C'yo.*"

I looked up to find Jenne staring at me in mild terror.

"What?" I dropped the towel and started to change. She'd given me one of her sweaters. It went down to my knees, but we both had narrow shoulders. No one had pants that fit, so I had to make do with a borrowed skirt. Everything was being washed, and all the undergarments were too big on me. So yes, I was going commando. I didn't care. My clothes would be ready before the committee made a decision anyway, and I was finding a bed to sleep in.

"Your hair is a bit..." She grimaced.

I touched my hair. "Oh fucking-A." I'd accidentally dried my hair. "I'm not going back in. Can you help me braid it?"

Still with a horrified look on her face, she nodded.

"Oh, it can't be that bad!" I hiked the skirt up and looked in the mirror. My hair looked like a black cotton ball. Curls every which way. Every strand had its own personal twist.

"Braids will be good." Jenne nodded, staring and not helping. "How are we going to untangle it, though?"

I thought for a bit. "Can you think of a light oil we can get our hands on?"

Ten minutes later, two *endaë* were in the room with me. Jenne was supervising because she wasn't good at braiding other people's hair, and the two others were braiding each side. Not that there was a lot to work with. The length was all in the front and got shorter until it settled at the nape of my neck. But at least my hair was thick.

"Well? What do you think?" Vaë, a *Zayuri* five years older than me, asked. She looked at me through the mirror, her lip between her teeth. They'd tried their hardest and it didn't look bad.

"It's good."

"Your face says otherwise." Jenne dropped her chin and dared me to lie again.

"I'm not used to my hair being in braids. I chose to cut it so I didn't have to mess with it. So, I like them, yes. Thank you, ladies."

Vaë set the brush on the table, disappointed by my lack of excitement. "It'll probably come out in your sleep anyway, but the oil should help."

I grabbed the ear cuff that my grandmother had given me as a child and hooked it to my right ear. "I do like them. They're intricate and very pretty." The cuff An'di had given me was next.

I pinched the silver little thing between my thumb and forefinger, remembering the day she'd given it to me: I was ninety-nine and a ball of nerves because I was about to start secondary school in a week. I'd been playing with her jewelry, and An'di had plucked it out of my hand to inspect it.

"A perfect ear cuff to start the new year. And it will look so pretty against your hair." She'd pressed it on next to Yalu's cuff and fluffed my curls. "You're such a pretty girl, Nevie."

"Hally?" Vaë had told me something. "Where did you go?"

"Sorry, I think I fell asleep standing up. Shit, I'm tired."

Jenne frowned at me in the mirror. "Yeah, well, it looks like that bed will have to wait."

"Tolwe just called for you. I think the committee came to a decision."

"Of course it did, because I can't catch a fucking break," I muttered in English and hurried to put on the rest of my jewelry.

"That's pretty," Vaë said. "I've never seen or felt anything like it."

I brushed the intricately carved flowers with my thumb. "I was told it's an empty *meril*, but I'm not sure if they were right."

"You don't know what it's for and you're wearing it? Hally, that's—"

"It's fine, I know the maker and I trust them undoubtedly." While I trusted Jenne, my dad kept his flavor of magic close. Not even his father knew how powerful he really was. But it made me feel closer to my dad, and that was a great power.

"Hally." Jenne called me back to the dressing room. "You forgot this." She held out the little stone box Gil had handed me before the *Zayuri* stormed the fortress.

With no time to go back to my bag on my bed, I decided to keep it with me. If he had told me the truth and I brought it to Charlie, it might be the key to her finding the cure. It could even be the cure. But if he'd lied to me, it could bring down every *Aeminan enda*. He couldn't lie to me. Or could he, though, to save his life?

Tolwe checked me from head to toe and stepped back. "That's perfect." Not a bit of sarcasm.

TOLWE LIKED TO WALK fast everywhere, and that meant I had to sacrifice my poor feet. How did Yalu do it? I thought back to the one time I'd seen them walking together. She'd had her arm hooked on his. I wasn't doing that.

"Are we on a deadline?"

Tolwe didn't slow down as he talked. "Deadline?"

Pushing my flyaway hair strands back, I stopped. He didn't. Eventually, he'd realize I wasn't following anymore. "Do we have to be there right this instant?"

Tolwe finally stopped and looked from me to where he'd stopped. "I suppose not. Why do you ask?"

Fists at my hips, I channeled my grandmother as hard as I could to hopefully get him to listen. I blinked at him with a long squeeze. "You are with my grandmother, who is the same height as me. Why do you think I'm asking?"

"Oh, *c'yo*." Tolwe bent his head and looked away.

I bit my tongue and gestured for him to keep going. Tolwe didn't match my stride like Nol always did, but at least he slowed down.

We found Nol pacing the small hallway near the heavily carved wooden door to a committee room. He didn't stop as we walked up, his fists clenching and unclenching, his thoughts turned inward. I could imagine a few things he could be thinking about. How to sneak in and murder Gileal if they said we couldn't stay, for one.

If they granted us a full stay, we might miss Sam and Mateo's wedding. What if Lewis proposed to Yumi before we came back? Charlie could have found the cure, and we had no way to communicate. If they didn't grant it, how long would Nol go on like this? At some point, I realized the hall had gotten quiet. I did seem to be falling asleep standing.

"What's in your hands?" Nol had stopped pacing and stood on the other side of the hall.

"Something..." I shook the box gently. "I'm not sure what exactly. Gileal gave me some small bottles before everyone came in. He told me to get them to Charlie."

Both *endao* froze. Nol still had his emotions locked down, and his tight fists were the only indication that he was angry. Not that I didn't know already.

"And?" Nol never raised his voice when he was angry, and the abrupt loud word startled me. This brought out something in him, something scary and foreign. *Please, Nol, find your way back.*

Lowering the box, I fidgeted as they stared back, judging me. "He said she'd know what to do with them. It could help us find the cure."

"He is a traitor. You can't believe him." But things weren't black and white. He'd betrayed all of us. Then he'd come over, wanting to help Charlie find a cure. But he could have been attempting to sabotage her work like he had with An'di's. It didn't feel right, though. Aswryn was dead, and the curse had gotten out of control. His own father was dying. I knew he wanted to find a cure. Everything was so confusing!

"Throw it to the ground and break it. Break the box."

We didn't know what that would do. It could destroy our only chance at saving everyone. It could go airborne and infect us all. "Nol—"

"You—" This again? He was going to accuse me. I dropped my head and waited for the rest. "You still trust him. Pick a side." That was better than "You *did* help make the curse."

"It isn't about sides. We don't know what this is. I don't trust it, but my trust is skewed and so is yours. I want a neutral party to test it."

Nol closed his eyes and took a breath. His shaking arms and stiff shoulders radiated tension I could almost feel from across the small hall. We waited, listening to Nol's heavy breaths. A click of the committee door saved us from further argument. He'd see. He needed time.

"The committee is ready to answer your request, *Hinam* Twynolan, *Savilë* Hallanevaë." And with that, I knew they'd denied the request. The outcome didn't matter. It was how I chose to handle it that would make a difference.

The bright magical sconces blinded me as the three of us walked in, Nol first and Tolwe between us. We followed the capital guard and sat where directed. The members were arranged on a dais in a semicircle, not unlike the large assembly room that Onaeris had shown me. Except there were twenty-two members, with three chairs to represent the rest of the committee joining in through *Olauvë*. Holy shit, the full fucking judiciary committee.

"Welcome to the three of you." The speaker eyed us, falling on Tolwe last. For a moment, I thought he'd make Tolwe leave, but he let it slide. "First, I am *Aore Memano*, the speaker of the judiciary committee. We would like to give our gratitude to you, *Hinam* Twynolan. You acted bravely and selflessly by coming here, prepared for the worst. You serve your country honorably. Thank you.

"*Savilë* Hallanevaë, despite the actions of your youth, you came with *Hinam* Twynolan so he could do his duty. That was honorable for a *savilë*. We're sure it required much contemplation."

That was it? Out of all the things I'd done for them, that was what they'd chosen?

"Even though today is the mid-season holiday, we chose to address this right away. We understand the importance of the issue and how Hallanevaë's stay here would affect our society. In that regard, we have prepared a few questions that need answering before our final determination. Are you prepared, *savilë*?"

I had not expected this. They wanted to hear my answers and not assume what my actions would be. They were making progress, or maybe it was only one or two who had fought for this. "Thank you for the opportunity—"

"Yes or no, *savilë*. Are you prepared?"

Oh. Not so surprised, then. "Yes." This was all pomp and circumstance, probably to make the paperwork look better and claim that they had actually done some due diligence before deciding.

"If we were to grant you a stay, would you resist detainment in the capital during your time here?"

My ears started to ring. Detainment? I would spend however long this took in jail? I swallowed and pulled myself together. This was no time to look weak. I wouldn't give them the satisfaction of seeing my pain. "No." The word was thick with emotion, and I cleared my throat. "No, I would not resist."

He was already past my answer before I strengthened my voice. "Would you resist wearing a dampening cuff for our peace of mind? As you know, you and your magic cannot be trusted."

Any hesitance and they wouldn't believe me. "No."

"During the time of your detainment, if we do grant you permission to stay, you will not be able to perform your duties as ambassador to *Rosava*. Would you agree to relinquish your title and asylum—temporarily, of course."

Oh, fuck me. They were going to keep me here. My heart was racing. I would never see my family again. Never see Mateo, Lewis, Sam, or Yumi again. Let alone see anyone here. They wouldn't allow visitations. I would never tattoo again.

"Honorable assembly members—"

"*Basean* Tolwe, these are questions for *Savilë* Hallanevaë to answer. You can listen quietly or leave. Do not interrupt again or we will hold you in contempt."

"Answer yes or no, *savilë*."

I looked from Tolwe to Nol. He was looking at me. Did he realize what they were asking of me or was he still too angry to care?

"If you don't answer, we will take that as resistance. Your answer, please."

"I...will. I must speak, your honor."

"Your comments are unnecessary."

"These questions are not for my benefit. They are for the fae and their reactions to my relinquishment. If you will grant me that, I beg you?"

"Proceed."

I licked my lips and settled my nerves the best I could. "Sending a letter to Queen Orlaith informing her of my choice doesn't mean she'll accept the new ambassador. She is the one who refused *Loret* Estwyn. If you grant my stay, I will respectfully recommend giving her a few *endai* to choose from."

"Your suggestion is noted and heard. However, understand that the host nation does not choose the ambassador of the other nation. Perhaps you don't remember that from your studies. That would be understandable." They would send Estwyn back. Holy fuck, we were screwed.

"If you go against your word at *any* point during your stay, we will act accordingly. Do you understand that?"

"Ye-yes."

"What would those actions include?"

Aore Memano's jaw clenched as he turned to look at Nol. "*Hinam* Twynolan, I give you the same warning as *Basean* Tolwe. These questions are for *Savilë* Hallanevaë."

"They may be her questions," Nol snapped back. "But the outcome also involves me. I have the right to have my question answered."

"You don't, as your right to stay is not in question. *You* are an outstanding citizen, and this is your home. What you are asking us to disregard, even temporarily, is the fair and just sentencing of a *savilë*, a person who chose to kill her friends with magic. She is a danger to every *enda* in the realm. Or did you not understand this when you asked us to stay? *Hinam*, I need an answer. Did you understand this?"

Nol clenched his fist resting on his knee and glared, his expression unguarded. "It is a small request for what she has done to save our people."

"Yes or no, do you understand? It seems you do not."

Nol was going to object again. I saw it in his eyes. Oh, this was not good. "I'll agree to anything you want, as long as my *muranildo* can stay."

"Of course *he* can stay. Have you been listening to anything we've said, child?"

My chin quivered. I would not give them the satisfaction. I would *not.* "I do understand. But you also know he can't stay if you send me back."

"It you want him to stay, perhaps another arrangement can be made." *Aore* Memano perked up as if he'd been waiting for just this introduction. "One that was discussed today. Life in prison, since the normal sentence for your crime would be death would also affect *Hinam* Twynolan. Would you agree to that if it gave your *muranildo* the ability to stay?"

"This is wrong," Tolwe interrupted.

"*Basean* Tolwe, you are now in contempt. Guard." *Aore* Memano pointed to a guard and waved toward Tolwe. "*Savilë* Hallanevaë, if you agree to all the terms, we will proceed with our decision."

The guard was almost on us.

"We're leaving. Now. Hallë, out the door." Nol shot up and made shooing motions toward Tolwe and me.

The twenty-two members stared in surprise as Nol and Tolwe defied them.

"She will no longer be your ambassador, and this may mean *Aemina* has made an enemy of an entire race of strong magical beings that already won a war against us. Think about that." Tolwe patted my arm to get me to move. "It is at the fae's discretion if they choose to include the other nations of *Endae* in their decision. I wonder what their reaction will be if all of *Endae* becomes the fae's enemy again."

"Wait!" A member stood.

We stopped.

"The floor recognizes *Aore* Jesdar," the speaker of the committee said.

"Let us vote," *Aore* Jesdar said. "If we say no, you will be sent back to *Rosava* immediately. Is that fair?"

Nol leaned around his uncle, his voice a quickened hiss. "Say no, Hallë."

"Are you crazy? We might not get out of here at all," I whispered back.

"Why should you agree? We're already leaving. This is bullshit. They're not giving you anything. This is a negotiation. Tell me Orlaith won't retaliate if you don't come home."

Twisting my lips as I thought of what Orlaith might do, I gave in. "No, we've already decided to leave. Find your own ambassador and deal with Queen Orlaith yourselves."

"An alternative?" another committee member called.

"The floor recognizes *Aore* Velbae."

"*Hinam* Nolan has acted honorably, and Hallanevaë did assist him. Perhaps they can stay until the group is processed? It will give them a day or two."

More time for them to grab me, throw me in a pit, and forget about me. Maybe throw a loaf of bread down there every week.

Nol didn't give me a chance to say anything, though, even if I knew what to say. "I want to come back for their sentencing and their executions."

"That can be part of the deal, as long as Hallanevaë agrees to keep working with the fae until a permanent ambassador can be determined."

I looked up at Nol and Tolwe for their thoughts. Was it enough? Nol got a look in his eye. He was going to go all out. "They'll say no, Nol. They would never revoke my exile."

He pressed his lips together, but I couldn't stop him. "I want a full assembly review of Hallanevaë's trial with witness accounts. I want you to give her a full *real* trial, which she never got before."

They brought their heads together to discuss Nol's demand. The speaker broke away. "We can only agree to bring the request for a trial to a full assembly. We cannot agree for the entire council."

"Are the three remaining members bearing witness in *Olauvë*?" They were obligated to speak truthfully. Just because their chair was here didn't mean they couldn't "step out" for a little while.

The speaker looked at the chairs. "They are."

"Then you've got a full committee. Convince the required additional ten *Aore* members and five *Loret* to sign. Then it *is* enough for a full assembly trial. I won't do it otherwise. I might even tell the queen how horribly you've treated me. And she likes me."

"Adores her," Nol added. "The queen comes to visit for coffee and tea."

She'd visited once, but they didn't need to know that.

"And I want it on paper, signed by all and dated," I added.

"You have until Gileal is processed to get it done. If Hallë isn't home by then, Orlaith might look into why her favorite ambassador hasn't returned."

"Nol!" I hissed. I mean, that was laying it on a bit thick.

They brought their heads together again. "Agreed, if Hallanevaë stays in the custody of a *Zayuri* other than *Hinam* Twynolan or *Basean* Tolwe, as they are biased to this issue."

"Agreed." The moment I said it, the guards backed off, not that they had been looking forward to arresting a *Zayuri*.

We walked out. Tolwe made sure it was at a steady pace and not rushed. Oh shit, this was crazy.

24

Nol seethed as the three of us walked back to the barracks. After leaving the moon phase courtyard and going down to the ground floor, we turned the last corner and came to a halt. I wouldn't have been surprised if every *Zayuri* in *Aetyru* stood in front of the doors to the barracks. All their heads perked up, their conversations muted the moment they saw us.

They wanted to know the outcome? All of them? They respected Nol a lot, no matter how much of an asshole he could be toward them. Their unity humbled me. I'd had no idea before this.

Tolwe looked at us. Nol and I weren't in the mood to announce anything to anyone, no matter who it was. Tolwe rolled his shoulders back and made eye contact with every one of them. "It's complicated."

The whole crowd seemed to sagged with disappointment, or maybe relief that I wasn't being kicked out and Nol wouldn't have to leave.

Jenne turned away, and Bren laid his head on hers. Tolwe went on to summarize the meeting, and after that, while not entirely happy, many of them came up and said something to Nol. By that time, he was wavering on his feet, and he was stubborn enough to stay there and talk to his friends in a subdued manner. I made sure I stayed close enough to hear, but also far enough away to give him space.

"Nol is going to pass out," I whispered to Jenne.

She lifted her head and stared right at him. "That's his problem."

"Yeah, but—"

Jenne's eyebrows shot up as she kept pushing back. "You should take care of yourself."

"He—"

"Come on." Jenne and Vaë, my self-appointed guards walked me back to the female barracks. "Take that nap you were gonna take earlier. Jenne and I won't let the council take you out from under us."

"Ah, so you get that possible ploy of theirs, too?" It was sad that we knew our own government would consider pulling this shit. Then I thought of the human governments. We were just like everyone else. I smirked to myself as I crawled under the covers and closed my eyes. The council would hate to know they weren't better than everyone else.

GIL'S PROCESSING WAS SCHEDULED bright and early the next morning. It wasn't soon enough for some who'd felt as betrayed as Nol. *Some* was putting it conservatively. Every *Zayuri* who'd arrived outside of the capital when Nol and I had arrived had flown to the fortress to save Gil. Which was larger than the *Zayuri* stationed in the capital. So, instead of dwelling on Gil's betrayal and the frustration with the pause on his processing *Sudome* Tamden had added the visiting *Zayuri* to the capital's rotations. Jenne had woken me up way too fucking early in the morning to make sure I knew that Vaë would have to walk me down to witness Gil's processing, because she had rotation duty at the same time.

She was not happy.

Neither was I. There was no need for me to be up, too. At least *she* had something to do.

Two hours later, Vaë walked with me around the courtyard where Tolwe had taken me and Estwyn had thrown a hissy fit. I'd never gone all the way down, as Estwyn, Onerous and I had only gazed at them from above.

In the main room of the Hall of Justice, Nol was waiting against the
wall where he'd stood before to glare at Gil, but it also kept him far
away from several council members, all in *Aemina* blue. My grandfather's was an intricate vest today, featuring a white scarf embroidered
with a trail of *Aemina's* blue trillium down its length. We stopped in
our tracks. I wouldn't let them force me into a prison. But here they
were, confronting us—and with my grandfather?

Onaeris stepped out of their group of five and walked closer but
stopped an arm's length away. It could have been the *Zayuri* standing
between us, or it might have been his own choice to stop where he
did. "Hally, do not be alarmed." At the use of my name, the tension in
me dropped from high to medium-high. "We're here to give you your
answer. As agreed? And I must say, your grandmother and I are proud
of the way you handled yourself. We were given full memories of the
entire meeting. You should be proud of yourself, *Catia* Hallanevaë."
He winked, and I about dropped. They were going to agree.

"All the signatures?"

Onaeris's eyes didn't fall, nor did that look of pride in his eyes waver.
"Let's go talk before Gileal's processing begins."

I followed Onaeris behind Vaë. She hadn't been kidding. There was
no way they were going to take me if she had anything to say about it.
Today was looking so much brighter than yesterday. Nol waited until
we'd walked up to meet the council members before coming close.

"Good morning." Memano started the moment Nol stopped in
front of them. "*Hinam* Twynolan, *Savilë* Hallanevaë. As agreed, we
are here to discuss the terms we talked about yesterday."

"Terms? We settled this. You get the signatures or you find your own
way of communicating with the fae," Nol snapped.

"It's all just the right vocabulary, Nol. Or it better be." I stared the
council members down.

"You are right, *savilë.*" The speaker handed me two rolls of natural-colored paper. I opened one, then the other. Two copies. One for
them and one for me to keep. "All that is required is your signature."

My eyes darted from the paper to the waiting *endai*. I couldn't
read this. A few words looked familiar, but it'd been too long. I did

recognize where the signatures started, however. My heart leapt. I was going to get a trial. A real trial. *Keep it cool, Hally.* "Interesting." I nodded and traced the signatures of the council members with my finger. "Nol, would you mind confirming it? Another pair of eyes?"

He frowned and looked at the paper and up to me. He wanted to tell me no. Politics wasn't his thing.

"Nol?" I continued in English. "It's been a long time, and I…I don't recognize all the words. Just…"

Nol gave in, and with mild annoyance, he took the paper and skimmed it. "Some of these members aren't in the capital. You have *Aore* Zella's signature…"

I perked up at my grandmother's name. If she'd signed it, where was she?

Aore Memano lifted his chin. "You wanted signatures, your uncle found signatures—"

"Using *Aore* Zella is bias—"

"But these were all who were in a few hours ride distance," Onaeris snapped back at the snooty, taller *endaë* that hadn't spoken yesterday.

Then she wasn't here, which was a relief but also a disappointment. I would have loved to see her, but she was safe. That was what mattered. "Where's *Basean* Tolwe?" I asked.

Onaeris lifted his hands, gesturing to the two *Zayuri* beside me. "Doing what *Basean Zayuri* do during the day, I suppose. It wasn't discussed when he dropped off the agreement."

"*Basean* Tolwe is with the royal guard until midday," Nol said as he studied the paper and *tsk*ed as his eyes ran back up the paper.

"Is something not to your liking?" Memano asked, interrupting Nol's lengthly scroll down the document.

"This looks to be everything we discussed yesterday," Nol said, talking to the paper. "All twenty-five council members from yesterday, ten more seniors, and five junior *Amura Ore*. There aren't specific dates set for your investigation, however. I'd like that communicated personally through *Basean* Tolwe or *Aore* Evazella."

"Like what?" a younger *Amura Ore* council member asked. "You're getting your trial. That's more than you ever could have hoped to get."

Nol snapped the paper forward, almost bending it. "We expected that the first time. It didn't happen. This is her trial, and we want to be informed of developments."

The fact that Nol saw all the agreements settled in the document was good enough for me. "I assume there will be a schedule drawn up as they get into it." The government ran slowly, and they had more things to work on, too.

"Yes, but when, Hallë? They haven't given a start date. What if they choose to start their investigation in a decade, but you are in Seattle having talks for them"—he pointed to the members—"as early as tomorrow."

Fair. We looked at the members before us. "*Aore* Onaeris," I said, singling out my grandfather. We had family issues, but I trusted him to make sure they treated me fairly. I was his granddaughter, and Yalu would be so far up his ass if he didn't follow through. "Can I trust you to keep them accountable, or do we need to draw up another agreement?"

"Writing up another agreement won't be necessary." Onaeris looked around at the judiciary committee members, settling on each of them and giving them time to object. "The committee can put your trial on the docket for our next *Amora Ore* meeting and get you a better idea of what the timeline will be."

I sighed. "That's good, but until I see a schedule, I don't see a reason to perform the duties you expect of me in the agreement."

I signed *Hally Dubois* on both copies, with Vaë and Nol as my witnesses.

My grandfather stepped close and reached out his arm. The moment I grasped his arm, his forehead was against mine. Eyes closed, he took a moment to settle his thoughts. "Every time they try to tame the Inara family, you roar back up again, the fire even more intense. I'm proud to be part of that legacy. The first report of events will be sent next week, then one report every week after that. I will make sure of it."

An announcement at the front counter brought Onaeris's head up. They were calling us back. I waved to my grandfather and eyed the other council members—not in a menacing way, but they did look a tad guilty.

Gileal had admitted everything, and it was still hard to grasp when I wasn't actively thinking about it. Nol walked into the processing room first and found a spot away from the barrier they'd cast to keep Gil in and us out. All standard, of course.

Vaë and I found a closer spot so I could hear everything they said. Nol's hearing was better than mine. That's what happened when mortars were dropped within a few kilometers from where I lived. Not fun. Don't recommend it. I touched the stone box and vials Gil had given me. After this, I was going to get them tested. I'd even had Tolwe tell Nol my plan.

A creak on the far side of the barrier alerted us that they were bringing Gil in. He didn't look worse than yesterday. A little rumpled from sleeping in his clothes, but they hadn't done anything to him. Gil turned as his jailer pulled him to the back counter where he would get his new clothes. His eyes were the deep teal of icebergs. My chest squeezed. This was really happening. He'd done this. The jailer told him something, and Gil ignored him, staring at me. That Gil didn't even glance at Nol broke my heart. How could he have lied to Nol all that time?

Something moved behind me, and then I felt Nol's familiar warmth against my back as he placed a hand on my shoulder. Gil's face relaxed, and his gaze rose to meet his ex-best friend's stare. Nothing happened until the jailer told him to take off his shoes. He nodded. I couldn't hear what they said, but the jailer moved back, and Gil leaned over.

I grabbed Nol's hand on my shoulder and squeezed. Issues be damned, we'd be united on this. Nol squeezed my shoulder back. A moment later, the jailer yelled, and the *endaë* behind the counter gasped. Wait, Gil had just been untying his shoes. Where'd he go?

"Majut!" Fuck! Vaë yelled. She stepped against the barrier and demanded to be let in.

Nol was next to her in a flash, but he didn't lift his hands or say anything as he looked around.

Somehow Gil was gone. He'd vanished. My stomach dropped. How?

"He can vanish like Aswryn!" Vaë shouted. "Be on guard!"

"He's not coming back, *Ginem* Vaë." Nol didn't sound like himself. No panic, but it wasn't his threatening, calculated monotone that I swore he practiced in the mirror every morning.

"Check the others, now!" Vaë told the jailer who bolted at her words.

Where would Gil go? I hardly knew him. He couldn't go back to the mountain. That would be the first place they checked. Or maybe it was so obvious that no one would think to look there. Where else, though? Home to see his father?

"His resources have been frozen," Nol mumbled to Vaë. "Everyone he knows has been alerted."

"That we know of," I said.

The jailer came back in, his breathing uneven but not urgent. "They're there. The dampener in their cells are engaged."

"Did you give him a dampening cuff?" Nol asked.

"Yes—I always do. It's required." The jailer thought back. He didn't sound too convincing.

Vaë looked around the room on both sides of the barrier. "We have to find out if someone helped him."

"We need to think ahead, to where he might be, not how he did it. That is a job for capital guards."

Oh no. Oh no, no. "Nol?" Vaë and Nol turned to me. The others stopped as well. "Charlie and Ray."

Nol's eyes widened, the fear too great to hide. "We must go. Vaë, we must leave for the other realm immediately. Update Tolwe, everyone. There is a high likelihood that Gileal has gone after Hallë's family."

We were out the door, running up the ramp to the courtyard. "Where's the tree that connects to my house?"

"Twenty minutes from the capital. Five on Sanae."

25

Sanae got us to the tree in three minutes. *"Go! We will see each other again. Save the younglings!"*

"Goodbye, Sanae. I loved being with you!" I thought before Nol grabbed my hand and pulled us through. One step in *Endae*, one in between, and one into *Rosava* and we were home.

Our early morning processing appointment meant it was predawn in Seattle. The moment we tumbled out of the tree, Nol let go of my hand. I looked up as he faded out of existence and into the shadows. In an instant, he was swallowed and gone. The lack of noise from inside my house as I sprinted up the back stairs sent my mind spiraling.

They could still be asleep. Don't panic! I repeated again and again.

Gil wouldn't hurt them. But he'd let Nol's family die.

I got up to the porch just as Nol shoved open the back door. "They're not here."

My world stopped. "Not again. Please, Mother, not again."

Losing Ray for those few hours had been a nightmare. This couldn't happen. Nol moved past me, mumbling something. The next second, Nol pushed my hands away from my face and lifted them so I had to look up at him. "Look at me." He waited, staring at me as I tried to focus on the here and the now, instead of going everywhere, thinking of all the what ifs. He came close until he was the only thing I saw and I calmed. "No matter how livid I am with you, there is no change in what I swore to you when you introduced them to me. I promise I'll be back soon."

"Where are you…" But he'd thrown himself into the shadows again.

I dropped to my knees at the top of the deck stairs. I stared down at the wood grain as it darkened in the light drizzle. It couldn't have started up more than a few minutes ago. What the hell could I do? I had no phone— Wait, was the Volvo here? If the pavement was wet where the Volvo was usually parked, that would tell me if they had been here if and when Gil had come. Mindful of my steps, I made my way down to the ground and through the backyard, narrowly missing Ray's bike and wagon tied together with a jump rope. I fumbled with the latch and pushed the gate open. The Volvo was parked in its normal spot. My mind started racing. He'd taken them? Would he hurt them? Hold them for ransom?

The fence shook. Startled, I spun, ready to defend myself. I was done worrying about hurting people that had no issues about hurting me. I'd blow the asshole into next Sunday.

The gate slammed into the garage. Nol stopped it before it came back and hit him. He caught my mix of ready to take him on and annoyance at his disregard for my poor damn fence. He grimaced for a moment before coming up to me, without a no clue what I'd just decided to do. "I checked on everyone, and they're all safe. Sam and I called Charlie. You don't need to worry, she's on her way to the manor with Ray."

My shoulders, knees, and body sank in relief. "That's not right, the Volvo's here! Gil has them."

"Stop. Collin, the fae from the lab, is driving her. I don't know the details on that." He waved his hand, flicking away the unimportant details. "Gil was here for a few moments just to give her a bag and then left." Nol sighed, slowly letting out his air. "She has many questions."

"Don't we all," I muttered. "Let's get going then."

Nol glanced at the Volvo, but didn't even scowl at it.

Quinn's black Porsche waited for us on a partially deforested small mountain top when we arrived almost an hour later to the veil where Orlaith's manor. If I'd driven another hundred feet, I'd have gone down into the trees below. The Cascade Mountains were past us, down this little mountain and through the rest of the foothills. But what we couldn't see was the entrance of Queen Orlaith's fae manor and the sprawling grape fields on the edge of Faerie with the Cascades as a backdrop. Quinn tried to explain that Orlaith's manor was not fully in Faerie but was still behind the veil. I didn't understand it, but I didn't need to.

We waited behind Quinn as he revved his engine, waiting for Faerie to respond to our arrival. The air in front of us wavered. Instead of driving off the top of the mountain, we drove into a Tuscan-style vineyard in the morning sunshine. The gravel pinged on my wheels as we hurried on through the gate and past the yellow walls surrounding the queen's manor. Several smaller mansions were laid out in a neighborhood style layout on either side of the winding gravel driveway, with a cul-de-sac at the end to boot.

Quinn stopped the car right at the main mansion's steps. Nol was out of the car, with Quinn jumping out and following on his heels. I turned off the Volvo and slammed the heavy door shut and ran after the two that had left me behind. I mean, Quinn could have waited, it wasn't some hostage situation.

"Hi, Hally!" Anna, a young fairy whom I'd met on several occasions, sprang out of the front door that was guarded by two tall, silent fairies. Her pink pigtails bounced as she tiptoed over the gravel on her bare feet. "Quinn told me to take you to the lab. Nolan didn't want to wait."

Sure, not that Quinn would've put up a fight about waiting, anyway. Sixty seconds, they couldn't have waited sixty seconds? "Tha—Perfect, that would be great." I didn't know where a lot of things were, except for a few conference rooms, the kitchen and the medical wing.

Anna smiled, she didn't spend too much time out of Faerie. I'd never asked how old she was and I wasn't sure how full-blooded fairies aged. But she knew the thanking rule and loved to enforce it.

"So, I took Ray to play with Seamus past the kitchen. Faerie made them a play area." Anna rambled and I nodded and hummed when she expected a confirmation of sorts. She took me through the south wing. I knew we were getting close when the smell of rubbing alcohol came from my right. Around the next corner, Anna opened the door with a flare. "Here we are. I don't know where they're at in here. Do you need any more help?"

"I've got it from here, Anna. You've been most helpful." The first room had a large glass window with a desk and chair. Not a lab. I kept going.

After the room, it opened into a larger space that came right out of a zombie movie. White everywhere, large glass windows showing empty rooms. Except zombie movies didn't have fairies and *endao* arguing at the door to my right.

"I told her to wait."

"I don' reckon she needs to be takin' orders from anybody. Don' you?" Collin's Irish accent thickened as he defended Charlie. "I think your worry was for not, though. I reckon the results might interest you."

I ran up to the two fae and one *endao*, frustrated that they'd left me behind.

Quinn snaked his arm around me and turned so I could see a lone brown-haired girl in the middle of a large lab. Her little home lab that filled three walls of our small formal dining room, with a light microscope, all the glass and measuring equipment that I thought she'd need, even a little refrigerator. Take all that stuff and triple it and that was this lab. No wonder she liked coming here more.

"Hally?" Collin, who had a brown-haired mess on top of his head and blue eyes to lose myself in, came up to me. He was somewhere between Quinn's height and Nol's. He waved his hand for me to follow him. "Would you like to come with us? The results came from Dublin two days ago."

"I...I guess. But Charlie—"

"She wanted to get a head start." Collin tipped his head back a smidge to encourage me to follow him. "Come, I'll show you."

Nol was not happy, but things seemed to be fine. Charlie was the only one in the room as she prepped slides on the counter next to a microscope. Several sets of test tubes were next to a large white machine. She was ass-deep in lab work, and I wouldn't bug her. But why was she the only one?

"Charlie was ready to roll before Nolan even called and wanted to get started right away. Everything is professional and ready for any magical or mundane threat. Your niece is safe." He kept reassuring me, like I was the one pissed off and not Nol. "Then, when Charlie's done, we'll compare tests."

"Tests on what?" I looked over to see Charlie again safe and unaware of how much danger she'd been in. "What was in the bag?"

"We're not too certain what all he gave her, except a load of vials, bottles and paperwork. He didn't wanna stay long. But as Charlie canna speak your language and vice versa, they were in a bit of a pickle. Now, I don' agree with his next choice, givin' her a good kiss right on the lips, but she says he didn't mean anythin' by it. But then he disappeared as fast as he came." Collin shuffled from foot to foot. He was gone before I—" Collin cleared his throat. "Now, let me just fast-pace this for you. Otherwise, we'll be here all week."

"Charlie told me the virus you have in your labs is similar to the *Pae-lesoda* virus."

Collin held his breath, uncertain how to respond. He'd been all geared up to give us a tour of their work. "Ah, actually, we have an update on that."

He walked over to a door with the same kind of long narrow windows in zombie movies. And schools, too. I thought he'd bring us to a microscope where we'd have to look and try to figure out where on the slide he was referring to, but Collin grabbed a remote, switched the light off with a thought, and turned on the screen. "This one is the fae virus." Collin went on to talk about proteins and DNA and everything that was way over my head. But he didn't say anything that I wanted to know.

Quinn went closer to the screen, squinting at all the details. "But it isn't the same."

"Correct." Collin answered immediately, getting excited. "Moira, another scientists on my team, found some books on it in the Dublin library. We are ninety-nine percent certain they are related to the virus inside of the curse." He scratched his chin and rambled. "Ours obviously doesn't have a curse—"

"Is there a cure for yours?" I interrupted to get back on track.

Collin's eyes flashed around the room. He grinned a broad smile and he clicked the remote. "Yes, that we do."

"Will it work on the *Pae-lesoda* virus?" I asked.

"Unfortunately, no..." He sucked on his teeth as he scrunched his nose up.

Chewing on my lip, I walked closer to the window to see all the doodads on the table. She had a lot more than a few of Gil's vials sitting there. "He showed me these vials. There were dozens in the fortress. They had both viruses. I don't remember which color is which. And he never showed me a yellow one."

"You're telling me we have samples of the *Pae-lesoda* virus in there?" Collin asked.

I shrugged. "That's what Gil told me. I even have a few in the Volvo. Two each."

The three guys looked up toward the front of the lab like they could see out at the Volvo. "Is all that what Gileal brought?"

"He did leave that letter and a lot of hand written notes." Collin pointed to a piece of paper in Nol's hand, which I hadn't noticed before.

I scoffed at Nol. "Unbelievable, we've been talking this whole time, and you've been holding a letter from Gil?"

Quinn grabbed my hand and tapped the back of it. There was no way I was fucking calming down. I was tired of Nol not communicating and getting angry at me over one thing when there was so much he hid from us. Nol looked down at his hand with the letter. He lifted the note higher, staring at it from different angles, as if just realizing he was holding something. From here, I couldn't tell if there was a seal, but the folded paper seemed to stay closed. It could have been another one that only Nol could open.

I walked up and stood in front of him. "Is it addressed just to you?"

He shook his head, staring. Shit, if it was for my eyes only, we'd never know what it said.

"I want you all out when I read it." Nol stared down at the paper and shook his head. "We can't trust anything from him."

I glanced over at the sealed lab with Charlie dropping liquid into one of their test tubes.

I looked at Collin, then Quinn. Quinn nodded, and I leaned in and caught Nol's very tired eyes. "Fine, but you better stay alive after this, because we're still mad at each other. Got it?"

One corner of his mouth twitched, but he locked it down and nodded. After a moment, to make sure he knew I meant it, I backed out the door.

"What's going on, Hally? What's wrong with him?" Quinn asked, staring into the room.

"He's been up for days."

Before I could explain anything else, Nol unlocked the door. Still not focusing, he stared off somewhere in front of him. "He...couldn't trust that the vials he gave you would make it to Charlie. After he saw us together, he couldn't risk it." Nol took a step back, then another.

Collin grabbed a chair and slid it under him before he fell.

Nol pointed toward the lab where Gil's bag of goodies were on the table. "He wants Charlie to use Doctor Serin's notes to find the cure—for me."

My brain was starting to hurt as I tried to sort through the technicalities. "Gil told me about that." The world made less and less sense by the hour. Raj and Camber, Gil was a traitor, committee threatening my life—oh wait, that was every other month—Gil escaping. Now apparently we were supposed to find a cure for Nol? Not the people of *Aemina*?

Nol raised his head and searched for me, taking too long to focus on my face.

Quinn came up behind me and touched my arm. "Nolan does *not* look healthy. There's something going on."

Yeah, heartbreak. "There's..."

"Hey, guys?" Charlie's voice came over the intercom, loud, clear, and unexpected. She waved for us to come closer to the glass.

Nol didn't budge, just stared in her general direction.

Collin walked over to the counter with a microphone and pushed a button. "Charlie, anythin'?"

"It'll take time, but..." Charlie looked at me, then at Nol. "I was hoping one of you could read Gil's notes on the vials? This one I'm testing is the one he was most adamant about. What was he in such a hurry for? What the hell is going on over there?"

I bit my lip as I thought about how to explain. Not through a damn intercom. "It's a long story, love. Will this take a while?"

Charlie tipped her head down and gave me a look of pure disbelief. A stupid question didn't deserve an answer. But come on, she wanted to know, and I needed a time frame. "Gimme an hour. Is Nolan okay?"

I turned back to Nol, who was still staring off into the lab behind Charlie. "No."

NOL HAD BEEN ON a loop of barely moving to pacing the room for forty-five minutes. Charlie brought a few of Gil's things over for us to inspect. Whatever Nol had read in the notes had riled him up, and his mumbling wasn't making much sense. Charlie had gotten a half hour of work done before Nol's dizzying movements became too much of a distraction.

Collin stood near the intercom, Charlie and I sat at one of the tables, and Quinn leaned up against the door, blocking off the room. Nol paced from the TV to the door, almost running into Quinn every time, except Nol never seemed to touch him. I had my suspicions Quinn had him in an illusion, and I was beginning to think Quinn was right.

"You need to sleep, Nol."

Nol clenched and unclenched his fists as he paced. "There will be another time for sleep. Gileal is out there—"

"And there are two huge worlds to look through. We won't find him anytime soon. There's no way to know if he is on his own or has any support. You haven't slept in almost five days!" But it was like talking to a wall. He wasn't listening to me, but I had to keep trying.

"I've had some naps."

I set my hands on my hips and glared. "The few hours last night were not enough. If you're going to be of any use, you gotta sleep."

"Hally?" Quinn whispered in my ear. I looked up but found Quinn still standing at the door. Did Quinn have us in the illusion, too? Quinn didn't move, but neither did his lips when he whispered again. "Would you and Charlie step out for a minute? I think I can convince him to rest."

"How?" I whispered.

"Give us a minute for some...guy talk? Collin and I want to check something."

I watched Nol turn, once again, too close to where Quinn still stood, staring at Nol.

"Please, darling?"

"But Collin, too?"

"He's the one asking."

My eyes darted to Collin. I watched Nol mumbling under his breath.

I felt ghost hands on my arm and a tug, all while Quinn stayed against the door. Charlie got up next. The door opened, and we were...in the room still? The door was an arm's length away, and when I looked back, Collin sat in his chair and Quinn was against the door. So fucking confusing.

Quinn appeared between Charlie and me. "Sorry, I know I promised never to use my illusions on you again. There is no fucking way I'm making Nolan do anything, though." He kissed my forehead.

"Go, get something to eat, and once Collin and I talk to Nolan, then we can talk about whatever is going on. Agreed?"

I looked over at my *muranildo*, still pacing the room. "But Nol—"

"Hally? He'll be okay. I swear." Quinn kissed me, a chaste one on the lips, and then he was gone, standing by the door-not-door again.

Charlie yanked the real door open. "This is weird." She had that right.

We went to a small room with several comfortable couches, an Xbox and PlayStation, plus a bunch of other entertaining distractions. She grabbed a bottle of water from a little fridge, picked a corner of the fluffy white couch, and plopped down. "What the fuck, Hally?"

"Would you believe me if I said Gileal is the one who hired Aswryn?"

Bottle at her chin, she froze, seething as I explained to the best of my understanding what Gileal had said to me at the fortress.

"That's diabolical. I thought he was your friend, the three of you against the world. That's fucked-up shit. And he was in my house." Charlie stood, her hand to her mouth. She threw the door open and ran. No explanation. She came back in, moments later, arms across her chest. "I think I know what the third one might be. And if it is—"

The door opened and Quinn poked his head into the room. "We have a problem."

"I think I might know."

Quinn studied Charlie for a second. "Nolan's infected."

"With the curse?" My voice squeaked. "He can't, he's immune."

"No, with the *serilesoda* virus."

"Oh shit! That's…Gil said that's how Serin got the cure for *serileso-da*. A few *Zayuri* became infected. Their bodies produced something that helped them heal really fast, but I don't know what. But how? Nol never went in the fortress."

"He must have modified the virus to make it more infectious to the *Zayuri* help us find a cure." Charlie stared at the carpet as she considered the possibilities. "How else could he be sure Nolan got sick? But that doesn't make sense. Gil would never endanger you."

Oh, what a relief. I wouldn't get sick. I'd just watch Nol suffer. Great, thanks, Gil. The thought came with the reminders of who Gil really was and the depth of his betrayal. The *Amura Ore* would kill him for this. I shoved the thought down to the pit of my stomach. My mind kept asking whether Gil would have been better off dead? I wasn't sure. Did thinking that make me a horrible person? I didn't have time for those thoughts.

"Why would he care if Hally gets hurt?" Quinn asked.

"Because he loves me, and because of that, he chose to help make this curse. I could say this means the curse *was* my fault, but I can't give myself that much credit. We are all responsible for our own choices. Gil chose to hire Aswryn to find a way to get back at the *Amura Ore.*"

"Could the third one be the cure for the original virus?"

I shook my head at Charlie's question. "No. He said he needed help finding the cure. I'm sorry, it's something else. It could be in the letter with Gil's notes."

Charlie deflated.

"Would you guys mind getting me up to date here?" Quinn asked.

I inhaled and prepared myself for what I had to tell them. "Let's get Collin and I'll tell all that I know."

26

CHARLIE CAME BACK INTO the room where she had put me after taking samples of my blood. Everything was too unbelievable to think about. Nol was fighting this ancient virus somewhere in this mansion, and they wouldn't tell me where. The more symptoms he presented, the more contagious he would become, and I couldn't see him until Charlie was certain I couldn't get infected.

"There are no signs of the virus in you yet, Tatie." Charlie plopped down onto the bed. "That doesn't mean it's not there. It could be incubating."

"Or it really could be modified, like you suspect."

Charlie sighed. "Sure, but we can't assume that. We're working on it." Charlie chewed on the inside of her cheek, thinking.

With Nol sick, I wasn't planning to go back to work or to France, but staying here at the mansion didn't sound like fun. "How long before you know if it's different?"

She dropped her head back. "I don't know. We'll test you every day."

I groaned. "At least Quinn's going to go get mine and Nol's phones from his condo."

We both laughed, and I asked, "So what's going on next? I can't read Gil's notes. Do you think Nol would be up to it?" I highly doubted it.

"Orlaith is reading Gil's notes now. She says his handwriting is crap, but legible."

Well, that was nice of the queen. She did have shit to do. "Did you check for the cells in Nol's immune system that Gil mentioned?"

"It's too soon for that. This virus started fast. The body wouldn't have had time to react yet." Charlie laid back and looked up at the ceiling. "Even if Nolan's body does change the curse like Gil thinks, there's no way we can collect enough changed cells to cure an entire population."

"Don't get ahead of yourself, love." I reached over and petted her hair. "Like you've said before, it's a long road. You need more information, not speculation. I'm curious if anyone else was infected. I can't imagine everyone who was at the fortress is as sick as Nol."

Charlie touched my arm and shook it. "There's nothing you can do about it. Maybe it'd do you some good to get some sleep. You haven't had much of that lately." Charlie stood and kissed my head. At the door, she turned around. "Hally?"

"Yes, love?"

"Congratulations on the new trial. If anything, that's something to look forward to." She blew me a kiss and backed out.

THE SUN OUTSIDE THE long windows turned the dust in the air gold, in a place I thought I'd never see again. To my disappointment, I couldn't smell anything. Not here. At the front, the librarian worked on something...writing on a paper no one would ever see. On the first floor in the back, kids were listening to a talking book. Again, it didn't matter. They weren't really there. I knew where I'd find him. We had our place on the second floor, left side. In a heartbeat, I was there, staring past the shelves to the table under a smaller second-story window.

A boy sat hunched over in a chair, his cinnamon-red hair glowing in the sunlight streaming in the open window. My breath hitched as I remembered the boy he used to be. His legs were pulled up, his feet on the edge as he pushed on the table to lift the front part of the chair off the floor.

He held a large book in his hands, his nose maybe six inches away, with a finger on a line as he squinted. And as dreams went, he knew what it said, but he couldn't read it. His age was indecipherable, younger than when I'd left him, but that didn't mean shit. He could know everything, or nothing, or anything in between.

Nol turned a page, not worrying about his nose being too close because it was his dream. It would work for him. And since in this dream he was young, and considering our location, I needed to change my appearance. All I had to do was pluck it out of his memory, and I'd look just how he remembered me.

The first memory of a young Hallanevaë that stuck out included the green vest Wennië had made me after I'd turned a century. Damn it, I didn't want to be this young. I searched for another. I was...with Raj in the library. When had this happened? I'd tried to get his butt in here with her many times, and he'd *never* shown up. But we were across the room, and he hadn't started walking farther inside. I felt him shift to leave the library, and I grabbed the vision of me he saw.

A much younger version of myself with dark freckles across my face, my black hair in an intricate braid that my mother had done, probably by bribery. I wore a traditional *endaen* shirt, long in the back and waist level in the front. Before Nol could leave, I pulled the memory back and looked at Raj. Her golden hair lay loose over her shoulders, split between the front and back. Her *endaen* blue sweater warmed her light brown skin tone and deepened her periwinkle eyes. Nol thought she was pretty. I pulled back. This was wrong, getting so far into his psyche that I could feel his emotions. The memory of myself was all I needed. Using that memory, I skipped down the bookshelves and grabbed his shoulders, tipping him back a fraction to tease him about the librarian.

"Jedyen would have you sorting books for hours if she saw you like this."

"Hallë?" Jeez, his voice. I hadn't realized how much it had changed. Late one-twenties? Had to be. He only had up to his third decade honors.

"What are you doing here? I thought you were supposed to be out with Jemi and Enyco."

His brow furrowed as he tried to think that through. The dream changed, and more book stacks appeared.

"What are you researching?" I reached for a book, knowing he wouldn't find what he wanted.

"I'm not sure. Would you help me find it?"

"Sure." I pulled the book into my lap and opened it. Then I watched him. His eyes roamed up and down the book instead of right to left like *Aemirin* writing read. "Can we find it here?"

"Maybe...but if I find the glass, I'll know I'm there."

"A glass, huh? That's what we're looking for?"

"No. I'm not sure what we're researching. But I'll find the glass." Whatever it was, it made sense to him here. Dreams were so weird.

I crisscrossed my legs to better perch the book on my lap. We looked for a little longer. He wasn't waking up anytime soon. Collin had made him sleep when the fever hit.

"How ya feeling?"

"Cold. That's why I have the books. They'll work."

"Nol?"

He didn't respond.

After a few more pages, I tried again. "Nol, would you look up, please? I need you to see me."

"I always see you. But if you look enough, you'll find yourself." He tipped his chair again, and his book changed to a piece of paper. He kept reading like there'd been no change, but he looked angrier.

"Look at me. See me."

He lowered the paper until he could see over it. His brow furrowed, bringing out that crease between his eyes that I always pressed away with my thumb. "You..."

"It's me, Nol. We need to talk."

"You're"—his head tilted to the side, his mind puzzling it out. This was the first time I'd ever gone into his dreams—"here, visiting my dream."

Nodding, I crossed my arms. Visiting someone's dreams without permission seemed immoral, and I hated the invasion of privacy.

"There are a bunch of things happening right now. Do you remember?"

He scowled at me. "I'm mad at you."

I dropped my arms in my lap to lean forward. "You are. And I'm mad at you. That doesn't mean we can't talk."

"You left me. And you stopped me from killing Gileal."

There was nothing to say to that. "And what did you do to make me mad?"

Nol looked down at the table and shook his head. "I don't want to talk about it."

"We're talking about it later. As in, later soon. Not later never."

"Like you are trying to do with our other conversation? Later never?"

More avoidance and distraction, but it wouldn't work. I shrugged one shoulder. "I don't know what to think. But those are for another conversation." I threw back his favorite saying whenever he wanted to avoid a topic. "Do you remember the lab in Orlaith's mansion?"

Nol wiggled to get more comfortable in his chair. "Yes. Charlie was looking at Gileal's equipment. What's wrong with me? Quinn asked if another fairy could look at me because I don't feel well."

"You aren't well. Collin took your blood and found something that should be almost impossible for you to have."

Nol twisted until he could see me, an eyebrow raised in suspicious curiosity. "The curse?"

"No. The *serilesoda* virus."

Nol pulled a book off the stack and opened it. "It's not impossible, just rare."

"The only place I can think that you caught it is at the fortress when Gil came out. Bren shackled him, and you had him on the ground. Those are two contacts. You were never inside."

"No...that's not where." Nol dropped his head back, taking in the sunlight. After a while longer of silence, he took in a breath to talk. "*Mujut*, why didn't I see it before? The vials on Charlie's lab counter were the same as the ones at the Starborn Palace. When I touched the device, it opened on its own. We thought it would go off, but there was only an unopened small glass bottle of liquid, with an empty vial beside it.

"I assumed the combination of chemicals had caused a reaction, and since the glass box was intact, it was over. That empty vial was the same kind of yellow as the vials Charlie is working with. The one she said Gil was adamant about. I think he sent that bomb to infect the *Zayuri* at the Palace."

"Who came with you?"

"Everyone who was in the room the night before. They need to be informed of what this is. People may mistake it as the curse, and fear that Aswryn's goal has been achieved will spread. If no one thinks *Zayuri* villages are safe, families will leave and be more susceptible to the curse. Perhaps this was Gileal's plan to create panic within the people who trusted him. For their families to suffer from the curse in front of them..." Nol squeezed his fists on the table next to his book, trying to keep his pain inside. "You have to tell them or their children and family members without the *Zayuri* gene will be at risk of catching the curse. If they stay in the villages, they might contract the *serilesoda* virus, but at least they'll have a good chance of surviving."

"I'll tell them, but this is great news. Do you remember me telling you what the vials were?

Nol frowned as he thought. "No."

"It's okay. Now that I know where you got it from, it solves one mystery." And possibly created a huge panic in the *Zayuri* villages.

I didn't explain more, because there was no way to know how much he'd remember from the dream. I stood, moved around the table, kissed his temple, and let Nol fade back into his dream state. He'd remember talking to me later, but his subconscious would take over and help him rest more.

First, I'd talk to my grandmother to ensure the *Zayuri* families stayed in *Jinatrau*. After that, I'd tell Charlie what Nol had learned.

"Oh, Hally, thank the Mother you're safe in *Rosava*." Yalu stood in her garden behind her house in *Jinatrau*. In her dream, she wore a pretty purple dress and apron for gardening. Her tools lay on the table near us. "Things are getting bad here, little crow. Tolwe won't come home, even though he hasn't developed symptoms. Are either of you showing signs of the curse? Everyone is being evacuated. We are all trying to understand how Gileal got through the immunity—"

"Yalu, stop." I grabbed her hands, sort of. They weren't *her* hands, and I couldn't feel them. She might have, though, as it was her dream. "It isn't the curse."

"My child, it is."

"No. It's the *serilesoda* virus." I explained what Nol had figured out with the help of Gileal's notes. As I did, she stayed the same, looking calm in her lovely garden. I could imagine how the stress had frazzled her in real life, though. "Nolan has it, too. Tell them all for us. If they stay in the villages, they won't contract the curse. Charlie has help and is looking for a solution. Keep everyone from leaving."

"You're certain?"

"Nol is, and you know we can trust his logic. I'll send you back now. Go tell everyone. Love you." I helped her wake up along with myself, too fast to say goodbye.

27

Quinn and Seamus stayed with us on the manor grounds the first night. Seamus and Ray *loved* the idea of having a sleepover in Faerie. Faerie loved it, too, judging by the fort it'd made for them, which I would take time to go see later. My awesome boyfriend had also brought me pastels and charcoals from my art studio along with my phone.

The latch to my room clicked. "Guess what I've got?" Charlie came in holding a plate high. I hadn't seen her since last night. I'd told her what Nol and my grandmother had told me and gone back to bed. My amazing niece walked over, her grin plastered on. She lowered the plate as she came closer. "Quiche. Your favorite kind, too." Quiche was good, but not if it didn't have the perfect companion. "Did you bring me coffee?"

"No. Your boyfriend's got that."

"Oh goodie." I slapped the charcoals down into the box and grabbed a tissue in my art bag. "Am I infected?"

She'd said it would take a week, but if she found out earlier, I'd be free—maybe. Charlie shook her head in annoyance. "Patience." She reared back when she noticed my sketch pad. "What is that?"

Blowing air through my pursed lips, I tossed the crappy sketch on the floor. "Not good enough to show my client."

"Hmm. It looks like zombie werewolves."

My lip curled. "It kinda does, doesn't it?"

She stepped over my crappy art and offered me the plate. "I've got some news, too."

I pulled the plate out of her hands and grabbed the fork. "What's that?"

She raised her shoulders once. "The crew from Dublin arrived early this morning. They brought their virus and their cure." Charlie grabbed my fork and took a bite of *my* quiche.

I snatched my fork back, wanting my coffee. "So they'll try their cure on the *Pae-lesoda*?"

"The uncursed version and the one Nolan has."

Charlie chewed her bite, watching me. Then my slow brain caught up to the conversation. "Wait, *and* the one Nol has? It's different?" We were never going to win!

Charlie nodded, stealing my fork again. "We were right."

"Charlie, *you* had the idea first. You are right."

Charlie lay on her back at the foot of my bed and closed her eyes. "Orlaith read the labels and some of the notes he had." She paused and held up a finger. "Both say *serilesoda* on it, but she couldn't read his handwriting. Turns out the green vial says *Zayuri serilesoda*. I'll tell you, that guy labels everything, thank god."

My head was already spinning so much that I'd stopped eating just to keep up. Couldn't she just get to the point already? I set my fork on the plate and lowered it to my lap, not even a quarter of the way through.

"What's the matter? You full?"

"No, love. I love the story, I do. What you've done is amazing, but—"

Charlie rolled her eyes. She knew I never followed along. It was why she'd been so excited and willing to work with the fae on this in the first place. She had someone beside me to bounce ideas off of. Poor Nol had tried, but when she talked over his head, he'd look up the meaning and figure it out on his own. It pissed her right off.

Charlie dropped her arm onto her face. "Fine."

Finally on the same page, I took another bite.

"The *Zayuri serilesoda* is suspended in a stabling serum." Charlie lifted her hands and twisted like she was holding an invisible Rubik's Cube, or possibly sorting out science stuff in her head from the shit I'd understand. "It only allows it to infect *Zayuri* with the active gene. It's a potion."

"What?" I gasped and choked on my breakfast.

Charlie took the plate and set it on the side table while I got a few good coughs in. There was a brief point when I thought I'd choke on my favorite dish. Death by quiche. Blasphemy. After drinking some water and assuring my body I wasn't dying, I tried again.

"When did you learn this?"

"After you came in and told me about the Jinatrau info. There was no way I was waking you at three in the morning."

She had a point. Mornings and I didn't get along. "So I *can't* get infected?" The little shit had waited this whole time to tell me this. "Charlie, I've been up since six. My body has no fucking clue what time zone to follow." My mind was already planning ahead. An *Olauvë* meeting with Yalu needed to happen after breakfast. Updating Nol—that could come later.

"Sorry, but I wasn't going to risk getting throttled for waking you up too early. Besides, you'd think your body would want to make up for the three days you didn't sleep."

I took my first cautious bite after the choking incident. "I slept very well last night, thank you. After talking to Nol and Yalu, of course. Let me be certain, as this science shit always confuses me. Are you saying I can leave if I want to?"

Arm over her forehead, she watched me eat the last of my food. "You can't catch the virus in Gil's serum, so yes. But I can't let you go anywhere, yet." Her chocolate brown eyes grew rounder and her lips pursed as she waited for me to ask why.

I set my empty plate on the table and pulled the blankets around me. She hummed with frustration and the need to tell me. Giving in after a few seconds more—she looked too damn adorable to say no to—I asked, "Why, love, do you need me to stay?"

"Because *I* get to use your magic for the greater good."

"Oh? Not me?"

Charlie scoffed and waved her hand at me with a *psh*. "Kevin, the Dublin historian, helped Orlaith get ten times farther in Serin's work last night."

For *Aeminan endai*? The fae owed *Aemina* nothing. Owed Nol and me nothing. My thoughts got away from me, and I missed what Charlie was talking about.

"...he's so hot. Oh my god." She fanned herself. "Wait until you see him, Hally. I couldn't string two words together in front of him."

Wait. Who?

"I wonder if Collin noticed, though."

So Collin wasn't the "so hot" guy. Interesting. "What's up with Collin?"

"Huh? Nothing." Charlie's cheeks turned a rosy pink as she held her break. "He's nice, but I-I..." She sagged and growled in frustration. "I don't know. He stayed all day that day and he flirts with me sometimes. He stayed the night last night, we were up late...just talking. He's cool, but he won't make any moves."

"He likes you. I think he's just shy. Ask him out."

Charlie huffed. Oh, the work it would take to ask the poor guy out!

"Maybe. I think Kevin and Orlaith know each other. They work well together, too. Anyway, enough about the sexy historian and Collin. Are you ready to find out what you're doing for me?" She sat up, flushed pink and animated. "Duh, of course you do." Charlie slapped my thigh over the blanket. "Get up so I can show you. And you can meet the sexy historian." She squealed and rolled off the bed. "I'm so getting the scoop with Orlaith."

"Do I have time for coffee?" From my experience, labs and food did not mix, except for my little spot in Charlie's home lab where I was allowed to drink coffee when visiting, or while being poked for tests.

Charlie blinked, and I noticed the darker circles under her eyes. "I told you, your boyfriend has it. Get your ass up."

She frolicked out the door—there was no other word for it. Charlie didn't have to tell me twice. I threw the covers off and yanked on some pants before following her to the lab.

My fingers curled around the warm ceramic. Coffee with sugar. Yep, Quinn was a keeper. He kissed the top of my head and snuggled in the chair next to me with his own hot cup. I paused. The lab classroom Collin had brought us to yesterday seemed smaller with six more people in it. Orlaith, Collin, and the five fae from the Dublin crew, Moira, Danny, Kevin, Mac, and Finn, had stuffed themselves inside.

"You can begin," Orlaith instructed Collin, who had waited to start until Quinn's arrival.

Collin hesitated, looking between the two of us. Unsure what Prince Quinn kissing the top of the head of an *endaë* meant, possibly? This would go viral in the fae world.

The historian, who I had to agree with Charlie, was amazingly good looking, with wavy brown hair tied back in a ponytail and smoky eyes that I couldn't decide whether they were gray or brown. He seemed oblivious to his appeal as he helped Collin explain a few details about the fae virus and how it differed from the *endaen* virus. They were much more interested in their virus than ours and it was a little annoying.

Collin pressed the tiny remote, and a picture appeared of the viruses in the lab room next to us. He took a deep breath as he stared at the little pinkish-purple glob.

"So is the bunch of dots and the squiggles a virus?" It looked like a row of little dots with squiggles on the sides. Oh, no, there was a squiggle in the middle.

"Squiggles?" Collin's brow wrinkled in confusion or maybe frustration. Hell, weren't we all?

"She's talking about the solution," Kevin the historian said in a bored tone that made him lose sexy points in my book.

"These dots here, they're the *serilesoda* virus Gileal used to infect Nolan." Collin tapped the pink dot on the screen. They all looked the same to me. "There are multiple individuals in this frame. Is that what ya mean?"

I nodded while I blew on my coffee. "You can't zoom in some more?"

"Eh, the screen isn't big enough?"

"Tatie, this is as close as we can get. Collin, go on. She'll get it."

"What we will need to know is how quickly Nolan's immune system will alter the virus."

"Not that quickly," one of the Dublin crew mumbled. I looked around at the five who'd come over. They all showed attitude whenever I asked for clarification.

"Doesn't science take a lot more time than a few days? Gil's work..." I sipped to hide my pause. The goal was not to praise his findings, but to look at the facts. I could do this. "He and his buddies didn't find this overnight. And he used Serin's and Aswryn's work. Serin developed his cure six thousand years ago. Aswryn cast her curse thirty years ago. And that was just the launch. Now you want Nol's body to grow some super virus-eater in two days? Really?"

They looked away like scolded children instead of the thousands of years old I assumed they were.

Someone snorted a laugh, and everyone looked over. Orlaith held her hand to her mouth as she tried to keep quiet. "Super virus-eater."

Charlie laughed when Orlaith couldn't hold it in, which had a domino effect. Soon the scientists, plus Orlaith, were laughing, while Quinn and I stared on. They'd been up all night. Ignoring their giggling fit, I stood and walked over to the screen as if this distance would give me a better advantage. It did not.

"Can we look at the *Pae-lesoda* under the microscope?"

They all shut up. I'd stared at Aswryn's curse in pictures before, many pictures, but never got to see it live.

"I'm dying to know how Aswryn's curse attached to these things. Does it just come in and engulf them like Pac-Man? Or wiggle in like a sperm to an egg? It'd be interesting to put the two together and see what happens. Maybe we'd get baby cursed viruses." I sipped my coffee and stared at the pink dots. If we dyed Aswryn's virus blue, we could make purple. We had time, sitting around until Nol's body started fighting the virus. They were scientists. Wasn't that kind of thing they did?

"Well?" I turned away from the picture of the stained *serilesoda* virus and found them gawking at me. Was it the Pac-Man reference? "Charlie, you're always saying we need more samples for research. We have both the original host and the evil one. Why not try?" For Pete's sake, they weren't even susceptible to the curse, and they didn't want to mess with it. "Does it need food to grow? We can put a few of my ME cells in there and see if it gobbles them up."

Collin looked at Charlie, then at his crew. "We could hook it up for a live feed."

"You'd hafta stay in here," Kevin said like I was slow or something. I didn't understand science, but I wasn't stupid.

"I asked to look under the microscope, not go in the lab and offer it my finger!"

"It wouldn't hurt to grow a few more," Collin agreed.

Finally! "Let's keep this away from Nol though. He gets grumpy whenever I'm involved with the curse."

MY COFFEE WAS ALMOST gone, but I'd have to leave the lab to get more, and this was interesting. The *Pae-lesoda* liked my magical energy cells a lot. That evil thing got a taste and bam! The little guys went wild on the original *serilesoda*. The poor wavy things on the surface of their bodies couldn't propel them away fast enough. They fluttered around like some freaky jellyfish. All it took was a petri dish with culture, aka, my blood, and a pipettete full of liquid.

"You're never getting closer to that curse than here," Quinn said beside me as we stared at the screen. "When they told me it attacked *Aeminan's* magic, I didn't imagine this destruction."

While he meant how fast it ate at my magical energy cells in the culture, it was hard to associate what happened after about ten minutes. The *Pae-lesoda* didn't engulf the *serilesoda*, nor did it wiggle in. It cuddled right up to the virus like they were the best of friends. Then they merged, like a reverse National Geographic cell division video. The *serilesoda* wiggled as it realized the danger too late, and it was gone, coated in a barrier of the curse. Creating the *Pae-lesoda* cursed virus. Flashes of pretty rainbow-colored light crackled like a nerve storm on the surface from the different energies. "Do you think they're gonna want more?"

"They have three vials of blood. They're not getting any more. Nolan might kill us anyway for letting you in the same building."

"Nah, he was okay with it in Charlie's lab, so long as it stayed locked up when not being used. Do you think I can do this?"

Quinn plucked my coffee mug from my hands. "Let Charlie use your magic for the greater good? Sure. Annihilating that son-of-a-bitch *Pae-lesoda* virus? Once you put your mind to something, I don't think there's any stopping you." He kissed me in front of anyone who might turn our way. Not a little peck either. One that sent my insides fluttering. He pulled back and asked, "You okay with this?"

Licking my lips, I tasted his sweetened coffee. "How much will this cost you?"

He came in for another kiss, this time less involved. "I'll get you more coffee. You think of ways you can dissect this evil creation while I'm gone," he said, then left the room. I was thinking of his kiss when the little flashes of magic brought my attention back to the screen.

"I think this'll be a good thing," Queen Orlaith said.

I jumped in my seat. "Your Majesty!" I hadn't heard her come in. Her silver hair looked darker in this light. Today, she was fancied up in a beige and pink pantsuit, but she'd come into my house for coffee in a sweatshirt and jeans once. I dipped my head, but she was watching the screen. "I hope it will. You don't think I've created a monster with this, do you?"

"A monster? Quinn? No. This is good for him."

"Oh." I gave a nervous chuckle. "I thought you meant the virus. Why do you think that?"

"You and Quinn showing your affection for each other shows that His Royal Highness approves of your presence. Some will fight it, but more, I think, will see it as a peaceful transition into a time of communication and cooperation between our species."

"Right, politically. What about personal? Do you approve of it?"

"You know his parents don't. They called me, concerned about the elven hussy entrapping their son."

I snorted a laugh. "I'm such a hussy."

"No, but he didn't give Katie's death a lot of mourning time. That, more than anything, will be an issue with some. Did he tell you they'd always been friends? They complained for centuries about their betrothal."

"He told me, but I think he was told to ask me out to learn more about the elf in your queendom."

Orlaith *tsk*ed with a smile. "Only because I saw he was interested." The queen walked in at a steady pace, her hands settled in front of her. She had a purpose, something on her mind, and she hadn't given me an answer. "Look at those pretty lights it gives off. Do you think you can manage what they want you to do?"

I sighed a huge sigh, wanting to be one-hundred-percent confident. "Break the curse? No. But five people's spells are holding the curse together, so severing that link between their *imolegin* to make a hole in their curse...maybe. I think I'll have to use a lot of magic in that tiny space and I have to hope that the band behaves." I thought back to how much it had let me use in *Endae*.

"Are those new?" Orlaith asked.

I squinted at the screen, but nothing was different...

"Your cuffs. There are four more than normal."

Touching them with my fingertips, I smiled, thinking about Edvic coming back with them. "Only one is. They took these three when they exiled me."

Orlaith nodded her approval. "And you got them back. Marvelous."

"The wooden one, my father made it, along with this ring. He's a carver, and infuses his magic into each touch of his tools."

"May I see?"

I handed the ring to her. Orlaith looked at it for a moment, then at the cuff. "Amazing. He's very talented. I can feel the energy pulsing through the ring. What is it meant for?"

"Nol's dad said I can use it like a *meril*, but I feel something more than my dad's *imolegin* in this."

"I agree, it's more than one of your *merils*. It's powerful. Do you mind if I have someone look at it? A small analysis?"

"Go ahead. I'd love to hear what your people find."

She bounced the ring on her palm. "Your father has power, maybe as much as you."

I pressed a finger to my lips. "Don't tell anyone. Really, if you ever see any of my people and the topic comes up, as unlikely as that is, do not mention my father's strength." I waved at her. "It's hard to explain. If this works, I can save my father."

She squeezed my shoulder. "Why do you think we're all helping? You will get your dad back."

My heart overflowed with joy and gratitude at her words. She wasn't doing it for *Aemina*. She was doing it for me—Hally Dubois. "Thank you, Orie," I managed in a whisper.

She didn't tell me not to thank her like the first time I met her. She looked back at the light show with a pleasant look on her face. I'd thanked the Queen of the Fae of the Pacific Ring of Fire, and I now owed her, and I knew she'd collect. "I hope I can one day help you save someone you love."

"Child?" Queen Orlaith came close, brushed my hair off my shoulder, and tucked it behind my ear. "You already have. This has fulfilled a debt to you."

My mouth snapped shut. She'd already done so much for us by saving the children. "Your Majesty, while I do not discredit their lives—they are all precious—I hope you don't think I expect a debt to be repaid for each child. I thought the permission to stay here was the boon for saving them."

"Just enjoy it, Hally."

As we watched our scientist group work and the virus sparkle, I gathered the courage to ask again, "Your Majesty? *Do* you approve of Quinn and me?"

She thought, or waited, and after a while, I gave up expecting an answer. "No, I think you would be better as friends. But for now? You're enjoying it."

Her answer surprised me. From what I had heard, she was the most forward-thinking queen of all the sovereigns. If she didn't approve, I had little chance with any of the others. "We are having fun. And your honesty is appreciated."

The queen smiled and turned. "Just remember," she said at the door, one hand on the handle. "Eventually he must find a co-ruler."

"Yes, Your Majesty, we've discussed it."

"Possibly sooner than he thinks."

With that tidbit of news, she slipped out to do whatever it was queens had to do during their busy days.

28

WHEN I SNUCK OFF to the kitchen to drop off my mug, Seamus captured me. It didn't take much convincing to go with him. I needed the distraction. A quick look at the fort Faerie had helped them make would be excellent. The place off the kitchen that Faerie made Seamus and Ray was an enclosed yard with a six-foot cobblestone wall connected to the mansion. May flowers, including lilacs, were blooming all around. The scent of dirt and flowers, even if it was in Faerie, took my stress level down by about a hundred notches.

A stepping-stone path, lined with blooming purple heather, led to a little multicolored patchwork quilt tent. Next to it was an ancient tree, complete with knots and a low palm perfect for hiding in. I'd need to tell Ray to show Nol the tree. It looked like a miniature version of the one Nol and I used to climb in *Rudairn*.

Six strands of Edison lights hung from the old tree to the walls around the yard in the afternoon sunlight. And my favorite, the blue, green, purple, and pink fairy fireflies flitted about as little birds, and other fae critters swooped past to land on the bird feeder set up close to their tent.

"Come see our tent," Ray demanded.

I crawled in after them. The kids pushed open the blanket and tumbled inside. Sleeping bags and pillows galore filled the space. They giggled and enjoyed showing me every little part.

"Pretty cozy."

Seamus smacked me with a pillow.

"Oh, you did not!" I reached for the closest pillow and threw one at Seamus's tummy. Ray joined in, and soon we were all giggling. I'd needed this.

"Hello?" Charlie called from somewhere in the yard, saving me from the onslaught of pillows. Ray went running to her mom. I let Seamus up so he could follow. Seconds later, I'd caught up in time to see Ray stomping and whining.

"I'm sorry, Ray, but I have to take her." Charlie tried a few more times to reason with the four-year-old. "Oriane Roux, if you don't stop right now, you'll go in a time-out."

She chose to storm off. Smart choice.

"You found me."

"Sorry, but I thought you'd want to know that Collin found the *Z. serilesoda* in Nolan's blood. And um…they wanted me to ask you to get Nolan out of the chill-out room. He's intimidating when he's sick."

I looked back at the paradise the kids had made and wished I could say no, climb into the little palm in the tree, and sip coffee while the kids played below. But if we could get this started, if this worked, we'd be one step closer to curing my dad. Besides, who didn't want to watch a six-foot-four grown *Zayuri* warrior complain like a baby about getting his blood taken? Me. I'd rather be in the tree.

NOL SAT IN THE cushiest chair, covered in a fluffy pink blanket, sipping his sister's magic-infused healing tea that she'd developed years ago. Pink was not his color. "You made some of An'di's tea?"

"Obviously." Only his head and one hand were outside the blanket.

I sat on the edge of the couch farthest away from him. A pint of blood was a lot, and if he hadn't eaten anything, he could get light-headed or nauseous. I had when Collin had taken just those three vials. Or maybe we needed to talk about the dream-walking. Had he felt violated? Or was this attitude only from what had happened at the fortress? He acted civil when others were around but ignored me when we were alone unless absolutely necessary.

"I'm not talking about it."

Oh, straight to the root of our problems. I'd hoped he'd delay and want to talk about our work here. I stretched my legs out and rested them on the coffee table littered with Xbox controllers. "Fine, we won't talk about *them*. But I want to know why you thought I'd be petty enough to be mad about something like that."

"It's not about you. If you've noticed, I don't want to talk to anyone about it."

"About them?" I corrected. Maybe I was pushy and insensitive, but it had been twenty-five years. Raj would want him to have closure and live. She wouldn't want...this.

"It," he corrected again.

I dropped my head back, groaning with frustration.

"Why are you afraid to talk about our situation?" Nol asked, turning the tables, making it about us. There was nothing to discuss!

"We don't need to *talk* about any reaction. It stopped when you moved out. Lots of people who've been apart are confused on how to treat each other at first. It isn't a unique concept. We're fine."

"Maybe you're wrong."

"Maybe I am." Considering what I knew now, about Raj, I had to question why he'd flirted with me the way he had during his first month in Seattle. "I know what you're doing; You're turning the tables because you don't want to talk about Raj. Fine. They aren't the reason I came in here."

Nol tipped the mug to his mouth again. It was already at face level, keeping his nose and mouth warm.

I closed my eyes and searched for calm. "I came in for more recent problems."

"Problems? There's no problem. I'm sick, my body is working through it. End."

"They took a whole pint of blood. How do you feel?" No answer. "Did you see their setup? They got a colony of Aswryn's *Pae-lesoda* virus growing in the lab." Nothing. I counted to ten and tried one last time. "Collin found and isolated the changed virus from your blood. They're calling it *Z. serilesoda*." With no answer again, I was done. Let him be mad at me longer.

I pulled my legs off the table and rose from the couch. "When you're done sulking and hating the world, come over to the lab. They should have me working on the curse by then. Just thought you'd like to see. Oh, and if you can't stand to be in the same room as me, you need to go to your room. You're scaring the locals."

He twitched but ignored me.

THE MICROSCOPIC VIRUS DIDN'T look any different from the other one, but as I watched on the screen, one of those altered viruses of Nol's went over to its neighbor, in slow motion no less, and first broke a hole in the side. Then, like watching a flower bloom, the super virus-eater, aka *Z. serilesoda*, began crumbling the original *serilesoda* virus from one side to the other.

"*C'yo*," Nol huffed, unable to take his eyes off the screen.

"That's it!" Danny of the Dublin crew smacked Nol on the back. Nol stumbled, bumping into me. "You did that, mate. Congratulations."

Nol, still standing there like nothing had happened, licked his lips and squinted. "We still have a long way to go."

"Nah, we're sidestepping the *serilesoda* virus. You're healing up fine."

Nol scowled. He'd finally started acting his age and came to look at the advances we'd made. Nol's blood had given us a good amount of *Z. serilesoda*, but they weren't lasting long outside his body. It was crazy to think that this powerful virus could kill the *serilesoda*, but they died so easily outside its preferred environment.

"So, when can I try?" I asked. "I'd rather try messing with this first before any more of the *Z. serilesoda* viruses die off."

The group looked at me. Collin turned to Charlie and shrugged. "Well, I guess you could start getting a feel for the *Pae-lesoda*

Nol poked his head out of the blanket. "Hallë's not getting near that curse."

I waved him off. "I'll be in the other room, safe and sound."

"As your magic is in contact with the curse? No. Find another way."

"Nolan, it can't transfer through glass," Kevin said, explaining what Nol already knew.

"It might exhaust you quickly," Moira confessed. "Because of the slave band."

This was what I'd wanted to explain to Nol earlier, but he'd been so irritating. "Right, and I'm okay with that."

Charlie grabbed my hand, and her eyes darted to Nol. "I'll get some samples set up for you." She gave me a tight smile and slipped out of the room. The others soon followed, with some excuse or another. No one wanted to be in the room with the crabby *Zayuri* not getting his way.

After two minutes of him glaring at Charlie in the lab, I reached for the tablet and found the recording of the *Pae-lesoda* feasting and multiplying in my blood. "Here. Watch what we did yesterday when you were asleep."

Nol frowned and took the tablet, glancing from me, to the tablet, and over to Charlie. "What's on it?"

"You'll see." I sat back down on the end of the table and watched Charlie set up the cursed virus under the microscope. The fact that we had these results the next day and not a year or more later humbled me.

Nol sighed, his eyebrows going high as he watched the screen with contempt. "And you think *you* can go in there and play with microorganisms?"

I narrowed my eyes at him as he stared at the tablet. "Why do you say it like that?"

Nol didn't even lift his head. "Say it like what?"

"You're doubting me again. You always do this."

Nol looked up and focused on me. "I'm not doubting you. You're—"

"No. You tell me I can't do things more than you tell me you believe in me."

He set the tablet down and crossed his arms, wrapping the blanket around him tighter. Lips pressed into a thin white line, he shook his head as I told him how I felt.

"The first time I've ever heard you say I have control of my magic was with Sanae."

"What about at the house?" Nol lifted his chin in challenge. "Fixing my jacket. Hallë, the problem isn't me. You are the one who has to believe in yourself, and I cannot stress this enough, stop seeking my approval. You cannot keep up with me, and that is okay."

"Seek your approval? When was the last time I did that? Certainly not since you've been here. And it's been a long time since I've tried to beat you at anything." I'd always been proud that I could beat him in the subjects of languages, civics, and politics.

He was the genius kid who skipped grades. Nol earned his honors ear cuffs earlier than the rest of us. I was proud of myself when I earned my third decade three years early. Meanwhile, Nol was close to earning his fifth decade honors. Had I tried to keep up with him in school? Somewhat, yes, in places I knew I could. Mathematics? No. Science? Absolutely not.

"You seek my approval all the time. For example—and I realize this is a shitty example considering what we're currently fighting about—you not telling me your magic was blocked. You didn't want to tell me because you thought I'd think less of you."

"Oh? You're right, that is pretty shitty. No, there's a difference between seeking approval and being ashamed of what I did. Why didn't you tell me about Raj and Camber? You said the same thing! We care about what the other thinks of us. You flat-out said you thought I'd see you differently. We both do this. It's just you're smarter than I am and that transfers to shit like this."

I pointed at Charlie and Collin, unaware of our argument as they went along preparing. "I hear the doubt in your voice, and because you're almost always fucking right, I doubt myself. It's that simple. I respect you and trust that you know what you're talking about. So when I hear you ask 'you think *you* can go in there and play with microorganisms,' it makes me feel like crap. You know my magic better than anyone. If you think I can't do this, say so. But that's not seeking your approval, Twynolan. I stopped that long, long ago."

"Hallë," Nol said after a while. "That's not—"

I wouldn't look away from Charlie and Collin in the lab as I asked him something I'd never thought I'd say. "Would you leave the room, please? I need to work on this soon, and I can't…I can't do this right now."

Without another word and with very little sound, Nol left. My tension ratcheted down, and I pushed our arguments aside.

"Hally, where'd Nolan go?" Charlie asked, looking into the room, having completely missed the argument. "I thought he wanted to be here."

The less drama at this moment, the better, so I put on a smile and shook my head. "Let's get this started."

I sat on the table in front of the screen, legs up and crossed. Several individuals of the *Pae-lesoda*, stained green, floated in a small amount of fluid. I pictured what we'd seen before, the curse next to the *ser-ilesoda*. That picture, I broadcast loud and clear to the tiny thing a room away. They all vibrated the moment I pushed the image of what I wanted. Pulling back on it after all they did was shake, I watched as they stilled. A few shot out a crackle of light. Could that be Gil's magical energy? Crap, now that I knew who Nyda, Savis, and Leda—wait, five, I'd forgotten about Pickles, I couldn't get their faces out of my head as I saw a few more sparks.

After a minute, I went back in, focusing on that vision of separation again, but it didn't feel like the right way. Clicking my tongue as I thought of how to get more individualistic, I scratched out all my ideas. I wouldn't mess with the screen or the microscope to enhance the magnification. I got up and tapped on the screen, picking a place with the least amount of dots with fuzzy edges. I was looking at the virus through a camera, not from above like they were. Like hell would they let me go in there, though.

"You good, Hally?"

Giving Collin a thumbs-up, I swished my hair off my shoulders and cleared my mind. Okay. I wanted one virus to mess with. Maybe telling it to divide was too difficult. But if I could push the curse away from the protein casing I could possibly create an opening for the *Z. serilesoda* to get in and have a chance to destroy the *serilesoda* virus under the curse.

"Hey, Charlie? Do you have a sample of the *Z. serilesoda* handy?"

She hesitated. "Yeah?"

"What if you got one ready in case I can make an opening? Is that worth a shot?"

Collin shrugged. "Uh, we can, but donna expect much to happen. This is your first try."

"Third time's a charm, and I already tried to split them twice." They didn't move for a while, and I got fed up. "Just do it. What will it hurt?"

"Nothin', really. We just haven' talked about it with the others."

The Dublin crew were in charge? "Then get them in here. I want to try."

Collin grabbed his phone, and in a few short minutes, they came piling in with food and drinks. Quinn brought me coffee again.

"What a surprise!" I took the offered coffee and a peck on the cheek.

"I hear you want to go all out?" Quinn took a seat behind the desk at the front and crossed one ankle over a knee. "I gotta stay up to see this."

"It'll probably flop now that everyone is watching." Except Nol—and I did not want his approval. "Seriously, low expectations, okay?"

They all found their spots, two staring at their damn cellphones looking only at the Mother knew what, the others actively watching.

"Here goes nothing." Instead of watching the screen, I pictured the viruses in my mind's eye. My magic went out, and like the door lock in the fortress, I played with it. Something tugged on my magic, but I knew only the energy could come through. It was my imagination. As I dismissed it, my magic latched on to a *Pae-lesoda.*

"Whoa, did you guys see that?" Danny said. "It twitched. Hally, was that you?"

"Maybe. Not looking. Concentrating." The moment felt like all those years ago when Nol liked to distract me during my *Olauvë* lessons with my grandmother. "One more sound out of any of you and you're out."

With the virus in my "grasp," I rolled it around like an eight-ball, feeling every part. Then I thought about what it looked like as it cuddled with the *serilesoda* and did the same. Someone behind me shushed someone else, and my magic dropped the virus.

"Out. Both the shusher and the one whispering." I waited until the door had closed to start again. My magic grasped the virus, but it didn't want to play nice this time. "Damn it."

I picked another one and started again. I felt the energies push at my magic next to it, not wanting to budge. Tough for it. My magic wrapped around the entire thing. There had to be a weak spot somewhere. The five *endai* who'd really cast this curse were keeping this thing active. What had Gil said about how they cast it? They each had their own section. Where was Gil's section, then?

I purged everything else from my mind and kept hold of the virus, searching like I had on the night I found Gileal's magical signature. There, on the other side! Like ripping a seam, I played with Gil's energy, tugging here and there until it loosened just a fraction. More pulling, but it wasn't going any farther. Clenching my jaw, I added more energy, tugging on a larger surface. Another tug and the curse threw my magic back in my face.

I hissed and shook my hands.

"What?" Quinn asked.

"It slapped me. Gimme a second and I'll go again." I rubbed my fingertips together, then shook them. Even my toes and the tip of my nose stung. My body mellowed out, the tingles left, and I sat back down. I needed something for it to bounce off of if it tried that again. My magic snatched the first one it came across, no messing around.

It found Gil's magic easily, and I got back to work, except this time, I layered my magic a few times, once around that virus, then around the little dish they were in, and last, around myself.

The curse didn't like this less gradual prodding, and it tried to buck me off. I knew what it wanted and went around it, like a parent with a child in the bathtub. They had to get their ears washed, no matter how hard they fought. And this was pissing me off. I intensified the strength of the tugging, adding more magic until I felt a pull on my arm and backed off just under that threshold.

Then, as I was mentally complaining about the band, part of Gil's magical energy loosened, and my magic slipped through. The others' energy did not like that, and I fought to keep the ground I'd made. The band pulled again as I concentrated harder to keep Gil's energy at bay. The shield around the dish dropped so I could use that energy to focus on the curse. Another *imolegin* came right up to me, pushing back. Instead of fighting, I reduced my magic enough that it moved into the space I'd created. Gil's magic fell like a popped bubble.

The band was really starting to pull now, but I was so close. I plucked at the energy that interacted with me, prodding it, two steps back, one step forward. The magic started to loosen its hold on the virus as it took more energy to fight me. I was the annoying gnat flying around inside, between the virus and the curse. Instead of fighting the next push, I searched for the gap it had left unattended and with one tiny push, I popped that one. Two down, three to go.

If I gave up now, I wouldn't find the thing again, so I paused. The energy in the curse hummed around my magic as I waited, not going forward, but not giving up any room either. The band calmed, and the pull lessened. It seemed wrong that I could use so much more magic in *Endae* than here. Still in a resting state, another energy shoved mine. I stood my ground, and the band siphoned at full force, pushing me all the way out. But because I'd wrapped the little thing in my own magic, I was able to hold on.

My magic crept along the surface to find the weak spot where Gil's magic used to be. Instead, I found the three energies spread thinner to coat the virus. I hadn't spent much time with the rest of Gil's real friends, but I brought their faces to my mind.

My magic pushed on everything, squeezing it like an orange. I felt the "dents" in the peel. "Got you," I whispered and shoved. Leda's *imolegin* was going down. It did not like that plan and reacted. But instead of a full-blown force, I shoved hard, then backed off, like I'd done with the second one. One more push and it fell a lot sooner than I'd expected. Three down.

"Charlie, add the *Z. serilesoda*."

As I waited for the entry of the changed virus, the two remaining magics pushed and pulled. At one point, it felt like two kids pulling me in different directions. This would not end well for them.

"There, Hally. Done."

I expanded my senses, looking for anything with Nol's magical signature on it. Nothing. The energies within the virus snapped, and my energy was thrown out again. This time, my layer of protection fell, and when I was forced back, it wasn't just my fingers that were tingling. My slave band was having a hissy fit.

I jumped off the table. My arms and legs itched on the inside as my magic tried to resettle inside my body. Worse, my band still thought I was using magic.

"Shit, shit, shit," I hissed. Once I got myself under control, I found the rest of the room staring at me like I'd lost my mind. I threw my hands up. They had no fucking clue.

"It didn't work?" the quietest of the Dublin crew, Finn, asked.

I pointed to the screen. "Do you see a virus there?" Stupid question. They saw plenty. If I'd had the *Z. serilesoda* when I'd gotten through Gil's barrier, it might have worked. The most annoying part, though, was that no one had seen anything. "One of them now only has two anchors on the *serilesoda* instead of five. Fuck, that hurts." And my arm was still numb.

"What do you mean, *two anchors*?" Kevin asked.

I sat back down on the table and drew my legs up, trying to suppress the jitters in my body. "Five *endai* hired Aswryn to make the curse, and

I managed to pull three of their magical signatures free. If I'd completed it, the virus would have been susceptible to just about anything."

Tracing the lines in the stone tabletop, I thought about what I'd accomplished. It didn't feel like much. "I need to rest for a bit. The band drained a lot of my energy during the last try. But I want to put Nol's virus in there earlier." I stopped tracing the table. They were all still staring at me when I looked up. "You didn't see *any* of that?"

"A few viruses flickered."

"It did a lot more than that at a microscopic level, okay?"

"Hally?" Charlie spoke through the intercom. "You did your best."

I gave her a thumbs-up and found my little room. I could not individually kill off every virus in each and every infected person. One tiny virus wiped the floor with me. Even if Yalu worked beside me, we couldn't do it all. There had to be a way to streamline this. And I'd kicked out the best person to think of such an idea before he'd even seen what had happened. Fan-freaking-tastic.

I rolled my ass out of bed and went to find a peace offering before I groveled to Nol. It didn't mean I forgave him, though. Shuffling up to his door, I paused before I knocked. *Be the bigger person, Hally.*

My knuckles rapped the door twice. "I need your help." A solid minute went by before I knocked again. "Nol? I almost did it." Still nothing. He could've been asleep; it didn't usually take much to wake him, but he *was* still sick. That could have knocked him out pretty good. "Nol, please, I need to bounce ideas off of you. I got past three *imolegin* anchoring the curse. I probably had enough room to get the *Z. serilesoda* in there, but it was too slow." I dropped my head against the door. "Come on, Nol. I have dinner." Even the bribe didn't work.

Fine. I'd try in the morning. I set the chicken on the floor beside the wall and walked away.

29

Bright and fucking early in the morning, my eyes fluttered open. Something had woken me. I checked my phone. Five thirty. No one would dare. Another knock. Oh, I'd kill whoever it was. Another damn knock. Not giving a shit how I looked, I opened the door to find Nol leaning against the wall by the door. "What do you mean, *too slow?*"

"You—" I was too tired to think of words. I'd have called him a bastard if that hadn't reflected on his mom. I'd never do that to her.

Nol lifted an eyebrow, waiting for me to figure something out. When I took too long, he shoved the door wide open instead and then scooted in. This was *not* okay. I plopped on the bed and covered my legs while Nol took a seat in the chair. "Charlie added your virus when I asked her to, but I couldn't reach it before the remaining energies kicked me out."

He waited for more explanation. Groaning, I lay back down, blanket to my chin, and explained everything.

Several minutes later, with a few questions answered, he figured out what I was trying to explain. "That might not—"

"I know, but it feels right. If the band didn't take so much energy, I might have had enough to keep my magic in there."

"You're going to have to try again."

"That's not what I need your help with." I curled in and moved the blanket so I could see him sitting with his ankle on his knee, waiting.

"That will be one virus, and it takes a helluva lot of energy. I can't do that over and over."

"No, it's not sustainable." Oh, good, he got it. "You need a medium to repeat everything you actively do."

That just didn't make sense. There was no active or inactive with this. It wasn't a spell. It was my energy. I'd never made anything like that, like a... "So you mean like a potion?"

"Mmhmm." His eyes were closed. His elbow was on the arm of the chair, and he kept his head up with his fist.

"You don't get to fall back asleep. Not after waking me up at five thirty. Are you saying you think I could make a potion to copy what I do?"

"Is that not what the purpose of a potion is? Unless you can develop something similar to what my body makes that will eat the curse, that's the only thing I can think of at the moment."

I flipped the blankets over and scooted out of bed. Might as well get going. My mind would only drift back to what I needed to do. Coffee was needed to think better anyway.

Nol and I made it to the kitchen, only seeing three people on the way. There was no reason for this. Nothing that couldn't get done four hours later. Even three.

"What the hell are we going to do until someone wakes up to put the shit under the microscope? Why, why, why did you have to wake me up so early?"

Nol stirred his creamer into his coffee. The little clinks of the ceramic carried through the kitchen to the giant family room connected to it. "Charlie woke me up. Ray had a nightmare and Charlie asked for my help." Ah. My little niece still had the occasional nightmare from when Aswryn took her, mostly of losing her mom. Nol was sometimes the only one who could calm her, as he'd been there when Aswryn brought her to her lair, commonly known as the Lake Union Steam Plant in Seattle. "What about Charlie?"

"What about her?" I asked as we started walking, with no idea where we were going and not a clue what he was talking about.

"Didn't she say they were close to something a few weeks ago? Why did she think that?" The chocolate sweetener from his coffee drifted behind him, twisting my stomach. It did seem like I'd gotten him addicted to chocolate. "Come on." Nol made an abrupt turn toward the great room. He didn't wait for me, his strides much longer than mine.

My coffee spilled over the cup and dribbled down the side, burning my hand. "Nol!" I hissed.

He looked back, saw the spilled coffee, and rolled his eyes. "*Ai,* cover it and hurry."

"It's hot. Just because you put more creamer than coffee in there doesn't mean mine is the same!" I growled.

Nol stopped, looked at my cup, made a tiny hand movement, and winked.

"Hey!" The shit. I hurried after with my frozen damn coffee, almost at a run as we twisted down the halls.

"Charlie." Nol came to a halt in front of her space. She was checking through a book and reading some notes. "The solution you were last testing, why did you think it was closer than the rest?"

Charlie blinked up at us, her brain not following Nol's excitement. *I* hadn't been expecting his excitement, either. Looked like the chocolate with some coffee was kicking in.

"The fae antiviral? It didn't work," Charlie started slowly, glancing at me and back at Mr. Too Perky For the Morning.

"No, yours. You said you were close to something before they brought the antiviral over."

Charlie scowled. "That? They paused for a second, then went back to normal."

Nol deflated and gawked at her. "That's it?"

I smacked his arm. Charlie reared back and glared at him. "Well, excuse me. You try doing better. Collin said it didn't feel right, but *I* can't feel it the way he does. Yes, that's *it.*"

Oblivious to her irritation, he pushed. "But—"

"Twynolan," I snapped at his insensitivity. "Quit being an ass."

Nol stopped and looked between us, clueless until he recognized Charlie's irritation. "Sorry, Charlie. May I see what your medicine does to the cursed virus? Please?"

Charlie glared at Nol for a beat and scoffed. She organized what she was working on, and then we followed her to the lab. We headed to the classroom while Charlie went in and made virus cocktails. After ten or so minutes, Charlie signaled she was ready. We were, too, screen on and waiting. Nol's anticipation kept him fidgeting, distracting me.

"Pick a spot, Nol. You're starting to remind me of when we first came back."

"If Tatie says you're acting weird, I'll make you go back to bed. Don't expect this to happen right away. It took fifteen minutes for it to react with the curse before."

Waiting for some interaction, I thawed my coffee. I looked up, not a minute later, and saw something move. "You mean like that?" I asked, watching the screen

A dark speck floated toward a *Pae-lesoda* virus, and at the last second, it veered right into the virus, like it had sucked the speck in. We watched as the little speck dissolved on the surface.

"No. It latches on, but it'll take a while for something to happen. Like medication, it doesn't react immediately."

Bummer. Did I have time to go get my sketch pad?

Instead, I watched the action-inaction on the screen. All the little guys moved in a zigzag motion, not paying attention to each other. The specks soaked into several individual viruses and nothing else happened. Twelve excruciating minutes later my coffee was long gone and I was regretting my decision not to get my sketch pad. Then something on the corner of the screen caught my attention. The little fluttering things on the surface of the *Pae-lesoda* stretched and after a few moments the virus started vibrating, then it froze, just like Charlie had said.

"Charlie! Was that it? It stopped." But just as I said it, the little thing began vibrating and fluttering again. But then another one paused.

"Yep, that's what it does. See? It goes back to moving along."

Nol and I turned around at the click of the classroom door. One of Orlaith's assistants popped his head in. His smile couldn't decide if it wanted to stay on his face as he looked at us. "Hally?"

I nodded, even though he knew who I was. He always did that. "Hey, Peter, what's up?" Great, what were the other nations complaining about now?

"Um, Her Majesty wants you to have this back. She-she said not to take it off again while you have the slave band on."

"Why?" Nol asked, his attention, once torn between the show on the screen and Peter, now on hearing an answer.

Peter held out the ring.

I walked over to grab it, but Nol beat me to it in three long strides. "Would you please tell me why the queen said this specifically?"

He swallowed, his eyes darting to Charlie, then us. Poor guy. He had to talk to the scary guy with the sword. "She-she said— The analyzer said it might counteract the reaction to the band." Peter looked down at his folded hands in front of him and laughed at himself. "I might have that wrong. You should just ask the analyst."

"Your explanation was fine," Nol told him.

Again, Peter's face couldn't decide if it should smile as it reddened. He waved and backed out.

"My dad said it was a *meril*." Nol plucked it out of my hands again. "It is *not* that. What did Orin do?"

"It could be the ear cuff that's a *meril*," I suggested.

Nol leaned in, his nose almost touching my ear as he inspected it. "I think you're right. But this, you feel it, right?"

"Yeah. I didn't think much of it in *Endae*."

"We were too busy, but you did play with it a lot." Nol turned the ring over in his hand, examining the intricate work my father did. It might have fit on Nol's pinky finger.

"Not a lot, a lot."

"You messed with it ten times more often than you mess with your bracelet."

"Whatever." I plucked it back and slid it onto my finger again. It didn't feel powerful once on my hand, which made sense why I hadn't noticed the spell on it. It counteracted the band's power. Huh.

"I'd like to see you messing with the viruses with that on," Nol suggested.

"Do you think it'll be that much of a difference?"

"How many insanely powerful spells did you do in *Endae* with that on? I think it'll be quite a difference."

I shrugged. "Okay, let's try it."

"Charlie?" Nol called. "Would you add the *Pae-lesoda, Z. serilesoda* as Hallë makes a hole in the curse? The pause might slow the curse down enough for Hallë to get in there faster and be easier for my virus to penetrate it."

"Sure..." Charlie lifted some papers and set them down again.

"What are you looking for, love?"

"Um...I want to get everyone in here before starting.

Charlie turned to the other side, moving trays.

"Try your pocket."

Charlie frowned at me, and I winked. Happened to us all.

By the time Collin was in the lab and his lab crew was in the classroom, Charlie had added her medicine to the mix of *Pae-lesoda* and *Z. serilesoda* to the petri dish so they didn't have to wait ten minutes. Lucky them. Collin walked up to Charlie, and I almost missed the touch to the small of her back. Charlie hadn't said anything, but maybe she'd made the first move. Go Charlie.

"Ready, Hally?"

I nodded. "Sure." Worst-case scenario, the *Pae-lesoda* would kick me out like yesterday. Best case, we would catch a break and I could get in.

The frozen *Pae-lesoda* that I picked barely resisted my prodding. In fact, I felt no energy on their surfaces. Plucking Gil's magical energy out of the curse felt less like a thread and more like a wet noodle. A few more tugs and Gil's magical anchor was gone. Leda's oozed up to me. I didn't need to pull at it. With slightly more pressure, my magic popped it.

I spread my energy through the microscopic viruses in the petri dish searching for the *Z. serilesoda*. It wasn't far. I coaxed it over with a hint of energy and then pressed the *Z. serilesoda* against *Pae-lesoda*, hoping to push the *Zayuri* altered virus through the curse barrier and into the original *serilesoda* virus underneath. After a moment the *Pae-lesoda* began vibrating again. The moment it did, the curse started to push back. The *Z. serilesoda* slid in and I covered the curse with a layer of my own magic.

"I think it's..." I opened my eyes to look at the screen for the two connected viruses. Several things were going on. The viruses reacted when they bumped into each other. A snap of light, this one brighter than the ones we normally saw when the curse flickered. Another strong flash and the *Z. serilesoda* was winning. I could feel it under my magic. A few seconds later, the *serilesoda* virus inside the curse disintegrated. The curse imploded, not finding its host, and there was no resistance any longer. With another spark of light, the magic was gone.

"Was that it?" Collin pointed at a corner on the screen on the lab side. "Hally?"

"Was that a *Pae-lesoda*." Kevin walked up to the screen, a finger on his chin. "Where'd it...did you do it?"

"It's gone." I checked the corner of the screen, wondering if that was where it had been.

Quinn moved until he could see my face. "You did it?"

The slave band didn't even tingle. I looked down at the ring my father had made and smiled. "One down, a gazillion to go."

That's when they celebrated. A loud, boisterous cheer filled the room. I giggled, as Quinn spun me around. The crew patted each other on the back. Charlie grabbed Collin and kissed him. I looked around for Nol and found one of the Dublin crew shaking his hand. A smile on his face showed he was happy, but he wasn't as excited as he should have been.

"Nol?" I came up to him and crouched to his eye level in his seat.

"I'm tired, Hallë. That's all."

"We did it. It's starting."

"And we're not stopping until those fuckers are extinct once again."

I laughed, but I could tell he really wasn't feeling well. "Did you want to go lie down again?"

"No, I want to see this through."

Charlie came up behind me with a blanket in her arms. "Hey, how about some of your sister's tea?"

I took the blanket from her and tucked it behind him. Charlie gave me a thumbs-up. He was okay. Fighting off an old virus took a lot out of a person.

"We need to take what you did there and use something to replicate it...what is the word...automatically?"

"What if...you know how Gileal made that serum to keep his spell in?" Charlie asked. "Could you add it to something like that?"

Charlie plopped down next to me in one of the stiff chairs. I liked sitting on the table better than these crappy things. "Hally, you did it." She shook my arm.

"No, love, we did it. If it weren't for you, we'd never have come this far."

Charlie rested her head on my shoulder while we watched Collin messing with something in the lab. He came over to the microphone button. "You guys, this was the last of Nolan's *Z. serilesoda*. We need more, sorry Nolan."

Charlie pointed at the screen. "The *Z. serilesoda* are still zipping around the dish. When you were playing with it yesterday, Hally, we had to add more by this time. Do you remember?"

I didn't, but it didn't matter. "Any idea why?"

Danny walked up to the screen, his head tilted to the side. "The only new addition is Charlie and Collin's concoction."

"Medicine, Danny. We're calling it medicine," I scolded.

"Sure." Danny rolled his eyes then went back to studying the screen. "Regardless, testing the *Z. serilesoda* with their"—Danny leaned over and winked at me—"medicine, is the only way we'll know for certain. What if you are able to add the spell you just did to the *Z. serilesoda* so it can attack the *Pae-lesoda* instead of you having to?"

It wasn't a spell though. Could I come up with something like it? "I can try."

"Hally," Charlie lifted a hand, pointing at the screen. "Use the *Z. serilesoda* like an empty *meril*." As if that was an everyday thing. Infusing a quasi-living virus with magic felt slightly wrong when I thought about it too much. Charlie looked back at the screen, her thoughts either racing too fast or her mind blank. "We're going to need more ingredients."

"We're going to need more blood. Nolan can't possibly do this all." Collin said, still on the intercom.

"Do you think five other *endai* will be enough?" Nol rubbed his eyes. "And we're going to need people to test it on, too."

"Whoa, whoa." Charlie shook her hands. "This isn't ready for human...er...elven trial runs. That's gonna take some time."

"Time we don't have. Once our bodies fight off the *serilesoda* virus, we'll either have to infect other *Zayuri* with more of Gileal's serum—which is unethical—or hurry and fight. I want Orin and Balin to get the cure first."

"Nol...are you sure?"

"I want to kill Gileal for what he did, not his father. All Balin has ever done is help people, and all he's ever received in return is suffering. Balin is getting a cure along with your father." Nol stood and dropped his blanket. Though he seemed to have gotten a second wind, I could still see the exhaustion. He'd do it until he collapsed, again. "If I am feeling better, they are as well. It has to be done now."

Nol was already making plans for *Zayuri* to come over before I'd even started. "Wait a minute, Nol. I've only killed one virus."

"You can practice with the new blood they take. Quinn, I must ask you, please come with me to Charlie and Hallë's house. I will contact my uncle and start bringing *Zayuri* here. Charlie or Collin, come take blood before I go. Hallë, work on infusing the *Z. serilesoda* virus with your spell before those ones start to die."

"Nol!" I jumped out of my seat in a panic. "What if this doesn't work?"

"You've made a *meril* before. You can do this." He grabbed my face and made me look at him. "I believe you can do this. With all my heart, I will never doubt you again. You've, *c'yo*—" Nol pulled me close. The first hug from him in five days. "I'm still so fucking angry with you," he whispered in *Aemirin*.

I pressed my ear against his chest and found his heartbeat. "I know."

He squeezed me for another ten seconds, kissed the top of my head, and backed up. "That doesn't mean I'm not proud of you, Hallanevaë Inara. You and Charlie...you did it." No, this was her vision. I'd done what she needed of me, what she needed from all of us.

"Without Charlie, this wouldn't have happened." I searched for her in the excited group. "You'd never have introduced Charlie and Gil. You'd have killed Aswryn and left. If she hadn't convinced you to look under her microscope, we wouldn't be here."

"You have an amazingly talented and selfless niece. I have to go. Work hard, Hallë. This must happen quickly. Collin? Would you mind taking another bag of blood from me?" What an odd request.

Collin, standing behind a semi-dazed Charlie, raised his head and caught Nol's eye. Collin held up a finger—something was going on.

"Guys, this is too fast. How are we going to make enough to save an entire race? How many *Aeminan* people are infected?" Charlie grabbed the back of a chair and guided herself to a seat. "Holy shit."

"We'll find a way." Collin placed a hand on Charlie's back, rubbing little circles on it, moving her hair. He leaned over close to her ear. She looked up and scanned the room until she found Nol and me, then nodded. Collin straightened and left the room with Nol right behind him.

"The ingredients aren't that hard to get," Kevin was saying.

"Most of our labs have the DAAs," Danny said, going all science-tech on me. They began a conversation about antiviral ingredients. As I listened, all the ingredient names began to sound the same. They had multiple levels of plans and whatever. I watched and tried to wrap my head around the situation. This was going to be a lot of work.

"Hally, you okay?" Charlie shook me. I hadn't even realized she'd gotten up.

"I'm lost in thought, I guess."

She tipped her chin toward the door. Collin was back in the room and walking toward Danny. "Nolan's done with his blood donation, and Quinn and Kevin will leave with him soon."

Quinn was leaving without saying goodbye? I looked up, searching for the three of them. There in the back, holding on to the door handle, Quinn waved. His smile didn't reach his eyes. Something was wrong.

"Quinn?" I hurried over before he could sneak out like Kevin had. "Everything okay?" I asked, coming up to him and tugging on his sleeve to bring him closer.

"Yeah." He looked away, pressing his lips together. "We can talk about it later. You've got a lot to do."

"No, we're talking now. You should know this as well as me." Anything could happen, and the look in his eyes told me it was something important. I opened the door and pulled him out into the hall. "What's going on?"

"It's stupid." He shoved his hands into his pockets and turned so his sleeve was out of my hand.

No.

"You sure there's nothing? Between the two of you?" He shook his head, his slate-gray hair falling into his face. "We've been over this. I know. You've explained it." Quinn looked around the main lobby. No one else was here. "I'm being so goddamn selfish. I know your bond is special. I mean, it was literally given to you by a goddess."

"Nothing's going on. Nol and I are going to be close."

"Yeah. I'd never want to get between you. Promise me."

"I promise. Nothing is going on."

"No." He scooped my hands up and kissed them. "Promise me, when you start feeling different about him—"

"If—"

"When that changes between you two, promise you'll tell me?"

I wouldn't argue. He'd just keep correcting it, and this meant something to him. Quinn and I weren't serious. We couldn't be with his duties to his family.

"Quinn. Hear me out. If that happens, of course I'd tell you. What did your parents say about us? I hope you told them I know you'll have to find someone to settle down with eventually. Someone who isn't an *endaë*."

"I did, yes." He chuckled. "Úna talked you up a bit when we got back. But it could never be you. We all know. That's not what I'm concerned about. Nol, you, and I are becoming good friends..."

"Please don't break up with me right before I save my people."

He looked at his feet, smiling. "No. That's not it. You are both growing on me, and someday after I've settled into my role as king and wherever you two will be, I want to be friends with you both. I don't want to screw that up with Nolan."

"Then talk to him. Again." Seriously, Quinn refused to go on a second date until he got Nol's approval or permission or whatever. "He might need a friend other than me right now."

"He told me he's angry with you. I'm sorry you had to do that. That's why I'm confused. He's so angry with you, but he still talks to you, hugs you. If I didn't know you, I wouldn't have a clue."

I stood on my tiptoes and kissed his cheek. "Would you talk to him? Not about me, about—other things. And I promise, I'll say something if things change."

He kissed me back, a few small kisses on my jawline and under my ear like he knew I liked, before he let me go. I hadn't even noticed he'd taken hold of my shirt. "See you soon, then."

THE MOMENT QUINN LEFT, the others came out like they'd been at the door listening. I caught Danny's laugh as the five Dublin fae headed to the chill-out room. Why didn't they call it a game room or something? A light touch on my arm distracted me from glaring at the guys who I was almost positive had placed bets on us.

"Tatie, you okay?"

"I'm fine."

"What about Quinn?"

"Confused, but fine. Who won the bet?" I asked.

Charlie scoffed. "You can't guess by that giggle of his?"

"Danny." I shook my head in disbelief. "How is it they're so old and act so immature?"

"Who? Them? Danny's only twenty-two."

That earned her a double take from me. "Really?"

"Mmhmm. Collin is fifty-six. Kevin is the oldest, and they won't tell me how old. I have to guess. Seems like I'm good at it."

"Seriously?" They'd make her guess just to mess with her. Such a...*guy* thing to do.

"Weird, right? My talents are sensing fae and *endai* energies, and guessing ages. Though Kevin says it's not a talent."

"Magic?"

"Inert." She shrugged. "You ready to get this virus spelled?" She held up a finger, a thought forming. "A curse is a type of spell, right?"

"Yes. The only difference is the intent of what it's meant to do." I rolled my eyes. "And it is kind of the same thing we're doing now." Except with the total opposite intention, which was the most important part of magic.

30

By that night, Nol, Quinn and Kevin weren't back, and the *Za-yuri* still weren't on their way. I, on the other hand, was making great strides. Huge. In not getting the damn spell to do what I wanted. I imagined it like a code. You had to know all the keywords and crap for a computer to read it. The magic I performed needed to be legible for anything besides me. Maybe it wasn't a good analogy. Too bad it couldn't have been like a tattoo. I understood those.

"How's it goin'?" Collin came into the classroom, bringing the smell of food with him. He set a hot sandwich on a paper towel next to me and a cup of something. I hadn't expected him to bring food with him. Nor had I expected him to come in here at all tonight.

"Frustratingly." I accepted his gift of a late dinner. "Do you think Danny's theory has merit?"

"Aye." Collin stopped talking, chewed and swallowed. "If it's the same as earlier, we can definitely extend the *Z. serilesoda*'s lifespan. It would be a tremendous help."

I grabbed my food and slid off the table to find a more comfortable place to eat. My bones creaked as I stood from being in the same position for hours. Maybe I'd set a break timer when I got back to it. "Have you ever used an amulet?"

He hummed in the positive. "Who hasn't?" He brushed his hands off and looked down at the other stuff he had. Three sandwiches, one cup, and his huge bowl of soup. Charlie's probably.

I sniffed the soup tentatively and pulled the sandwich closer. It looked...interesting. Melted cheese and meat. Some vegetable in there of sorts. "Charlie? Humans—"

"I get it, fine." Collin waved my answers off.

"Have you ever *made* one?" I asked after I'd taken a bite. A deluxe grilled cheese of sorts.

Collin swallowed his bite of sandwich and wiped his chin before answering. "No. Have you?"

"Yeah, that's why this is annoying."I opened the bread to check on the vegetable. Zucchini? Odd, but I had no qualms about the squash. "The communication one I have with Nol was easy to do."

Collin set his bowl and sandwich down, preparing for an actual conversation. "Because it only has one purpose. What are you doin' with this one?"

Counting the ways... "Let's see, I want to somehow get the *Z. serilesoda* to find a *Pae-lesoda* faster, pull on Gil's energy to create a whole in the curse's defenses, stop other energies from taking its place, and push the *Z. serilesoda* inside the hole."

"That's it, huh?" Collin echoed my thoughts.

"Yeah...that's it." Not that those things were a walk in the park. Twisting my lips in thought, I stared back at the screen and imagined going through the steps it took for the *Z. serilesoda* to get under the curse. I thought about the feel of pulling on Gil's energy and the way it had felt like a limp noodle last time.

"Could you go about it a different way?" Collin asked. "Maybe you could think of it as teaching the *Z. serilesoda* how to use your spell, instead of making it work how you want it to?"

"You're treating it like it's alive."

"Don't the elves believe that?"

"Yeah, I guess. Nol says that, anyway." Finished with half the sandwich, I pulled the soup closer, dragging the spoon from right to left as I talked. "What is this?"

"Cream of celery, vegetables, and dumplings."

Collin slurped up a spoonful.

"Thank you for making the food, by the way." Yes, I didn't like it, but I'd never complain. Food was food. I'd just look for someone to donate the soup to.

"You're welcome." He slurped again, confirming my suspicion that he'd made the food himself. *Cream of celery? Really? That's a thing?*

The thump from the back caught our attention as Charlie strode into the room, frazzled. "Hey, guys. Sorry I'm late, Collin. Seamus and Ray were arguing. Turns out, after three days in the same mansion, they get tired of each other."

Collin snorted. "Kids. The manor is enormous. There's plenty of space they can give themselves, but do you think they'll do it?"

Charlie and Collin tilted their heads close. "No," they said together. Collin handed Charlie the other soup and sandwich.

"So, Tatie, have you figured it all out, yet?"

"Hardly, but Collin made a good point. I'll try looking at it in a teaching way. It's still the same, but my mind has to figure out how to glue the magic into the right places." Holding my breath as that gave me an idea, I went back to the screen. I tried to "show" the virus each step of what I'd done to help it kill the curse. Essentially, it was all in my head. I had to let my brain believe what it needed in order to import the process of what I'd done with the *Z. serilesoda*.

"Eat something first, Tatie." Charlie tapped my shoulder, breaking my concentration with the little viruses.

"Yes, mother," I teased before taking another bite of sandwich. I'd have to find a way to take this soup to the kitchen. No, cream of celery should not exist.

AT TWO IN THE morning, I was messing around with a dozen test tubes filled with a mix of the *Z. serilesoda* virus and medicine that everyone was now calling Collin and Charlie's antiviral. Danny was right. Since we'd added the medicine, none of the *Zayuri* viruses had died. On an even better note, Collin's idea to change the way I considered infusing my magic with the *Z. serilesoda* seemed to have worked.

Charlie had said we were limited on ingredients. The only way I could wrap my head around making their antiviral was imagining it like a cocktail. There were enough ingredients for two batches of margaritas. How the hell she knew it all worked was the miracle that was Charlie. Even Collin praised her, and I'd found out that he'd kicked out the other fae who were being dicks to her when I was in France.

Trusting Charlie, we set me up in my own lab room. I knew how to work the microscope and the monitor, and I got to use pipettes and Petri dishes. I felt like a scientist working on my own little project, wearing safety gear and everything. That's right. If only I were really that confident.

The first test tube, I was almost fully positive, maybe, sort of, had worked. By the fifth tube, my slave band was tingling, but I managed to activate all twelve test tubes. I looked at my latex-gloved hand and the wooden ring below it.

How the hell had my father done this? And he'd lied to Edvic, or Edvic had lied to us. My father had made the spell inside the ring the night before while I'd been sleeping. It was too specific. What if it had worn him down too much? What if it was the last magic he'd ever cast? The *Pae-lesoda* attacked the organ that created magical energy, our *dirlegin*. No *enda* could survive without one. What if his was so badly damaged from the curse and overuse that my dad never recovered? Or perhaps the organ would only be able to produce enough magical energy to keep him alive. No, I couldn't let myself fall down that rabbit hole. It wasn't too late.

I paused to give my body a break and keep the band from stealing more of my magic. I walked away from the table and touched the *meril* around my neck that connected with Nol's.

"How's it going?"

Nol didn't respond. Maybe they'd gone to sleep over there? Something stirred. It felt like it was in my head, but I knew it was the *meril*. He'd been asleep.

"They're waiting on the traveling *merili*. They'll be in at the start of the new day. How about your project?"

"Going well, I think. If it works." I showed him what I was doing and the progress I'd made.

"I am really proud of you."

"Thanks..." Even though he could sense my thoughts since I wasn't hiding them, he waited until I asked, "How about you? Have you had time to think?"

"Gileal killed them, Hallë. He was responsible for their deaths, and he got away. I had a chance to end him. You took that away from me."

I let go of the *meril* to give my mind a little space before I tried to help him see through this. My fingers fumbled for the little *meril*. "Be honest. Would killing him have stopped your pain? Would that have brought them back? Would killing him without an approved mission have given all the other *endai* that have suffered under his actions justice? Peace?"

"He got away. How will anyone find peace now?" Still so angry.

"We'll find him."

Nol paused. He'd seen *Sudome* Tamden and a few others. They'd formed a plan? "You will not. I don't want you with me when I go after him. All of the *Zayuri* are in this, not just me this time. Whoever finds him will assassinate him on sight."

Great, so it was an actual approved mission. "I want to tell the fae nations about him. Share the information so they are aware of the situation." I paused to give him time to comment. Nothing. "If they'll accept other *Zayuri* into their countries, then an inter-realm manhunt can proceed."

"But you don't want me to kill him." The hurt and anger in that one thought made me take my hand off the *meril* and I counted to ten.

I pushed down the pain of our argument, of Gil's betrayal, all of it, so I could talk to him. Reason with him. "I'd prefer you didn't," I told him when I was ready. "He was practically your brother, Nol. The fact that he betrayed you so deeply brings in anger and pushes the justice and punishment away. Are you supposed to feel that way when on missions? Somehow, I don't think so."

He didn't want to hear any more of my lecture. I wasn't old enough to know what I was talking about. Yeah, well, neither was he, then. Frustrated with the last few thoughts, I remembered what Quinn and I had talked about.

"Quinn's worried."

Through Nol's thoughts, I knew he was confused. "We talked about this before."

"He's worried again."

"Because I kissed your head?" If a thought could grimace, his did.

"I don't know! But he really likes being our friend. Maybe you could talk to him."

"Hallë."

"I mean, really. I doubt he's had the same experiences as you, but I know he's lost kids. Just please, think about it?" He hadn't said no, so I kept pushing. "He's new and almost a stranger. Sometimes, it's easier with ones who don't know our past."

"You don't know my past."

I waited, letting him think about those words before I responded. "But you still won't talk to me."

"I've told you why."

"No. You gave me a bullshit answer. You knew I never had a crush on you. Everyone else, I'm sure, pushed that into your head after I left. Is that what this is? Them talking?" I waited again. He didn't want to talk, and it was driving me insane. "Let me guess. Jemi and Enyco."

No, the feeling was that the bullies who had hated me with a passion had also hated Nol. But like all bullies, they strung him along and used him. Made him believe they were his friends.

"They're not as bad anymore. Enyco even said it wasn't right what they did to you."

He always made excuses for those two and I never understood why Nol always wanted to be friends with the two kids, both a little older and both using Nol to get better grades. "But they're the ones who said something, aren't they?"

I felt him hesitate as if he wanted to say something but didn't know if he could.

"Come on, Nol. Just—"

"It was Raj. Raj didn't want you to know."

I dropped the *meril*. Why? It must have had something to do with her seer abilities. She'd known I wanted them to be together. We'd always been honest with each other. Hadn't we?

With shaky fingers, I found the *meril* again. "Why would she—"

"I don't want to talk about it anymore. We'll be back by eight." He closed off communication and left me staring at an empty counter, wondering if I'd known my friend that well. Nol didn't want to talk to me because Raj hadn't wanted me to know? What if she never liked me? What was happening right now? I pulled my phone out and found the right number. Someone I knew would answer.

"Hally?"

"Mateo?" My voice cracked at the end of his name.

"*Ojitos*, what's wrong?"

I sat on the floor, wrapped my arms around my legs, and sobbed to my best friend about everything. He stayed on the phone, doing what best friends do, making me laugh and letting me know we'd never know and we couldn't assume—that was his mom talking, her favorite English phrase being, "Assumptions are like assholes. They make an ass out of you and me." She laughed every time she said it, which made us all laugh to hear his wonderful Peruvian mama.

"I think I need your mom's cooking to help me feel better."

"Mama's cooking is the best. Now get to work, lady. I'll talk to Mama and see when she can come out again."

"Maybe we could go visit her and your dad instead."

He stayed silent for a moment. "We could, but it'd need to be after the honeymoon."

"We have over two months to go. There's plenty of time. Is it vacation time?" He was using a lot of it for the honeymoon. "We'll go for a weekend."

"It's Sam. His parents want to talk to him before the wedding. He's going back to talk." Mateo's voice cracked at the end.

Oh, that pissed me right the fuck off. His parents would only ask Sam to come home to try to talk him out of marrying Mateo—or any man for that matter. Sam would try anything to get their approval, to convince them, and it would never work. I realized he'd been silent for a while.

"How are you feeling about this?"

Now it was Mateo's turn to be upset and have his best friend to talk with. Even with everything going oh so smoothly in my life, I'd be there for my friend. I listened, made sure he knew I'd kick anyone's ass for either of them, then made him laugh until he was too tired to talk anymore. "Love you, Mateo. Hopefully, this shit will be done soon."

"Yeah, I miss our family dinners."

"Me, too," I agreed.

Now that I'd purged all of my troubles and felt much better for having an outside perspective, I spent the rest of the night working on the last seven test tubes, less stressed and with no pull or tingles from the slave band.

31

SOMETHING NUDGED ME. I hit it back. I had work to do, and no one should have been bugging me. Giggling from my right made me lift my head from the arm of the couch. Oh, never mind.

"Good morning, Tatie!" Ray just about yelled in my face as I blinked my eyes open. "They're here, and Mommy told me to get you." Ah, send the adorable kids in to do the job because they wouldn't get yelled at for waking me.

"Thank you, *ma colombe*." I snagged her and kissed her face until she giggled some more and tried to get away. "Good morning, Seamus." The little guy smiled. Those baby teeth of his…how could I be grouchy with that face, his blue eyes, and blond hair? A deep breath helped settle me as I stood and rubbed my eyes. They wouldn't know the time, but Nol had said eight, so I guessed about that. "Go tell Mommy she owes me lots and lots of coffee."

"Okay." The kids were out the door before I could say *tickle*.

I rubbed my eyes again, bleary from sleep and dried tears, and I walked out in search of a group of sick *Zayuri* warriors. I prayed they weren't as grumpy as Nol when he was sick. I found them right away, as Nol was translating everything, explaining what Charlie needed to explain. They didn't like needles. Well, tough shit. I didn't enjoy draining my energy to make this either.

"Hally?" Jenne called from the group. She moved people aside and hurried to me.

"You're not sick, are you?"

"No." She scoffed and looked back at them. "Tolwe, Bren, and I came with them. It's been rough."

"I bet."

We stood shoulder to arm watching the fae and Zayuri mingle. I wouldn't want to mingle if I were sick. Thankfully that never happened—hung over though. Bug me and die.

"So you figured it out? This will work?" Jenne asked after a minute.

"Let's hope so."

We kept watching the unhappy group. You'd think coming over would have meant they were willing to do what they could. After showing them what a *Z. serilesoda* could do to the original *serilesoda* virus, they were more willing. But when I demonstrated my part in all this, I was a nervous wreck.

"It *should* work." I told *Sudome* Tamden after we'd all gathered in the classroom.

"Should?" Tamden's white eyebrows shot up high.

"I made them last night. There's been no way to test them yet."

"So, this isn't tested?" another *Zayuri* asked. "How do we even know if this is a success?"

"Nolan said you found a way past the curse. Now we hear this?" Tamden said.

They all complained and complained. My hands hurt, I'd twisted them so much. Finally, I'd had enough. "Would you all shut up and wait? Fucking-A," I said the last in English. "How old are they again?" I muttered to Charlie. The biggest, scariest moment of my adult life was about to happen—because it was a thousand percent scarier getting exiled as a kid.

Quinn shuffled up behind me and kissed my temple. "Sorry, I had to deal with an issue at work."

"Should you be there instead?"

"Yes." He snaked an arm around my shoulders. "But I want to see this."

"If this doesn't work, I'm hiding in the Himalayas for the rest of my life."

Quinn pulled on a curl and kissed me again. "It's going to work." I wanted to ask him if he had talked to Nol, but it was out of my hands.

Charlie added a full pipette of *Pae-lesoda* first and showed everyone how the curse crackled with energy every so often. Nol made eye contact with me from across the room as Charlie started to explain. I couldn't translate, not when breathing was difficult.

"Did I miss it?" Queen Orlaith scooted in between Jenne and me.

"No," Quinn whispered.

She winked a taupe eye at me as she almost hid behind us. I got the impression she didn't want to be noticed.

Nol was still explaining how we could tell the viruses apart, how the equipment worked and on and on. Charlie added our spelled antiviral *Z. serilesoda*—really, the names were getting ridiculous.

"Hallë? Can you explain your part?"

"Fuck," I hissed. No one understood me when I explained how my magic worked, but that didn't mean I couldn't try. "As I haven't tested it yet, I...um...balanced the feel or the harmony to the *Z. serilesoda*. Nol, I'm not good at this," I explained. Okay, I whined. No sympathy. None.

"Look!" Jenne gasped and pointed at the screen.

The spelled *Z. serilesoda* started sucking in the cursed viruses, which I'd wanted it to do. I hadn't realized how well that part would work. The cursed viruses sparked and vibrated as my spell inside the *Z. serilesoda* picked away at Gil's magic, then slipped past the curse. One cursed virus popped—itty-bitty bubbles popping away. It was working.

I glanced at Nol, standing next to the screen on the opposite side of me. Mad as he was, his chin dipped down, and I knew he'd meant it when he'd said he was proud of me.

Someone jumped on me, their arms going around my shoulders. "You did it!" Jenne all but screamed. "It's working."

Her excitement made me laugh, and I let myself accept that we'd done this together. But it wasn't the end.

The *Zayuri*, while happy and excited, discussed how this was going to go and asked actual important questions.

Charlie began answering the first question that Nol had translated—"We don't know if one dose will be enough. Often, antiviral medication is given in a series of doses. So yes, there may be more than one session."

Two other questions: "How many doses, did she think?" and "What would that entail?"

I was only half listening.

Orlaith and Quinn waited for me where I'd left them, both with smiles on their faces, just like everyone else. Jenne came along with me instead of listening to the back-and-forth *Aemirin* and English. It was enough to make my head spin.

Orlaith held her hand for me to shake. Even though this was of no consequence to her and she had no reason to care, she'd stayed informed. "Congratulations, Hally. What a breakthrough."

"Your congratulations mean a lot to me, Your Majesty. I'm excited to start making this at full capacity, if you're still okay with us using the lab? We never could have done this without your support and the amazing people who helped Charlie do it. They worked so hard."

"I have to admit, there is always an ulterior motive. It wouldn't hurt to hang a boon over your government's head, just in case."

"I think they'll be more than happy to oblige, Your Majesty."

"Again, congratulations." Orlaith left, just as inconspicuous as she'd come in. I loved that she didn't have all that pomp and circumstance crap that the others had. From the video chats I'd taken part in, she appeared to be the only down-to-earth ruler.

"I have to go, too, darling. Congratulations. Would you like to have coffee later? I'm in the Lilly house today." While Quinn's office was officially in this mansion, he enjoyed the Lilly house at the end of the lane to avoid noise, traffic, and people interrupting him when he was on the phone. Who didn't?

"Yeah, if I can get away." I kissed him goodbye and walked him to the door.

Ten minutes later, the high-ranking, unwell warriors sat down and allowed a pint of their blood to be taken and I was walking with Jenne and the others in the garage.

"We'll see you in a few days." Jenne hugged me again. Tolwe, Bren, and Jenne were going back now that they'd made the delivery. I felt like a mother sending her kid off to college as she got into one of the white vans. While she was only eleven-years younger and a *Zayuri*, Jenne seemed so much younger than me. I wondered if I'd stayed, how much younger I'd have acted.

Nol was already going back inside before I realized he'd left. The guards held the door open, and I followed him back toward our rooms near the lab. Nol veered off to his room in silence and closed his door. Great. How long would this go on? We'd never been mad at each other for more than a few days.

THIS WAS THE LAST batch we could make until more ingredients arrived. Dublin was sending ingredients over, which would take a week or so. We'd ordered the rest from a drug manufacturer. Not just anybody sold wholesale raw antiviral ingredients. They'd arrive at Avalon Winery in two and a half to three weeks.

"Will the freezers really work?"

Charlie chewed on her cheek, thinking. "Freezing works with every medicine, virus, and bacteria I know, so yeah, it better." We didn't have another solution. The *Zayuri* would donate a pint of blood a day until they were better, but when they were done, we were done.

I leaned my elbow on the counter and watched her walk to the giant freezer in the back. "Hey, you know how you become immune to some diseases after you've been sick with them?"

"Sure?" She shut the door and locked it down.

"Will this be like that?"

Charlie came to lean against the table beside me. "There's no way to know that, unless there's more information on the original virus." She placed her hand on my head. "You okay? Wanna go lie down?"

"I want to go home. We've been at the manor for four days and in *Endae* just as long. I'd like to be in a place that's mine." My head was getting too heavy for my elbows to prop up. "I never knew I'd miss my art so much until now."

Charlie flipped my hair around, playing with the short curls. "Then let's go home."

"Really?"

"Sure." She shrugged. "Until we get those ingredients, your job is done."

"What about you?" I got off my chair before I fell asleep.

Charlie held the door open and waved me over to get me moving. "I'd like to go home for a bit, too. Let Ray sleep in her own bed."

I chuckled at that. "Today, when we had coffee, Quinn heard her tell Seamus that she misses her princess nightlight."

"She has literal fairy-flies buzzing around her tent and she wants her nightlight? Only my child."

We laughed together, walking out of the lab, shutting down lights, and locking up.

"Do you think Collin can handle everyone tomorrow on his own?" I asked.

Charlie scoffed. "Piece of cake. The Dublin crew is leaving tomorrow, though. I'll drive in later if you'll keep Ray?"

"Do you really need to ask? Normalcy would be lovely."

"Okay," Charlie said. "She's been a little brat, being spoiled by all these fae around her."

"I noticed. Just wait until she's had a talk with her Tatie Hally."

On the way by, I knocked on Nol's door. "Nol? Do you wanna come home with us?" Nothing. Ugh, this bipolar treatment was really starting to get to me. I hadn't seen him since midmorning when the other *Zayuri* left.

"Just text him a note. If he wants to come home tomorrow, I'll take him to visit."

She was right. Nol would have to come back here anyway to donate his share. I did not envy the *Zayuri's* part in all of this. Give me draining magic over drawing blood any day.

I CALLED LÉON ON the way home to make sure they were doing okay. Léon had picked a nurse—a lady in her forties. Nicole liked her, and she didn't put up with any of Léon's shit. I couldn't wait to meet her.

"All right, call if you need me, or even if you don't need me. You know I love to hear your voice, old man."

"I will, old lady." And Léon hung up before I could say anything else.

"You almost got the goodbye in," Charlie teased. "I got a goodbye out of him once."

"Oh?"

Charlie turned off the ignition and the old Volvo shuddered to an end. "Turns out it takes your husband dying in order for him to say it."

"That is not funny." I slammed the heavy door shut and waited for my nieces at the back gate.

Léon wasn't right, but he wasn't wrong either. I didn't need to leave Emma's children and find a new life, but maybe I didn't need to hover so close. Even though I lived in Seattle, I always checked in on them at least once a week. Things with the fae and *Aemina* were taking more of my time, weighing on my mind more than the kids in France. After Léon was gone, maybe I'd distance myself a little, but I'd let them know I was always there for them. Maybe I'd get Charlie's opinion on it first.

Charlie picked up Ray so she could reach over and unlatch the gate—something Nol had started. The gate swung open. The lilacs had already bloomed. They were so fast! Not much else had changed since we'd been away.

"Huh, Quinn left the mudroom light on when he got my art supplies. Damn, I left them at the manor."

"He does know that was a special occasion, right?" Charlie asked.

We followed the broken cement path around the roots and Ray's toys. "Yes, I made sure he knows my art room is off limits."

Charlie unlocked the back door to a warm mudroom. It smelled like cumin and peppers. Ray pushed through, kicked off her shoes, and was gone. Not even five seconds.

I reeled on Charlie. My mouth almost hurt, my smile was so wide. "You're so sneaky!"

Charlie grinned from ear to ear. A ploy! "We knew you were homesick. You better go hug Mateo. It was his idea." It was Sunday, after all, and he knew I needed this. I didn't even have my shoes off before Mateo was through the hall door. He didn't say anything, just hugged me—one shoe on, one shoe off. We stayed there, me resting my head on his collarbone, him on my shoulder, both of us knowing each other's worries.

"Wanna talk about it?" he asked with his mouth buried in my shirt.

I shook my head. He knew everything except for the shit today. "I wanna not think about it for a little."

Mateo let me go, and I dropped the other tennis shoe. "Do you want to talk about Sam?"

"Later, maybe. I can't convince him to stay."

They wouldn't accept him because of who he was. No matter how much Sam wanted it. Why couldn't people accept who others were? Accept the choices they made for their lives? It didn't affect his parents' daily lives. Ugh, no rants.

Everyone was there. Lewis had made our favorite fajitas. Ray piled on the peppers but left the shrimp. But the dinner wasn't complete without Nol. Quinn and Seamus, while I loved having them over, weren't regulars yet. But Nol always played poker with us after Ray went to bed, and it just wasn't the same without him there.

"He's gonna be better soon." I set a five of clubs down in front of me. "Hopefully our rift won't affect everyone else."

"I can't believe he's grown on me so much," Mateo said, washing the last pan.

Yumi lowered her Corona and scoffed. "What are you talking about? I have no doubt you liked him before you even met him."

Mateo lowered the pan and glared at Yumi over the kitchen peninsula. "That's not true."

"Nol thinks it is." I couldn't keep the laughter out of my voice over Mateo's fake denial. "When you said 'I like him already' as he was being a pain in the ass the first night? Yeah, he believes that."

"I don't know what you're talking about." Mateo went back to the dishes.

"Were you drunk?" Charlie asked, setting a nine of spades down.

"No! Hally canceled on us."

"You do remember!" I stood at the dining room table and jabbed my finger at him.

Everyone at the table laughed until Mateo gave up and laughed with us.

We talked about the wedding in July and work. When I flew to France, Lewis had rescheduled all my appointments until June. But the real shocker...the man had written the new dates, and the clients' names, down on the schedule!

I loved my friends.

Things weren't good with Nol, and it hurt. It hurt because he hadn't told me, and it hurt that Raj hadn't wanted me to know. It hurt that Gileal had betrayed us all. It hurt that Nol was more focused on getting better to go hunt for Gil. And I feared what I'd done would affect our relationship forever. I'd taken his revenge away from him, and I feared I'd never get my Nol back.

But I couldn't give up. Everyone said Nol would come around and admit I'd done the right thing. When that would be was anyone's guess. But I had other things to worry about until he came around. Like going to a meeting with the fae heads of state.

Quinn's mom hadn't been kidding. She was gathering support from the other fae nations about a meeting with *Endae's* heads of state. So fun, but even better, I still hadn't briefed *Endae* on the assassination attempts. That was going to be an interesting conversation: "The fae want to meet you all, and also, they tried to kill me twice. How does next fall sound?"

Even crazier, I'd used *Olauvë* twice now to search for Gil. Nothing in either realm. It was like he didn't exist or was in a place I couldn't find him, the latter being more probable. But where? If I couldn't find him that way soon, I was going to talk to my grandfather about finding his dreams. Gileal needed to be found.

Big what-ifs, big plans, and even bigger hopes for the future. Just as long as my family and friends stayed safe and I got my *muranildo* back soon, things would work out okay.

32

Nolan

Nolan stopped and tightened his grip on his sword. He heaved as he searched for his water bottle. *C'yo*, it was empty. Oturan hummed with the urge to practice his favorite combinations, but practicing such complicated spells was dangerous when Nolan wasn't at his strongest. And at his strongest he was not, even with another five days of rest at the fae mansion. He could still feel a sluggishness in his reflexes and responses.

After dinner, Nolan had come out to the south orchard practice yard that Quinn had Faerie make for him. He scratched his nose with the back of his hand and looked at the evening sun, just below the horizon. The last set needed redoing, and then he'd go in. He didn't like the lack of strength behind his straight cuts, and the initial thrust was garbage. The whole fucking thing was a mess.

"Nolan!"

As quickly as he could, he covered Oturan in shadow and searched for Quinn. He sighted him on his left, jogging out into the field. No one was supposed to be out here with him. Damn it, the old man was going to get himself killed. He sheathed his sword and walked toward him.

Quinn came to a halt, his breathing heavy from the run. "Jesus, I caught you before you started again. Fuck. Remind me to never take you on in a duel. Your diagonal to horizontal transition cuts are seamless." He waved his hand in front of his face. "Sorry, I know you didn't want to be bothered, but it's been three hours. Aren't you supposed to be in *Endae* at eleven? It's ten forty-five."

Three hours? Damn this Faerie place. The sun and moon rose and set when they wanted to. He checked his phone. Dead.

"I apologize. Faerie killed my phone. Again." He was running out of his savings. From the money Hallë had given him in the beginning and the amount of his paychecks he had saved, he had just enough to cover the rent and electricity this month. He needed to go back to work soon, especially if he wanted a new phone.

"It doesn't fuck with me. I guess it's trying to get that stick outta your ass." Quinn smirked.

"Or you're a prince."

"Nah." He backed up, expecting Nolan to go with him.

"I'll take the shadows—"

"If you don't mind, I'd like to talk to you before you leave?"

"*Sercae cumo,*" he cussed. "If it's about Hallë, I don't want to talk about it." No. Seeing her tonight would be a challenge. This entire plan was going to be a challenge. The bond already wanted him to forgive her. *C'yo,* if it was anyone else...and that was why she'd been the one to stop him. Nolan knew she knew that and that pissed him off all over again.

Quinn held up his hands placatingly. "You know I've tried to be Switzerland."

Nolan pursed his lips. "Fine, but if you fucking say her name, I'm leaving you out here."

"Twice. Give me two times before you run away."

Nolan seethed. Yes, Quinn had worked hard on not talking about her, except for the occasional "I'm headed to Hally's later." The old man was accommodating, backing off when Nolan needed him to and helping him find an outlet for his anger—hence this area for practice away from everyone.

Maybe I shouldn't be so mad at him for coming out here. "What is it?"

"It's been just over a week since you've been back. I've given you some space, but considering where you're going tonight, I wanted to suggest a different kind of outlet. Let's face it, this isn't working well." Quinn pointed to Nolan's practice yard. "If you can't talk to anyone, I know someone. They won't judge, won't even make you talk. Fuck, you two could just sit and stare at a wall together. Her name's Ness—Venessa. Have you ever heard of a therapist?"

Nolan shook his head and would have pulled out his phone to look it up if Faerie hadn't fucked with it.

"They're a type of doctor who helps with all sorts of issues. Now, I don't know much about what happened. From what I do know, I get it. I really, really do. Centuries ago, I killed one of my brothers."

Nol's head shot up. He had not expected that. He knew not to assume others didn't understand, didn't have similar experiences, but he hadn't wanted to hear it from Hallë. *C'yo*, she was right. Thirty-two hundred years old was a lot of baggage for Quinn to carry.

"Do you regret it?" Nol asked as Quinn opened the side gate to the vineyard.

Quinn scoffed. "No. The fucker...killed my family. But he didn't betray an entire country on top of betraying you because he loved Hally so much."

"Wait, what?"

"Yeah." Quinn slowed and paused, like Nolan should have known this, but he hadn't. "He gave her the lame-ass excuse of 'I loved you so much and I wanted the council to pay.' She says she doesn't blame herself. Gileal made his own choices. A mature way to look at it."

"But..."

"Yeah, but..." Quinn shoved his hands in his pockets. "Listen, I'm not trying to get you on her side with that. I'm just sayin' it's fucked up of him to try that shit."

Nol agreed. "I never considered that aspect. Hallë is right. She isn't to blame. I'm only angry with her for stopping me."

Quinn didn't argue either way. Was that the Switzerland analogy again? Now he would dwell on it. They climbed into the four person utility vehicle—the only type of vehicle allowed in the grape fields.

"It's sad that you brought this out here." Nolan gave him shit.

"Is it, though? Faerie doesn't like to fuck with vehicles. If we walk back, Faerie might try to keep us out here all night, and then where would we be?"

Nolan's left eyebrow rose at the ridiculous question. "Here…"

Quinn scoffed and started driving, resting one wrist on the steering wheel. Nolan liked these vehicles better than the large ones on the roads. Out here, if he needed to, he could jump out. And the wind felt nice on his face. He breathed in the aroma of the dirt and grapevines in the evening air.

"Besides, Faerie doesn't fuck with princes, remember?" Nolan said.

"Ha-ha. Anyway, Ness is a good friend." Quinn pulled into the garage with several other covered vehicles like this one. "I've never been her client because you don't become friends with your therapist."

"Do you have a therapist? Is it common?"

"Seamus and I both have one. It's a new human thing, and I'm confident it's common with them."

"Is it helping Seamus?"

"Yes. But he still misses his mom."

Nolan could understand that. They got out of the utility vehicle and walked into the mansion. He liked the twilight here. The manor was peaceful, even with the guards at the front door. Orlaith had to give them something to do.

Quinn followed Nolan through the main manor to the room Nolan had been given while he recovered. While he wasn't at full strength, the *serilesoda* was out of his system, and it was time to go…home. Not home home, but for the time being, the loft worked.

"There was one more thing I wanted to say before you left. I've wanted to ask for a while. And this is where the two mentions come in. It'll be three mentions now, but you're leaving, so screw it. I need you to promise me something."

Nolan threw the rest of his clothes into his satchel and flattened it. The *Zayuri*-issued bag folded to the size of his palm and could hold almost anything.

As he waited for Quinn to ask, Nolan attached Oturan to his jacket. The feature was an ingenious addition, but Hallë could *never* make it for anyone else. Nolan shook his head at the thought of what that had almost been. And her boyfriend was standing at his open door. He was glad Quinn had helped her share energies, so she'd now understand why it wasn't a good idea to try anything like that with anyone else. Nolan turned as he shoved the satchel in its place on the back of his *Zayuri*-issued shirt.

Quinn leaned on the doorframe, his hands in his pockets as he looked down at his feet. They stood in silence for a full minute. Nolan wouldn't say yes until Quinn told him what he wanted him to promise. Quinn smirked, knowing Nolan wasn't going to fall for it.

"When your feelings change...tell me. I swear, I'll back off. Hally and I are just having fun."

"Quinn—"

"Just promise me, okay? Don't tell me it's not happening, because it will. You both are...shit, maybe I should break it off."

Nolan walked up and set his hand on Quinn's shoulder. "Don't." He made sure Quinn really saw how much this meant. "Don't. I'm in love with someone."

Quinn stiffened, and his hands came out of his pockets. "You're fucking with me, right? You don't look at a woman like you do Hally and love someone else."

"I'm a mess and I'm not good for her."

"Does Hally know?"

"She found out some things in *Endae*. Things I was too cowardly to tell her." He squeezed his new friend's shoulder. He *had* to explain this in a way Quinn would understand. He'd trusted Nolan with some of his pain. Nolan could give him something that he'd never given anyone before. "Things my wife made me promise never to tell Hallë before she and our daughter died of the curse."

They stayed silent for a long time. It was probably past time to be there, and Tolwe, Zella, and Onaeris were waiting on them in *Aemina*. But Quinn had to understand. Hallë needed someone else so Nolan could stay away. The bond had mellowed out once Quinn had come into their lives, and it needed to stay that way.

"So, promise me, when you have to leave her to find your future co-ruler, warn me. It's hard to refuse the bond unless there's someone else. My wife is gone, but I love her still. Do you understand? I *can't* be with Hallë. It's not fair to her. I'm a fucked-up mess."

"My friend, I will swear that, but please, do the same. Because now it makes more sense than ever why you're stuck here."

Nolan dropped his arm, groaning at the stupid shit Quinn was about to say. The same damn thing his uncle had told him.

"Fine, I won't say it." Quinn laughed at Nolan. "Obviously, you know what I mean, but I'm not getting in the way when you figure it out. Go to Ness, unfuck up that mess in your head, and make peace with yourself somehow. However that is, you need your *muranildë* to help with that. Your Mother Anara's wants have made that clear."

This was not the way that confession was supposed to go.

"You have me, too. The asshole friend who isn't going away. So tonight, when you go see her, fucking fix this shit and forgive her. Seriously, she did that to protect you."

"I thought you were Switzerland?"

"Yeah, well, I lied. Get going. It's ten fifty and you probably don't want to keep your uncle waiting, he's a scary ass dude. And Nolan, swear it."

"I swear I'll tell you." With that, Nolan stepped back and dropped into the shadows. Under a minute inside and his fingers were cold. He needed to be back to full strength by next week. Thank the Mother tonight's plan didn't involve using the shadows. They just involved illegally sneaking Hallë over to *Endae*. He dropped off his bag at the loft and went to Hallë's house.

He came out of the shadows in her bedroom. She lay in her bed, sound asleep, and she'd left the curtains open again. He knew Hallë would complain about the sun beaming down on her in the morning, waking her up. If she'd stop opening them during the day, this wouldn't be a problem. But the light warmed the room, she said. *C'yo, save me the whining.* With an exasperated eye roll, he stepped over to the window, leaned over her bedroom hammock with all the pillows, and closed the curtains.

Nolan came back to her bed, took a deep breath to prepare himself for her wrath, and shook her. "Hallë?" He waited for a moment, hoping that was all it would take. "Hallë, we have to go." He shook her harder.

"Nol?" she said in her groggy, grumpy, just-woke-up voice.

"Yes, we have to go." Nolan hoped she was decent. Sometimes, she wore those big shirts to bed. He wouldn't care, but she might.

"You're not talking to me. Go away." She rolled over and lay her head on her arms, away from him.

Nolan counted: one, two, three...

"What the fuck are you doing in my bedroom?" But she hadn't sprung up like he'd expected her to. Her words were muffled by the arm covering her mouth.

"There's something we must do."

She didn't answer. Nolan dropped his chin to his chest in annoyance.

He searched for a way to tell her without scaring her or saying exactly what they were doing. If he told her, it would be her choice to go. If it was her choice, they could accuse her of breaking her exile. Onaeris had said it would work. "Hallë? There is an emergency, and...I need you to come with me."

"Screw off."

"Don't make me carry you." That would get her up. She hated it when he carried her anywhere. "Three, two, one..."

"Twynolan, don't you fucking dare!" She kicked him when he grabbed her. An elbow to the face was next. He dodged it, but she got his ear instead.

"Then get up."

"Get out of my room!"

She fought and wiggled, but he had her and her blankets off the mattress. "Get dressed and don't take forever. You have three minutes before I come in there." He shoved her, blankets and all, into her closet.

She hit the door three times and cussed at him in several languages.
"Two minutes."

"It has *not* been a minute."

"One and a half!"

"Fucking-A!" she growled. He heard hangers moving and drawers opening.

"Thirty seconds."

"So help me, Twynolan, if you come in here before I say you can, I will blast you out of my fucking room."

"I've got coffee."

"I want sleep!" She threw something solid at the door. "I just went to bed an hour ago."

"How would you know? You don't even know what time it is." He'd missed this. It had been almost eight days and already he missed their banter. While she wasn't as carefree—Mother, help him, she could win a challenge against Tiaë sometimes—she was his pain in the ass.

"Hallë?"

"Leave me alone."

"I'm coming in. Three, two, one!" He grabbed the handle, but she shoved the door open like he'd known she would.

"Damn it all to hell, Nol. What the fuck do you think is so important that you just have to talk to me? By the way, don't you remember that you hate me? Is this part of it? You hate me so you wake me up at ungodly hours? I don't know what's worse, ignoring me or this!"

"I don't hate you." Nolan meant that, too. Anger didn't mean hate.

"Bullshit. I took away your revenge and now..." Hallë pointed to the window as her words fumbled. She hated crying. "You don't think I want him found? I'd wish he were dead if I knew that would hurt him. It's not just *you* he hurt. He hurt everyone. I want him to pay for everything he did, okay? I hate him so much. An'di was my sister, too. Raj was my friend."

He could barely understand her now, and he didn't want her talking anymore. Nolan pulled her close until her face was in his jacket, until she stopped struggling and just cried. The others would have to wait.

Fuck. Why had he waited until now? Because he'd been wallowing in his own pain and couldn't see hers.

When her crying slowed and the little hiccups that came afterward started, they always had, ever since he could remember. He knew he had to say something. What, though? She was better at this shit. "Hallë?"

She didn't respond, but he didn't want to speak louder. Didn't want to upset her more.

"Hallë? I was wrong."

She nodded and turned her head so her face wasn't in his jacket. "And?"

He laughed quietly. "You're right. He hurt more people than me. It wasn't fair of me not to see through my pain and ignore yours."

"Go on." She sniffled, pulling out all the stops here.

They didn't have much time, and yes, she was important, but this was urgent. "Can we discuss this later?"

Hallë stepped back and glared. "Not another of your deflections. I'm tired"—she hit his chest, her arm in her long-sleeved sweater. Not too hard, but enough to get his attention—"of you always changing the subject. No more other conversations. I hate that."

Nolan grabbed her hand the next time she when to hit him and held it to his chest. "I know. We're having a good conversation, but we truly don't have time. You'll understand in a few minutes." He looked down to check on her clothes. "You're still wearing your pajamas."

"I threw leggings on. I'm not going anywhere."

That's what *she* thought. "Fine." Nolan picked her up, jumped into the shadows, and took her to the redwood in the backyard. She gasped once they were out, coughing and rubbing her eyes. Shit, he'd forgotten she couldn't stand the cold. "Are you okay?"

"Of course I'm not okay. You kidnapped me, you jerk."

Nolan groaned, grabbed the *meril* around his neck, and walked through the tree with her in his arms.

"What is—" Nolan clapped a hand over Hallë's mouth and pulled her closer.

"You're late," Tolwe grumped. He hated tardiness. But it had been important. Plus, if he knew, he wouldn't complain—maybe.

"We had an issue."

"Why isn't she walking?" Zella asked.

As soon as Hallë heard her grandmother's voice, she stopped fighting and grumbling. Then she wanted down for a different reason. There wasn't anything in any realm that would stop him from letting her see Zella. As Hallë held her grandmother, her breathing sped up, sounding raspier.

"Hallë? You need to take a deep breath," he told her as calmly as he could, leaning in. "You're going to hyperventilate." She wasn't listening, and she wasn't letting go of Zella either.

"We have to go. My colleague could only secure the spot for so long," Tolwe said. He kept a hand on Zella's back, supporting her as Hallë refused to let go.

"What about on the way back?" Nolan asked.

"If we keep to the schedule, we will be fine."

"What are you talking about? Yalu, why am I here?" Then at once, she came to a horrible assumption. Nolan saw it plainly on her face. Before she could cry out, he leaned over and covered her mouth. This time, she didn't fight.

"It's not what you think. I promise," Nolan whispered in her ear. "Try to stay quiet. Everyone is risking a lot by sneaking you in like this. He's not dead." She settled again. He released her but stayed close. "Ready?"

The three older *endai* nodded, and Onaeris took the lead, placed his traveling *meril* in his hand, and stepped through. One by one they followed, Nolan guiding Hallë since she didn't have one. She didn't speak, not after that warning.

Once they stepped through the Tree of Connection in *Rudairn*, Nolan breathed a sigh of relief. The threat of discovery was ninety percent less likely now. But only here. Returning to *Aetyru* was a different story. Nolan pulled his bag out from behind his back. He reached in and thought about what he wanted.

"Uncle, here." He handed Tolwe one vial of the serum and shoved the other one into his front inside pocket. When he looked up, Tolwe was gone, leaving Zella and Onaeris behind. Zella knew what they'd planned. Onaeris, however, that was up to Tolwe and Zella to decide. "I'll take her through the shadows and meet you there."

"Nol? What are—"

"Wait to ask." He pulled her close once again and left, coming through in the home he had spent half his childhood in. After Hallë's exile, he'd hated coming over, but he couldn't stay away at the same time. Sometimes, being in Hallë's room had been the only way he could sleep. Those memories weren't helping him now.

Hallë was already trying to scramble out of his arms. He didn't blame her. Nolan grabbed her face and made her look at him. Most of the time that was the only damn way to make her stop for five seconds. The *endaë* never held still. "Stop and let me explain now that we're relatively safe."

Hallë held her breath to calm herself. She took in two full breaths and tried to move again. He refused to talk until she could stand there on her own without fidgeting.

"Your father took a turn three days ago. Charlie and Collin have been working constantly on a medium for dosages since then." Nolan pulled out the vial from his jacket. "The time is now."

"Why-why didn't you tell me?" she asked through her squished cheeks.

"The less you knew, the better. I literally kidnapped you. You can't be blamed."

"But you can. My grandparents and Tolwe could get in trouble."

"Our choices. Are you going to keep freaking out, or do you want to cure your father?"

Hallë snatched the vial out of his hands, bouncing with excitement while she held the small glass thing close to her face. "Thank you, Nol." She jumped, kissed him, and ran up the stairs. He doubted she even knew what she'd done. Nolan shook his head, smiling to himself. The pain in the ass.

"*Oiy?*" Tolwe came in, Tiaë at his side. "What's wrong with you?"

Nolan ignored him, not wanting to hear his uncle tease him. "Tiaë? How are you doing?"

"Nolan? Sweetie, what are you doing here?"

Nolan grabbed Hallë's mother's hands and brought them together in front of her. "I brought Hallë home. She's upstairs, and you should go see her."

"Nevie isn't here anymore, remember? Did you bring Cam? I made cookies yesterday."

Nolan glanced at his uncle. This was bad. Maybe Hallë was right. Tiaë's body could have been masking the curse and these were her symptoms. Balin's symptoms were odd, as well. "Can we go see Orin?"

"Of course, sweetie. Watch your step on the stairs. You know how you miss the first one."

As a klutzy teenager everything made him fall, but that step was the bane of his childhood. Nolan followed his second mother to the bottom of the stairs, all the while terrified about Tiaë's behavior. Cam? She didn't remember? If it wasn't the curse, then what in the Starless Abyss was going on with her memory?

"If she doesn't recognize Hally, you're taking her back and having Charlie look at her," Tolwe said from beside him while they watched her climb the steps.

Nolan agreed with his uncle. They might just take her back regardless. "Did Balin accept the medicine?"

Tolwe glanced up at the ceiling to where the family was reuniting. "I explained about the cure. He said he had nothing else to lose and took it. I told him I'd check in on him tomorrow."

Nolan wanted to get up there. "Where's Onaeris and Zella?"

"They're waiting outside. I'm still not certain Hally should be in here. You don't know if that cure is effective in the form it's in."

"I wasn't keeping her from her father a day longer, Tolwe. It was torture for her when I pulled her away from Tiaë. She's had enough taken away from her. The cure will work."

Tolwe wasn't a pessimist, but he was more than extra cautious when it came to Zella's safety. Why would her granddaughter be any different?

"Why were you all goofy when we got in here?" Tolwe asked as he took the first of the stairs. "Did Hally say something?"

Nol turned his head until he could see his uncle below him. "I got a kiss for bringing her here."

"Weren't you trying to avoid that?"

Nolan grunted. He'd known his uncle would take it there. "This was different. I don't even think she realized what she did."

"Makes sense. You did something nice for the person you love. She thanked you in a way that meant more than words could express."

"Shut up, you ancient bat."

Tolwe laughed and shoved his nephew up the last step. They went to the first room past the staircase, where Nolan rarely went. Hallë was sitting on the bed, holding her dad's hand as she nodded. Tiaë sat on the other side of Orin, watching her daughter and husband with a blank expression, blinking as if her mind was trying to come up with an explanation for what her eyes were showing her. The bottle lay empty on the table in the corner. Their conversation was quiet, only between the three of them, if Tiaë was listening. Nolan gave his *muranildë* several more minutes while he and Tolwe watched Tiaë, unchanged and staring off into nowhere. She'd seemed better last week.

"Go tell them. I'll talk to Tiaë."

Nolan sighed. This wasn't enough time to visit. He wanted to give Hallë up to the last second of time with Orin before they had to leave.

"Hallë?" Nolan whispered.

She lifted her head, her eyes wide and fearful that he would take her back now.

"Orin?" The *endao* wasn't old. They'd had Hallë young, in their early third century if he remembered correctly. But now, Orin looked as old as Zella. His eyes had sunk into his skull, and his hair was limp and dull. When was the last time Nol had visited? He was ashamed to admit he didn't remember.

"Nolan," Orin rasped. "It's nice to see you. Who let you in? Nevie won't tell me the truth."

Nolan laughed. "I kidnapped your daughter, and then your mother and father brought us here."

Orin curled his lip. "That doesn't sound right coming from either of you." He looked at his daughter, who nodded but didn't say anything.

"How's that serum taste? Charlie didn't have time to make it taste good, and it smelled"—Nolan scowled and licked his lips, attempting to get the scent out of his memory—"distinct."

"Oh, yes, distinct to its own. Perhaps adding some of your father's wine might help get it down."

The three of them laughed. According to Edvic, everything was better with his wine in it. Nolan reached for Hallë and swept her hair back. She was so happy. So much had happened. He brushed the puffy skin under her eyes with this thumb. He always seemed to make her cry. "I didn't want to intrude on your time with her. I know it's precious and won't be long. Tolwe and I need to know if you've noticed Tiaë acting absently? Forgetting?"

Orin looked up at the ceiling and nodded. "She won't let anyone examine her. Balin has tried, but she won't. She's scared they'll take her away from me."

Nolan looked at Tolwe, who was guiding Hallë's mom out of the room and asking her for some tea. "I understand. Tolwe wants me to bring her back to Earth. The girl who made this cure could look at her, maybe get her the help she can't get here with no healers anymore."

"Thank the Mother," Orin said.

"Nol?" Hallë cleared her throat and glanced at her father. "Do you think they both could? It would be good to observe him and...um...watch for changes as he improves."

Nolan tried to keep a straight face as she fumbled her *Aemirin*. She tried so hard and made it work ninety-four percent of the time. He would never tell her, but her pitches and pauses were off. It was too adorable and he'd miss it when she figured out what was wrong with her e and ë, as she liked to say. The other part was lack of vocabulary, like his with English. It wasn't her fault. Too bad there wasn't a phone app for *Aemirin* to English translation. He could imagine Mateo making one.

Watching their faces, this peace it gave them to be together again, he couldn't take that away now, not when Tiaë was going, too. "Screw it. Yeah, if you're up to it, Orin, I'll take you back."

"Nevie, dear, would you grab my traveling kit out of my workshop while I get dressed? It'll take these tired bones a while."

Orin and his carvings. Always bringing his traveling kit because there was no telling where inspiration could come from. Hallë hurried out the door.

"How's the ring working?" Orin whispered the moment Hallë was gone.

Exactly as he had thought. Orin was getting Hallë to leave so he could sneakily pry for answers. "She knows, Orin. It works. I don't know how you did it, but her band barely gives her any trouble. She helped develop this cure, thanks to you. That band wouldn't have let her do it."

"My baby needed help. You'd do the same."

"I would, yes." Nolan helped him get out of bed and get dressed. Orin didn't apologize or get embarrassed about any of the functions he couldn't perform because of his illness.

Orin's parents didn't give him any grief or argue once about the decision to take Tiaë. She needed help and Orin wasn't leaving her side. Hopefully, Orlaith wouldn't mind a few more *endai* on that side. They were Hallë's parents, after all. And the queen liked her elven ambassador. Tolwe would watch over Balin, and he and Hallë would watch over Orin and Tiaë. And he'd— How had Quinn put it? Unfuck up that mess in his head and make peace with himself. Peace? No, probably not, but maybe he could fix it so he didn't make Hallë cry so much. He'd give that friend of Quinn's a call, then.

EPILOGUE

I SHOOK THE NERVOUS tingles out of my hands as I paced. It wasn't doing a damn bit of good. Nol did this all the time when he was anxious or nervous, or pissed. He did it way too often, but I needed to do something while we waited.

"We're here!"

My pacing stopped when Wennië's voice filled the antechamber next to the *Aemina* assembly room. I looked at Nol. "Did you tell them?"

Nol's loose hair swished as he shook his head. We were talking, but things were still rough between us. We still weren't over our hurts. Nol left the house when he grew contemplative, and in the past three days, he'd barely been around. He had "work" to do. Except Mateo said he wasn't coming to work.

Edvic released the door and followed his wife into the room as she jogged over, holding a long blue piece of cloth. Not just any blue, either. The national blue of *Aeminan.* Um...then I remembered. She'd said she was going to make me a vest, something that signified our country.

"Oh, Wennië, you didn't have to." But I was dying of excitement inside. Even the nerves were gone. She'd made me something for the assembly meeting. No fucking way. I loved my second mother.

"Yes, I did," she said as I pulled the soft *endaen* silk out of her arms. "I heard they weren't giving you any fancy council clothes. Now you have some."

No, I had something better. I held it up high and gasped. It wasn't a vest and not just blue. It was the most important garment I could ever have the honor of wearing. There were no words for what she'd given me.

"Murë," Nol whispered in shock.

"You don't like it. I know I said blue, but you're more than just *Aeminan* now. I put the blue on the bottom so it won't show the dirt it picks up, but I put a repelling spell on it, too. If you have any problems reactivating it, get him to do it." She jabbed a thumb at her son. "White's at the top to signify—"

"Unity, sacrifice, and hope," I said.

"I thought of that." Edvic chuckled. "*Endae* stands united. You've sacrificed so much to become the strong, brave *endaë* you are today. And we stay hopeful for the peace you will bring to our realms."

That was a lot to unpack. A lot of pressure. My mind wanted to sprint out of here until I found a deep cave in the woods and never come out. How did any of them think I could do all of this? I wasn't even an official ambassador.

"Oh! And look," Wennië said, distracting me. "My favorite. I got the idea from the flowers your dad etched on your ring and cuff. I know night stars are your favorite, but look." She picked up a sleeve and pointed out the hem. A trail of flowers lined the hem and collar. Not just the night star trillium of *Aemina*, but she had dyed all the flowers of *every* nation in *Endae* and their colors: *Aemina's* blue with one white speck on each petal, *Mellori's* gold and purple midnight lily, *Pequwyn's* white star poppy, *Ajelara's* sunset yellow peony, *Dartayen's* red iris, *Luctanez's* white moon blossom, *Ja'hene's* dawn rose, and the *Terren's* deep green clover.

Nol tugged it out of my hands. For a moment, I clutched it close, but he only wanted to see it. Then he spread it out and laid it on my shoulders. "They could call us in at any time. You should probably have it on when they do." He wrapped it around me, made me slip my arms in, and buttoned the wooden toggles on the side. My father's toggles. I couldn't see, but I had a feeling they were the same carvings as my ring.

"We have something for you, too, Nolan."

"Me? I'm not a part of this. And even if I was, I'm required to wear..." Nol shut up as she pulled out a sash of the same design as my robe. White in the middle, bleeding blue at the ends with embroidered national flowers. I wouldn't ask now, but I didn't quite get why he needed a sash. "Oh."

Wennië looped it over his head and set it down over his shoulder and under his left arm. "There. It suits the cuff well."

"Murë, I haven't told her. I wanted to wait."

"Wait for what?" I asked. The hesitation in Nol's voice made me nervous. "What are you talking about, Wennië? Which cuff?"

Annoyed, Nol didn't look at me until Wennië had pinned him with her glare. "I received a new cuff."

Wennië scoffed. "Really? That's it?"

"Wait, you made *Lidean*?" My eyebrows shot up as I realized what this meant. This was better than exciting. Being promoted to *Lidean*, two ranks below Tolwe, was an amazing accomplishment for someone so young. "Let me see it!"

Nol screwed up his face as if he were afraid of what I'd say but knew he had to admit it, anyway.

My mini-celebration stopped. "Why do you look like you're gonna get into more trouble?" I set my hands on my hips. "What aren't you telling me now, Twynolan? Did you really get a new cuff? I've had just about enough of your secrets and hiding."

Edvic's laughter distracted me for a second. "You sound like Tiaë."

Shocked for a moment that he'd ever think I acted like my mother, I settled as I thought about the challenge she was facing right now. I shrugged with a smile.

"Twynolan." I glared until he caved.

"I didn't want to tell you today. This is more important."

But I didn't give in, even as Nol sagged and looked at his parents for help. He wasn't getting out of this. "*Ai*, can we wait until after your speech?"

"No! This could go on all day. Is this a bad thing? Just tell me!"

Nol shoved his hair back. "Stop freaking out. See?" He leaned over so I could see his ear. At first, I thought it was just a plain blue cuff like his *hinam* cuff, but upon touching it, I realized it was a Celtic blue stone with veins of silver.

I stepped away and looked him in the eye. "That's not *Lidean* rank, is it? What does this one mean?"

Nol wiggled his eyebrows. "Wouldn't you like to know?" Technically, I wasn't supposed to know the cuff ranking, but growing up around him, I knew more than most *endai*.

I crossed my arms over my chest. "What's going on?"

"Hallanevaë? *Hinam* Nolan?" A staffer assigned to bring in guest speakers interrupted my little interrogation. "They're ready for you."

I grabbed Nol's arm before he could even think of leaving without an explanation. "Wait—"

Nol leaned in close to me. "I promise, I'll tell you after the meeting. It isn't bad, if that helps."

No, it did not. It would bug me the entire time. And that was the reason Nol had wanted to wait. I didn't need the distraction. I turned to Wennië.

As soon as she saw my face, she stepped over and held me. "It's going to be okay." She pressed her hand to my head, her fingertips at the nape of my neck. "You will get through this just fine. And they're letting Nolan in, just for you. And you look official."

"More than official. Thank you so much, Wennië. I can't wait until my parents see my robe."

Before the staffer got too impatient, I hugged Edvic. "What a wonderful idea about the white. It's perfect."

"Thanks. Don't let them intimidate you." He kissed my cheek.

Wennië kissed the other one. "You're stronger than all of them."

I hurried over to where Nol stood by the doorway, waiting with his hands at his back.

"I like your sash." I gave it a tug as I walked by. Now for the hard part, the thing I'd been working on since we got back to Earth: the request of Queen Brigid and all the fae nations on Earth.

Endae's national leaders sat before me. It had been over seven hundred years since a *Mellorin* and an *Aeminan* were in the same room together. And soon, the nations of both realms would be meeting in the same realm after six thousand years.

I looked down at the robe Wennië had made me, all the nations' colors fluttering as I stepped to the middle of the dais. This was really happening. And they were looking at me.

They needed me. I looked up at Nol on my right, with the sash that matched my robe. And I needed him.

"Good morning, people of *Endae*. I'm honored to be here in front of you today. For the past week, it has been my privilege to tour this realm and meet the people of the other nations. Even as a child, I never imagined I'd get to do that before my third century. Or my fourth, for that matter. I understand this wasn't your choice, that I wasn't your choice, but until you choose your own ambassador, I will do my best to represent you in *Rosava*. As such, I have demanded answers on your behalf, which they must provide on or before the meeting they requested. And speaking of that meeting, you all agreed upon the autumn equinox and"—I gave them a sly smile—"they came around to it."

In the first row, I saw some shoulders shake with laughter.

Came around to it was a mild way of saying most nations had bitched up a storm. How could they prepare to go to another realm in one-hundred days? The horror.

"I must say, they thought I meant next autumn but I assured them we wanted answers now. You're getting them. However...they have asked you to make your choices for ambassadors at the banquet." The assembly of nations rustled, but did they think the fae would roll over and give them everything? The biggest shock was that *Aemina* had volunteered to host a banquet for all of *Endae* and the fae of *Rosava* during our equinox celebration.

Hours later, after twenty-thousand and two arguments, discussions, and all the bullshit they could think of, Nol and I walked back through the small door on the side.

The hushed quiet of the room felt false, like the assembly members were going to barge in here and demand more information. Nol inhaled, and I turned to see him puff out his cheeks. "This won't be easy, watching after you. Not only do you not pay attention to anything, but you will have other attempts on your life. I guess someone's got to do it, though."

"I've told you before, Nol, this isn't your job. You don't *have* to protect me."

"Actually, it is." Nol reached out and touched my nose before I realized his hand was out. "My new mission is protecting you in *Rosava*. The Starborn King and Queen just agreed to it. Seattle will receive several other *Zayuri* to accompany you on any foreign visit. *No one* was pleased about the attempts on your life."

He preened. "You should be proud. I had to talk to all the fae nations to get unilateral permission to bring *Zayuri* to Earth once again. I, and any *Zayuri* stationed there, am getting paid by a collection of the fae nations."

"Shut up." He *had* been working.

"And now I am giving you notice. This is my last month at the loft."

"Why? I thought it was growing on you."

He tipped his chin up. He couldn't have been prouder of himself—wait, yes, he could. "Because I found a place closer to you."

I rolled my eyes. At least his new duties would keep him busy, whatever those duties might be when *Zayuri* weren't hitting people over their heads with swords. "You are *such* a pain in my ass."

"Not as much as you are in mine." Nol thumped my nose lightly. "Are you ready to go home?"

I took one last look around the antechamber of the *Aemina's* assembly room. My gaze landed on Nol, patiently waiting for my answer. "Very much so."

Author's Note

Enjoyed this book?

I'd be so grateful if you could leave a quick review wherever you buy your books. Reviews help other readers discover The Exile's Paradox — and they mean the world to me.

Thank you so much for reading. The QR code will take you a link to find your favorite place to leave reviews and ratings. Thank you so much for reading.

Don't miss future books! Subscribe to my mailing list https://subscribepage.io/kristineendsley and you'll get new release alerts, behind-the-scene sneak peeks, book giveaways, and more. Would you like to know what Hally did that was so tragic? How could she have possibly killed her friends? Sign up for my mailing list and you'll get a free copy of Shattered Fate.

Hally's and Nolan's story will continue in book 4, coming out in 2027.

Acknowledgements

If it weren't for the people here, I would never have published my first book, let alone the rest. Thank you.

My critique group at Café Noir in Silverdale. My partner at CritiqueMatch, Rachel. Katie Cross, you are super woman! I wouldn't have done this without your encouragement and advice from you and G.S. Jennson. Thank you both.

My betas! I begged and bugged you to read this and give me your honest feedback. April, Cassie, Yeal, Sarah, and Lauren. Thank you so much.

My ARC team, much like my beta team, thank you for putting up with my emails and reminders. Thank you for your honest reviews.

Adam, I love you. Thank you for coming with me to Miscons; listening to me rant or ignore me when I talk to myself; not complaining when you get up for work and I've just gone to bed and for being my partner for the past twenty-three years.

My boys, you are my world. You amaze me; you inspire me. How did I get so lucky to be your mom? Thank you for being there, for the hugs and Eskimo kisses.

My editors, Elizabeth Darkley and Jennifer Griffin. Thank you for making it look professional, you know it'd be a mess without you.

My cover illustrator/designer, Cristiana Leone, thank you for making this book look so magical!

ABOUT THE AUTHOR

Kristine Endsley is an urban fantasy author from Washington State. When she's not writing Kristine can be found spending time with her friends and family, enjoying a Seattle Sounder's game, or hanging out at her local coffee shop. She lives a ferry ride away from Seattle with her husband, two boys, one lazy, old dog, and two crazy kitties. Kristine works as a substitute para-educator to fund her writing habit.